"A hil… t-
hearte… s.
The p… n
will h…

—*RT Book Reviews* (Top Pick, 4½ stars)
on *One Hot Summer*

"Melissa Cutler is a bright new voice in contemporary romance." —*New York Times* bestselling author Lori Wilde

"Sizzling." —*Publishers Weekly* on *One Hot Summer*

"A fun contemporary Western romance. Cutler brings Texas ambiance and color to this delightful and sexy tale."
—*Booklist* on *One Hot Summer*

"A red hot romance with a sexy cowboy and a great story!" —*Fresh Fiction* on *The Mistletoe Effect*

Also by Melissa Cutler

One Hot Summer

One More Taste

ONE WILD NIGHT

Melissa Cutler

St. Martin's Paperbacks

This is a work of fiction. All of the characters, organizations, and events portrayed in this novel are either products of the author's imagination or are used fictitiously.

ONE WILD NIGHT

For information address St. Martin's Press, 175 Fifth Avenue, New York, NY 10010.

ISBN: 978-1-250-07188-0

Our books may be purchased in bulk for promotional, educational, or business use. Please contact your local bookseller or the Macmillan Corporate and Premium Sales Department at 1-800-221-7945, ext. 5442, or by e-mail at MacmillanSpecialMarkets@macmillan.com

Printed in the United States of America

St. Martin's Paperbacks edition / March 2017

St. Martin's Paperbacks are published by St. Martin's Press, 175 Fifth Avenue, New York, NY 10010.

10 9 8 7 6 5 4 3 2 1

Chapter One

If only Skye Martinez could run a fever on command. Or, after a few bites of the eggplant parmesan that Mrs. Biaggi of Vito's Eatery just delivered to the table, maybe she could fake food poisoning. *Anything* to get her out of this disaster of a blind date, the latest in a string of them. That was the trouble with living in a small Texas town. All the good men were taken—along with most of the bad ones too.

"And here's your meatball, Sweetums," Mrs. Biaggi said.

Sweetums, in this case, was Vince Biaggi, Skye's date—and Mrs. Biaggi's son.

Yeah.

Skye was gonna kill Granny June for this one.

"It looks great, as always, Mother," Vince said, digging in. With a mouth full of meatball, he poked his fork in Skye's direction. "Now you see why I wanted us to eat here. There's no sense paying for dinner when we can eat for free."

Naturally.

Mrs. Biaggi gave Skye a nudge and a wink. "Vince brings all his first dates here. It gives his Pops and me a chance to check out the merchandise."

And now she was merchandise. Good to know.

She took a despairing glance at her phone, which she'd positioned strategically at the opening of her purse. Twenty minutes until her sister, Gloria, was scheduled to call, a Plan B in case Skye needed to fake an emergency and escape. When she raised her gaze, it was to find Vince and his mother beaming at her.

"Go on and try the eggplant parmesan," Mrs. Biaggi said. "It's been Vince's favorite since he was just a little squirt."

Skye made slow work of slicing the eggplant as her mind scrolled through possible ways to make Granny June pay. Maybe she'd reprogram the horn on Granny's riding scooter to play chicken noises. Or set her up on a disaster of a blind date of her own. God knew there were plenty of toothless or senile senior men at church. Or maybe Skye could get her mom to whip up one of her old-world curses to turn Granny's hair bright blue.

Then again, Granny June would probably approve of that one.

Granny June Briscoe was the matriarch of the family-owned Briscoe Ranch Resort where Skye worked in housekeeping, and where Skye's family had worked for almost four decades. Usually, Granny June had a knack for matchmaking—which was the only reason Skye had agreed go on a date with the son of one of Granny's Bingo buddies. Plus, Skye had recently made a decision to abandon her rebellious side and settle down like the good Catholic woman she was raised to be.

She had a bite of food halfway to her lips when, miracle of miracles, her phone chimed with an incoming text. It was all she could do to hide her relief. "Oh Gosh, I'm so sorry. I didn't realize I'd left the volume on. Excuse me."

The text read, *this wedding is bananas.*

It wasn't from her sister, but from her friend Remedy, the head wedding planner at Briscoe Ranch. In Skye's lifetime of experience at the resort, all weddings fell somewhere on the crazy spectrum, so tonight's affair would have to be extra gonzo for Remedy to text something like that. This wasn't a fake emergency; it was even better.

Skye waved her phone at Vince. "Sorry, it's my mom. Just a sec." Oh, how the lies rolled off her tongue. But she couldn't find it in her heart to care as she let her fingers fly over the touch keys.

Crazier than the date I'm on? She texted.

Looking at Mrs. Biaggi and Vince, she forced her smile to stay apologetic while waiting for Remedy's reply. It came less than a minute later.

Better hurry if you want to see the maid of honor doing tequila shots from the best man's belt buckle flask with no hands.

That did sound bananas—and exactly what Skye needed to salvage her Saturday night. A zing of delicious, addictive adrenaline pulsed through her veins. It was only a small fix of her preferred vice—nowhere near enough to satisfy the hunger for rebelliousness she'd been cursed with—but it was way more of a thrill than she'd expected out of the night.

"Aw, shoot," Skye said, taking her purse handles in one hand and waving her phone in the other as she stood. Her napkin fell from her lap to the floor, but she didn't dare risk losing momentum by stooping to pick it up. "My mom needs me. My dad, with his bad back . . . he fell again and he's stuck. She can't get him off the floor on her own." Which was kind of the truth. Sort of. He'd fallen a few times lately and they'd needed Skye's help to hoist him up again.

She sent up a quick mental prayer for forgiveness for using her dad's disability as an excuse. Then she dashed off a second prayer for forgiveness about lying in the first place, covering all her bases. One thing she *wouldn't* feel guilty about was running out on her free meal.

Vince looked as lost as a boy who'd just been told his dog had gone to visit a farm far, far away. He poked at his half-eaten meatball. "But our date's not over."

Yeah, buddy, it is. "I'll text you."

Another lie, another prayer. Such was life.

Skye grabbed a dinner roll from the table and dashed through the front door. She'd driven herself to the restaurant, a rule she'd learned the hard way a few years back while on another excruciating blind date. In fact, she'd come to think of the act of inviting a guy to pick her up at home for a date as a big relationship step—one that the guys she'd dated had seldom made it to.

Racing the clock, hoping to catch the maid of honor's and best man's belt buckle antics, Skye arrived at Briscoe Ranch Resort in record time. After tossing her car keys to her cousin Marco who was working valet that night, she hot-footed it through the lobby and ascended the grand staircase, headed to the ballroom on the second level.

What she saw as she crested the stairs didn't disappoint. With a small crowd surrounding them, Remedy and her assistant Tabby were pushing a luggage trolley through a small crowd of onlookers. Seated on the base of the trolley was a very, *very* drunk young woman, slumped against one of the trolley's brass poles as her eyes fluttered open and closed. The voluminous yellow bridesmaid's dress she wore billowed out around her like she was being eaten alive by Pac-Man.

Skye froze in an open-mouth stare—until the yellow dress caught in the trolley's wheels and she roused herself to rush over and free the material. "Is this the maid of honor?"

Remedy flashed a wry smile. "Oh, yes. And it's time for her to turn in for the night." She patted the woman on the top of her elaborate, hairspray-crispy updo. "Sound good, Kimberly?"

Kimberly groaned. Her head lolled to the side.

"I think it's a little past time," Tabby muttered.

With Skye clearing the crowd from their path, Remedy and Tabby wheeled the trolley to the elevators, where Remedy got on her phone to request that someone meet them at Kimberly's room with the master key to let them in. They hadn't snagged her clutch purse during their hustle to remove her from dancing on the bride and groom's sweetheart table because they needed to get her out of the ballroom before she threw up or flashed even more skin to the attendees or both.

"So, your date was a bust?" Remedy asked Skye once they were in an elevator, headed to the fifth floor.

Skye pressed her fingers to her temples. "This guy was even worse than the last one, who kept steering the conversation back to his plant collection and making double entendres about propagating succulents."

Remedy snorted out a laugh. "This guy was worse?"

"He took me to dinner at his parents' restaurant so he wouldn't have to pay and so they could scope out 'the merchandise,' as his mother called me."

Remedy gave her a playful hit on the shoulder. "Ew!"

"Right? I know I said I wanted to settle down with a

nice, vanilla Catholic guy, but Vince Biaggi was a little too vanilla. I have to believe that in the danger-and-drama spectrum of Vince on one end and Mike the Mistake on the other, there's got to be a guy in central Texas who's somewhere in the middle ground."

Mike the Mistake was Skye's ex-husband. Except she couldn't quite get the word *ex-husband* past her lips. Partly because, eight years later, she was still reeling in disbelief that she'd ever been that out-of-control twenty-year-old who'd allowed the thrill of rebellion to intoxicate her into marrying a lion keeper with an international traveling circus—even if they'd only lasted for three months. And partly out of respect for her faith and her parents, both of which strictly forbid divorce. That three-month marriage had caused her nothing but pain and had resulted in the greatest sin of her life—a sin she could never afford to make again. Which was why she had to get it right next time when it came to choosing a mate, because next time would be forever, for real.

On the fifth floor, they rounded the corner and found Skye's mom leaning against the wall just outside of Kimberly's hotel-room door. Clad in the resort's standard-issue middle-management uniform of a burgundy skirt suit, she held herself with the noble bearing that came with being the fierce loving, no-nonsense heart of both the resort and the Martinez family. She'd put on some pounds since Skye's dad's health had deteriorated a few years earlier, and they'd pleasantly softened her compact, athletic build in a way that made Skye want to hug her every chance she got—not that her mother appreciated any random display of affection.

"Hey, Mom," Skye said. "What are you doing here? What good is it being in charge if you keep working Saturday nights?"

Her mom flashed the key fob at room 524's door, then shouldered it open and held it for Remedy and the luggage trolley. "Your father was driving me crazy. You know how grouchy he gets when his back's hurting. I made him a poultice of herbs, brewed up my mama's special tea, and sent him to bed." She frowned sympathetically at Kimberly as Remedy and Tabby wheeled her in. "Poor thing."

"Kimberly made some bad choices tonight," Tabby said as she pushed.

Her mom shifted her focus to Remedy, a brow raised in a bid for more details, but Remedy just shook her head. "It involves the best man's belt buckle. You don't want to know."

"You're right," Skye's mom said, following them farther into the room. "Where are her friends? Why aren't they taking care of her?"

"The DJ had them busy running through the gamut of eighties dance styles at the reception," Remedy said. "Kimberly was attempting the Running Man on top of a table while a couple of groomsman were filming up her skirt when I found her."

"Bastards," her mom muttered. "Speaking of which . . . Skye, I thought you were on a date tonight."

The trolley wheels snagged on something, giving Skye a chance to look around while Tabby rushed forward to clear the carpet. The room was a wreck, as though a wedding-supply store had sneezed all over it. Every horizontal surface was covered with discarded champagne flutes, makeup, plastic dry-cleaning bags, and glitter. So much glitter.

Skye groped down around the trolley's rear wheels for anything else they may have snagged on and pulled up a blonde weave. Nasty. With a shudder, she tossed it onto the nightstand. "I ditched him to hang out with Remedy."

Remedy, Tabby, and Skye made careful work positioning the trolley next to the nearest queen-size bed with the hope that Kimberly could be roused enough to crawl up into it.

Her mom cringed. "Your date was that bad?"

Skye was spared from answering by a sudden retching sound. The next thing she knew, Kimberly projectile vomited tequila and God-knows-what-else all over her dress, the floor, and the duvet.

Remedy and Tabby sprinted for the hall, shrieking and gagging in disgust. But Skye and her mom merely groaned at the idea of what a pain in the ass it was going to be to clean it all up. Polished Pros, the housekeeping company started by Skye's grandmother more than thirty-five years ago and passed to her daughter, Skye's mother, when she retired, had done wonders for their tolerance in coping with every manner of bodily fluid.

Gesturing to the mess, Skye shot her mom a wry look. "Still more fun than my blind date tonight."

With a roll of her eyes, her mom got on her phone. "Hey, Annika? It's Yessica. Would you bring your cleaning trolley and a new duvet to room 524 please?" To Remedy and Tabby, who stood in the hallway, eyes averted from the room, she called, "You two can get back to the wedding. We'll take it from here."

Some might not like working with their mothers, but Skye didn't mind. Except for a brief stint as a waitress during high school, she'd worked for her mom all her life and fully expected to take over the business as the third-generation owner when her mother retired. And she was damn proud of that legacy. Side-by-side with the Briscoe family itself, Skye's family had been the backbone of Briscoe Ranch Resort for nearly four decades. Besides Polished Pros, which exclusively leased its services to Briscoe Ranch, Skye's father had run the resort's maintenance department until his back forced him onto disability, and innumerable other extended family members worked around the resort in various capacities, from the accounting department to the stable.

Skye made short work of helping Kimberly off the trolley and out of her dress, leaving her in Spanx and a strapless white bra, while her mom fetched wet washcloths and towels.

"You're too picky about men," her mom told Skye as she toweled off Kimberly's hair.

Yes, Skye was picky. She had to be. The next man she fell in love with had to be forever, no mistakes. "This is rural Texas. There are only so many men. Of all the eligible bachelors who work at the resort or go to our church or live in town, I've either dated them or they're not interested in me. There's no one left, mama."

She swabbed Kimberly's face and arms with a wet washcloth, cooing to her as she worked. Skye had endured her fair share of drunken regret back in her early twenties, so she knew how awful the poor girl must be feeling.

Annika arrived pushing a housekeeping trolley. She assessed the situation with a frown and a shake of her head. "Every weekend, every wedding," she grumbled as she walked to the bed.

Skye's mom left Skye to attend to Kimberly while she and Annika stripped the soiled duvet from the bed and stuffed it into a laundry bag.

"I can help you with your man problem, mija," her mom said as she pushed the voluminous skirt of Kimberly's bridesmaid dress into a second laundry bag.

It was an offer her mom had made before. There was just one problem. "I don't believe in magic, Mom."

With Annika busy mopping, Skye and her mom helped Kimberly crawl between the bed sheets and tucked her in. "It's your generation. You don't appreciate tradition. If there isn't an app for it, it doesn't exist."

Skye had heard that argument before, but she knew better. If her mom's old-world magic actually worked, then her dad would be pain free and back at work. If the old magic worked, then maybe Skye's marriage would have too, along with everything else that went wrong during those fleeting months. Her arms, working of their own accord, wrapped around her belly. "Mom, I'm telling you, there's no one."

Her mom grabbed a water bottle from the trolley and set it on Kimberly's nightstand. Then she squared up to Skye and took her hands. "Then there's no harm in trying a little magic. Let me help you find someone to love."

Annika mopped around their shoes. "Yessica helped me last year when Nicco wouldn't commit. She gave me this magic coin that I stuffed in my bra and—*bam*—he proposed."

Never before confronted with an actual, living person for whom her mom's magic had worked, Skye's resolve started to crack. She took a long, hard look at Kimberly, slack-jawed and drooling and going to bed alone—the perfect embodiment of Skye's wild, rebellious, drama-addicted, terminally single past. Not a very pretty picture. Not at all.

She was done being a bridesmaid. Her career's future was all mapped out and she owned her own house, so there was just one thing missing. "Okay, Mom. I give up. Let's do this your way."

Even if it didn't work—which it wouldn't, she was

certain—then at least her mom would stop needling her about trying such ridiculous, old-fashioned methods. Then she could get back to her equally ineffective, often ridiculous modern-day methods of online dating and ill-advised blind dates arranged by eighty-year-old Bingo players. The thought nearly made her wince.

Annika gave a quiet golf clap at Skye's agreement, while Skye's mom straightened up. The impish gleam in her eyes reminded Skye of her fondest memories of Mama Lita—her dad's mother, Edalia—when the two of them were sneaking cookies in the kitchen for breakfast one morning while her mother was in the bedroom ironing.

Without warning, her mom reached out and plucked a hair from Skye's head.

"Ow!"

Impervious to Skye's shock, her mom dropped the hair into a mug lifted from the coffee caddy near the television. "This is going to be great, mija. You'll see."

Skye rubbed the tender spot on her scalp and gathered around the coffee maker along with Annika to watch. With Kimberly's snores as their soundtrack, Skye's mom brewed a cup of coffee right into the same mug that contained Skye's hair. Then, from the housekeeping trolley's mini bar replenishment kit, she pulled a bottle of bourbon and poured it in while chanting under her breath in Spanish, the words said too low and quick for Skye to understand. Then she pinched silver glitter from the bathroom counter and sprinkled it over the magic brew.

"Glitter?" Skye hissed, because *really*? The bourbon and hair, she could sort of understand, but glitter? *Oh, please.*

With eyes closed, her mom waved the cross pendant on her necklace over the mug. "No questions."

Skye darted a look at Annika, who only shrugged.

After another minute more of chanting, her mom's eyes flew open. "The rest of the ingredients we need from the day spa."

All right. That sounded totally legit—*not.* Because what old-world magic didn't require volumizing shampoos and nail polish?

Still, she and Annika followed her mom from the room like eager students. After stowing the trolley in a housekeeping closet near the ice machine, they descended in the elevator to the ground level. They'd only taken a few steps into the lobby when they were stopped in their tracks by none other than Granny June, five foot nothing and sitting astride her hot pink riding scooter, dressed in an emerald jogging suit and with a lowball glass of liquor in her hand.

Skye's mom put her hand on her hip. "Aren't you up a little late for an old woman?" The teasing line was said with a heavy dose of affection borne from forty years of familiarity.

Granny June hoisted her drink, the ice clinking merrily. "I can sleep when I'm dead. What are you kids up to? Skye, shouldn't you be out with Pearl's son right now?"

"Vince Biaggi is a dud. No more dating advice from you," Skye said with a wag of her finger.

Granny June replied, "But his Facebook picture is so handsome!"

Skye's mom stepped between them. "She's listening to me now, June. We're doing this my way, and I have just the spell to help her find the perfect man. All we need are a few final ingredients and we're off to get those now."

Granny June stood from her riding scooter with a spryness that belied her age and extricated a knobby wooden walking cane with a bejeweled handle from behind the scooter's seat. "I'm in. Let's go."

What a motley crew they made, marching through the lobby, past wedding revelers and clusters of hotel guests, then down a flight of stairs to the basement level where the resort's day spa was located. Skye's mom waved her master-key fob at the spa's main door, then led the way into the darkened spa, flipping on lights as she blazed a trail through the hair salon room and into the corridor of private massage rooms.

In the first massage room, her mom went straight for the row of aromatherapy vials on the counter. "A drop of lavender. Two drops of cedar. And, finally, the secret ingredient . . ." She hunched away from the group, but Skye swore she saw her spit into the mug.

Gross. But Skye couldn't find it in her heart to mind. She was having a blast connecting with this side of her mom that seldom made its appearance anymore.

Then her mom was facing them again. "Skye, get a coin from your purse."

Skye dug through her purse and found a quarter loose in the bottom of it. She held the coin out, but her mom shook her head. "Kiss it first."

Her mom held out the mug. "Drop it in."

Skye said a quick prayer as she released the quarter from her fingers. *Bring my true love to me.*

"Hold the mug and tell the spell what you're looking for."

Skye knew the answer without thinking. She cradled the mug in her hands and stared down at the brown, oily liquid. "A man with a solid career. And I'm not going to move away from my family in Dulcet, so he has to be local."

"And handsome," Granny June said.

"And Catholic," her mom added.

It would be nice to meet a man who shared the religion she'd grown up in, but that was hardly mandatory, seeing as how Skye herself had long ago given up trying to follow the strict rules of the Church, much to her mom's chagrin. "And a kind heart."

Now *that* was mandatory.

Her mom gave her a side-eye, but Granny June gave a snort of incredulousness. "Think bigger. Sexier. You deserve it."

She did deserve that. Funny how low Skye's expectations had sunk over the years. "Someone handsome and daring, with dark, soulful eyes, and who makes my toes curl every time he kisses me. Someone who's the staying kind, but that's all right because he'll be all the adventure and thrill I need for the rest of my life, and, most importantly, someone who loves me more than anything else in the world."

Granny June gave a sage nod. "That's more like it."

Skye's mom smiled. "Good. That sounds like a man I'd want for you. Now, reach in and find the coin. Don't dry it. Just stick it in your bra, left cup, as near to your heart as you can."

Skye dipped her hands into the cool liquid and did as she was told, though the coffee was sure to leave a permanent stain on her white lace bra. The wet coin was chilly against her breast, but other than that, she felt nothing new. No magic zings rippling through her. No swirls of glittery magic surrounding her like Cinderella's fairy godmother had accomplished with her wand before the ball. Instead, she felt like the same old Skye Martinez—relationship loser, rebellion junkie, and Polished Pro's assistant manager.

"What's supposed to happen next?" Granny June said.

"We wait," Skye's mom said. "Your perfect man will come. You'll see."

Another silent moment passed, waiting . . . waiting. And then the doorknob turned. The door opened wide.

Skye and her mom whirled toward it, using their bodies to block the view of the spell ingredients scattered on the counter, while Annika pretended to fluff the doughnut-shaped pillow at the head of the massage table.

"We're with housekeeping!" Skye called with a manic tone. "Just finishing up." The last word died on her tongue as she took in the interloper.

A tall, broad-shouldered man filled the doorway, all muscle and tawny skin and dark, smoldering hotness.

"Oh! Didn't expect to see anyone. I, uh . . ." He scratched his head, tousling his inky-black hair in the most adorably sexy way. "I'm Enrique. I'm new at the resort, and I have my first massage client scheduled for the morning, so I wanted to get set up." His attention slid to Skye. There was no mistaking the heat in his eyes as his gaze swept over her. Then his lips curved into a hint of a lopsided smile, just enough to reveal a dimple on his right cheek. "I think I'm going to like this place."

Skye's mom nudged her in the ribs with a whispered, "It's working."

That was fast.

Skye's body lit up with the all-consuming thrum of adventure and drama—her own personal call of the wild. Except this time, there wouldn't be any negative consequences or shame brought onto her and her family, no repentance needed. This thrill was mother-approved. Skye was going to find a sweet, sexy local man to settle down with and then she wouldn't ever be tempted again to run off in search of trouble. She'd have everything she needed right there in Dulcet—in her home and in her bed, forever.

She reached out her hand to Enrique, dizzy and breathless with the realization that tonight's little spell was the first step in making all her dreams come true.

Chapter Two

Four weeks later . . .

Of course there was a mechanical bull. There always was.

Gentry Wells peered out across the bar at the bull from backstage at the Hitching Post Bar of Briscoe Ranch Resort, minutes before show time. Smoke streamed from the bull's nostrils, and its beady eyes glowed red. The pissed-off expression was in discord with the crass appreciation etched on the faces of the men who'd gathered around the arena to watch a long-legged blonde in cut-off shorts straddle it and hold on tight. A few seconds later, Gentry, along with the rest of the men in attendance, admired the sight of her ass flying through the air and landing on the red mats surrounding the bull.

He was still watching with rapt attention as someone slapped him hard on the ass. "Ready to hit another home run, champ?"

That would be Larry Showalter, Gentry's agent, who was at Briscoe Ranch Resort for the same reason Gentry was: to witness the wedding of country music producer Neil Blevins' only daughter, along with just about every other producer, agent, and recording artist in the industry. But unlike every other performer in attendance, Gentry had the singular honor of being tapped by Neil to perform both for the rehearsal dinner and during the wedding ceremony the next night. Lucky him.

"For the love of God, Larry, I've told you a million times. This isn't baseball."

He'd already tried to convince Gentry to overcome his song-writing block by breathing through his eyelids and wearing a garter belt like Tim Robbins did in the movie *Bull Durham*, something to jar him out of his stagnant state of mind. Gentry had flatly refused, until one night, in a fit of panic because he hadn't written any new material in weeks, he'd gone online and bought men's bikini briefs in every color of the rainbow—not that he'd ever admit as much to Larry or anybody else, for that matter. The banana hammocks were way too snug around his junk, but he *had* experienced some sparks of creativity while wearing them. More of the sparkler kind than fireworks, but he'd take it.

Larry smoothed his hand over his salt-and-pepper goatee and peered past the stage to the famous and well-connected crowd. "Might as well be, this industry is such a mind game."

The man did have a point, with one minor clarification. "I think the term you're looking for is mind fuck. And you're definitely right about that."

"Speaking of which, you've got quite the crowd tonight. I counted three producers and the head of Appaloosa Records out there. Not to mention Neil Blevins and his whole crew. That home run I mentioned? Tonight, it'd better be a grand slam. Break the fucking bat." With that, Larry pushed a can of Budweiser into Gentry's hands.

Because what would Gentry Wells, the bad boy of country music, be without his favorite prop? Especially under the watchful eye of Neil Blevins—the man who'd discovered Gentry all those years ago in a going-nowhere bar in Nashville and the reason he was about to go on stage at a bar for free on a Friday night instead of performing for crowds of thousands like he'd become accustomed to. It was a giant middle finger from Neil all wrapped up to look like a touching gesture of affection.

Whatever Neil's motivation, it had been a proposition that Gentry had been unable to turn down, especially after his last album flopped, and with only a month until his deadline to deliver to Neil the passion project he'd fought Neil tooth and nail over. All Gentry had wanted was the chance, for once, to write an entire album of his own songs, something that was about as common in country music as unicorns at a rodeo.

Gentry nodded to the mechanical bull. "Think I should ride it tonight?"

Nick, his band's tattooed, long-haired drummer, strolled by on his way to the stage. "What, the bull? It's named Johnson. One of the bartenders told me earlier." He twirled a drumstick, studying the bull with a cringe. "Mean motherfucker, isn't he?"

Gentry's eyebrows shot up. "They named the bull Johnson?" Gentry had seen more than his fair share of mechanical bulls over the years, but that was a first.

Larry held out a pair of aviator sunglasses and a set of brass knuckles, Gentry's other signature props. "Nothing wrong with watching a pretty girl ride a johnson."

Gentry slid the glasses on, instantly feeling more in character with his onstage persona. "Not sure I want to ride it now. Not too keen on johnsons, myself."

Neil Blevins himself clamored up on the stage and

took the mic, launching into a glowing introduction for Gentry, giving no hints about how strained their relationship had been for the past year.

"That guy blows more smoke up people's asses than Johnson the Bull," Nick muttered.

Larry took the brass knuckles out of Gentry's palm and wedged them on his right hand, his guitar strumming hand. "Either way, it's go time. Bottom of the ninth of the World Series, bases loaded, two outs."

Gentry adjusted the hardware, then flexed his arm and watched his tattoo of his family's Oklahoma wheat field undulate beneath the torn-off sleeves of his black T-shirt. "Jesus, Larry. Give it a rest, would you?" he growled with the heavy twang that was a signature of his stage persona. Mr. Bad Boy of Country himself. *Hell to the yeah.*

But all that earned Gentry was another slap on the ass. "Go get 'em, champ."

Nick snickered as he followed Gentry toward the stage. Gentry was two steps from the stage when the panic hit, right on cue. He ground to a stop, and Nick smacked into his back.

"Sorry," Gentry said. "Gotta get in the zone. You go on ahead."

Nick gave a salute with his drumstick and walked past him with a loping stride.

Gentry waited for him to get out of earshot, then let out a long exhalation. The rails were starting to come off his career and he couldn't shake the feeling that maybe he shouldn't have pressed so hard for the chance to write his own music. He'd already proved himself an ace at being a puppet—the hard bodied, tough persona of the Gentry Wells business, but not the brains or the artistry. Yeah, he could sing and play a mean guitar. And, yeah, he had enough charisma to fill a football stadium. But that was about it.

It didn't help that the Hitching Post Bar was packed with music executives and recording artists, a veritable who's who of Nashville dropped into the Texas countryside for the weekend.

There's a reason they're out there enjoying themselves while you're up here, playing a goddam wedding rehearsal, his battered ego whispered seductively. *They all know your last album flopped.*

Could they smell blood in the water? Were the newly signed musicians in the crowd salivating, eager to take his place on the charts and airwaves?

They all know you don't write your own music. They all know you don't have the chops. It's just a matter of time before they figure it out.

Damn stage fright. Damn insecurities. He had every right to his fame and fortune, no matter what his traitorous mind tried to convince him.

He was Gentry Fucking Wells.

The reason he was playing this wedding rehearsal was because he was the chosen one. He was the one that Neil Blevins' daughter Natalie had personally requested as the soundtrack for the most important day of her life. That was a big deal. Just like *he* was a big deal, bigger than any one flop of an album. Big enough that he'd shot to stardom all those years ago with his very first single, despite that he'd been singing someone else's songs. When all the chips were down, he hadn't needed anything to conquer the country-music industry but the power of his personality and the good looks he'd been born with.

Larry stepped in front of him. "Here. You almost forgot." It was that open can of Bud. Because the proud creator of the party anthem "Beer O'Clock" could never be without one. With that prop, his persona was complete. He might be Neil Blevins' puppet, but he was a badass puppet, the baddest around. Bright pink bikini underwear notwithstanding.

Holding up the beer like it was an Olympic torch, Gentry took the stage amid the cheers and calls of dozens. Instead of dozens, he imagined a football stadium full of thousands of women screaming his name. Been there, done that. And he might be in a bar, performing for a wedding, but he was going to give them the show of his life, just like he did every single time.

"Y'all ready to party?" he crooned, low, into the mic. Because beer swilling, hard partying, womanizing Gentry Wells was too cool to shout.

Setting the beer on the drum platform, he lifted his acoustic guitar from its stand and strapped it on. It wasn't mic'ed and the band took care of all the instrumental heavy lifting, but guitar playing was a big part of his musical process and it gave him something to do with his hands during his shows, so he tried to never be without it on.

Sure enough, with the strum of the opening riff to his biggest hit, "Beer O'Clock," the noise level in the joint went into overdrive. The song had shot him to the top of the charts, helped him win Album of the Year at the ACMs, and bought him his dream ranch, but the kicker was that it was the greatest con job in history. Gentry hated the feeling of being drunk and out of control and couldn't stand the taste of beer. Never had and never would. And, like most of his songs, he'd had nothing to do with the writing of "Beer O'Clock." Fraud central.

But Gentry's rendition tonight kept the crowd electrified

and singing along, all the way to the end when he held up his can of Bud. "To Natalie Blevins and Toby Weissman! May you always find time to crack open a cold beer with the one you love."

The young men in the front row started chanting, "Chug! Chug! Chug!"

Kill me now, Gentry thought as he brought the can to his lips. Thanks to all the practice he got with this persona, he was able to squelch a shudder and stink face as he drank a long swig, but, damn, he hated the taste of that shit.

After "Beer O'Clock," he worked through the rest of his hits—judiciously leaving out his anthem to his long, pattern of commitment-phobia titled "Built to Leave." For his second-to-last number, he lit the crowd up again with the start of his hit single "Well Hung." The audience went ape shit, as always. Gentry let waves of cowboy attitude pour off him as he launched into song . . .

Girl, I hung around like a puppy dog
Hung up over you
Until you hung me out to dry
What's a man to do?
So I hung a U-turn back to this bar,
To toast to our good-bye
But all I got as my reward was too hung over to cry

"If you know the chorus, then sing it with me!" he called, holding the microphone toward the crowd. All thoughts of failure and fraudulence were gone. It was just him and his fans and the songs that had helped him achieve this crazy-amazing life. In unison, every person in the place shook the walls with their voices.

Oh, It's big
And it's long
That list you made of all my many wrongs.
Oh, it's thick
And it's strong
That relief that I'm feeling now that you're
done gone.
And it's hard, so hard, for you, I know
But, babe you're never gonna find another
man who's so well hung as me.
Oh, you're never gonna find another man,
Who's as damn well hung as me.

After the second verse, the guitarist launched into an extended solo, as was their usual practice when performing it live, to give Gentry time to interact with the crowd. Except this time, he thought, *fuck it.* Time to ride the bull.

He set his guitar aside and leapt off the stage into the crowd with his microphone in hand. The people parted, catching on that he was headed to the mechanical bull at the back of the room. Up close, Johnson the Bull looked far less intimidating. Its mangy hide was fraying at the edges, and it bore scuffs on its sides from countless boot heels. But if the crowd in the bar cared about its phoniness, they didn't show it.

Not the mechanical bull, nor Gentry.

He sang the final verse and coda of "Well Hung" while straddling the bull, then let the band rip into another extended instrumental solo while he nodded to the bar employee waiting for his signal to start it bucking.

With the microphone in his raised right hand and his left hand holding fast to the bull's leather straps, he managed to hold on for the whole eight seconds of jerky motion, much to the delight of the onlookers. He fell from the bull to the mats with as much style as he could, though his back had started to spasm. Looked like his mechanical bull riding days were done. *Oh darn.*

On his way back to the stage, someone stuffed a Texas state flag in his hand. With a wink, he handed it off a few steps later to the very same blonde who'd gotten tossed off Johnson before the show. Once upon a time, she'd been exactly his type. But his blood hadn't boiled for any woman in quite some time, not since his last girlfriend, Cheyenne, had dumped him very publicly the year before. Still, he faked a sizzling moment of connection with the blonde, capped with a kiss to the back of her hand, then jogged to the stage.

For his last number, he located the bride-to-be in the audience. He wasn't known for his slow songs, but he did have in his arsenal a dirty little ballad about a couple on their wedding night called *Garter Belt.*

Natalie Blevins and her fiancé, Toby, made their way through the crowd from their seat of honor on a raised seating section in the back. Gentry had watched Natalie grow up from afar, mostly through photographs on Neil's desk and the tales he told of her. Gentry knew absolutely nothing about Toby Weissman, but he seemed nice enough, though way too spineless to handle having Neil Blevins as a father-in-law.

Both kids looked way too young to get married, but that was probably only because Gentry was no spring chicken himself, as his back twinges during the bull riding had reminded him. They were probably in their early twenties, which was the age Gentry had been when he'd gotten married—and gotten divorced, for that matter—so he wasn't in any position to judge. But, damn, did their youth make him feel every one of his thirty-six years.

Natalie and Toby mounted the stage stairs tentatively, clearly uncomfortable in the spotlight, which was odd given that there were five hundred guests expected at their wedding the next night. It made Gentry wonder how much say Natalie had gotten for her own wedding or if she and her intended groom were as much puppets in Neil Blevins' country-music empire as Gentry was.

Two chairs appeared from somewhere, probably thanks to a bar employee, and Gentry directed the couple to sit while he serenaded them. It was fun to watch both the bride and the groom's cheeks go bright red with every bawdy lyric. The crowd ate it up.

As the song ended, and with the audience cheering and the band playing an extended coda, Gentry hugged Natalie and presented her to the crowd for applause. He then peeled off his aviator glasses and stuffed them onto Toby's face. To top it off, he gave the young man his brass knuckles, which looked absolutely ridiculous on Toby's slim, pale fingers. As a final touch, Gentry held both couple's arms up like they were champion boxers and he was the ref, much to the crowd's delight.

Then Gentry beat it the hell off the stage, leaving the happy couple in the spotlight to the great delight of their family and friends—and leaving him to shed the remains of his stage persona and take his first deep breath in hours.

Larry handed him a cold water bottle the minute he stepped backstage. "I'd call that a grand slam, all right. The bull was a great touch."

"Glad you enjoyed it because I think that was my last

time on a mechanical bull. I'm lucky I didn't throw my back out. That Johnson's kind of an asshole."

"Most Johnsons are," Nick tossed out.

True enough. Before he could say as much, a bright-eyed young man got in his space, smiling up at him. "Gentry Wells! This is awesome. I don't care what they said about your last album. You still got it."

Gentry used to be caught off-guard by backhanded compliments like that, but no longer. "It's all good," he said instead. Easy-go-lucky, that was him. Not a care in his badass country music world.

"You'll always be one of the great ones," the guy tossed out as he handed Gentry a magazine for him to autograph.

Shee-it. Gentry ought to just stamp *Has Been* on his forehead.

"I'm still bummed that you and Cheyanne split up," the guy continued. "She's so hot."

"Well aren't you just a bag of sunshine," Gentry said as he signed the magazine and handed it back.

Cheyanne, the sweet and sexy lead singer in an up-and-coming country band, had been his latest in a long stream of short-term monogamous relationships since his divorce more than a decade earlier. He and Cheyanne had made headlines as a country-music power couple, which had been great for both their careers in the short term, but even that hadn't been enough to keep him from getting bored and checking out, until Cheyanne had finally had enough of his neglect.

Striving to make lemonade out of lemons, he'd turned the experience into an epic breakup anthem that turned out to be not-so epic, if the sales figures and lack of airplay were any indication. How ironic that he hadn't been able to turn a country album about heartbreak into a hit, a hard truth that had him feeling more like a fraud than ever. At least he'd had one positive decision come out of all of that. He finally realized that healthy long-term relationships weren't in his nature and it was time to stop pretending that they were.

So he was done with monogamy, done with pretending to be the kind of man who stayed. Ironic, that. "Beer O'Clock" might be his biggest hit, but it was also the furthest from the truth. And his most honest single, "Born to Leave," had been his least successful. Well, his second-most-honest single after "Well Hung." A man's got to tell the truth sometimes.

Larry shooed the stagehand away, then dropped a pint of beer in Gentry's hands. Another prop drink for his grand exit. "Don't listen to them. You can't win 'em all."

"They're right," Gentry said, staring at the foam. "Look at me, playing a wedding rehearsal dinner. Guess this was a glimpse of my future, coming full circle. Rise and fall of a country music giant."

Nick rubbed his thumb and index finger together in the universal symbol of the world's smallest violin. "Boo Fuckin' Hoo."

Larry brushed imaginary lint off Gentry's shoulder. "Nick's right. You've got to stop talking like that. Everybody knows there's no crying in—"

Nick speared a finger at Larry. "Don't say it. Don't you dare."

But it was too late. Gentry's funk had been lifted, and he was smiling despite himself. Larry and Nick were always good about bringing him back down to earth when he got lost to his anxieties.

"You wanna hang around and watch the other acts with me?" Nick asked. "Plenty of tail to catch. I saw you winking at that blonde. Weddings do have their perks. All these bridesmaids and women who are in the mood for romance. I definitely plan to capitalize on that all weekend long."

That was one thing about Gentry's girlie underpants—they kept him celibate, his mind on his music and nothing else because there was no way in hell he'd strip down in front of a hot little number while wearing those. Gentry slapped Nick on the back and handed the untouched beer to him. "If they're looking for romance, then I don't know why they'd mess with me."

To Gentry's trained musical ear, there was a country song in that "chasing tail" phrase—something about catching lizard tails as a boy to growing up and catching tail in the clubs as a man. Now that he'd committed to Neil Blevins that he'd write his own music for the next album, he owed it to himself to sit down and get the lyrics on paper. Just what he needed, another oversexed, innuendo-laden song to add to his portfolio. But if it kept his star burning and kept his producers and fans happy, then what did he care?

Man, oh, man, was he jaded.

"Think I'll get some fresh air." He'd never spent much time in hill country, but what he'd seen since his arrival at Briscoe Ranch Resort, he liked. Maybe he'd rent out the villa the resort had put him up in for the rest of the spring. God knows his empty ranch didn't do a thing for his sanity. "Catch you two tomorrow. And don't do anything I wouldn't do."

"Jeez, don't wish that on me. You're damn boring these days," Nick called out after him.

With a chuckle, Gentry set out across the darkened resort grounds in the direction of the equestrian center. With any luck, he'd find it unlocked because there was nothing like looking a horse in the eye to get a man right with himself again—and maybe come up with another hit song in the process.

Skye took a sharp corner at a speed that would've been way too fast for someone who hadn't been driving the same winding, two-lane country roads of Dulcet all her life. The speed got her heart racing a little, which was pleasant enough, but it was hardly the cure she needed, given the date from hell she'd just escaped from.

And by hell, she meant the most boring hour and a half of her life, spent at a barbecue joint in Fredericksburg listening to her date drone on and on about his car repair garage. He'd talked so much that he'd barely had time to eat before his food got cold. Skye had counted the drops of condensation that had slipped down the brown bottle of his beer to pool on the gray Formica table, only losing count when he decided he'd done enough talking and it was time to put the moves on Skye.

With a kiss to her hand, he declared, "I've never felt this way so instantaneously about a woman before. I'm spellbound with you, and I think you and I are going to have a real future together."

That was enough of that. She'd slid off her stool and grabbed her purse. One flippant excuse and five long strides had her out the door and on the way to her car.

It was her third date that week alone and the tenth new guy she'd gone out with since she'd agreed to that damnable spell her mom had conjured. She should be more grateful for the sudden influx of eligible bachelors in her life, shouldn't she? But she'd never felt so suffocated before.

Around the next turn in the road, she spotted a man standing next to a broken-down truck on the side of the road who was trying to flag her down. He looked like his engine had overheated. He was handsome and rugged—and would probably want to marry her within moments of her stepping out of the car, if the last few weeks had taught her anything. But even if she wasn't already fed up with the male gender that night, Skye didn't make a habit of pulling over to help strange men after dark when she was driving alone.

"Not tonight, buddy. Sorry." Hopefully someone else would be along soon to give him a hand.

She tapped the radio's power button. "Halleluiah!" blared the speakers, mid-chorus of what was apparently her new theme song, "It's Raining Men."

She growled out her frustration as she smacked the power button hard. The coin in her bra dug into her skin. True to the song, her world had been raining men since her mom conjured the spell. But Skye was beginning to believe the adage "Be careful what you wish for" because, though every man she met fit her parameters—local, good looking, kind, and ready to settle down—none of them were quite right. Not one of them inspired her to want to take a chance on forever—or even a second date.

Skye was in no mood to go home and deal with her sister, Gloria's, hunger for every juicy detail about her love life. Normally, Skye didn't mind that Gloria had taken to living vicariously through her since her husband, Ruben, had died in combat three years earlier. It had to be tough being a working single mom, especially with her two rambunctious kids, which is why Skye had invited Gloria and her two kids to move in with her after Ruben's death. Normally, Skye loved living with them, but she just didn't have the patience to sit and detail her evening to Gloria every single time she went on a lousy date. What Skye needed was a thrill, a fix. Something wild and just for her. What she needed was a late-night trail ride.

Smiling, her nerves instantly less agitated, she started planning the route that she and Vixen, the horse she regularly borrowed from James Decker, the owner of Briscoe Ranch's equestrian center, would take that night. Out in the field on her favorite trail, there would be no way any men would surprise her. She could be alone with the wind and the night and her need for speed. At the fork in the road that led north to her neighborhood or west to Briscoe Ranch Resort, she lingered at the stop sign while she texted Decker to let him know her plan.

Moments later, he replied. *I'll unlock the stable for you. Have fun.*

Suddenly, the night air felt electric. The leaves of the oaks she passed shimmered a crisp, deep green in her headlights, and the moon shone in stark brightness against the fathomless sky as she drove west to the resort. But mostly, the thrill came from realizing that there were no more bewitched men waiting to woo her around every bend in the road or certainly none on the well-trodden trail through the canyon to the south of the resort. Just her, Vixen, and Mother Nature.

She turned on the radio again. This time, it was playing "Proud Mary." Skye cranked it up, rolled down her window, and sang along all the way to the stable. In the parking lot, she'd only taken a few steps when she heard her name. Thinking it might be Decker, she turned. Her heart sank. So much for her man-free evening.

"Oh, Enrique. This is . . . a surprise." She and the resort's new masseuse had gone on two dates, on the first of which he'd revealed to her that he was writing his great American novel in his spare time and on the second of which he'd spent half their time together reading excerpts aloud to her.

"The stars drew me here to you tonight, my lady."

She closed her eyes. "I am not your lady."

He brushed his fingers over the tips of her hair. "So modest. Like a flower waiting to bloom."

Okay, that was one word that should *never* be used to describe her, which highlighted how screwed-up this spell was. The men it had brought her weren't falling for her because of who she was or what she brought to the table. They barely registered anything real about her. She jerked her head away. "I have to go."

"As you wish," he murmured.

She took a step, then whirled around, her finger spearing through the air. "Don't follow me." She wasn't usually so harsh, but her nerves were frayed.

She stomped the rest of the way to the stable, taking her irritation out on the dust and gravel path. On the way, she reached into her bra and took out the blessed—no, *cursed*—coin. She was *so* over this little experiment. On the other hand, maybe the spell really had worked. She certainly didn't need a man in her life anymore.

The first thing she noticed when she rounded the corner to the stable was that the light was streaming through the cracks of the wood. That was sweet of Decker to leave the lights on for her. But the moment she pushed the door open, she bit out a "Oh, hell no."

In the middle of the aisle stood a tall, strapping man. He was holding a broom, and it looked like she'd caught him mucking out a stall.

Not another one. She couldn't get away from them.

It didn't matter that this one was the best-looking man yet who'd been sent her way. He wore a backward ball cap over dark blond hair just a shade too long to be respectable, a black T-shirt with the sleeves torn off to reveal several expansive tattoos and that had been tucked haphazardly into a pair of low slung, distressed jeans that fit him just right in all the places and ended with dusty brown cowboy boots.

He noticed her right away and, for a beat, they stood and looked at each other. She watched his blue eyes rake over her. "Didn't mean to trespass, but the door was open and I couldn't help myself. You a hotel guest too?" He chewed each word with a sexy growl of a drawl. Behind a dusting of stubble, his chiseled jaw tightening with approval of what he saw in his assessment of her.

Nice try.

She'd seen that look before. Way too often lately. "No. But I came here to be alone." Before the spell had been cast, she would have never been so affronting, but the barrage of men had frayed her politeness. She now found it impossible to demur.

With smiling eyes, he leaned against the broom handle. "I suppose we're at an impasse 'cause so did I. But, uh . . ." His gaze turned languid as he perused her body again. "I'm pretty sure there's room in here for both of us."

The drawl didn't sound Texan, if she had to guess. "So you're a guest at the resort?"

"Yes, ma'am."

That *yes, ma'am* was like a lasso around her hips, urging her toward him a step at a time. Was it possible that he wasn't a local, which meant he hadn't been summoned by the spell? "You're not from around here."

He shook his head. "Oklahoma. I'm in town for a wedding this weekend."

Hope and interest surged through her. "Random question: are you Catholic?" Not that Skye cared, but thanks to her mom's interjection while they were casting the spell, every prospective date she'd encountered since that night had been.

The question tugged his eyebrows together, though the heated interest in his eyes never wavered. "Lutheran."

Not a local, not Catholic. And he was not dark-haired and dark-eyed, to boot. *Three strikes and you're out.*

Relief relaxed her shoulders and peeled away at her armor. This sexy, corn-fed Oklahoma cowboy was not part of the spell. She was in no danger of falling for him. Or him for her. She took a final step that brought her close enough to catch the faint scent of his aftershave and trace the curves of his lips with her gaze.

"I'm Skye. What's your name?"

The muscles in his cheeks tugged those lips into a straight line and his gaze slid past her as he considered the question. "Tell you what, Skye. I don't think I'm gonna tell you my name." With a sweep of long eyelashes, he focused those baby blues on her eyes again. "Call me crazy, but tonight I just want to be that guy you caught mucking stalls in the barn."

Even better. After the month she'd had, with the smitten, puppy-dog eyes and fawning from the men she'd dated, not to mention the several marriage proposals she'd fielded, it came as a thrill to know that she could flirt with this guy—she could even sleep with him if she wanted—and yet there would be no price to pay, no *forever* to worry about. Never mind that becoming involved with resort guests was strictly forbidden by Polished Pro's contract with Briscoe Ranch. If anything, that particular rule infused her blossoming interest with a sharp edge of danger. And Skye Martinez could never resist a little harmless danger.

But to make absolutely certain, she asked, "To be clear, you don't want to marry me?"

He gave her the side-eye, as though she'd asked him a trick question. "No."

Excellent. "And you're leaving town again after tomorrow night's wedding, right? We'd never have reason to run into each other again because you'll be gone?"

"Uh . . . no? I mean, yes? My man-brain isn't following what you're getting at."

"Nothing. Never mind." Allowing her expression to turn flirty, she slid her fingers along the broom handle. "So, why are you out here mucking stalls instead of with your wedding party?"

His attention darted to an acoustic guitar leaning against the wall. "Looking for a little clarity."

"Your guitar?"

"Sometimes a little clarity requires a song," he said on a shrug.

She gripped the broom handle and gave it a jiggle, though with his weight resting on it, it barely budged. "And sometimes it requires mucking a stall."

"Now you're feeling me. What are you doing here so late on a Friday night, dressed so fine?'

"Same as you. I come here when I need to clear my mind," she said.

"Yeah? What do you have on your mind that needs clearing?"

She flickered her eyebrows, playing it cool, even though her arousal was a thick, heavy force bubbling in the cauldron of her belly. The sensation was almost foreign, it'd been so long since a man had lit her up like that.

"Let's make a deal," she told him. "I won't show you my baggage if you don't show me yours."

He leaned the broom against a stall door and faced her

square on, crossing his arms over his chest in a way that made his biceps round into solid curves. "Best deal I've heard in a long time."

The thrill of adventure coursed through her, potent and wild. More intoxicating than a trail ride in the dark with Vixen. Flirting with a man who wasn't under a spell, whose name she'd didn't know, whom she'd never see again. And a resort guest on top of all that. Then again, who was to say she couldn't have her cake and eat it too?

"In that case, stable boy, I have a question. You want to go for a ride?"

Chapter Three

Not that Gentry was questioning his good fortune, but riding through the dark night on a horse with a beautiful woman who had no idea who he was and didn't care was almost too surreal to believe. But there they were, on a trail ride that hugged the hills and crossed through meadows and streams, with nothing but moonlight and stars to light their way.

Gentry had been skeptical of riding out into the backcountry like this, but Skye had reassured him that she knew the trail by heart, just as the horses did with their superior night vision, and that the trail was pristinely kept by the equestrian center, with no hidden rocks or holes to trip the horses up. So far, he'd found her reassurances true in every way.

The trail they were on had narrowed to single-file through a field of bluebonnets as high as his ankles that he was sure were lovely, but he only had eyes for the way the saddle accentuated Skye's curves and the way the movement of the horse rocked her hips, all the way down to where the simple black cotton dress she wore bunched up high on her thighs. The dark copper hue of her skin glowed golden where the moonlight kissed it from the tops of those thighs until where her slender legs disappeared into black boots with intricate turquoise and gold stitching.

But his favorite part was the way her dark-as-night hair whipped around when she turned to look at him with eyes that danced with seductive mischief. It had gotten so he was dreaming up questions just to get her to turn.

"So . . . this is Frosty I'm riding? As in 'Stay Frosty, my friends'?"

She turned in the saddle and smiled at him, and just like that, his body pulsed with carnal awareness. "As in the snowman. The holiday season is a huge deal at the resort. All the animals have Christmas-y names."

Which gave him new understanding of why the private villa he was renting for the weekend was named the Poinsettia Suite. "Then your horse, Vixen. You're sayin' that's not just a reflection of its hot-as-hell rider tonight?"

"No. But thank you."

"The gratitude's all mine, believe me."

His mind wasn't only filled with questions he wanted to ask her to keep her turning and talking to him. The longer they rode, the more he was dying to ask about what she did for work at the resort. What her full name was. How did she learn to ride like this? But every time a question about her welled up, he bit his tongue.

I won't show you my baggage if you don't show me yours.

Far be it for him to be so curious, when he'd opted not to share his name with her.

That in itself made him freer. He was just a man spending the evening with a beautiful woman. He wasn't Gentry the performer. Gentry the celebrity.

Gentry the washed-up star.

Just a man on a horse, riding in the dark.

Inspiration sparked in his mind like a sunburst. This night, this woman, was begging for a song to be written about her. "Riding in the Dark." Perfect.

She turned again, her eyes bright. "The trail's opening up. I thought we might get our giddyup going, if you think you can handle your horse."

Handling the horse wasn't a problem. It was its rider he was having trouble getting a handle on. Or, more accurately, he was having trouble getting a handle on his urge to pull her down off that horse and right into his arms. And he might have done it if the thought of galloping side-by-side with her in the darkness didn't hold such appeal.

But appeal it did. It'd been a long time since he rode like this, carefree and just for the fun of it, and even longer since he'd ridden in the dark, but it was a rush of freedom to submit to their horses' night vision and the moonlight. How could he have forgotten something so wild and wonderful? Of course, he knew why. He'd been so busy hustling for his career for so long, touring and recording, then doing it all again. To top it all off, Cheyanne hadn't been into horses, which, looking back on it, should have been a red flag.

"You tell me when," he said. "Let's open her up."

Another smiling look over her shoulder, another painful pulse to his heart and his groin and all the places in between. "Then let's go. Ride with me."

She gave a click of her tongue and the slightest nudge of her boot—and she and Vixen were off. Gentry nudged Frosty into motion, but the horse was already speeding up to catch his friend. Neck and neck, their horses tore through the countryside.

The wind in his hair, the not-unpleasant off-kilter

feeling of riding in the darkness on an unknown trail in an unknown land. Gentry had never felt so alive. Blood pounded through his veins, his lungs filled and emptied with air, the wind nipped at his cheeks, and every footfall of the horses hit his ears with crystal clarity.

Just like that, the puppet strings that had been binding Gentry snapped off. He was a free man. Was it the riding or was it the woman? Or was it the magic of hill country and the balmy Texas air? All he knew was that this experience was one-hundred-percent authentic—everything his performance tonight, hell, his life, hadn't been.

They barreled around a bend in the hills, but slowed slightly on the other side of it. Skye spread her arms wide and tipped her face up to the heavens, eyes closed. Her body swayed with a loose-hip grace in rhythm with her horse's stride. "This is it. This is what I live for."

"Amen to that."

She dropped her chin and smiled at him, broadly enough that her teeth glowed white with the moon's reflection. "Thank you for this. I needed to step out of myself for a night."

What did that mean, that she'd needed to step out of herself? For the first time, he recalled her words when she'd first discovered him in the stable. She'd been looking for a place to gain clarity, though she hadn't said from what. What was going on in her life? What wasn't working for her?

Gentry was filled with a sudden, inexplicable urge to fix whatever it was. But that wasn't part of the plan. Their whole time together tonight was predicated on the fact that he didn't want to reveal his identity and her obvious relief that they'd never see each other again after this weekend.

So, then, this ride—and whatever came to pass between them after it—would have to be enough. And wasn't that a damn shame?

"Think the horses can handle another run? Do you think you can?" he asked in challenge.

This time, she gave him no signal before bursting forward into the night. It took Gentry and Frosty the lengths of two meadows to catch up with her, and by the time he did, they could both sense the horses fatiguing.

Which meant it was time to head back to the stable. As much fun as Gentry had on the ride, he had the unmistakable feeling the best of the night was yet to come.

Back at the stable, they worked in charged silence to tend the horses, the air thrumming with the knowledge that as soon as Vixen and Frosty were tucked in their stalls, something was going to happen between Skye and Gentry and it was going to be fireworks. He knew it; she knew it. And he couldn't fucking wait.

"That was incredible," he said as she latched Vixen's stall. "It almost makes me want to get back to my ranch, my horses."

"Almost?" Skye's cheeks were flushed from the ride and her dress was wrinkled. If possible, she looked even sexier in this disheveled state, a true cowgirl with an untamed spark in her eyes that were the color of the earth after a rainstorm.

Fire and earth. And Skye. Everything he hadn't known he needed that night.

He tucked a strand of her hair behind her ear. "Yes, ma'am, because there's nobody like you there waiting to ride with me."

When she tipped her chin up and her lips parted, he didn't even try to fight the urge to kiss her.

Their mouths came together, hot and hungry, as

though their trail ride had been an hour of foreplay leading very specifically, very deliberately, to this moment of connection. There was nothing exploratory or tentative about it. Their primed bodies pressed together, the perfect chemistry of her body's soft curves and his hard edges. Gentry's hand splayed over the small of her back to worship the flared curve of her hip as her hands explored his neck and hair.

Brand new lyrics and guitar riffs raced through his head at lightning speed as the kiss got dirtier and sloppier, their hands more frantic in their exploration as desire throbbed between them, thick and elemental.

His dick hardened painfully in the maddeningly tight pink bikini briefs. That's when it hit him: no matter how much fun he could have with Skye, it had to end here. And not just because he was wearing a ridiculous pink plum sack as underwear. The heart of the matter was that whatever he and Skye did, the pleasure would be fleeting, ultimately meaning nothing to his future or his career unless he could take all that raw, erotic power and repurpose it to fuel his creativity. As much as he longed to lay Skye down on his bed and make down-and-dirty love to her for the rest of the night, the hard truth was that he had an album's worth of songs to come up with in a month's time, and for the first time in months, he felt saturated with inspiration and fresh ideas.

Skye and their midnight ride had been the key, but it was time for him to take the reins and turn toward his future, which meant it was time to bid good-bye to the sweetest surprise he'd encountered in a long, long time.

He peeled his body away from hers and stepped back. When he opened his eyes and looked at Skye, it was to find her clutching the wall behind her. Her lips were dewy and pouty, fully kissed. Her chest heaved with every labored breath. He looked into her eyes and let a languid smile curve his lips. Damn, she was a sight to behold. Ravishing was the only word that came to mind to describe her.

It took a moment for Gentry to rebalance himself and find his voice. "Skye, I hope you'll forgive me for saying this, but I'm gonna need to stop right here and leave it like this between us. As bad as I want more of you, this has been a perfect night with you, and I need to hang on to the memory of it." He straightened his thumbs and index fingers into a frame and gestured from her body to her face. "With you, just like this. Does that make any kind of sense?"

Her languid smile fell and she nodded. "All that baggage that we agreed not to share."

"Exactly. You know what I'm talking about."

"I do. I don't like it, but I get it because it's the same for me." Her voice was husky, and a hint of a Hispanic accent had crept into it.

He'd done that to her. He'd stripped away all her pretenses and made her melt into this supple, sultry beauty. That knowledge would sustain him through what he knew would be a sleepless night of song writing. And there was nothing saying they couldn't return for an encore the next night, generate some more heat—and perhaps even some more inspiration. "And, hey, there's always tomorrow night. Are you free to meet again?"

Her smile turning aloof, she rolled her eyes to the ceiling, as if her weekly schedule were posted there.

He stepped closer, reminding her of how charged the air between them got when they were near. "Say you'll be here, Skye. Nine o'clock. Give me one last night with you before I pack up and go home to Oklahoma."

Her eyes fluttered closed. On a breathy whimper, she

leaned in for a kiss. Gentry groaned as his willpower snapped. He braced his hands on the wall behind her and lowered his mouth. But before their lips could do more than brush, she ducked under his arm and out of reach, playing hard to get.

He whirled to face her and found her smile one of flirty aloofness. She let her gaze linger on his lips before rolling it up his face to meet his eyes. "I guess you'll have to wait and see if I show up tomorrow night."

He watched the seductive sway of her hips with each step as she walked away. So much for aloofness; he had all the evidence he needed that she was feeling it too.

He adjusted himself in the underpants. Man, had he gotten it wrong. He hadn't needed any special underwear or to try breathing out of his eyelids to break him free from his writer's block. He'd needed a midnight ride with one of the hottest strangers he'd ever laid eyes on. As soon she was out of sight, he sat down on a bench near his guitar and whipped his phone out. He opened an email to himself, getting all those lyrics and song ideas out before he lost them. Frosty stuck his head out of his stall and nuzzled Gentry's head as he typed with urgent purpose.

When he'd gotten all the ideas out of his head, he stood and gave Frosty one last pet, then grabbed his guitar and headed back out into the night. Skye was nowhere to be seen, but then again, he hadn't expected her to hang around after an exit like that. He walked with long, quick strides across the resort grounds to the resort's cluster of lakefront private villas, eager to get busy crafting all those songs that his sexy new muse had inspired.

Chapter Four

Another weekend, another celebrity wedding, which meant there were way too many entitled, famous people at the resort this weekend for Skye's taste. She loved Remedy and was so grateful for the friendship that had evolved between them since Remedy had relocated to Texas two years earlier, but Remedy was the daughter of two insanely famous actors and, as the resort's wedding planner, she'd turned Dulcet into a bona fide celebrity hot spot.

Great for business, but not so great for Polished Pro's staff's morale. While actresses and celebrity couples were hit-and-miss about tipping and their various levels of obnoxious entitlement, musicians were a whole different animal. They partied the hardest, left lousy tips if any, created the biggest messes in their rooms, and kept vampirish hours that screwed with Skye's housekeeping schedule. But even this weekend's influx of five hundred guests for some country music mogul's daughter's wedding couldn't erase the skip in Skye's step as she went through her workday.

"Last night's date must have been a winner. You're

practically glowing," her mom commented in their shared office on the basement level of the resort's main building. She speared her finger at Skye. "Just don't tell me that glow is because you slept with him. If you treat yourself like a hussy, then men will too."

Right. She'd been on a date last night. She'd nearly forgotten. The truth was, she was pretty damn pleased with her hussy-like behavior the night before, not that she was ever going to share the story with anyone, least of all her mom. Her late-night rendezvous with the mysterious stable boy was an erotic present all for her. "Oh, yeah, the date was great. He was really generous." With his words and talking about himself.

"Good. The spell is working. I told you, mija. All you had to do was believe in it."

"Like I'm Dorothy in the *Wizard of Oz*?" The power was in her the whole time, and all she had to do was believe in it?

"Just call me the Good Witch Glenda," her mom said with a smile.

Skye loved moments like this when she could joke with her mom. When her dad's back pain was stable enough for her mom to let down her defenses and relax a little, she even made a joke sometimes. And ever since Skye had agreed to the spell, her bond with her mom had seemed to strengthen. For that reason alone, Skye was so glad she'd given up the fight and agreed to it, even if it'd turned her life into a zombie movie—except with eligible bachelors instead of actual zombies. Close enough.

The radios they used to communicate with their staff beeped in unison from their desks. "Skye or Yessica, are either of you in the office? It's Laura."

Skye was the first to reach for her radio. "This is Skye. What's up, Laura?"

"I'm only on my second villa and I'm already wiped out of Jack Daniels and Johnny Walker Black. These country music people must be crazy about their whiskey. Any chance you could swing through with more so I can stay on schedule?"

If only Polished Pros got a cut of the tabs from the minibar. Skye might have to contest that point when their contract with Briscoe Ranch came up for renewal. "No problem. I'm on my way."

Laura was right to radio in that request. With forty employees and hundreds of rooms and suites to clean every day, the more Skye kept her ladies on schedule during their shifts, the better their operation ran. So far, this bunch of country music people weren't as bad as other groups of musicians the resort had hosted, but the real test would come that night during and after the wedding they were all in town for.

Skye didn't know the first thing about country music except what she heard as background noise in restaurants or when she flipped past the country station on the radio in search of her Top 40s or classic R&B stations. But this weekend's guests had been so unexpectedly pleasant that she might have to give it another listen sometime. Maybe she'd even duck into the reception that night to listen to the live band that was going to be playing, according to the people talking in the break room.

Ten minutes later, she was walking along the sidewalk that ran between Lake Bandit and the villas, the box of mini bottles she carried jangling with every step, when Annika stuck her head out of another villa and called her name.

"Skye!" She hissed in a harsh whisper, as though she

was trying to keep it on the down low. Her eyes scanned the sidewalk all around Skye as though to make sure the coast was clear. "Come check this out."

"Just a sec. Let me deliver these to Laura in Villa Three."

Laura stuck her head out of the door next, looking both ways just as Annika had. "I'm here too. You've got to see this." She said it all from behind her teeth, without moving her lips.

What was up with the sneakiness? As if the housekeeping staff was trespassing or something. The honest truth was that, after a lifetime spent in the housekeeping industry, nothing that anyone could find in a hotel room would surprise Skye anymore. She'd seen it all. "Don't tell me there's a celebrity passed out in there. It's none of our business, and I don't care."

"It's better," Annika said.

"Is another duck trapped behind the fridge? Because seeing that once was enough for me. Call maintenance if that's the case."

"Just get in here!"

Skye faked a look all around her like Annika and Laura had, then tiptoed into the villa, hamming it up. Nothing wrong with a bit of fun. "Is this a musician's villa too?" she asked in a lowered voice as she transferred the whiskey minis to Laura's arms.

"Yeah," Laura said. "Gentry Wells."

There was a reverence in Laura's tone, but Skye had never heard of the guy. "Doesn't ring a bell."

Laura smacked her shoulder. "Are you kidding me? He's . . . he's . . ." She flexed, hands hovering in front of her chest, as though to indicate bulging pectorals and biceps. "He's hella hot. And he sings these really racy country songs that just . . . mmm . . . you'll have to

Google him. Better yet, type in 'Gentry Wells on a motorcycle.'"

Motorcycles. Now Laura had her attention. The only thing better than a midnight horseback ride was a late-night motorcycle ride—all the thrills, no men required. What a motto. Come to think of it, why *didn't* she own a motorcycle? As soon as she was out of this Gentry guy's villa and her arms were free of minis, she'd have to look him up. And maybe pay a visit to her local Harley dealer.

"Look, you two. This is what you had to see, even though it's a little lost on you, Skye, since you've never heard of him." Annika appeared in the bathroom doorway with a pair of bright pink bikini briefs pinched between her rubber gloved fingers. "Check. These. Out."

Laura gasped. "Did he have a booty call last night? I mean, he broke up with Cheyanne last year, so he's on the market . . ."

Annika wrinkled her nose. "I think they're men's."

With a gasp, Laura gave the briefs the side-eye and walked over for a closer look.

So this guy had a thing for underwear that was . . . pretty. While Skye appreciated that the occasional guest-related oddity reinvigorated the staff and helped them breeze through the afternoon grind, there was a line in the sand that had been crossed here. Details of a guest's romantic life were strictly none of their business. Especially given the high-profile status of this particular guest combined with all that paparazzi that was buzzing around this weekend.

Oh, how they'd love to get a load of a story. Skye could see it now, how they'd use the bikini briefs to stir up rumors that a motorcycle-riding, bad-boy country star was gay. She'd seen enough of those stories on the tabloid stands at the supermarket. But, a story like that would also trace back to housekeeping, which would be ruinous for Skye's business.

Skye shook her head. "Uh-huh. Nope. We are not going to stand around and comment on our guest's underwear. It's unprofessional and you both know better than that. Please don't tell me you found those by digging in the dresser drawers."

"Oh, come on. It's just a little fun. He's busy with a band rehearsal in the ballroom for Natalie Blevins' wedding reception tonight. And I didn't snoop. You know I'd never do that. These were on the bathroom floor. I had no choice but to move them. Plus, this is Gentry Wells. *The* Gentry Wells. Mr. Well Hung. And he's got a bright pink sausage sling."

"Mr. Well Hung? That's his nickname?" Between that and the motorcycle, she was definitely Googling this guy the first chance she got.

"It's a song he sings, so everyone just assumes there's some truth behind it. That's what I want to believe, anyway," Laura said. "You mean, you've never heard it?"

Skye didn't bother searching her mental database for it. "I think I'd remember that one."

"The song makes total sense now because these have got a big ol' bulge in them." Annika reached back into the bathroom, then dropped at least three shampoo minis into the underwear. "See? Extra roomy."

Laura gasped and bit her lip. "Oh, my Lord. The prophecy is true."

Skye stifled a laugh. It really was a funny discovery, given that the guy had a song about being well endowed. But rules were rules. "I'm serious, you two. This is not cool. We had our fun, and now it's time to put them back exactly where you found them. Oh, and I don't think I need to remind you to keep your lips sealed about this. If I see an image of these . . . these . . . sausage slings, or whatever you called them, on Facebook or on TMZ, I'll know who to—"

Laura looked past Skye and her face paled. "Gentry Wells," she breathed.

Out of the corner of Skye's eye, she watched Annika toss the underwear behind her back into the bathroom, the mini shampoos clattering when they hit the marble floor.

Skye spun around, too mortified to do anything but open her mouth and gasp, her eyes on the man standing in the doorway.

Laura nudged Skye in the ribs. "That's him. That's Gentry Wells."

What the actual, ever-living hell?

The mysterious stable boy. The best kiss she'd had in years. The hotel guest she'd been planning to rendezvous with again that night against company policy and maybe even take their make-out session far beyond another scorching kiss.

In the light of day, he was just as sexy, just as chiseled and edgy with all those tattoos and the guitar slung on his back and those worn-out jeans that fit him just right. Of course, he rode a motorcycle. Everything about him oozed wicked, wanton danger—the kind of danger any woman would dream of getting into. She would have never guessed that he was a famous country rock star, but it fit.

She had been right about one thing last night, though. He was *definitely* not part of her mom's spell. Not in any way, shape, or form.

The expression on his face was unreadable, down to

his Mona Lisa smile. "I prefer the term banana hammock, actually."

Skye's heart whooshed down through her body like an out-of-control elevator and landed in her legs. He'd seen them playing with his underwear. Oh God. "This is impossible," she whispered.

His jaw rippled. "Hello, Skye."

"Hi" was all she could think to say in return.

"You know him?" Laura and Annika blurted in unison.

"You're a maid?" he asked, ignoring the other women's outburst.

It took Skye a few tries of opening and closing her mouth before she'd processed his question enough to answer. "Housekeeping manager. And you're a singer. The guitar makes sense now." She blinked rapidly. "A lot of things make sense now."

Such as why he hadn't wanted to tell her his name. All it took was thinking about Annika's and Laura's reactions to his underwear to know why. Nothing about his lifestyle was private. He probably rarely got to just be a regular guy—*just a guy you found mucking stalls.*

Then again, what if the reason he'd wanted to remain anonymous was less noble? What if the bikini briefs belonged to a lover? A stab of jealousy sliced through her at the notion that she might not have been the only person he'd locked lips with last night. She wanted him all to herself.

Don't go there, girl. He didn't owe her anything, especially his fidelity.

"We didn't mean any harm with the underwear."

"I didn't take it as such." He lifted the guitar strap over his head, then propped the instrument up between a table and the wall, then he crossed his arms over his chest and gave her a pointed look. "Something tells me you still don't know who I am, now that you know my name."

No matter who he was in real life, he was still the same guy she'd made out with the night before, which garnered a lady certain privileges, such as not gushing over his celebrity status. Easy to do since she had no clue who he was. On top of that, Gentry hadn't wanted her to know who he really was, so why make a thing out of it? She shrugged. "Country's not my style."

"That's a shame. Here I was thinking you and I were really hitting it off."

"I guess not." She loved that they weren't. He was definitely not part of the curse, which meant none of this counted. Like how eating broken cookie bits made them calorie-free.

Laura nudged her with a tsk. Common wisdom held true that it was poor form to not gush about how impressive a man or his career was, but Skye didn't think that would play very well with the stable boy—er, Gentry. What an odd name. "Can I ask you a question?"

"Shoot."

"The underwear—"

"The banana hammock," he corrected with a wink and a smile.

"Right. Does it belong to you? Or your lover?" She might not have any hold on him, but she refused to be "the other woman," if that was the case. So, she figured, might as well get that out of the way if she hoped to make out with him again that night. *If* he still wanted to, given that she now knew who he was and he'd seen her making jokes about his underwear.

He didn't seem fazed by the question at all. "That's right forward of you."

"I'm a pretty forward person." At least, she had been lately with men, for better or worse. Ever since that love spell was cast.

At that pronouncement, his features softened, turned affectionate, even. "I noticed that. It isn't every day that I get back to my hotel room to find the housekeepers admiring my underwear. I've come back to the room to find them in my bed on occasion, but this is a first."

She wagged her finger at him. "Don't go getting ideas about my staff."

He gave her a wolfish grin. Like the rest of him, it was sexy and a little bit dangerous. He was definitely putting out all kinds of alpha rocker, flirtatious vibes, so, then, the pink underwear probably meant he wasn't gay, but it was totally incongruous with everything else she knew about him. "Naw, I don't have any designs about your employees, Skye."

The way his eyes raked over her body as he spoke, combined with the sound of her name said in his gravely drawl, let her know loud and clear that she hadn't been misreading his attraction. Yes, they were definitely still on for their repeat rendezvous that night.

But she was still curious about the underwear. "You didn't answer my question," she ventured. With a raised eyebrow, she added, "Hot pink?"

"Got 'em in every color, if you must know. My agent's idea to get me out of my head and get my creative juices flowing again."

"Is it working? Are your juices flowing?" Yes, she said it. No regrets. She wasn't about to dwell on how she ended up flirting with a country star about pink underwear and flowing juices, but she was owning the moment. And honestly? It was refreshing, flirting with a man who didn't have marriage designs on her. Someone completely outside the curse.

On a low, deep chuckle, he looked at his boots, his eyes demurring behind impossibly long eyelashes. "Not until you walked through that stable door last night, they weren't."

Interesting. She liked that—a little too much, perhaps. "I thought of another question." Was she really going where her mind was telling her to? Asking this was bound to push her past the point of no return. Ah, fuck it. She was owning this moment, for better or worse. "What color banana hammock are you wearing right now?"

There was that deep vibrato of a laugh that curled her toes. "Are you trying to trick me into showing you what I've got?"

Wicked, wicked man. Lucky for him, he'd met his match. "You're a famous musician, right? I thought the deal with rock stars was that it didn't take much to get them to drop their pants."

Gentry didn't miss a beat. "Well, I certainly wouldn't stop you if you wanted to find out for yourself, but maybe we should ask your employees to leave first."

Oh, shit. She'd completely forgotten about the audience—of her employees. Terrific.

She turned to find Annika and Laura looking utterly agog, mouths lolling open and eyes as wide as saucers. With a pounding heart, Skye braced a hand on Annika's shoulder and the other on Laura's. "You two didn't see anything, do you hear me? This never happened. Not you two admiring his underwear and not my un-boss-like conversation just now."

In other words, she was asking her employees to lie

about her inappropriate exchange with a hotel guest. Super-duper terrific. Great job, boss.

Mouths still wide open, they nodded in unison.

"Good. Back to work, ladies. It's time for me to leave." Of all her possible next moves, that option seemed the best. Get the hell out of there and pretend nothing was awry. She couldn't even look Gentry in the eye as she hustled past him and out the door.

"Skye," he called after her. But she was out of there.

Gentry had a long stride, but it was no match for Skye's brisk pace. By the time he let himself out of the villa's gate, he had to jog to get within shouting distance of her.

"Skye!"

She kept moving.

"I never answered your question," he called. If that didn't get her to stop and look at him, nothing would.

Luckily, this time, she stopped walking, but she didn't turn.

He'd spent the morning in the stable's tack room, scribbling in his notepad. Working off the sexual energy he'd harnessed the night before from his time with Skye and his anticipation of a repeat performance that night, he'd drafted song after song. All this time, he'd thought his creative well was dry, but it turned out he was just trying to tap into it all wrong. And all the thanks went to the dark-haired beauty who'd rocked his world. He'd be damned if he was going to let her skip out on their meet-up due to a little harmless embarrassment.

He cupped his hands around his mouth to project his voice her way. "I'm wearing blue today."

She pivoted to face him. With a bemused smile, she shook her head, as though she couldn't believe she was acquiescing to his bid for her attention because she found him too charming to resist. At least, that was his hope.

He took a chance and stepped closer.

"Royal or navy?" she asked.

Glad she asked. "Sky blue."

Fighting a smile, she tucked her chin into her shoulder and rolled her eyes as if his answer was so corny it caused her physical pain.

He stepped ever nearer, until they were only an arm's length away. Up this close, in the sunlight, her hair took on a reddish tone that he hadn't been able to see the night before, and with it gathered in a ponytail, he could admire the delicate structure of her neck and the little wisps of hair that framed it. She was stunning, inside and out—and he had one more night with her, God willing.

He was in completely uncharted territory, but there was one line that seemed to melt the defenses of every girl he'd met, whether they knew who he was or not. He extended his hand. "Hello, my name is Gentry."

Sure enough, her whole body relaxed and she didn't try to fight that smile anymore. She shook his hand. "Skye Martinez."

"The pleasure's all mine, Skye. And I mean that sincerely."

A man could lose himself in eyes like hers—soulful and brazen, and still the dark, rich hue of the earth after a rainstorm, even in the light of day.

"So, you're the housekeeping boss?" he said, because while looking into those eyes, he couldn't think of a single intelligent thing to say.

"My mother owns the company that leases its services to the resort. I'm her second in command."

"You work for your mom?" No way, no how would Gentry have ever been able to endure that.

"I know. It sounds like a nightmare for most people, and sometimes it is. I'm not going to lie. But it's usually pretty great. And when she retires, I'll buy her out and it'll be mine."

Good for her. She was made of the right stuff to be a boss, even if she'd just broken a few of her own rules with Gentry. "I'm guessing you broke a few rules last night fraternizing with a guest."

"Very much so."

There was a lilt in her tone that almost sounded like an invitation, like she enjoyed dancing on the edges of respectability. Time to test his theory. "Then would you feel more comfortable tonight if I found us someplace nice and private to meet away from the resort?"

She bit her bottom lip. "Not necessarily."

Well, well, well. Little Miss Midnight Rider got off on breaking rules. She looked honestly aroused at the moment. Her blood must have really been pumping while they flirted in front of her employees. For a man who'd started to feel like he was merely going through the motions of living, the prospect of hitching his wagon to a muse with a rebellious streak, even for a night, was exactly what the doctor ordered. "I can do that too."

He was brainstorming options when she looked over his shoulder and cursed.

"What?" He turned to follow her gaze and saw a tall, young pretty-boy type in a Briscoe Ranch polo shirt walking in loping strrides toward them, his eyes on Skye and a goofy grin on his face.

"That's Brent from the entertainment department and I cannot deal with him right now. Or, like, ever again."

Gentry cracked his knuckles. "Is he harassing you? Because I have a few tricks up my sleeve to get him to stop." Been a while since he'd tuned a guy up on behalf of a lady, but he was sure it was as easy to pick back up as riding a bicycle.

"Uh. I wish. I'm going boy crazy, and not in a good way."

"Huh?"

"It's complicated." She looked around as though in search of a hiding spot. "Follow me," she said, tugging his sleeve. They jogged between buildings, then ducked into an old-fashioned barn, complete with worn wooden boards and peeling white paint that looked more artfully distressed than actually weather-beaten.

Gentry pulled the sliding door closed behind them. The air inside was dusty and warm, but the space was tidy, with rows of fresh straw bales lined up facing a stage up front as though the resort held concerts there. Actually, it was a pretty cool venue, now that he was looking around.

Skye sank onto a bale. "Thanks. That was close."

"What is this place?"

"A barn that the resort built for weddings and other events. We get lots of couples who come here specifically for a shabby-chic country wedding right in this very spot. But it's another space I like to come to when I need a moment to myself."

Gentry took a seat next to her. "Yeah, about that. Why are we hiding from that clown, Brent?"

Her shoulders sagged. "Long story."

"Ex-boyfriend?"

"God no. I've been cursed."

"By that guy?" Brent didn't look like he was old enough to shave, much less curse someone.

"By my mother. About a month ago, she convinced me to let her help me find a man to marry, so she cast a spell on me. A love spell. Or a curse, as I've come to think of it." She buried her head in her hands.

Gentry wasn't sure what he expected Skye to say, but that certainly wasn't it. "A love spell? You're joking, right?"

She looked up again and the distress in her eyes told him loud and clear that she wasn't. "I wish. There are men everywhere I turn now, and they're all perfect for me on paper, except that none of them are actually right for me. In any way. That's how I ended up in the stable last night, escaping another bad date."

"And there I was, invading your space. You really can't escape us men."

"But see, you're different. My mother and I set up the spell to help me find a very specific kind of man—and you're not it."

"Let me guess, you wanted tall, dark, and handsome? 'Cause I'm only two of the three. Which isn't bad, all things considered."

She nudged him playfully with her shoulder. "No. I'm looking for a local man, someone vanilla and kind, with a normal job, and who's ready to settle down. And, not that it matters much to me, but if my mom with her spell gets her way, Catholic."

What the hell would someone as untamed as her who had a kink for breaking rules want with a vanilla guy? It didn't add up. But she was right about one thing. "Okay, yeah, that doesn't describe me at all."

She leaned in toward him, her hand on his knee. "I know. It's wonderful."

He couldn't help but laugh, it was such a crazy-ass conversation. "Wait . . . you're into me because I'm nothing like what you want?"

"I know how that sounds. But after the month of men fawning all over me and proposing marriage on the second date and all kinds of insane stuff, it's just so . . . refreshing to be with a man who doesn't want a future with me."

Huh. All right. Who was he to argue with that, given the promise of a night with her on the horizon?

She leaned the rest of the way over and kissed his cheek. "And in case I hadn't mentioned it to you yet, thank you for that. For being the break I needed from my life right now."

He wasn't about to let her stop at that chaste contact and cupped her cheek, holding her face near his. She splayed her hands over his chest as he took her mouth in a hot, wet kiss that picked up right where they'd left off the night before.

It wasn't long before he needed more from her, more tongue, more contact, more heat. He reached his hands under her ass and hauled her up to straddle his lap, notching her thighs around his steel-hard erection. She ground her hips against him as they kissed, driving him out of his mind.

He broke their kiss and did a quick calculation of how much time he had before the wedding. Not that much. Not nearly enough time to do to her what he wanted. A quickie would only leave them both unsatisfied. He wanted all of Skye and he wanted to make it last.

"Call time for that wedding I'm in town for is in an hour, which doesn't give me nearly enough time to do with you what I have in mind. I hate to do this, but we're gonna have to wait."

She panted into him. Her fingers toyed with his neck as she locked her dilated, half-lidded eyes with his. "Tonight. We'll meet in the stable again and figure out where to go from there. I want to take you on a midnight ride of another kind."

"Sweetheart, that's the best damn offer this cowboy's ever gotten."

He gathered her hair in his hand and tugged until her chin lifted, granting him access to her parted lips. "I'm gonna kiss you again now."

She arched, pressing her ass into his hand and grinding against his cock again. "Speaking of damn good offers."

When she aimed her lips at his, he tugged her hair again and growled, "I didn't say on the lips." He dove into the sweet, tender skin of her neck. Her body undulated and jerked with every lick and bite.

The trouble was, while he was down there working his lips along her collarbone, he got to thinking of her ridiculous love spell again. What did a woman like her need a spell like that for? Any man in his right mind would kill for a chance to win her hand, no magic required. Yet, here she was, hiding out from all of them in a barn with Gentry, who was definitely not the marrying kind. Never had been and never would be.

"Something's still rattling around in my mind," he murmured against her throat. "I still don't get it why, if you're so desperate to settle down with a nice, upstanding family man that you'd cast a spell to find one, are you hooking up with a rambling man like me? I know you said it's refreshing that I don't want you like that, but you either want to settle down or you don't. Am I wrong to think that?"

Looking at her hands, she took a moment before answering. Gentry was frustrated with himself for wrecking the mood, but that was probably for the better too. He still had to shower and change into his tux. "You don't have to answer that, you know."

"I know. Let's just say that old habits die hard."

That he could understand. "One last thrill before you turn into someone mama can be proud of?"

"Exactly."

"Guess that kind of makes me your Mardi Gras." Lyrics to another new song exploded in his mind like fireworks. This idea gave him a whole-body shiver, a sure sign that it was going to be a hit.

Unaware of his wandering thoughts, Skye took hold of the top button of her uniform and worked it open. "Does that mean you'll toss a necklace to me if I show you my—"

The creak of the barn door opening caught their attention. Skye jumped to her feet, smile gone. "That'd better not be a man."

Maybe there really was something to that spell, because the sound of a male voice floated through the air.

On a weary groan, Skye took his hand and pulled him to the far corner of the room, behind a folding screen where the lighting and sound equipment was stored. The sound of footsteps on the hardwood floor echoed through the barn.

Gentry glanced at Skye, taking note of the heat in her eyes, her red-stained, swollen lips, and the top button gaping open to reveal the smooth copper skin of her décolletage. She was so fucking sexy. He pressed a finger to his lips in a suggestion that she stay quiet. "I'll get rid of him," he breathed. "Don't you dare move one muscle." He hooked his finger on the vee opening of her shirt, right between her breasts. "I want to come back and see you just like this. Then we can get back to business."

"Yes, sir," she purred.

The words went straight to his groin. He had to do some quick thinking about mucking stalls to tame his body back down to a presentable state. Before Gentry could take more than a step around the corner, he heard a woman sniffle. Whoever the intruder was, he wasn't alone.

Another step, and the couple came into view. When he saw who it was, he couldn't believe his eyes. Natalie Blevins and her soon-to-be husband Toby, sitting on a pair of hay bales near the stage, dressed in their wedding attire. Toby's crimson bowtie had been tugged crooked and looked on the verge of coming undone. Natalie's wedding gown fluffed up around her like marshmallow crème. The veil added to her air of innocence along with her tears. He'd known her since she was a little kid, when Neil used to bring her to work with him. She looked that way again. So young. Too young and precious to be crying on her wedding day.

Toby was the first to spot Gentry. He wrapped a protective arm around Natalie, who looked up with a frown. "What are you doing here? Did Neil send you?" Toby said.

"No. I'm . . . this is just a coincidence, trust me. Natalie? Are you okay, darlin'?"

She started to nod, but couldn't hold it together and broke down into a sob. "Oh God. I didn't want anyone to see me like this. What are you doing here?"

Gentry knelt before them and took Natalie's hand. "I think a more important question is what are you two doing here? If I recall, you're supposed to be getting hitched in an hour or so. Did something go wrong?"

Natalie and Toby took a long look at each other as though silently discussing whether they should share their troubles with Gentry. "I won't tell anyone. I promise. I just want to help."

Out of the corner of Gentry's eyes, he watched Skye

make her way to where they were. Natalie's spine went ramrod straight as she swiped the evidence of her tears away.

"It's all right," Gentry said. "This is Skye. She's with me. She won't tell, either. Back to what you two kids are doing in here on your wedding day looking like somebody killed your dog."

Toby clutched a handful of his hair. "It's a mess out there. Natalie's mom's trying to take over," Toby said. "And my parents both showed up with dates who weren't on the guest list, so they're at each other's throats."

Skye sat on a hay bale across from the couple. Gentry eased off his knees and joined her. "Skye, this is Natalie and Toby. Natalie and Toby, this is Skye."

"Your date tonight?"

He almost said no, but Skye beat him to it. "I am, yes."

All right. In a way, she was, he supposed.

Skye continued, "But it sounds like this wedding isn't going to be much fun for you."

"Got that right," Natalie said with another sniff. "There are five hundred guests out there, and I maybe know a hundred of them. It's just a sea of strangers. Strangers walking an actual red carpet that my dad set up. It's a total circus."

"You looked like you were having plenty of fun last night at the bar," Gentry ventured gently, trying to boost their moods.

"It was all for show. To make my dad happy."

Gentry knew all about that when it came to Neil. Hell, when it came to just about everyone. Rarely did Gentry feel like he could be himself because so many people were always watching and analyzing his every move.

"I didn't want a wedding that was all about my dad, like everything else in my life," Natalie said. "But he still managed to get his way. He turned my wedding into a media circus. He's so busy trying to control the spin that he doesn't care what Toby and I want. There's a paparazzi helicopter hovering around, so he says we can't take pictures outside because he wants to control the spin. And I heard my mom talking to my aunt that she wants to sell the official wedding photos to the highest bidder to help offset the cost."

"That sucks." But Gentry wasn't surprised. He'd known the Blevins for a long a time.

Natalie smoothed her hands over her skirt. "I don't care. I just want to be married and get on with our life together. All of this . . . I thought I wanted the fairy tale, but this doesn't feel like a fairy tale."

Skye knelt before Natalie and picked a piece of hay from the dress. "You're getting your beautiful dress dirty."

"I don't care about that either. It wasn't the dress I wanted. It was the dress my mom and my maid-of-honor insisted on. This is my mother's dream wedding, not mine. She's parading me around like I'm . . . I'm . . ."

Toby set his hand over Natalie's. "Like we're puppets."

Gentry cringed at the analogy. He'd felt that way for too long. A puppet, a sell-out. "I know exactly how you feel. You have this fantasy and you think you want it more than anything else in the world, but when it becomes real, it's not like you expect. It's not nearly as much fun."

"Tell me about it," Skye said. "That's my life right now too. Overbearing mother and all."

Gentry hadn't put that all together with Skye's love-spell-gone-wrong, but he could see how she felt the same way. What a sorry crew the four of them were.

"No, it's not any fun at all," Natalie said. "And we

didn't see a way out of it that either of our parents would accept. Five hundred people traveled here to see us get married. They're all waiting, but it's not right. This isn't what I wanted for my wedding. Not even close."

"Me, neither. So we ditched the photographer and that's how we ended up here," Toby said. "We're going to elope and get married on our own terms. We know our parents aren't going to be happy with us, but we can't make choices about our wedding and our marriage based on our parents' feelings or opinions. So we're going to elope."

Damn. Gentry hadn't seen that one coming. He never would have guessed it in a million years. Too bad Natalie and Toby couldn't have figured that nugget of wisdom out a few weeks or months ago and saved their parents thousands and thousands of dollars. But Gentry wasn't about to bring that up.

Skye stood, her eyes shining with compassion. "We're going to help you."

We're what? Gentry couldn't just betray his allegiance to Neil—his boss, for all intents and purposes—by helping his daughter skip out on her wedding. "We are?"

Natalie gave Skye a watery smile of gratitude. "You are? Thank you. Thank you both."

Well, hell.

"Look, all we need is a car," Toby said. "We'll go to the courthouse and get it done."

Gee, how romantic.

Skye must have been feeling the same way because she tsked and smoothed her hands over Natalie's dress again. "That's no different than this circus wedding you're running away from. Neither ceremonies are about celebrating your love the right way. You deserve better.

You deserve for your wedding day to be one of the best days of your life."

The hope fizzled in Natalie's expression. "It's too late for that."

Neil was going to kill Gentry for this. Or worse, kill his career. Gentry was shocked by the force of his panic over that thought. Shocked that one man had the power to lord over Gentry so completely.

Since when had Gentry gotten so afraid to take chances? Since when did Gentry Wells—Gentry *Fucking* Wells—bow prostrate before another man's will, a victim of his own success? Gentry really had sold his soul for the sake of achieving his lifelong dream. Some dream that was anymore. He looked again at Natalie and Toby, the latest victims of the Neil Blevins machine.

Screw that shit. Skye would probably be risking her job to help the couple too, but she had the courage to do the right thing, so what the hell was keeping Gentry from doing the same? Or Natalie and Toby, for that matter? Gentry stood in solidarity with Skye. "She's right. That ain't no way to start out your life together. What if we helped you get out of town for real so you could elope in style?"

Toby raised his eyebrows. "You would do that?"

Skye looped her arm around Gentry's. "We would."

She felt good at his side. Good and right in a way that Gentry refused to analyze. Sure, they were compatible, but that didn't mean they needed to take that baton and run with it all the way to monogamy. He'd only break her heart, and they both knew it. But that didn't mean he couldn't appreciate her for the brief time they had together or for the inspiration that her mere presence filled his creative well with.

Already, the beginnings of new songs were starting to take shape. If nothing else, helping Natalie and Toby elope, with Skye as his partner, would give him one hell of an adventure. His creative well would be full for months—or, at least, until his next album was done. Neil couldn't stay pissed if Gentry presented him with an album full of potential hits, could he?

Gentry looked Natalie in the eye. "We'll do all we can to help—but only if you're serious about this. Because you can't take it back once you pull that trigger."

"We're serious," they said in unison.

"Then it's settled. Do you have the rings?" Gentry said.

Toby patted his jacket.

"What about the marriage license?" Skye asked.

Natalie's face went long. "No. We gave it to the wedding planner last night."

Luckily, Skye happened to be the best of friends with the wedding planner. "Okay, I'll take care of that. But I don't have access to a car because I caught a ride from my sister this morning."

"Naw. If we're going to do this, then we've got to do it in style. We need a limo," Gentry said. "Leave that up to me."

"Okay, then we have a plan. I'll go get the marriage license while Gentry gets us some wheels. Natalie and Toby, get on your phone and start looking up elopement venues within driving distance, see if anything catches your eye. We'll rendezvous here again in a half hour. You two stay put, out of sight," she said to Natalie and Toby.

Leaving the couple embracing and whispering their plans to each other, Gentry and Skye stepped through the barn door and into the blinding sun. The sound of a helicopter buzzing the building eclipsed all other sounds.

The paparazzi Natalie had mentioned. Neil Blevins and the celebrities on the guest list more than warranted a full-court press by the media. The rest of the resort would be crawling with them too. Not to mention the five hundred guests who were all probably on the lookout for the runaway bride and groom.

And Gentry had just agreed to help smuggle them off the resort. No problem.

"You ready?" Skye asked on a whoosh of an exhalation.

Gentry adjusted his ball cap. "Easy as pie," he faked. "Let's go make some wedding magic."

Chapter Five

Skye wasn't doing this because of an addiction to risk taking. Nope. This was about helping a young couple break free of their parents' overbearing love. Yes, that help included smuggling the couple off of the resort undetected and against their parents' wishes and potentially aggravating Skye's working relationship with Briscoe Ranch, should anyone discover her involvement. But no one was going to be hurt, and Natalie and Toby had planned to escape regardless of Skye's involvement, so she was completely absolved of responsibility. One might even call Skye's participation a good deed—and it was pure coincidence that this good deed got her blood pounding with juicy, sinful adrenaline.

Feigning nonchalance, she hopped into one of the golf carts staged near the barn for employee use and drove to the resort's wedding chapel, which was situated on a grassy hill on the northwest corner of the resort, smiling and greeting guests and tourists as she passed. *Nothing to see here, folks. Just a housekeeping worker making her rounds . . .*

The grounds surrounding the chapel were swarming

with people, as expected. The chapel itself was too small to accommodate five hundred guests, so the ceremony was being staged in the chapel's rose garden and would be spilling out into the flat, perfectly manicured lawn that was maintained for just such an event.

Due to the high-profile nature of the wedding, Skye's uniform was apparently not enough for the two beefy bodyguards controlling the flow of guests into the cordoned-off event. She flashed her hotel ID and all they did was frown at her until she smiled sweetly and said, "I got a call that there was an incident in the women's restroom with feminine products. Blood and tampons everywhere."

That made zero sense, but she'd learned on the job that nothing made men disintegrate like the thought of menstruation. Sure enough, their faces contorted and all pretense of toughness vanished as they waved her through.

She didn't see Remedy outside, which meant she was probably in the chapel, where the bridal party was usually assembled before the ceremony. Sure enough, Remedy was in the vestibule, sitting with a middle-aged bleach-blonde in a skin-tight lime-green dress who was worrying a tissue into little bits that rained down on her impossibly tanned legs. Her puffy, cosmetically enhanced lips trembled as tears rolled down her cheeks.

Skye caught Remedy's attention and motioned with a tip of her head for Remedy to join her outside. After a few quiet reassurances to the woman, Remedy followed Skye out the chapel doors.

"Who was that?" Skye asked.

"The mother of the bride. She's freaking out and tried to start a fight with the mother of the groom. And I don't mean a fight with words. I had to literally pull them apart before they tore each other's earrings off. So I don't really have time to talk. The bride and groom ditched their photography session and no one can find them—and the wedding starts in a half hour. What do you need?"

Skye braced her hands on Remedy's clipboard. "I know where they are."

"The bride and groom? Thank God because this was on the verge of turning into a dumpster fire. Where are they?"

Dumpster fire, ahoy. "I'm so sorry, but I can't tell you. They're canceling the wedding."

"They're—*what did you say?*"

"Natalie and Toby are calling the wedding off. They said they're overwhelmed by the scope of it and how crazy their parents are getting. It's not how they want to start out their lives together. So they're eloping. And . . ." Here was the tough part. "Don't hate me, but I'm helping."

Remedy lowered the clipboard on a sigh, nodding. "I could see cracks in their happiness, but I ignored it. What else could I do? A lot brides and grooms get anxious. I did my best to keep them out of the loop throughout this whole process except for big decisions, so they wouldn't get stressed, but I can't control their families."

"This isn't your fault. It's just two kids figuring themselves out and finding their voice."

"All right. I guess I'll go tell their parents. Those mothers are definitely going to get into a fist fight now. At least the paparazzi that's lurking around will get an even better show than they came for."

Remedy turned toward the chapel, but Skye snagged her sleeve. "No. Please. Not yet. We were hoping you'd help us stall until we get them off the resort grounds."

"We? Who are you working with?"

That was the fun part. Skye wished she had the time to tell Remedy all about it, but that would have to wait. "Gentry Wells."

Remedy just about fell over sideways. "Gentry Wells, who's supposed to perform during the ceremony and then again at the reception. Gentry Wells, whose music producer is Neil Blevins, the father of the bride? The 'Beer O'Clock' guy?"

Skye had no idea what that last part meant. Beer O'Clock? "That's him."

"And you know Gentry how . . . ?"

Oh, the stories she owed Remedy over a glass of wine when this was all said and done. "I don't have time to explain. But I need your help with one more thing. We're going to need their marriage license."

"I don't have it. I already gave it to the chaplain." She nodded to the rose garden, where an older man in religious robes was standing near a flower-covered archway and podium, talking up a silver-haired man wearing a boutonnière pinned to his finely tailored suit. "And right now it looks like he's talking to Neil Blevins, the bride's father. I'm not sure we can get the license without tipping him off about the elopement. What we need is a ruse."

"Whatever it is, I'm in," came a voice behind Skye.

Skye and Remedy both jumped at the sound. They turned to find Granny June grinning up at them in a bright purple sequined skirt suit and a pillbox hat perched at a jaunty angle on her hair and leaning heavily on a cane.

"You sure have a knack for sniffing out trouble you can get into," Skye scolded with a heavy dose of affection.

"Keeps me young."

Anyone else, Skye would have told them to mind their

own business, but Granny June was perfect for this job. "We need a distraction."

Granny June snorted. "Does this have anything to do with the bride and groom I saw running across the lawn a little bit ago?"

Remedy gripped her clipboard like she was imagining wringing Granny June's neck. "You saw that and you didn't come tell me? I thought you and I were friends!"

"Oh hush. Of course, we are. I assumed they might be sneaking away for a little pre-wedding necking."

It was *so* Granny June to think that. "Not quite."

"The only person who's ever ditched out on their wedding, as far as I can recall, is my granddaughter Haylie, and she had plenty of reason to. What's this couple's excuse? Are they calling it off?"

"They're eloping."

Granny snorted her disapproval. "They're not going to get the Briscoe marriage luck if they don't get married at the resort."

She had a point. There was no denying for anyone who'd spent a little time at the resort that Briscoe Ranch carried with it a heaping dose of mystical power in the love department. Love was in the air, and in the soil, and in the walls of every building. It sometimes felt as if people just couldn't help falling in love there. It's where Skye's parents had met, as well as where her aunt and several cousins had found their mates. Skye's sister and Ruben too. It was a charmed place that had all began with June and her late husband, Tyson Briscoe's, wedding so many years ago.

"We need to get the chaplain and Neil Blevins away from the podium where the marriage license is," Remedy said. With a stern point of her finger, she added, "Without tipping anyone off."

"I'm on the job." Granny June speared her cane at Skye. "But you owe me. My friend Meryl's grandson is new to town. He'll be at the Spring Kickoff Barbecue in two weeks, and I want you to make him feel welcome."

Of all the blasted things. But Skye gritted her teeth and nodded. What was one more man in the sea of them she was surrounded by? "Fine. But he'd better not be a dud like Vincent Biaggi."

"Then it's settled." She pushed her purple sequined sleeves up her forearms. "Leave this to me." And off she went, a little skip in her step.

Remedy gave a beleaguered sigh. "I don't know why I'm helping you with this."

Skye hugged her. "Because you're a good person?"

"That's true. But I think it has to do more with how overbearing the mother-of-the-bride has been. She's a special breed of mothers-of-the-bride. That fight was the last straw. If I were her daughter, I'd want to elope too."

The next moment, the grating strains of a horn bleating out the notes to *La Cucaracha* drowned out the subdued sound of the string musicians performing near the bar.

"Holy shit," Remedy muttered.

Granny June barreled through the crowd in her riding scooter, which was pointed straight for the front of the rose garden where the chaplain and Neil Blevins stood. The two bodyguards from earlier were hot on her tail, but they didn't seem to have any kind of strategy to stop her beyond flapping their arms and shouting.

Granny June paid them no mind, shouting, "Yoo-hoo! Chaplain Dickerson, I have a question!" As she threaded her way into center aisle between the rows of white folding chairs, she discretely dropped her cane to the floor of the scooter where it stuck out a foot on either side, snagging the two wide silk ribbons that had been strung along the innermost chairs in the rows to line the aisle like garlands.

With the buckle of the first chairs as it dragged along behind her scooter, the guests leaped out of the way while others just stood, stunned. Some called for her to stop and others joined the bodyguards in their arm flapping, but Granny June would not be deterred. One after another, the chairs collapsed and trailed behind her like tin cans behind a *Just Married* car. Except these took out everything in their path, including a few guests, who had to leap out of the way.

Remedy groaned and held her clipboard over her face. "I knew she couldn't just do something easy and clean, like fake a heart attack."

Skye sympathized, but she kept her eye on the podium. The chaplain and Neil Blevins planted themselves in front of the podium, waving their arms and calling for Granny to stop, but she merely pressed her *La Cucaracha* horn again and waved to them. "Yoo-hoo!"

The leather-bound folder on the podium contained the marriage license, Skye assumed. Holding her breath, she skittered across the temporary flooring that the podium rested on and threw open the folder. She nearly had her hands on the stack of papers, ready to dash away with them all and sort it out later, when the chaplain whirled around and threw his arms around the podium. "Quick! Get this out of her way!"

He gave Skye the briefest of glances as he pushed the podium out of Granny June's runaway scooter path. Skye could do nothing but stare after him—which is why she didn't see . . .

"Move it, Skye!" Granny shouted. The tires squealed as she yanked on the safety brake lever.

With a yelp of surprise, Skye lurched to avoid hitting the scooter and stumbled backward, landing on her rear. "Ow."

Granny June stood on the scooter and grinned down at Skye. "Oops. My bad. But it looks like the brakes work, so that's a plus."

"My bad?" Skye said. "That's all you have to say?"

The chaplain helped Skye up, which is how she noticed the leather folder tucked under his arm. Damn it.

"Are you okay?" he asked.

Skye watched Granny June attempting to execute a three-point-turn in her scooter, much to the horror of the guests who'd gathered around her to try and unsnag the chair ribbons.

"I'm fine," Skye said. "Just a little sore from the fall."

Neil Blevins blotted his forehead with a handkerchief. "Okay, good," he said, almost to himself. "This buys us some more time while they get this mess cleaned up. Where's that damned wedding planner?" he barked, storming off.

Skye whipped out her phone and dialed Remedy. "Head's up. Neil Blevins is headed your way."

"I see him. Did you get the license?"

"No. What are we going to do? They can't get married tonight without it," Skye said.

"Not in Texas they can't. There are enough states that don't have a waiting period to get married after applying for a license, but it's already five o'clock on a Saturday. Outside of huge elopement destinations like Vegas, Nashville, or Niagara Falls, most county clerk offices are closed for the weekend."

"Got it. And thank you again. I owe you."

Remedy sighed into the phone. "It would have been such a beautiful wedding. But okay. I'm glad they're happy with their choice. Don't forget to text me when the coast is clear so I can tell their parents. And, hey, tell Natalie and Toby congratulations from me. Oh shit, there's Neil. Got to go."

There was not a moment to spare.

"Bye, Granny June!" she called. "Thank you for trying."

"You bet, kiddo! And don't forget you're still on the hook with Meryl's grandson."

Oh joy.

As soon as she rounded the corner near the barn where the bride and groom were hiding, she saw a long, black stretch limo idling out front. She parked the golf cart and jogged over. The driver's window rolled down.

Skye's heart skipped a beat at the sight of Gentry behind the wheel, looking cool as a cucumber in aviator shades and a ball cap, oozing that bad boy charm that she was fast becoming addicted to. And of course she was. There was a reason he was a rich and famous country music rock star, and it wasn't because he was dull and hard on the eyes. No, he had an *It* factor that crackled with charisma and otherworldly good looks. Skye wasn't the first woman to fall under his spell and she certainly wouldn't be the last. "Please tell me you didn't steal that."

He stuck his elbow out of the rolled-down window. "I think the proper word is commandeer. Climb on in. Let's roll."

"Natalie and Toby are already in?"

"In the back, plied with champagne, and totally into each other like almost-newlyweds should be."

She dropped into the passenger seat and Gentry reached across to wrap a not-so-gentlemanly hand around her knee. "You ready to ride with me, beautiful?"

Man, oh, man, did he light her fire. "With you? Anytime."

Her only regret was that in helping Natalie and Toby, they'd be missing out on one last night together. Ignoring the pang of displeasure at the realization, she winked at Gentry. They might not have much time left together, but Skye planned to make the most of every minute of it.

While Gentry navigated to the road leading away from the resort, Skye lowered the privacy window to the back of the limo. "Natalie and Toby, I've got some good news and some bad news for you. The good news is that you can still totally get married tonight."

"Uh-oh. I'm afraid of the bad news."

"The bad news is that, if you have your hearts set on getting married tonight, it won't be in Texas because I couldn't get the license without tipping your parents off. And believe me, I gave it my best try."

Natalie snuggled into Toby's side. "But you said that the good news was that we might still be able to get married tonight? How?

"We'd have to put you on a plane to a popular elopement destination where a county clerk's office would still be open on a Saturday night. According to Remedy, your wedding planner, that includes Vegas, Niagara Falls, and Nashville."

"That won't be as big a problem as you might think, because I have a plane on standby at a Ravel County private airstrip," Gentry said.

"You do?"

"Yeah. I reserved a private jet for later tonight after

the wedding so I could get back to Oklahoma. I'm sure the pilot would be more than happy to switch destinations if we threw enough money at him. Which I'd be perfectly happy doing for you. You could consider it a wedding gift."

That was . . . *wow.* Generous beyond measure. But Skye was getting stuck on the fact that he'd been planning to leave that night after the wedding. So much for the tryst in the stable he'd intimated about. Had he been leading her on? She masked her disappointment with a searing look and an arch of her eyebrow. "You were leaving tonight? Interesting. Because I thought otherwise."

Though he kept his eyes on the road, the hand on her knee inched higher to tease her inner thigh. "That reservation was made months ago. But let me be clear that I wasn't gonna leave without taking care of some unfinished business first. My plane wasn't supposed to depart until nearing midnight." His words were said in a low, throaty twang that seemed to emerge when he let his guard down, as though arousal brought out the cowboy in him.

Unfinished business it looked like they weren't going to get to, after all. What a shame. Even if they were doing the right thing by Natalie and Toby.

"You'd do that for us?" Toby asked.

"Are you kiddin' me? This weekend's been the most fun I've had in months. Years, actually," he added so quietly that Skye doubted Toby or Natalie had heard.

Skye studied his profile. How could that be? Sure, the last twenty-four hours had been the most fun she'd had in years, but he was an internationally famous rock star. How could it be that they'd both been so starved for adventure?

Toby took Natalie's hands. "It's your choice. Where do you want to go?"

Natalie tugged on her bottom lip with her teeth and cast a questioning look at Toby. "How about Nashville? That's where my parents eloped to. Maybe if we did that, they'd have an easier time understanding why we have to do this."

Toby cupped her cheek and gave her a slow, tender kiss. "Nashville it is."

"Leave it to us, you two. Just enjoy the ride." Gentry raised the privacy window, then pulled out his cellphone. "I'll give the pilot a call. And while I do that, you have a special assignment."

"What's that?"

He clicked on the radio. "It's time for you to acquaint yourself with the glory that is country music."

Gentry had called it right, Skye discovered. It turned out people were willing to do just about anything for a person if they had enough money thrown at them. Which was why, only an hour after Skye and Gentry had absconded with Natalie and Toby, a private jet and pilot were waiting for them at Ravel County Airfield. Gentry preceded them into the plane to talk to the pilot while Skye followed behind to help Natalie with her dress's flowing train as she mounted the stairs.

At the top of the stairs, she caught Natalie's arm. "Hey, I need a hug before you go."

Natalie seemed to panic. "You're not coming with us?"

"To Nashville? Oh, gosh, no. I'm still technically on the clock at work, and if I took a one-way jet ride to Nashville, I'm not sure how I'd get home."

The two women embraced. "Okay. I understand. Thank you so much for everything," Natalie said.

"The pleasure was all mine. You and Toby are going to have the most magnificent life together. I can feel it."

Gentry appeared behind Natalie. "What's going on here?"

Natalie moved aside, wiping a tear from her eye. "Just saying good-bye and thank you."

Gentry lifted an eyebrow at Skye. "Good-bye."

"Yes." Her heart gave a painful squeeze at the word. She held out her hand. "I'll drive the limo back to the resort."

He tilted his head to the side, studying her like she was a piece of art he didn't understand. "I don't think so. I'll call the driver and let him know he can pick it up here himself at his convenience."

Okay, so he was going to make her spell it out. Fine. "What I meant was—"

But he didn't let her finish. "Natalie, would you give us a minute?"

With a nod, Natalie disappeared into the recesses of the jet to join Toby.

"Listen, Gentry, this adventure with you has been great, but I can't just blow off my life and run away with you." She'd tried that once upon a time and all it had led to was heartache and shame.

He waited to reply until Natalie was out of earshot, and when he turned his focus onto Skye again, there was an invitation in his eyes that could only be described as the call of the wild. "You think I'm gonna let you go so easily?"

"You don't have a choice." This was her call to make. But even as she said the words, a wicked little voice, her inner thrill addict, whispered to her. *What if . . .*

"Come with me, Skye. It's just one night. Let's get these kids married and then have a little fun of our own in my favorite city. Then I'll fly you home tomorrow and you can get back to your masochistic search for a dweeb who won't give you the life you want."

"It's more complicated than that." He might be all kinds of wrong about the life she wanted for herself, but he was right about one thing—the search was definitely masochistic.

"I'm sure it is, but you and I have unfinished business and I fully intend to make good on my promises. Mardi Gras, remember?"

"I have to work on Monday." Damn, she sounded old.

He shook his head, frustrated. "I'm not talking to the Skye who wants to settle down with a boring, church-going guy. Tell her to scram. I'm talking to the Skye who dared me to ride horses with her last night. I'm talking to the Skye I flirted with in my villa and kissed in the barn today. I'm talking to the Skye who just helped me smuggle a couple away from their own wedding. Give me that woman for one night. I'll have you home in time for work on Monday and you can get back to trying to tame yourself."

She shivered at his words, every one of them loaded with unspoken hedonistic promises. The trouble was, she *wanted* to tame herself. She was tired of the morning-after guilt, of feeling like a bad Catholic and a bad daughter. She was sick and tired of being alone, without real love. These flings and wild moments didn't get her one inch closer to the person she wanted to be or the life she wanted to lead.

But what if it didn't have to be that way? What if she could prove to herself that she was capable of having a little fun without wrecking her life?

"I can see the wheels turning, Skye. I don't have any promises about the future I can make you, but I have tonight and my promise to you is that I am going to brand myself into your memory so that every time you hear my name or hear my song on the radio, your cheeks flush like they are right now and your eyes turn dark and hungry when you think back to the night we spent together. Let me give you that, baby."

Those words, coupled with the way he crooned the word *baby* in that low twang, made the last chains of her resistance snap. Suddenly, acutely, the idea of turning him down and walking away was unbearable. She deserved this. She deserved one last thrill before she gave it all up—the reckless choices, the fear of commitment and the unmarriable men she was attracted to because of it. On Sunday, after he'd returned her home, she'd get serious about staying on the straight and narrow path. True to her family and her faith. But not tonight. Tonight she would bid a final farewell to her old ways, and she'd do it in style—private jet, rock god, and all.

He held out his hand, beckoning. "You know you want to."

More than anything. Which is why she left Good Girl Skye standing on the top of the staircase as she took Gentry's hand and followed him into the plane.

Chapter Six

Skye couldn't take her eyes off Dolly Parton's mole. She wasn't exactly a Dolly Parton expert, but she definitely didn't remember the singer having a beauty mark the size of a chocolate chip on her upper lip, nor did Skye think the real dame was quite as thick in the waist. But, Fake Dolly had the accent down pat, along with eyes that blazed with Southern fire in a way that was unmistakably Parton.

Besides, Natalie and Toby seemed to be having the time of their lives, which was all that mattered. They hadn't taken their eyes or their hands off each other since the jet had taken off in Texas. The lovebirds had chosen the Islands in the Stream Chapel because, apparently, one of their best dates had been to the Dollywood amusement park. Go figure.

Skye's first wedding had been at a courthouse in front of a justice of the peace. At the time, that had felt so rebellious. She'd been high on the rebelliousness of the act, and on her love for Mike. What a joke.

The kitschy neon-lights-and-silk-flowers charm of Islands in the Stream captured Skye's romantic, if restless, heart. She would love to get married in a chapel like this, if only her faith and her family were a little bit more flexible about how a couple could tie the knot and keep their good standings. She'd texted her sister from the plane to let her know she was safe, but had turned the phone to *airplane mode* before her sister could text back with her judgment, which so often mirrored their mom's. Standing in as the maid of honor next to Dolly Parton and the ceremony officiant, Skye was acutely aware of the rift in her soul, the good Catholic girl who honored her family and their traditions and the free spirit who craved the novelty and thrill of nights like this, chapels like this, men like Gentry.

Gentry stood across from her as the best man. Skye looked across the backs of the bride and groom at Gentry. He'd slicked back his shaggy, rock-star hair as best he could after removing his ball cap for the ceremony and had borrowed a blazer from the officiant, and he'd cleaned up pretty well, though there was no disguising his cowboy swagger beneath that tenuous guise of respectability. Case in point, his guitar was up at the altar, propped against a chair, and Gentry was ready to perform as soon as the vows had been said.

For a man who'd sworn he wasn't the marrying type, he'd sure gone all out to make tonight as flawless and romantic as possible. After he'd called the clerk's office from the limo to make sure they'd be open, and while Natalie and Toby were getting their marriage license, he'd reserved a hotel room for the newlyweds. He'd even sprung for the chapel's most expensive package, the "9 to 5 deluxe," which included an award-winning Dolly Parton performer, a bouquet of flowers for the bride, and even an end-of-ceremony performance from the dancing waters fountain behind the podium.

Skye couldn't wait to check out the dancing waters, but at the moment, Dolly Parton was reading a blessing—which happened to be the last verse of her song "I Will Always Love You." When she finished, the officiant opened a leather folio and began the actual ceremony. It was a little bit of a bummer that Dolly herself couldn't marry them, but those were the rules.

As the officiant read the vows, Skye experienced her first moment of regret at her role in the elopement. Those vows were such a profound promise of forever and ever, no matter what—the very same promise that Skye had made when she was only a little younger than Natalie and Toby. What was she doing, encouraging these kids to pledge their lives to each other when, clearly, they weren't yet mature enough to speak up for themselves to their parents? She knew better. She should have advised them to wait.

Then again, who was she to give such advice? She was the one who'd hopped onto the private plane of a sexy musician she'd only just met the night before, aiding and abetting with two resort guests' ill-conceived elopement plan in a way that might compromise her business's contract with the resort. But there was no regret about how alive she felt that night. Vital. This impetuous, risk-taking flight of fancy was as intoxicating as a drug.

The regret was useless anyway. She was here, and Natalie and Toby were getting married, and that was that. No more thoughts of Mike the Mistake or their ill-fated wedding, she scolded herself. Tonight was about fun and forgetting. One last thrill. She could keep this—whatever this was—in its tidy box, separate from her real life. Maybe that's what the wild woman inside of her needed: the occasional relief.

Skye tuned back into the ceremony in time to watch Natalie and Toby exchange rings and those huge, binding vows. As they kissed, the Dolly impersonator and the officiant broke out in a rousing rendition of "Islands in the Stream," which Gentry joined them on with his guitar. The next moment, the dancing waters sprung to life behind them in a blaze of pink and blue, waving like hula dancers in time to the music.

Skye's heart was bursting with love and hope for the newlyweds, and she sent up a silent prayer that they always return in times of struggle to their memories of tonight and how they fought for their love to unfold according to their own visions instead of anybody else's. Their kiss dissolved into laughs of pure joy that only ebbed when Toby shifted Natalie in his arms for an impromptu dance.

As the song wound down, Gentry sidled up next to Skye. "I think our work here is done."

She held up her hand and he high-fived her as they shared a smile of accomplishment that made Skye's heart do a flip-flop. How could it be that Skye felt such a strong bond with a man she'd known for two days? "We did good, partner."

"I'll say. There's just one more thing." When the song ended, he raised his guitar with a whistle to get everyone's attention. "May I be the first to congratulate the bride and groom?"

Skye, the officiant, and Dolly clapped. Gentry kissed Natalie's cheek. "Skye and I are about to take off, but before we do, we have a gift for the bride and groom."

Skye didn't remember any gift, so she wasn't sure where the *we* came from, but it was certainly sweet of Gentry to include her.

Toby shook his head. "You've already given us too much."

But Gentry waved away the protest. "The limo we rode to get here is yours for the night. But I suggest you have it take you straight to the Four Seasons, where we reserved a room for you, our treat. Just tell the front desk your names. They're expecting you."

Whoever said money didn't buy happiness would change their tune if they could have felt the giddiness radiating off Natalie and Toby. Not that Skye faulted them. It really was such a generous gift. But that seemed to be Gentry's usual M.O. He was generous with everything—except his promises. As he'd told her their first night together and then again in the plane, he couldn't promise Skye anything more than this night.

That was fine with Skye because it mirrored her vision for the two of them—didn't it?

With a squeal, Natalie threw her arms around Gentry. "Thank you, Gentry. I love the Four Seasons! I'll never forget everything you did for us today. You made tonight so special."

Toby shook his hand. "That's . . . wow. I'll be forever in your debt. Both of you," he added, smiling at Skye.

"We're happy we could help," Skye said. Which was true. She may not have gotten them a room at the Four Seasons, but she'd done everything in her power to make sure they had the wedding of their dreams.

"What are you two going to do for the rest of the night?" Natalie asked, looking between Gentry and Skye.

Gentry turned to look at Skye with a smile that was pure wolf. "You two are already having the best night of your life, and I think it's time Skye and I take a shot at that too. I've got big plans for this one."

He set his hand on the small of Skye's back, his splayed fingers dipping measurably lower than what would have been polite. Skye's whole body heated. She arched her hips, filling his hand. Hot damn, she couldn't wait to find out what he had in mind.

Chapter Seven

"Like most good stories, this one's gonna involve a bar. And not just any bar."

They strolled down Broadway, arm in arm, through the heart of Nashville's Music Row, past one famous spot after another, including the RCA Studio B, where Elvis famously recorded more than two hundred songs and that also served the likes of Dolly Parton and a bevy of other indelible musicians that seemed to be near and dear to Gentry's heart.

There was no mistaking the affection in his tone as he schooled Skye on Nashville's illustrious musical history, interspersing the story with tales of his own rise to fame after years spent paying his dues in the dive bars and nightclubs that dotted the city. Despite the late hour, the sidewalks hummed with the promise that the night was just getting rolling.

"A special bar?"

"Not just any special bar, but the Wild Beaver Saloon, the bar Neil Blevins discovered me in."

Skye had never heard such a ridiculous name for a bar. "Wild beavers aren't that exciting, you know. They tend to keep a low profile and keep themselves busy damning up rivers. But I have a hunch this honky-tonk joint is nothing like a wild beaver."

"You'll see soon enough," he said with a boyish grin that made her heart do a flip-flop.

Her gaze drifted over the neon lights of the gift shops and other stores that they passed. Open late for retail establishments, they were probably trying to catch a few sales with the late-night crowd. There were certainly plenty of people on the street to justify the extended hours. At the sight of a woman's clothing shop, a sudden burst of inspiration hit her. "If you're taking me to a honky-tonk bar, then I need a better outfit. This uniform isn't gonna do."

She grabbed hold of his shirt and pulled him inside. She wasn't usually one to spend a man's money willy-nilly, but she wouldn't mind if Gentry shared a little of his generosity with her, especially if she paid him back with a hot little number like the slinky red dress that first caught her eye.

She made a beeline to it and flipped through the hangers, searching out her size. "Come on, come on . . ." she muttered, losing hope. Then, *bingo*. She snatched the hanger from the bar and held the dress up to her body. "What do you think? Is red my color?"

His jaw rippled as he swallowed hard. "What do I think?" He looked over his shoulder at the cashier who was distracted by another customer. Then he grabbed the dress away from her and walked toward the curtained fitting rooms at the back of the store. "I think I can't go on another minute without seeing you in it." He flung the curtain open and ushered her in, pressing the dress into her hands as she passed.

Alone in the stall, Skye made eye contact with her

reflection in the mirror. The sight had her holding her breath. She looked like she was fresh off a daring rollercoaster ride full of 360-degree loops and steep drops. Her hair was in disarray, her cheeks were flushed, and her eyes had an unmistakable sparkle to them. Tonight, with all its crazy twists and turns, was even better than a rollercoaster. Even better than midnight horseback rides through the dark countryside.

She peeled her work uniform off, feeling lighter and freer with each layer gone. She loved her job, but it didn't breathe life into her, not like this did. Gentry had called it right when he'd referenced the two different Skyes—the one who was beyond ready to settle down and the one who could never be tamed. Once undressed, she stood in her panties and bra and regarded her reflection again. All her life, she'd thought of her two sides as in war with each other, a battle to the death, with her brain clearly on the side of the settling-down Skye, the make-her-family-proud Skye. The noble, faithful Skye who honored her heritage and church and her family's legacy at Briscoe Ranch.

But this . . . running off with a virtual stranger to another state, helping a couple escape their wedding, breaking the rules, going too fast, too dangerously, too hard. It lit up her senses and set her free. But Skye knew there wasn't room in her for both sides to flourish indefinitely. Because the part of her that made her feel the most alive was the same part that would destroy her, as it had tried to all those years ago with Mike the Mistake and the baby she'd lost, the devastation of shame and sin gnawing away at her heart.

"This is my Mardi Gras," she whispered. "After tonight, I'm saying good-bye to this addiction," she told her reflection. But until then, she was going to make the most of this one last thrill.

Thus resolved, she shimmied into the little red dress. It fit her every curve like a glove and showed off just enough cleavage to leave Gentry wanting more. Perfect.

"Ready?" she called over the curtain.

"Can't wait."

She pushed the curtain aside and emerged. Gentry gave a low whistle. "The only way you could look better than with that dress on is with that dress puddled around your ankles."

Oh my. "Be careful what you wish for."

With a glance over his shoulder to make sure nobody was paying them any mind, he stepped closer and tipped her chin up. "I know exactly what I'm wishing for." He brushed a kiss across her lips. "And I'll tell you all about it." His hand swept from her chin to trace the outline of the dress's strap. "First, I'm going to show you around this town I love, break a few rules with you . . ." His fingers grazed the dress's scoop neckline, bumping lightly over the swell of each breast. "And I'm gonna keep you slow-burning until all you can think about is me and how badly you need me, and only me, to put out that fire inside you. And then you know what I'm going to do?"

"What?" she said with a shiver.

"I'm not gonna put that fire out. I'm just gonna keep feeding the flames and keep you going all night long, burning bright and hot and all for me. Think you can handle that?"

It wasn't in her nature to sit back and let a man take complete control of the night. Heck, she rarely even trusted a man to drive her around on dates. But tonight, she'd never wanted anything more than to let him take the wheel and give her the time of her life.

Sniffing, he stepped away from her and scrubbed his face, clearly as affected by their little talk as she was.

"Pick out some boots to go with that dress and let's get on with it. It's time for me to see you ride a mechanical bull," he said in a gruff voice, moving toward the cash register.

A mechanical bull? With any other man on any other night, Skye would have cringed at the thought. She'd ridden a bull a few times, mostly in her early twenties, with one notable exception last year when she and the other Briscoe Ranch employees had the chance to ride the bull after hours at the brand-new Hitching Post Saloon at the resort. She'd nearly bitten her tongue off on that particular ride and had decided she was too old for those antics anymore. But she wouldn't dream of turning Gentry down.

She made short work of selecting a pair of inky black boots with gold embroidery that felt great on her feet. They cost hundreds, but Gentry merely nodded his approval and reached for his wallet.

On her way out of the store, Skye gave one last look through the racks of clothes to the open dressing-room stall at her uniform, balled into a crumpled pile of beige on the floor, and smiled.

Mo the Bull was nowhere near as whiz-bang as Johnson. No smoke out of his nostrils or red glowing eyes. Just a hide with a handle on hydraulics. But Mo, with its fraying hide and greasy frame, fit the dive bar vibe of the Wild Beaver to a T. And Mo had the dubious distinction of being the first mechanical bull Gentry had ever ridden, in the bar where Neil Blevins had first caught his act all those many years ago.

While Skye waited her turn to ride Mo, Gentry sidled up to the wooden bar that stank of spilled grenadine and cheap whiskey and ordered Skye's requested margarita and himself a beer. He didn't even think twice about it. Having a beer in hand was all part of the costume he wore every time he was in public.

Skye was about halfway through her glass of liquid courage when her number came up to ride Mo. Gentry held her drink as she made her way across the mats and straddled the bull in one strong, fluid motion that made every hot-blooded male in the room perk up.

The dress straps slid over her shoulders, revealing a white bra beneath and inching the neckline down enough to reveal quite a lot of cleavage. Her hair fell over her shoulders in cascading waves, as fluid and dark as a river on a moonless night. Gentry had seen a lot of pretty women in his life, but Skye just kept upping the bar.

He was busy contemplating her legs when she looked over at him, all bravado and sexiness. The minute he locked gazes with her, she blew him a kiss.

Sweet Jesus. Gentry's breath caught in his throat. His beer bottle slipped through his fingers a few inches before he remembered he was holding it.

He couldn't wait to have his way with her—every which way he could dream up. He wanted to memorize every curve of her body and every sound she made. He wanted to leave his mark on her memory so she'd never forget how thoroughly ravished she'd been by Gentry Wells. He hadn't been exaggerating when he told her he wanted to brand himself to her memory. He wanted her to hear his name or his song on the radio and get instantly wet, remembering what they'd done together.

After the wedding, he'd thought about taking her to a hotel room, but she spent most of her life at a hotel for work. Plus it wouldn't tap in to how turned on she got by the idea of breaking the rules of the resort and consorting with a guest. He did not, under any circumstances, want to be her vanilla lover. She could resign herself to that kind of man once they'd parted ways.

A siren sounded, and, with a snort of artificial smoke, Mo the Bull started bucking.

Skye's yelp of surprise rang in his ears, but she kept smiling, even as she was vaulted off of Mo after only two short seconds. She flew ass-over-tea-kettle onto the foam padding, laughing the whole time. And when she stood, adjusting her skirt down, a handful of men who'd been watching gave her a slow clap. With that tousled hair and her dress askew, the flushed cheeks, he could well imagine what she'd look like in his bed.

She melted into his arms as soon as she crossed through the pen's gate and leaned heavily against him as she swayed, catching her balance. "My brain's scrambled."

"You want to sit down?"

She cast him a seductive look and burrowed into his neck. "No, I think I want to stand right here with you."

Not a problem. He backed them up into the shadows, out of the way of the bull-riding crowd, and stroked her back while they swayed in a kind of slow dance in time with the two-step the live band was playing. When the song ended, she turned her face up and smiled at him, the perfect invitation to kiss those sweet strawberry lips.

He notched his mouth with hers and let the shared warmth of their lips mingle. He kept it slow and sensual and full of promise, and he kept on kissing her until she moaned and parted her lips in a plea for more. But he wanted to keep her hungry for him, so he ended the kiss and nuzzled her nose. "Been a long while since I've done anything like this, Skye Martinez."

"Helping a couple elope? Or inviting a random girl to spend the weekend in Nashville with you?"

He'd had plenty of weekend flings with plenty of random girls, some in Nashville, even. But this—with Skye—was different, though he wasn't exactly sure why. He nearly bit out a joke about how he was an old hat at helping kids in love elope, but he didn't feel much like joking at the moment. He wasn't sure why that was, either. "More like I enjoyed someone's company so much that I forget who I am, and all my cares just float away."

She matched his smile. "In that case, me, neither."

"Hey, that's Gentry Wells!" someone shouted.

A handful of college-age kids had gathered around them, slack jawed, grinning like fools. "No way!" one of them said. "Are you really Gentry Wells?"

So much for forgetting who he was. Gentry left a loose arm around Skye as he turned to face the fans. "That's me."

In a true snowball effect, the band on stage stop playing. "What's the fuss back there?" the lead singer asked.

"Here we go," Gentry said under his breath to Skye.

"What?"

"Gentry Wells is in the house!" one of the college kids bellowed.

"Well, holy shit," the singer said. "Mr. Well Hung himself is in the house tonight. Back home to the bar that started it all. Get the hell up here, man. Sing us some songs!"

"Why do people keep calling you that?" Skye said. "Have you leaked some secret sex tapes I don't know about or something?"

It was too perfect of a set-up for Gentry to ignore. He winked at her as they made their way through the crowd, saying, "You'll find out soon enough."

"Let's get him up here, everyone!" the singer said. Then he broke out in a chant of his name, which the rest of the bar-goers caught on to fast. "Gentry! Gentry! Gentry!"

It had been bound to happen eventually, especially in Nashville, in this bar where an autographed photo of him performing graced a wall. He might have refused, but his ego was just big enough to want to show off for Skye. She said she'd never much cared for country music, but he wanted to sing to her anyway. Maybe she'd learn to love his music.

That was a dumb thought to have about a woman he might never see again after they parted ways and she got back to her bullshit pursuit of some kind of boring Dulcet schlub to attend church picnics with as they raised two-point-five children. Frankly, he wanted to be as far from one of those guys in her mind as possible. Maybe he'd even start his set with "Built to Leave," just to put her mind at ease that he had no designs on her beyond being her fantasy man.

"You mind if I leave you alone for a few minutes so I can sing you a song or two?"

Skye looked around, clearly dazzled by the crowd's enthusiasm. "I don't think this crowd will let you get away with not singing a song or two. I mean, listen to them. They're chanting your name."

That was a part of his job that never got old and never made him weary. He had the best fans in the world, hands down. "Cool, ain't it? You didn't know you were hanging out with such a big deal tonight, did you?"

She pinched his chin. "Guess you don't need me to stroke your ego. You're stroking it plenty on your own."

That's what he loved about her—she gave as good as she took. She'd never be one of those moony-eyed groupies that was only with him because of his money and famous name.

Gentry clutched his heart. "You wound me, woman."

"You'd better get up there before the crowd picks you up and carries you to the stage." She held her hand out. "I'll hold your beer for you."

"Thanks, but it's part of my act." Which was the understatement of the century. "You stay right here, okay? Don't get lost in the crowd. I want to be able to see you while I'm singing."

Leaving Skye at the edge of the stage, Gentry jogged up the stage stairs, his still-full beer bottle aloft, much to the glee of the crowd.

After shaking hands with every member of the band, he launched right into "Beer O'Clock," singing along with just about everyone in the audience. He loved that they knew the words. Hell, he loved that Skye was there to see that a crowd of people knew the words to his song. Standing in the front row, she danced to the music and even sang along on the final chorus, truly the most stunning woman in the bar—and she was his.

For the night, he had to remind himself. Good thing he'd already planned to sing her "Built to Leave," only not for Skye's sake, but for his. He was the one who needed the reminder that she didn't want him like that, and even if she did, he'd only break her heart. She was too lovely and full of life to be dragged down by a rambling man like him.

He pulled a stool from the side of the stage and sat. "Time to slow it down and get real with a song I helped write last year. Let's go."

I rebuilt that Chevy's engine
If you have a leak, then I'm your man
And every cabinet and shelf in my mama's house

Was built with these two hands.

But there's a messed-up part inside of me
That's been brokedown from the start
You see, when a man is built to leave, like me,
He's destined to break your heart
And that's something I can't build back.
Naw, baby, it's nothing I can build back.

Loneliness washed through him, as it did every time he sang this song. He couldn't look at Skye, but he hoped she got the message loud and clear. He really was no good for her, not in any real sense.

It was hard to shake the mood off when the song ended, but he had a bar full of people watching him, waiting to see what he did next, including one beautiful vixen in the front row. It was time to shake off.

But he wanted to end the mini-set on a high note, get her primed again for the rest of the evening. He might be the leaving kind, but here was something else about him that he wanted her to know.

"Ladies and gentleman, you're a great crowd and I thank the Whistling Dixies for letting me jam with them tonight. I've got one more song for y'all, and it's a big one." He hammed it up on those last two words, and the audience got the hint. Their cheers shook the building. "All I need now is a special lady to sing it to." He walked to Skye and held out his hand, not so different from when he'd reached for her from inside the private jet. "Let me serenade you."

After a tentative look around, she set her hand in his and let him pull her up on stage, where he sat her on the stool he'd used for "Built to Leave."

"Skye, these are my fans. Fans, this is Skye. Give her a warm welcome, would you?" She looked a little uncomfortable, but smiled at the crowd and gave a charming little wave.

"Y'all know the words, so I want you to sing it with me now, folks." With a signal to the band, they were off.

Girl, I hung around like a puppy dog
Hung up over you
Until you hung me out to dry
What's a man to do?

By the chorus, Skye's face had turned a becoming shade of pink. He gyrated in a kind of lap dance for her, much to the delight of the crowd. And Skye, who got in the spirit, started to move along with him. By the last verse, she was on her feet, dancing, and singing along with the rest of the bar, loud enough that he felt the vibrations of their collective voices all the way to his heart. Honestly? He felt like freakin' Superman.

While the band ground out the closing coda of the melody, Gentry muffled the mic and whispered in Skye's ear, "Are you ready to make our grand exit? I'm ready to be alone with you."

Chapter Eight

When Gentry had told Skye he was ready to be alone with her, she'd expected their next stop to be a hotel, but Gentry surprised her again by taking her through a VIP entrance into a club that pulsed with techno dance music. Strobes flashed. Beautiful people preened and held martinis like accessories along with the wristlet purses dangling from their arms and their five-inch stiletto heels.

"I thought we were going to be alone," she said.

"Working on it. You wait here." He left her alone to talk to one of the hostesses standing at a podium near a glass staircase. When the hostess left to check on something, Skye looped her arm through Gentry's. "I don't think we're up to dress code," she said, looking down at her boots.

"Baby, you'd be up to code at any bar in the world in that itty-bitty dress. Besides, all these people, none of them are gonna see you for very long."

Then the hostess was back. They followed her up the stairs and through a hallway of black walls rimmed in neon pink lights. The hostess opened a door and stepped aside. "Your VIP suite, Mr. Wells."

Skye had never seen a club's VIP suite before. Much like a private box at a football stadium or a box seat at an opera house, the room was walled on three sides along with a balcony that looked out over the dance floor.

The hostess lingered by the door. "May get I get you anything else?"

Without taking his eyes off Skye, Gentry handed the waitress a hundred-dollar bill. "No. And see that we're not disturbed. If we need anything, we'll ring for you."

The waitress took the money and disappeared with a nod.

Skye walked to the balcony and ran her hand along the curved metal rail. The balcony itself was glass, giving a dizzying view of the dance floor below it and a peek into the other VIP suites that lined the upper level. A blonde young woman in a black dress standing in a balcony directly across from them caught her eye. They shared a brief smile before Skye turned again to take another look at their suite from this new angle.

A horseshoe-shaped black leather sofa took up the center of the room. In the middle, on a black-leather ottoman sat a tray with a bottle of high-end vodka, low ball and martini glasses, an ice bucket, and garnishes. Mandatory bottle service, if she had to guess. She'd seen enough television to know about that.

Gentry must have noticed her eying the setup, because he leaned forward and touched the bottle. "May I mix you a drink?"

"Sure. Vodka and soda with a twist." She'd only had half a margarita at their last stop, and she didn't plan on drinking much at this stop either. She was far away from home with a man she'd just met the day before, so she wanted to keep her wits about her. And she also wanted to be running on all cylinders for whatever the night had in store for them. But he'd gone to the trouble of paying for the VIP suite and bottle service, so a few sips of vodka wouldn't do any harm.

"Gentry, what are we doing here? I said I wanted to go someplace private with you. Are you dragging your feet?"

He mixed her drink and handed it to her, then poured himself a club soda with lime.

"You didn't add any vodka to yours."

"That's because I don't drink."

"You had a beer at the bar, then got up on stage and sang a song called 'Beer O'Clock,' which everyone seemed to know the words to, so I'm guessing it's one of your big hits."

Sitting back, he rolled a sip of soda water around his mouth. "You ever wear a persona like a suit of clothing?"

She wished she could claim she couldn't relate, but she knew exactly what he was talking about. Far beyond her job, she could never quite shake the feeling that she was playing at being a good Catholic daughter. It was an ill-fitting suit, that persona, one she was determined to adopt for real. Just as soon as this weekend was over.

"Yeah, you know what I mean. Because I watched you abandon that housekeeping uniform in the fitting room in favor of this little red dress. Me and my stage personality are like you and that uniform. Every year, every album and tour, it gets a little bit less me and little bit more fiction. The beer was a decoy." He winked. "Which can be our little secret."

"Are you an alcoholic or something?" She regretted

the question instantly. They had this one, hedonistic night together and there she was wasting it with far-too-serious and personal questions. But she couldn't help it. There was so much more to Gentry than he'd seemed, and the more glimpses she got of the man beneath those tattoos and bad boy smirk, the more she wanted to know.

He didn't seem to mind the question, though. With a shake of his head, he leaned close to her ear. "Not an alcoholic, but I'm not a great guy when I'm drunk, something I figured out when I was a senior in high school. The drummer of the band I was in at the time, Nick, who's still my drummer to this day, told me I was getting to be just as mean as his old man when I was drunk, which was saying something. He threatened to quit the band if I didn't shape up. That was all it took for me to lose my taste for the stuff." He pushed up his sleeve and angled his arm out to show her his tattoo of a farm. "This cornfield, it's the farm I grew up on. An homage to my downhome roots, is what I tell the press. But to me, this tattoo isn't an homage, but a reminder of how far I've come from all the shit I left behind when I decided to pursue this career, everything that isn't good for me."

Her expression softened as she studied his eyes. Beyond the tinge of weariness, she was most struck by the determination blazing in them. She scooted closer on the sofa and stroked his cheek, then kissed the spot.

He turned his head and captured her lips. She'd had months of tentative end-of-date kisses with staid, respectable men, but the way Gentry kissed her was nothing like those. The bristle of his five o'clock shadow. The hard planes of his body. His scent was that of dusty leather, and of chicory and sage, the spices of her mother's potions. So familiar, and yet, somehow, on him, the scent heightened his exotic appeal, this musician.

When the kiss ended, she snuggled in close to him. "What are we doing here? Because I thought you said you wanted to be alone with me. Did you get cold feet?"

The suggestion seemed to amuse him. "No cold feet, trust me. I'm taking my time, making the most of our night together."

"I had the same goal, but mine involved a bed." And maybe the shower if they were feeling adventurous.

In a flash, he rocked up to his knee, looming over her, caging her between his arms. A provoking heat infused his expression. "Don't sit there and pretend you're with me tonight because you want to play it safe with the same old, same old. If you'd wanted to make quiet, vanilla love in a bed with the lights off, then you would've picked a different man. God knows you've got enough of them beating down your door." He brushed his finger over her chin. "But you didn't pick one of them. You picked me. And what I want is to see what your skin looks like under these strobe lights. I want to fuck you in time with that booming bass."

Skye's breath caught in her throat. He was right, and it scared the hell out of her. She wasn't with him that night to play it safe. She'd wanted a thrill, and he was delivering it to her beyond anything she could have imagined for herself. The edgiest fantasy she'd conjured for the two of them was doing it in the shower.

But he wanted her here in this semi-public space. Anyone on the dance floor could look up and see them through the balcony glass, and just because he'd paid the waitress to leave them alone didn't mean she would.

She flashed back to the bar, when Gentry was singing, and how the women in the front row had practically tossed their tops on stage to him. What was it like to go on tour and have that constant barrage of women lusting after him? Did that turn him on? Did he select a special one each night the way he'd brought Skye up on stage, then take her back to his trailer with him after the show? The idea turned her on as much as the unexpected flash of jealousy.

His hand dropped from her chin to her outer thigh. His fingers teased the sensitive flesh. "Now that we're clear about what I want," he growled, sliding his hand up until it bumped into her dress. "What is it that you want?"

With that look on his face, the heat of his hand, her answer was an easy answer. She knew what she wanted, what she'd wanted from him since the first time she'd laid eyes on him. She pressed his chest, pushing him back onto the sofa. Then she stood. She bullied her knee between his two and nudged his legs open wider. "What I want is for you to treat me like one of your groupies."

That hard expression didn't dissipate, even when the corners of his lips kicked up into a dangerous smile. "See? I was right about you. Dirty girl."

Gentry Wells' Dirty Girl. She liked the sound of that. Then again, it was easy to push the envelope on a night like this, so out of context from her life, another world, another version of herself that she knew wasn't real. But if she was only playing out a fantasy with him, then why did she feel so alive? It scared her shitless to wonder whether she had it backward—that this side of her was real and honest, while her real, daily life was the fantasy.

She pushed the thought away. She had a lifetime to ponder that, but at the moment, there was a gorgeous man sitting in front of her, offering her anything and everything she wanted. Time for some fun.

She set a hand on his belt buckle. "Tell me what they do for you. Is it like this?" She unlatched his belt.

"That's a good start." He slouched even more, then lifted his right leg and, with his boot, pushed the ottoman away. The second she figured out why, a rush of arousal flooded her between her thighs. He was making room for her legs. He wanted her on her knees.

She grabbed a pillow from the sofa and dropped it on the floor between his boots. A girl had to stay comfortable, after all. And then she sank down to the floor, knees on the pillow.

He let out a ragged breath. "You are the stuff of fantasies, Skye Martinez."

She unzipped his jeans, revealing a shock of bright blue. She'd forgotten about those ridiculous bikini briefs, the ones that were meant to help his creativity. Their encounter that afternoon in his villa had seemed like a lifetime ago.

Refusing to remind him about his writer's block or anything else about their real lives, she ignored the finding. This was a game they were playing now, and she was determined to stick to the script. She wasn't going down on the earnest, sweet guy who didn't drink, but the badass, sexy-as-hell country star Gentry Wells—and she was merely a groupie.

She conjured up her best look of wide-eyed innocence. "I don't know what you're talking about. I'm not Skye Martinez. You don't know what my name is. You don't even care. You just want to take from me whatever I'm willing to give."

He held her gaze. His jaw rippled with tension as he swallowed hard. "Damn right, I do."

She freed his hot, heavy cock from the briefs. It curled up against his tight abs, hard and huge. "I knew it," she murmured, biting her lip. "It's just like your song."

With a wry smile, he gathered her hair in one fist and

the base his cock in his other. "Less talk. You know why you're here." And then with mock-force, he brought her lips to the blunt head of his cock.

She sank her mouth over him, feeling her lips stretch to accommodate his girth. She moaned with the pleasure of taking him into her, of the salty heat of him that made her mouth water. She let the vibrations of that moan carry from her tongue to his shaft. He hissed a breath out through clenched teeth and arched his hips, straining for more.

She teased him with slow strokes of her tongue and teasing suckles of his head until the pressure of his hand in her hair intensified, urging her to move fast, take him deeper. She felt like the most powerful goddess in the world when she rolled her gaze up and saw his eyes glazed over, lost in passion. Then she started to move, bobbing her head in time with the beat of the club's techno music, ready to take him right to the edge.

He gave a low grunt and rocked his hips in time with her, bumping his cock on the back of her throat with every thrust until, with a curse, he backed off, breathing hard.

He released his grip on her hair and stroked her hair like she was his pet. With his other hand, he took hold of his cock, glistening in the pink and purple strobe lights, and traced her lips with his cock head. "Tell me, baby, how deep into this groupie fantasy do you want to stay? Are you gonna swallow like one? If you don't, that's okay. I just need to know what to do. You tell me if you want me to be a gentleman or not. The choice is yours."

She loved that even though they were playing out a fantasy, he was still in control of himself. He was still letting her call the shots. With her lackluster dating life, it'd been years since she'd swallowed, because no guy she went out with ever seemed worth that kind of effort. But Gentry was, and it didn't feel like an effort at all. "You were right, before. I didn't get on that plane because I wanted to spend the night with a gentleman. Use me how you want. Let me have all of you." She licked her lips, then parted them and set her tongue on the underside of his crown.

"That's what I thought." His hand went to the back of her head again and he shoved his cock past her lips on a grunt.

Only this time, he scooted to the edge of the seat and pivoted, forcing Skye to turn with him until he'd pinned her head to the sofa with his cock. With a hand braced on the coffee table, he pumped his hips, fucking her mouth, taking what he wanted, but never violently, and never forcing her to take him deeper than she could handle.

Before tonight, she'd never gotten off on rough sex or blow jobs. It had always seemed so selfish, reflecting her lovers' unskilled, porn-fueled character flaws. But not with Gentry. He made sure she knew that he wasn't actually losing control, that he knew what their boundaries were and he respected them. She never felt unsafe or used, not really. It was all part of the game.

She reached a hand up her dress and fingered her panties. Soaking wet, they clung to her folds. But she didn't have time to do more than find her clit before Gentry's thrusts grew erratic.

"Take it," he growled. "Just fucking take—" His words dissolved on a grunt.

And then he filled her mouth with ropes of wet heat. She rubbed her clit, generating ripples of pleasure that radiated through her whole body. She was so aroused that she was only half aware of swallowing, half aware of her tongue cleaning him off.

After one last thrust, he stood and backed up, taking in the sight of her on the floor, her hand disappearing between her legs.

"Fuck," he breathed in appreciation.

No shit, she thought, her eyes on his still hard cock jutting out from his jeans.

Then he offered her a hand up. "It's time for Little Miss Groupie to get her reward."

With the driving thump of techno music as their score, he walked her to the balcony. Irrational fear of falling or the glass giving way kept her from getting too close—right up until Gentry pushed her up against the rail and gave her a dirty, wet kiss that went on and on, until the only thing on her mind was Gentry's tongue and the hard planes of his body pressing against her—that, and the wanton hope that someone in another balcony or on the dance floor might be watching them.

Twisting behind him, he grabbed an ice cube from the bucket on the table and set the tip of it on her shoulder, just inside the strap of her dress. He traced her collarbones with it, then drew a line of icy water between her breasts. Her nipples hardened. Chill bumps broke out all over her skin. She threw her head back and surrendered to sensation as Gentry drew lines and swirls on every exposed piece of skin, putting on a show of pleasure for whomever might be watching.

"All right, baby, are you ready to push the envelope a little more?"

She lifted her head and looked at him again. His nostrils were flared, and his eyes dark, oozing virile power. "I thought we already had."

He offered her a lopsided grin full of wicked promise, then he sank to his knees.

"I'm going to taste you now. I'm going to make you come." His hands roved over her legs. "Widen your knees. Let me in, baby."

Gentry's hands slid up her legs until they disappeared beneath her dress. His fingers closed around her panties, then pulled. The sensation of air swirling between her legs on her wet, heated flesh made her clench in pleasure. She cast a look over her shoulder. No one in the other balconies was paying them any mind, which was too bad, she realized with surprise.

He scraped a finger along the curls covering her plump flesh, one side and then the other, then right up the middle. "So beautiful. And so fucking wet."

He reached behind him for another ice cube, then traced the same path that his finger had. He pushed the ice in between her folds. It stung her hot flesh, bombarding her senses with pleasure and pain.

Then he held the ice cube up to her mouth. "Eat it."

She didn't think twice before accepting the ice on her tongue. It tasted faintly of her, but only a little. The cold made her shiver again as she held it on her tongue and let the water trickle down her throat. Gentry bunched the fabric of her dress until it neared her hips. Soon, the whole club would get a view of her ass. She was all for pushing the envelope tonight, but public nudity? Did she actually want to take it this far?

He buried his face in her curls and kissed her sweetly, warming her flesh again. "Don't worry. It's a one-way mirror."

She looked out across the room at the other balconies and confirmed that to herself. The sliver of disappointment she felt at his answer shocked her. She had her answer. "That's too bad."

His deep chuckle rumbled between her legs. He suckled her as though savoring a delicacy. "You really do have a kink for breaking the rules."

She rolled her head, face tipped up and eyes closed. "Yes, always," she breathed.

His tongue breached her folds. Ripples of bliss consumed her, and she cried out. The music fell away. The club, the other people, and all she knew about herself in that moment was that she was sexy and beautiful and a powerful, gorgeous man wanted her. There was no room in her head or her heart for anything but the way he made her feel. Just Gentry and his hand and his mouth, that hard body holding her while she quivered and bucked and descended into the madness of pleasure.

The buildup of her release was swift and potent. She gripped handfuls of his hair. "Oh, damn, Gentry. So close . . ."

Just like that, he stopped, removing his mouth and hands.

She whimpered and squirmed, a slave to the impossible pressure inside her screaming out for release. "What the hell?" she bit out between pants for air.

He looked up at her with eyes that were dark and intense to the point of almost seeming angry. "What are you going to do about that kink of yours when you marry your boring husband? You gonna pretend you don't need it? Pretend like that part of you doesn't exist?"

She mashed his face into her pussy. "Shut up. Finish what you started."

He resisted her efforts and stood. His lips were shiny with her juices and his shaggy blond hair was in disarray. "Or is that part of the kink? Maybe you like to put yourself in little boxes just for the pleasure of breaking out of them."

She fought against allowing his words to sink in. He knew nothing about her, so he had no idea what he was talking about. Why would she do that to herself? Make rules so she could break them. When she and her mom had conjured that love spell, Skye had meant every word. Unlike tonight, her life was no game and he was out of line to suggest that she treated it as such.

"Why do you care?" she said.

The question seemed to catch him off-guard. He blinked and rolled his tongue across his lower lip. "Hell if I know."

Their eyes locked. Skye felt her layers peeling back, revealing too much, even as she saw in him a raw, bald vulnerability that matched her own. They stared at each other, breathing hard. The music thumped as loud and fast as their hearts. Real. That was the only word to describe them at that moment. Real and honest. Two broken souls clinging to whatever rock they could in the storm of life.

But the moment could not last. Like walking on the edge of a cliff, one could only stay vulnerable as long as you didn't think too deeply about the danger of doing so. They startled back, as though they'd scared themselves with the truth.

"Not tonight," she said. Tonight was about forgetting. It was about getting lost in the game and the kink and the wild wonders of each other's bodies.

He nodded, hearing the truth behind her words loud and clear.

They came together in a clash of lips and tongue and teeth in a kiss that bordered on desperate. In a way, they were. She wrapped her leg around him, wrapped her arms around him, and battled to regain that lost, mindless descent into bliss.

His hand snaked between them and found her pussy as his other hand reached into his jeans pocket and came out with a condom. Beneath the low brim of his ball cap, heat and need radiated from his dark, half-lidded yes. "I'm gonna give you what you need. I'm gonna help you cross that line."

Yes, finally. "So do it," she challenged. "Just fucking do it."

He seized hold of her hips and spun her around so that she faced the dance floor. His erection dug into her ass. He placed her hands on the rail. "Keep them there and spread your legs."

The young blonde across the way was holding a pink drink in a martini glass and swaying to the music. She must have felt Skye's eyes on her because she squared up to the balcony and gave Skye and Gentry her full attention.

Gentry wrapped a hand around her waist and found Skye's clit, working it in relentless little circles until she was breathless again. Still, she held the pretty young thing's gaze, even when Gentry's cock nudged at her entrance.

Bracing her hands against the rail, her eyes on the blonde, she shifted her hips, arching for him, but the moment he started that slow push inside her, stretching and filling her, every nerve ending in her body lit up and she lost all sense of herself. She hunched into her hands, head lowered, lips open with a moan that went on and on and on.

He kissed her back. "You with me, baby?"

She lifted her heavy head and angled her chin over her shoulder to offer him a look that was half-smile, half-plea. *You're still fucking talking*, she wanted to say. If only she could get her mouth to form words. Instead, she rocked her hips, moving him in and out, figuring that if he wouldn't move, being so hell-bent on driving her crazy without release, then she'd do the moving herself.

His hand cupped her pussy, his middle finger pressing ever so perfectly against her clit so that it slid up and down as she moved. And then, finally, he took over, thrusting so hard that her hips hit the balcony, so hard that she wasn't sure how he was managing to keep that finger on her clit. Another look across the club revealed that the pretty young blonde in the black dress wasn't alone. Another woman was toying with the young thing's hair. Both sets of eyes were on Skye. Good. Let 'em watch.

The sex got raw and dirty fast as they devolved into their animal selves, thrusting and grunting. Nothing between them but slick heat and friction. Then his hand closed on her throat, lifting her up. She arched her back to keep him inside her and let him pull her up until his face appeared near her ear. His breath fanned out over her cheek.

"You are so goddamn hot. I need you to ride me."

Oh, she liked the sound of that, but there was one problem. "I don't want to say good-bye to my friends." She nodded toward the blonde, who licked her lips and sipped her drink. Her friend's lips teased her ear and her hand cupped the blonde's tits through her dress.

Gentry followed her gaze, then gave a growl of a laugh. "I can see why. I think I can make us all happy. You stay there for a sec."

He pulled out of her. She traced the swells of her breasts, purely for her friends' benefit. Behind her, glass rattled and tickled as Gentry moved the bottle service tray off the ottoman, then scooted it behind Skye.

Then he was standing behind her again. He spit on his hand and worked it over the length of his cock, then pressed into her, thrusting, once, twice, until he seated himself fully inside her, flooding her senses all over again.

"Come back with me, now," he said.

Taking her by the hips, he sat on the ottoman and then laid back so that Skye was straddling him backward, reverse cowgirl style. She braced her hands on his legs and found her friends across the club again. They were both smiling this time. Skye blew them a kiss, then, with Gentry's hands on her hips urging her on, she started to move her hips in a rolling, bucking thrust, around and around like she was back in the bar riding that bull like the cowgirl she was.

Gentry swore and smacked her ass. "You keep that up, I'm gonna come. Touch yourself. Get there with me."

No problem. She was so close, as it was, that all she needed was to flick her clit a few times while she bounced and she was there.

The young blonde and her friend had stopped moving, so enthralled were they with Skye, their faces the pictures of arousal. Skye looked the blonde in the eye and mouthed to her, "I'm coming." The blonde's lips parted at those words, but that was the last thing Skye saw. As her body shattered into a million little pieces, she gripped Gentry's wrists and threw her head back, crying out her pleasure for all the world to hear.

Whoever she'd been when she'd boarded that private jet was all but gone. And in her place, a wild, wanton force of nature, free of the bonds of time and faith and family—and with an equally wild bad boy beneath her, anchoring her and goading her on. They were so compatible, she and Gentry. Two reckless, hungry souls looking for escape, and at least for this one night together, they'd found it in each other's arms.

Chapter Nine

Sunday around noon, Gentry rented a car from the San Antonio airport to drive the hour and half northwest to Skye's home in Dulcet, just as he'd promised. The experience didn't compare to a private jet, but he'd flown them first class from Nashville, which was as close as he could get on such short notice. She'd insisted that she could find her own way home and he could fly direct to Tulsa, but he'd made her a deal that he'd make sure she got home all right from their jaunt in Nashville, and, by God, he was going to walk her all the way to her front door.

He'd have plenty of time afterward to return the avalanche of phone calls and text messages waiting for him on his phone, from Larry and Nick and even his ranch manager, Elias. But for the time being, he let the phone vibrate in his pocket as he enjoyed every minute he had left with Skye.

He had the feeling she was feeling the same way, because she'd insisted on giving him a driving tour of Dulcet on their way to her house. It was a sleepy, small town, with only a café or two, a bar, a firehouse, a feed store and a grocery store, and a church on every corner, much like the small town Gentry had grown up in. When she spoke of the places and stores that meant something to her, including her family's church, a somber, sand-colored building with an ornate wooden door and even more ornate stained-glass windows, there was no mistaking the affection and pride in her voice.

It was the reminder he needed that she had a real life, that the wild, wanton Skye of last night and that morning in the hotel room they'd collapsed in after the club was not the only side of her—nor, necessarily, the superior side, as he'd tried to insist. She'd been trying to tell him as much, but he'd resisted because he could see how conflicted she was to be living such a dual life.

But he'd clearly been projecting the pain of his own duality. The man who couldn't stand the taste of beer, but had made millions of dollars pretending to in song. The man who extolled the virtues of hometown roots, only to see his own as nothing but a warning about what not to do. The man who swore up and down that he had no interest in being in a relationship ever again, but was having trouble accepting that, as soon as he dropped Skye off at home, they'd probably never see each other again.

From Main Street, they headed northwest, where the terrain grew hilly and greener, save for the striking fields of bluebonnets. She directed him into an upper-middle-class neighborhood of well-kept, two-story brick homes set on a lot of land, their driveways accented with nice cars, rather than rusty old heaps on the lawn. This was a side of small town America Gentry wasn't all that familiar with growing up, the well-to-do kind.

"This is it," Skye said. "My neighborhood."

"I like it."

"Me too. I grew up here, went to school here." She looked out the window, an almost accidental smile tugging at her lips. "It's home."

No wonder she wanted to marry a man who was a local and settle down there. She was already settled down—she just needed a partner who wasn't going to pull her away from her family and her life. Suddenly, he was filled with gratitude that he'd insisted on driving her home. Beyond that, he now had a much richer understanding of her and what made her tick. This made it easier for him to accept that he wasn't the man for her. He would never be able to give her the stability she needed, not with world tours every other year and jetting all over the country wherever the interviews, performances, and awards shows took him. They were doing the right thing by parting ways, no matter how his heart wanted to play tricks on him that it could be otherwise.

At a four-way stop in the belly of the neighborhood, she set a hand on his arm. "I'd rather you let me out here. My place is just around the corner, and if we say good-bye here, then I won't have to deal with the prying eyes of my family."

"Your family?"

Her expression turned sheepish with a cringe. "Don't judge me, but I live across the street from my parents."

"Holy shit, girl. Are you kidding me?"

She tugged at his arm. "It's a good thing, most of the time. I love it. When the house went up for sale across the street, I jumped on the chance."

"And, here, I thought you and I were a lot alike," he teased.

With a bright smile, she shrugged. "In a lot of ways. Just not this one. I love my family."

That, she did.

"I'll make a deal with you," he said. "The outlaw in me needs one last dirty kiss good-bye, but the gentleman in me still insists on walking you to your door. So how about we have our kiss right here?"

"Deal. I'm just glad that gentlemanly side of you doesn't take over too often."

"Got that right," he growled as he cradled her cheek in his hand and lowered his mouth to hers. Random song lyrics tried to pop into his head about outlaws and gentlemen and kisses around the corner from his sweetheart's house, but he forced them away. He could write it all down when he got back to his ranch. This moment, right here, was just about him and Skye.

Damn, he was going to miss kissing her, the strawberry sweetness of her lips and the way her tongue slid against his, that little moan in the back of her throat, the way her cheek felt in his hand, and the way she gave herself so completely over to her own pleasure. It had been an honor to witness.

When the kiss ended, she sat back in her seat and caught her breath. Her cheeks were stained pink, her eyelids seemed a little heavier, and her lips were dewy with moisture. Everything about her, from the wispy, baby-fine black hairs that curled along her hairline to the faint freckles that dotted her nose and those soulful brown eyes. Jesus, those eyes.

She directed him to a two-story brick and yellow-siding house around the corner, with a neatly trimmed lawn and a lovely porch, complete with a swing bench.

"Your house?"

"Yep. Home."

He parked at the curb and walked around to open her door and help her out, along with a shopping bag containing last night's red dress, which she'd swapped out this morning for a breezy moss green sundress they'd picked up in the hotel lobby.

The closer he looked at her house, the more impressed he was. She'd done well for herself. Before he'd hit it big, he'd never lived in a home this nice. Not that he enjoyed the ranch-style mansion he'd bought with the first big chunk of money he'd gotten after hitting it big, the one that his ex-wife and girlfriends had cycled in and out of and that was more of a home to his ranch manager than him.

"I love it," he said as they walked up the driveway to the front door. "I guess your business must be booming."

The pride was evident in her eyes. "We do all right. My mom has a great business sense and I'd like to think she passed that to me. It's a good life."

She said that last part as though she felt like she needed to convince him. "Hey, I can see that. In fact, I'm jealous, truth be told."

Walking up the porch stairs, she smacked his shoulder. "You are not."

"No, really. My ranch, my house"—he shook his head—"it's big, but it doesn't feel like home. And when I get there, I don't look at it the way you're looking at your house right now. Not even close. So, yeah, I'm a little jealous right now."

She leaned in as though she was going to kiss him again, but the garage door started to open across the street and she pulled away, muttering, "Typical."

"Your parents' house?" he asked, nodding to an equally grand two-story gray-trimmed house.

"Yep. I'm surprised they're not out front pretending to water the lawn."

"But they're not, so . . ." He leaned in and brushed his

thumb across her lips. "I know this isn't very gentlemanly of me, like I promised, but I can't help myself," he said in a gruff voice. "One last little kiss before I go . . ."

Children's giggles froze him in his tracks. He looked around Skye and saw smiling, laughing kids at her window, including a girl whose nose and eyes were distinctly the same shape as Skye's. His heart sank. True, the two of them hadn't done a whole lot of talking in the three days they'd known each other, but surely she would have mentioned if she were a mom.

"Yours?" he choked out, nodding to the window.

She whirled around as the kids disappeared behind the curtain, though their laughter could be heard through the glass. "What nosy little things!" She knocked on the window with her knuckle. "Get away from the windows, kids. What did I tell you about spying on people?" To Gentry, she smiled. "Sorry. That was Teresa and Chris, my sister, Gloria's, kids."

"Ah." He wasn't sure why he was so relieved, but he was. "Not much into kids, myself. Never wanted them and never do. I have enough trouble managing myself and my career."

"Another reason you're not part of that love spell," she said. "Because I can't wait to have a couple of my own."

Okay, then. That was the perfect segue to his goodbye. Except, even knowing how different they and their life goals were, he still couldn't seem to lift up his boots and turn toward the car. How the hell did a man walk away from a woman like Skye, so beautiful and smart and sexy as hell?

There he went, romanticizing what they'd shared. It'd been the wildest night of his life—which was saying something because he'd been around the block a time or two—but the two of them had an agreement. He was her break from reality. Her Mardi Gras. And every Mardi Gras had to come to an end sooner rather than later. A pang of regret hit him.

He cleared his throat. "I should get going. I've got to get home and back to working on my next album."

"It's only noon. You might want to swing by the resort and get your stuff. Since you didn't check out this morning, it's probably in your villa. Including all your colorful underwear. I know you need it for inspiration."

He'd forgotten all about that, having ditched the blue pair last night in favor of going commando. "Not sure I do anymore, thanks to you and all the songs you inspired me to write this weekend."

"Then I guess I'll be buying your next album."

"I'll do you one better and send you a copy. As far as my belongings at the hotel go, I'm not sure I want to take a chance of running into Neil Blevins or his wife or anybody else who was supposed to attend the wedding last night. I think a call to the resort in a few days will be more like it. But, listen, when I call Natalie's parents to explain what happened and how I ended up flying Natalie and Toby to Nashville, I'm going to leave your name out of the story. I don't want to take a chance of you getting fired or hurting your business because you were fraternizing with a hotel guest and ruining a pricey wedding and all that."

"What about you? Neil's going to be pissed."

Yes, he would be. But that wasn't Skye's problem. He winked at her. "Don't worry about that. He can't fire me. I'm the talent." A gnawing feeling started up in the pit of his stomach, which he soundly ignored. "Good luck with your magic spell."

God damn, that sounded like bullshit to his ears. He wanted her to be happy, and he wanted her to live the life she dreamed of, and Gentry certainly wasn't the man to make that happen, but he still couldn't stop thinking about what a shame it was. The thought of Skye choosing to give up that fire in her eyes was damn depressing. Almost as depressing as thinking about the quiet, lonely ranch house he'd be sequestering himself in until his album was done. At least he'd live on in Skye's fantasies as the life of the party. Ironic, that. It was his fate to be nothing but a fantasy to those around him—for Skye, for his fans, for his label.

Save it for a song, man.

"Thank you for everything," she said. "For taking me with you. It was the adventure of a lifetime."

He tipped the brim of his ball cap. "Baby, the pleasure was all mine."

She tapped the brim of his hat. "Such a cowboy. Next time you're in town, you'd better call me."

"Then I guess I'd better pray that love spell of yours doesn't send you the perfect, upstanding Catholic local man anytime soon." He leaned in for a chaste good-bye kiss. "Until next time . . . I'll be dreaming of you."

When Gentry had gotten home from his weekend with Skye, he'd expected the words to flow. He'd holed up in his basement studio and tried to make the magic happen, but the more he forced it, the drier his creative well felt. After a few days of that and feeling like the walls of his ranch were closing in on him, he'd stomped to the barn and chosen the first horse he'd bought after his first album went platinum, the aptly named Wild Beaver.

He kept a skeleton staff at the ranch year-round to care for his property and animals since he was rarely home, which meant his horses belonged more to his ranch manager, Elias, than Gentry. But Wild Beaver, or just

Beaver, as Gentry called him, remembered him just fine. He'd planned to go on a trail ride to clear his mind with some fresh air, but he and Beaver were only on the trail for a few minutes when the lyrics to "Riding in the Dark" hit his brain all at once like a fireworks grand finale.

He'd raced Beaver back to his ranch where he strapped his guitar to his back like an old-school cowboy and stuffed a notepad in his saddlebag, then headed out on the trail again.

That had been three days ago, and the words had been flowing ever since. The longer he was out on the range with Beaver and his guitar, the more creative he got, writing song after song after song. The words and the notes flowed through him as though directly from the Man on High. He'd never felt so inspired.

Given how closely woven his songs were to Skye, she was never far from the forefront of his mind, but the more he thought and wrote about her, the less real she seemed until he couldn't shake the impression that she'd been nothing but a fever dream. There were hours that he lay in the shade near the banks of a stream while Beaver rested and replayed moments of their time together over and over, searching for the songs in her beauty and in the potency of their connection.

In the late afternoon of the seventh day, a full week after Natalie and Toby's elopement, Gentry rode Beaver back to the ranch after having been on the trail all day. He was hungry and tired, but even more satisfied with the progress he'd made. Today he'd tackled "Make Me Your Mardi Gras," as well as a song that hit a little too close to home to be comfortable and that he wasn't sure he wanted to include on his next album, titled *You're All I Need to Drink.*

A red Ferrari was parked in front of his house. Gentry had an immediate, visceral reaction to the sight—sweaty palms and a racing heart. There was only one man Gentry knew who'd drive such an audacious car.

The moment he'd driven out of Dulcet after dropping Skye off, Gentry had called Neil Blevins. He'd left a voicemail, saying he wanted to apologize and explain what happened, but Neil had yet to return the call. Guess he'd been waiting until he could confront Gentry in person.

Gentry puffed his cheeks full of air, then let out the air in a slow stream until the shot of adrenaline had dissipated. All he had to do was remember that he was the talent, not Neil.

In the stable, Elias caught up with him. He was a wiry, well-tanned man a decade or so older than Gentry, with a wife and young son who lived with him in Gentry's groundskeeper's house. "I tried to call you to give you a heads-up about Blevins, but you didn't have your phone."

"Thanks for trying. I was trying to keep my head down and focus on song writing. No such luck."

"Songs aren't coming to you, are they? I've sensed as much since you've been back," Elias said.

Gentry wasn't sure Elias considered him a friend, but the two men had managed to keep up a loose, if distant, camaraderie over the years. He couldn't decide if Elias preferred it when Gentry was away from the ranch or when he was around. Probably the latter. "Yeah, it's hit or miss. A lot like that old well in the south field."

"That's why I stick to livestock and wheat," Elias said with a sympathetic grin. He tried to take the reins from Gentry's hand. "I've got Beaver. You go deal with your business."

"If it's all the same to you, I'd like to tend to Beaver

myself." He wasn't about to admit to Elias that Neil's presence had him rattled, but he needed the time to calm his nerves and gather his thoughts.

Gentry took his time cooling Beaver down and getting him cleaned, fed, and put up for the night. He had nothing to be ashamed of and he would have helped Natalie and Toby all over again if given the chance. He stood outside his front door and closed his eyes, conjuring a vision of Skye lying in the hotel-room bed they'd briefly shared, looking so sexy and sweet, wearing nothing but a sheet and a sleepy smile, and he'd wished they could've laid there together forever.

Neil was waiting for Gentry in his formal living room. He'd made himself at home on the sofa, smoking a cigarette. Asshole. Gentry didn't even so much as own an ashtray, but Neil had created one out of a glass candle holder that Cheyanne had left behind. When Gentry walked in, Neil acknowledged him with a flicker of his eyebrows.

Gentry wracked his brain for something to say by way of a greeting, but the only words that sprang to mind were *fuck you*, and rather than waste those right up front, he decided to save that particular sentiment for later.

"Been waiting long?" Gentry said, dropping into the chair across from Neil.

"Long enough that I nearly opened this bottle without you." He nodded to an expensive bottle of tequila on the coffee table. Funny that, because Neil, of all people, knew Gentry didn't drink. But that didn't stop Neil from producing two tall shot glasses.

"I found these in your kitchen."

He'd been snooping. Lovely.

Neil poured two generous shots, then handed one to Gentry and clinked the two together. "Cheers."

Gentry waited for Neil to tip his shot back before emptying his into the nearest potted plant. Neil snorted his dismay.

"What I'm sorry for is that your plans for Natalie's wedding got messed up. I'm sorry that happened so publicly, and I'm sorry for the loss of money you've probably suffered."

"Suffered is a strong word."

"What I'm not sorry about is helping her have the wedding she wanted. I have no regrets for the role I played. She and Toby were gonna elope with or without my help, so I helped them do it in style."

Another snort of disgust. Neil poured himself another shot, tipped it back, then wiped his mouth with the back of his hand. From his worn brown leather briefcase, he pulled out a stack of magazines, which he tossed on the table between them. "Any truth to these?"

Gossip rags. A whole slew of them, and all with a cover story about Gentry going on a bender in Nashville with a mystery woman on the night he was supposed to be performing at his producer's daughter's wedding. Though Gentry was in the photos, the real star was Skye. Dang it all, he'd loved that little red dress. He wished he'd taken a picture of her, but these would do. Despite the harmful, invasive intent with which the shots had been taken, and they were low-quality and grainy in a way that blurred her face, they were enough to get Gentry's blood pumping again.

Gentry fought a smile at the sight of her and at the rush of memories the images filled him with. *All right, lover boy. Let's focus on getting Neil off your ass and off your property. After that, you can get back to daydreaming about her all you want.*

Gentry fixed a bored look on his face and shrugged. "There's some truth, I guess."

Neil tapped his fingers on his knee. "Let me get this straight," he said, over-enunciating each word. "You indulged my daughter's selfishness, broke any last shreds of trust I once had in you, and then you hooked up with some random groupie for the rest of the night and got yourself in the tabloids? Real smooth."

The word *groupie* made Gentry feel like Pavlov's dog. Goddamn, she'd been a hot little number in that VIP suite, on her knees between his legs.

Neil snapped him out of his thoughts. "Is she here?"

Only in his dreams. "No."

"Do you have plans to see her again?"

None of his goddamn business. "I'm a busy man, so let's get to it. What are you here to get from me? A pound of flesh? Groveling? You're not going to get it, so stop wasting both our time."

Neil stared daggers at him for a long, pregnant minute, then dropped another bomb. "The ACMs are the Friday after next. I know you, which means I know you were planning to ditch it, what with your last album not managing to garner a single nomination. But it's your lucky day because Kyle Crawley just had an emergency appendectomy so they needed another male vocalist to take his place in the line-up, so I secured his spot for you."

"You're kidding." The ACMs were the Academy of Country Music Awards, one of two big industry showcase nights. There had been years upon years of Gentry being the ACM's Golden Boy, earning Entertainer of the Year, Best Male Vocalist, and more. Two years in a row, in fact, he'd even emceed the event. But Neil was right;

he'd planned on begging out this year. The sting from the awards snub and not being selected to perform during the show for the first time in his twelve-year career had been too much, and this new album's deadline was coming at him faster than a runaway stagecoach. The perfect excuse to stay home and lick his wounds. But he'd be a fool not to take the opportunity, even if it dug him further into a debt of gratitude with Neil. He gritted his teeth and said, "Thank you."

On a fierce scowl, Neil gave the stack of magazines a shove with his boot heel. "You can thank me by performing the shit out of your set with one of the songs on your new album. Please tell me you've got at least one ready, since you fancy yourself a big shot singer-songwriter now."

Neil had always known exactly where to hit him below the belt to bring about maximum pain. Time to pull out those two little words he'd been saving for the just the right time. "Fuck you, Neil."

"I'll take that as a yes. And please tell me this song is about sexing up a woman or partying or something that lets us put a spin on this idiotic bender you went on."

Gentry ran through the list of songs he'd written since meeting Skye. Every single one of them fit that profile. "Yeah, I've got the perfect one. Called 'Riding in the Dark.' It starts out about a sexy horse ride in the moonlight, then gets dirty, with suggestive lyrics about riding her in the dark."

"That's perfect. And you're going to sing it to her. That's the hook. You get up there on that stage, you look right at the camera, and you burn down America's TVs with that corny smolder you do."

"You want me to invite her as my date?" Because,

damn, that would be cool. Or, at least, it would have been had Gentry been up for a single award. But still, having Skye on his arm for the awards show weekend in Las Vegas would be like getting a second ticket into heaven.

Neil threw his hands up. "God, no! Don't you get it? These piece-of-shit magazines are going crazy wondering about who she is. If you have her there, then they'll know. And then there'll be no more speculating." He backhanded the cover of one of the magazines, right over the image of Gentry's face. "You know how this game is played. You don't reveal your secrets; you give them a few crumbs so they'll have even more to talk about. It's time to make yourself relevant again."

Neil might be an asshole, but he was a damn smart one.

"I can do that. No problem."

"Good." Neil stood and hitched his pants up. "I'll send a driver to get you on Sunday morning. My secretary will be in contact with the details. And don't think this grants you an extension on the songs for the new album. You've got one month before we go into the studio to record it. May I remind you that this is the last album on your contract? This is it for you. Your last chance. It'd better be dynamite or you're finished. I have no interest in sticking around for your fall into music oblivion, so don't fuck this up, son."

Gentry didn't bother to show him the door or even rise and say good-bye.

Hours after Neil had shown himself out, Gentry sat in the same chair, staring at nothing, and contemplated that ultimatum. He'd really dug himself a hole this time. Neil Blevins was a force of nature in country music. When he said a performer's career was finished, he didn't just mean with his own record label. He meant in the business as a whole. He meant that if Gentry didn't put out the best album of his career, that career was over.

How was he supposed to work creatively while under that kind of pressure? He wasn't a robot. He was making art, not widgets. But was he really any good at making art? That remained to be seen. All those fears of being an imposter, of being discovered as a fraud instead of a real artist worth his salt, came rushing back at him.

"Hello, old friend," he said, his typical greetings to the feelings that were as familiar to him as breathing.

He had five great songs written already, but five songs did not an album make. He looked around his empty house, a mirror for his suddenly empty imagination.

Disgusted with himself, with the hole he was in, and with life in general, he grabbed his guitar again and headed back out to the barn. Because he sure as hell wasn't going to find any peace in that big empty house.

He fed the horses treats and groomed them, then he sat on a wooden bench and sang them some of his greatest hits. Not exactly the best use of his time, given what he had to accomplish in the next month, but at least it got him to stop panicking. The more he relaxed, the more the horses did, too, until he felt confident about saddling Beaver up for a late-night ride. With any luck, it would provide him with a fraction of inspiration that he'd had when he'd taken that midnight ride with Skye. What he wouldn't give to be with her again, out on that trail, drinking in her vivacity.

He pulled out his phone and stared at her contact information. He could call her up. He could text her to let her know he was thinking about her. But that didn't feel right, to call her because his creative well had dried up; it felt like using her in all the wrong ways. She might be his muse, but she had a life of her own. He'd already imposed himself into too much of it. It didn't matter how good she was for him because they'd both agreed that he wasn't good for her. And he didn't have time for women anymore, anyhow. He had a multimillion-dollar business to run.

With his guitar strung on his back and a notepad and pen at the ready, he and Beaver took off over the countryside, following the same path they had earlier that day. Out in the open country on his horse, Gentry didn't feel like an imposter or Neil Blevin's marionette. And he wasn't a no-good man whom respectable women like Skye should avoid. He was just Gentry, the Tulsa boy with a penchant for trouble and an ear for music.

It was time to take himself back to that humble beginning again, back to his cowboy roots. Because when all the chips were down, that's who he was. A solitary cowboy, through and through. Skye, with all her vivacity and sexiness, would have to just stay put in his dreams from thereon out. He couldn't afford to give her any more time than that.

Chapter Ten

Skye stood in the resort's employee parking lot and looked at the Spring Kickoff Barbecue in the distance, cringing. Time to pay her debt to Granny June with another matchmaking fiasco, this time to June's friend Meryl's grandson.

Stalling, she fished her phone from her purse and dialed Remedy's number. She picked up on the third ring.

"Hey there. I can't talk. I am literally herding cats over here!"

Nothing like a little wedding drama to take Skye's mind off her problems. "Where are you? I'm on my way."

"The amphitheater." After a pause, she shouted away from the phone, "Litzy, for the love of God, go buy some catnip at the feed store!"

Skye hitched a ride with one of the guys in the maintenance department and arrived on scene at the amphitheater that had been carved out of a hill behind the resort's main building. Usually, it was a shady and peaceful place where the resort employees liked to eat their lunches, except on weekends, when it was usually booked for weddings.

Sure enough, the amphitheater was in the throes of chaos. Skye counted at least seven cats—and one wedding planner who looked like she'd gone off the deep end, waving her arms and talking to the cats, trying to herd them toward a row of open pet carriers on the stage. And watching it all happen from various perches around the amphitheater were more than twenty cream-colored homing pigeons.

"Hey, Remedy. Oh my gosh, your pigeons are here. No wonder the cats are going crazy."

Remedy barely looked up. She had a gray-and-white long-haired cat cornered in the second row. "Hey yourself. Look, I got this one cornered. Grab me one of those carriers, would you? But don't make any sudden moves."

Skye crept with even, quiet steps to the carriers and brought the nearest one to Remedy. "Are all these cats part of the wedding?" Skye had heard of crazier things at weddings, but not by much.

"Yep. The ring bearers."

Skye had never owned cats, but even she knew that they weren't the best at following commands. "You're kidding."

"I wish. The couple runs a cat-training company and so they insisted that their perfectly trained felines would be up to the job during the wedding. One of these things is supposed to have the ring pillow strapped to its back. The bride and groom got the cats out of their carriers for the photography session this morning, but then my pigeons showed up and now the cats think they just died and went to heaven. The bride was freaking out about it, so I sent her back to the bridal suite for some champagne and told her I'd take care of it."

"I don't know how you do this job. I honestly don't," Skye said.

"I think the same about you every time one of the guests trashes their room."

Good point.

The cat that Remedy had corralled was sniffing the door of the carrier when she was startled by flapping and cooing as one of the pigeons landed a few feet behind Remedy. Faster than Skye could blink, the cat took off. Remedy tried to pounce on it like one might try to catch a pig, but the cat was too fast. Thankfully, the pigeon was even faster.

"Dang it all!" Remedy said, shooing the bird away. "I love those pigeons, but this is ridiculous." She ran after them, trying to shoo them away. "But they're not welcome here today. Do you hear that, birds? Shoo!"

The story, as Remedy had told it to her, was that during one of the first weddings that she'd planned for the resort, a group of homing pigeons that had been hired as makeshift doves took a liking to her and started following her around town. It wasn't long before she claimed them as her own. It wasn't unusual these days to find her feeding them on the front lawn of the firehouse, next to which she and Micah lived, and the birds had gotten so bold as to start roosting on her whenever they got the opportunity. It was quirky and crazy and so very *Remedy.*

"Skye, look to your left. I think you can get that calico cat."

Sure enough, Skye was in striking distance of a pudgy calico cat who was chewing one of the ribbons decorating the stage. She turned ever so slowly, then made a diving tackle. The cat gave a shrieking meow in response. Afraid of getting scratched, Skye released her.

"Sorry. I love you, but I'm not willing to shed blood for you over a bunch of cats. When is this wedding supposed to start, anyway?"

"Not for another three hours. Thank God." She collapsed onto one of the amphitheater bench seats. One of the pigeons wasted no time in landing on her knee. Once upon a time, that would have been a strange sight indeed, but Skye and Remedy had grown accustomed to the pigeons' presence. This one blinked at Remedy until she smiled. "Hi. You're a pain in the ass," she told it. "You and your friends. But I like you anyway."

It blinked again, then decided it was time to groom itself.

"We cordoned off the amphitheater exits so hopefully that means the cats can't escape, but there's not much we can do until Litzy gets back with the catnip." Remedy patted the bench next to her. "So tell me, what's up? What are you doing on this side of the resort today instead of at the Spring Kickoff Barbecue on the north lawn?"

Skye shooed a cat away from the pigeon, then set her head on Remedy's shoulder. "I am going, but I'm stalling. I think Gentry Wells ruined me for other men."

Remedy snorted. "He was that good, huh?"

"Yeah, he was, actually."

"Has he called or texted you? Or vice versa?"

As if Skye hadn't picked up the phone a million times in the two weeks since their weekend adventure hoping to see his name on the screen and stopping herself from reaching out to him. "Nope. Which is for the best." And she was going to keep telling herself that.

"Don't tell me he didn't give you his number. Because that would be shitty."

"No, he did. But we agreed to go our separate ways. He and I aren't right for each other, and we both know it. I love it here in Dulcet. My life and my family and friends are here. I've already fallen for a guy who lived like a nomad once and I swore to myself I'd never do that again.

I want a man who's here in Dulcet to stay too. That's not Gentry." As much as she'd started to wish otherwise. But she hadn't been able to stop thinking about his song "Built to Leave" since he sang it in the Wild Beaver Saloon. Since then, she'd downloaded the song and had played it to herself on repeat whenever she was tempted to text him.

"I know that's what you want, sweetie. I'm just so sick of seeing you miserable. And Gentry made you happy. No other guy has been able to accomplish that for you."

Skye was sick of her miserable dating life too. Beyond sick. "He only made me happy because we'd both agreed up front that we weren't right for each other and had no future. I was using him for the thrill of it and the distraction, and he was using me as song inspiration."

"Seriously? Because that's kind of cool. I want to be someone's song inspiration."

It *was* kind of cool, but that didn't mean it was in her best interest. "My mom threatened to fire me over the incident because I could have gotten Polished Pros' contract with the resort revoked." The memory of the reaming her mom had given her on the Monday after she'd returned from Nashville for breaking so many rules in their company's agreement with Briscoe Ranch gave her a fresh pang of guilt. She'd illicitly consorted with a hotel guest while on the clock and abetted in the demise of a scheduled wedding.

There was so much more than Skye's life at stake. Their company supported dozens of employees and their families. If the hotel dropped them, the repercussions would be staggering. Not only to Skye's family, but to their employees. "It was foolish of me on so many levels. I'm a grown-ass woman and it's time for me to act like it. I'm giving men up for the remainder of Lent."

"But I thought you were meeting with Granny June's friend's grandson today at the picnic."

"I agreed to meet Eddie Rivera in order to pay Granny June back for helping me, but that's all. Nothing's going to happen."

"That's a nice name. Eddie Rivera. Skye Rivera. I like the sound of that."

Remedy was teasing her, but it *was* a nice name, Skye thought begrudgingly. Who was she to say that he wasn't exactly the kind of guy she was looking for? What was her problem? Why was she so resistant to this guy—or any guy who was good for her, really? All she knew was that it was time to give up her terrible weakness for bad news, fly-by-night guys who were all wrong for her and her life. She'd already given her heart to a circus performer. She refused to add country rock star to that dubious list.

"I told Micah I'd try to swing by the barbecue too. He and the rest of the fire department will be there, as part of their community outreach. I'm not sure I can still make it because those darn cats put me behind schedule, but if I do, I want to check out this Eddie guy."

Micah was Remedy's husband and Dulcet's fire chief. He knew a zillion people in Ravel County. Some of them had to be male and gainfully employed and available. And Catholic. But Skye had never managed to connect romantically with any of them.

There had been a time, long before Remedy had come to town, that Skye had had a tiny crush on Micah. He was the best kind of good ol' boy—strong in his small-town values, with a sharp sense of humor, and easy on the eyes. They'd even flirted on occasion. But he didn't fit that bad boy profile that Skye had always been attracted to. Way too upstanding a citizen for her taste. And he wasn't

Catholic. So she'd let the attraction fade. And thank goodness, because he and Remedy were perfect for each other and very much in love.

In a clatter, Litzy and Tabby appeared on the amphitheater stage, with Litzy holding up a baggie of herbs like a kitty drug dealer.

Remedy gave a whoop of delight that startled all the cats to attention and convinced the pigeon on her knee to fly off. "Great job! What are you waiting for? Go drug those cats!"

Litzy sprinkled a trail of catnip over to the row of pet carriers, then a little inside each one. The calico was the first to take the bait, but once she'd rolled a few times, the rest of the kitties decided they couldn't possibly be left out of the fun. Working together, Litzy and Tabby managed to get every single cat into their carriers without much fuss. It was the triumph of the day.

Skye checked the time on her phone and sighed. "Okay, now that the cat-herding fun is over, I'd better suck it up and get over there. Maybe he won't be so bad." She waved her fingers at the pigeons roosting on a row of lights above the theater. "Bye, pigeons. Be good to your mama."

"For Pete's sake, I'm not their mother. Even if they think so sometimes."

"I know. I just said that to bother you, like a true friend."

They blew air kisses at each other and parted ways.

Skye strolled across the resort grounds, in no particular hurry to arrive at the picnic on the northeast lawn near the Winter Wonderland Garden. Not only because of her blind date of sorts with Eddie Rivera, but because her family would be there and the tension between Skye and her mom since she helped sabotage Natalie's wedding and ran off to Nashville with Gentry. Since their confrontation, they'd barely spoken.

The barbecue was an annual event at the resort, a cross between community outreach and guest entertainment. While a live band played, resort guests, employees, and Dulcet residents mingled under the trees while kids enjoyed the carnival games and petting zoo. The scent of tangy barbecue sauce and charcoal floated on the air along with the sound of crowd-pleasing golden oldies and pop hits that reminded Skye of a wedding reception playlist.

The Ravel County Sheriff's Department and the Dulcet Fire Department had both shown up en masse in uniform, their squad cars and fire trucks on display for curious guests and photo ops. She spotted Remedy's husband, Micah, among them, shaking hands and kissing babies and taking the time to greet anyone who wanted to bend his ear for a moment.

Skye's family had already arrived. Gloria was chowing down on a plate of food while standing and staring into a giant, barn-shaped jump house, where Skye assumed Teresa and Chris were. Skye's parents were headed away from the buffet line, with her mom holding both plates of food.

Every step her dad took was gingerly taken, but he was walking far more upright than usual. Only his grimace spoke to the pain that choice caused him. And he had no cane in sight, as was his typical choice when he was out in public, particularly at the resort, where he'd worked more than thirty years until his health forced him to quit. He still had a lot of friends there, and even though they all knew about his back and health issues, he was a proud enough man to not let them see him using any kind of crutch—much to her mom's consternation.

Skye assumed her cheeriest smile and joined them. “Hey, Mom, Dad.”

Her mom pushed one of the two plates of food into Skye’s hands. “Tell your father he’s being ridiculous.”

“Hush, woman. I’m fine. Stop clucking over me. We’re only walking to the table.”

“What if you fall?” her mom said. There was no mistaking the love and worry in her nagging.

Her dad was a master at letting it all roll off of him like water off a duck, but today, instead of ignoring her pleas, he stopped and cradled her cheek in his hand. “Yessica, listen to me. Stop worrying. Let’s have a nice afternoon together.”

“But you’re in pain. I know you are. I hate that.” Skye could hear the resignation in her voice plain enough.

Her dad shook his head. “Not when I look at you, I’m not.” He placed a kiss on her lips. “Let’s go find an open table to sit together.”

Her mom’s shoulders dropped. “All right. Let’s get you sitting down before the food gets cold.” Typical Mom. Anytime a conversation veered too close to emotionally real, she retreated to the safety of pragmatic, if superficial, worries.

Skye walked her parents to an open table, then went to join Mama Lita in line for the food. She looped arms with her grandma and kissed her cheek.

“My darling! You finally made it. And thank goodness. I needed a distraction from this horrible music.”

“You should go up there and show them how it’s done,” Skye said.

“If only I’d brought my keyboard.” She said it with complete earnestness, and Skye knew she wasn’t joking. If she’d had her instrument, she would have been up on the stage showing the youngsters how it was done.

Back in her day, Mama Lita had played organ and keyboard in a rock band in Mexico City, where she'd grown up, as part of the La Onda movement, which had always sounded to Skye like Mexico's version of America's hippie culture, all about rock 'n' roll and free love and political protest.

"Heads up," Mama Lita said. "June Briscoe smells love in the air today." She said it with an eye roll. Granny June and Mama Lita had developed a grudging respect for each other over the years but had never really meshed. Though they were both single, older ladies full of moxie, their world views were completely opposite.

Skye swallowed her groan. "I know. She helped me out with something and in exchange I agreed to help her friend's grandson feel more at home today."

"That's ridiculous. Want me to go have it out with her? Because I've been waiting for that day."

One of these days, Skye had no doubt that Mama Lita and Granny June would brawl, badass grandma style, but today was not that day. "I'm on shaky ground with my mom as it is. Better cool your jets for now."

Mama Lita dropped a drumstick on Skye's plate with a flourish of tongs. "Chicken."

Skye wasn't sure if she was talking about her or the food.

She was saved from asking by Granny June, who arrived at their side on her riding scooter, and was dressed in a cheery blue-and-yellow track suit, complete with yellow visor. "Yoo-hoo! Skye, you're late!"

Skye leaned over and gave Granny June a kiss on the cheek. "I know. Sorry. I was helping Remedy herd cats."

"Ha! Sorry I missed it. But listen, you and I have a deal."

"I remember."

"Good. Come with me. The man I wanted to introduce you to is standing over there, in front of the tray of ribs."

She speared her cane farther down the buffet near the corn to a pale man covered from head to toe in sun-protective gear, including a wide-brimmed floppy hat with flaps that extended over his neck and long sleeves despite that midday temperatures were pushing the high-seventies. Eddie Rivera, if Skye had to guess.

Mama Lita stepped between them, brandishing the tongs. "She doesn't need a man."

Granny June slid off the scooter seat and stood, extending her cane to touch the tongs as though the two grannies were preparing for a clash of swords. "It's not about need. It's about what Skye wants."

"Exactly," Skye said. "Thank you."

Mama Lita snorted. "Then what are you doing wasting time with these pendejos? And don't blame that spell my daughter-in-law put on you."

"Mama Lita! But the spell's working." *Sort of.* "I want to settle down with a good man."

Mama Lita threw her hands up and muttered in Spanish, too rapid and quiet for Skye to translate.

Granny June lowered her weapon and patted Skye's hand. "Eddie Rivera is a good man. You'll see. I didn't pick a dud for you this time like that Vincent Biaggi. Eddie's a doctor and he just got a job at the Tri-City Hospital. He moved here to be closer to Meryl. And this past Sunday he started attending Our Lady of Guadalupe with her."

That was Skye's family's church. He was a man of faith and a doctor—and here in Dulcet to stay. He checked all the boxes of the kind of man she was looking for. She gave him a second look along with Mama

Lita and Granny June. At the moment, Eddie was rummaging through the pile of barbecued corn with a pair of tongs. He'd pick one up and inspect it, then move on to another one with a frown, as though searching in vain for that perfectly grilled ear of corn.

"Men are such idiots," Mama Lita said on a groan.

Granny June shrugged. "Maybe he just loves corn."

Mama Lita spun to face Skye again. "I won't accept this. You don't need a man. If you want a family, start one. No man needed."

It was a wonder that Skye's dad had come to exist at all, given Mama Lita's views on men and marriage. By her own account, she'd gotten pregnant in her late thirties by a man whom she never named and who never stepped forward to claim his child, much to her relief. By all accounts, she'd been a decent mother to Skye's dad, but she never quite seemed to get over the forfeit of her freedom that motherhood inflicted. As soon as Skye's dad turned eighteen and joined the army, she'd gone back to being a hell raiser like she'd been in her twenties—vehemently single, playing in rock bands, and traveling the world, with an insatiable hunger for life.

"Remind me to teach you about the birds and the bees sometime, Edalia," Granny June said dryly.

"I know it'll drive you crazy for me to say this, Mama Lita, but I agree with Granny June. I know you were a great single mom, but that's not my path. That's not my faith. This is about more than having kids. It's about living the life I want, taking over Polished Pros from my mom when she's ready, just like she did from Grandmother. It's about caring for Gloria's kids and Dad and you. And mostly it's about giving up all the things that are bad for me—including the wrong kind of man."

Mama Lita waved the tongs under Skye's nose. "Just because you and that lion tamer didn't work out doesn't mean you were wrong to go after what you wanted. I mean, sure, you shouldn't have married him, but women are supposed to run with the wolves. That is our true nature."

No. It's not, Skye longed to say. Running with the wolves had never brought her anything but pain.

Granny June yanked the tongs right out of Mama Lita's hand and tossed them onto a pile of chicken. "Being married to the right man won't stop a strong woman. It'll lift her up. I believe in the power of love, and it's time for Skye to believe too. Go talk to Eddie. He's a fine young man. He'd love and respect you."

"Don't listen to her, mija. You come sit with me," Mama Lita said. "We'll talk about trips we want to take to faraway lands, and I'll tell you about running wild and free in Mexico City back in my day."

Skye felt the tug of yearning to follow Mama Lita back to the picnic table and daydream about adventure, but she and Granny June had a deal. "Sorry, Mama Lita. I'm going to go meet this guy. I promised Granny June I would. But if it makes you feel any better, I've decided to give up men for the rest of Lent."

"Fine. It's your life," Mama Lita said with a dismissive wave.

"Good girl," Granny June said, rubbing her hands together. "This is the start of something great. I can feel it."

Skye followed Granny June's scooter to where Eddie was standing. When they arrived, she leapt off the scooter as spryly as someone half her age and wedged herself between Eddie and the person in line behind him, with a brash "Cutting in!" which would have been rude if it had been anyone other than the Briscoe Ranch matriarch.

"Eddie, this is the girl I told you about. Skye, meet Eddie."

Smiling at Skye, he shifted his plate of food into his left hand and extended his right. "Skye. What a beautiful name to go with such a beautiful day."

It was a groan-worthy line, but somehow, Eddie made it work. Skye shook his hand. His grip was firm, his skin soft. "Nice to meet you."

Up close, she could see past his sun-protective gear to his nice, though slender, build and pleasing features. There had been a time when Skye might have been more nervous and demure while meeting a new, prospective romantic partner, but the spell had long since cured her of that. "Nice to meet you too. So tell me, did you find the perfect ear of corn yet?"

His smile was more of a cringe. "Almost. Sorry to hold up the line."

"You're serious about your corn. And sun protection, I see."

Granny June tsked her disapproval at that observation. "Ask him about being a doctor, for pity's sake!"

Skye wrapped an arm around Granny June's shoulders and gave them a gentle, affectionate squeeze. "Leave us, old lady."

Granny June looked longingly at Eddie as though reluctant to be anywhere but in the middle of the action, then sighed with a nod. "You're right. I'll give you two some space to get to know each other. I'll be right over there if you need me."

Eddie gave a good-natured chuckle when Granny June was out of earshot. "I like her. Young at heart. To answer your question, I like a good, charred ear of corn, lots of butter."

Skye held out her plate. "Since you're the expert, why don't you pick me out an ear too?"

He took his time rummaging through the pile of corn to pick her out the perfect ear.

"May I ask you another personal question?" she said while she watched him inspect ear after ear. "What's with all the sun protective gear?"

He set an ear of corn on her plate, angling it so it didn't touch the beans or chicken. In truth, it did look like an exceptionally tasty ear of corn. "I know I look like a total dork. But I'd rather be a dork with sun flaps on his hat than a beet-red total dork, which is worse. And painful. My father never lets me live down that I inherited my mother's fair Argentine complexion instead of his tough Puerto Rican skin. I've been living in upstate New York, so my skin's not used to the Texas sun. Hopefully I'll acclimate so I can ease up on the nerd fashion."

He handed her a bundle of plasticware wrapped in a napkin, then took one for himself. "Would you like to sit and eat with me? I'd love the chance to get to know you better."

She would have loved to claim otherwise, but she was charmed by Eddie Rivera. She liked the easy way he shared himself and talked about his family. He seemed totally grounded and comfortable with who he was. Unlike her.

And unlike Gentry.

Granny June was right. Eddie Rivera deserved a chance. Maybe Skye didn't need to give up men for the rest of Lent after all.

"How about that table in the shade over there," she said, pointing to the literal opposite side of the picnic from where Granny June sat with a table full of old ladies, all of them watching Skye and Eddie with unabashed nosiness.

"Aw, come on," Eddie said. "What are the grandmas going to do for entertainment if we sit all the way over there?"

"Oh, I'm sure they'll come up with something. Like I always say, Granny June has a way of sniffing out trouble she can get into."

At the table, they settled across from each other, Skye more at ease every second.

"I still can't believe this Texas weather," Eddie said. "In New York, some of the nights are still getting down to freezing temperatures. It's only April 2nd, but it feels like summer."

"It's April 2nd?" Time had flown by. Had it really been two weeks since she'd flown off to Nashville with Gentry? She would have sworn it was still March, but she checked her phone to find that Eddie was correct. Which meant that next week, on the ninth of April, it would be the anniversary of her miscarriage. Pain squeezed her heart, as fresh as it had been on the first anniversary.

With the twisted thinking of someone who was compelled to pick off a scab, she navigated to the calendar on her phone, just to see it written on there in the little square for April 9th. The entry read simply *Lost*.

Because that was the only word that came to mind when she thought of that time in her life other than *pain* and guilt. Pain for the baby she'd never expected, that she'd never known she wanted—that she was denied knowing when she lost it at five weeks. And guilt, because God never did anything arbitrarily.

She might not be a practicing Catholic any longer, but that was one lesson that had stuck. There was a reason she'd lost the baby, and a reason she'd caught Mike cheating on her the day she found out she was pregnant. She'd made some horrible choices, ones she'd accepted and tried to learn from so she could move on with her life—but once a year, on this anniversary, they were choices that she longed to forget. So that's how she'd treated the anniversary: a day for her to get lost, in booze or out at a club with friends, anything she had to do to forget about the pain until the anniversary had passed.

Not this year. It was time for her to stop running with the wolves once and for all. She was determined to let the day pass without succumbing to the urge to get lost, without her making any more decisions that she would regret. She just hadn't realized it was coming up so soon until she looked at her calendar. The sudden awareness gave her an off-balance feeling, like the table was tilting one way while she was falling the other.

She snuck another look at the calendar on her phone, reading the word *lost* one more time. Then another calendar entry caught her eye, one with a red font. It was the recurring note to herself of when her period was supposed to start. It'd been on the calendar for last Monday. *Huh.*

"Whatcha doing?"

Eddie. She'd forgotten that he was there. She blinked herself back to the present and realized she'd been staring absentmindedly at her phone, and probably for quite some time. Great first impression for the first guy who'd been prospective boyfriend material in a very long time.

Except Gentry.

Nope. Because he wasn't boyfriend material in any way, shape, or form. And furthermore, she'd already decided she wasn't going to think about him anymore. "Sorry, that was rude. I was looking up when Easter is. I thought I had more time."

Eddie bit into his ear of corn. "I know. This year is

flying. It'll be Easter before we know it, which is great for me since I gave up coffee. That's been . . ." He shook his head, cringing. "But I guess that's the point, right?"

While he'd been talking, her gaze had slipped back to the calendar on her phone. Damn. Her period was a week late. That never happened. "Uh, yep. That would definitely suck."

Gentry had used condoms. They'd been so safe. Well, the first time they'd done it, in the club, he'd had a condom in his hand, but she couldn't remember if she'd actually seen him with the condom on. He'd taken her from behind and then in reverse cowgirl. She scoured her memory for a clearer image, but that night had been a whirlwind and, even though she hadn't had much to drink, she definitely had spots in her memory.

"Earth to Skye. Are you okay?"

Shit, she was flubbing this meet-up. "Yeah, sorry. Coffee would be torture for me to give up too. Last year I gave up listening to music in my car, which nearly killed me."

"That's a good one. Brutal, but effective."

Of course, Gentry had used a condom in the club. He didn't want to have kids and made a point to tell her that, to prove how incompatible they were. So, really, she couldn't be pregnant. Because Gentry didn't want to settle down, and having a baby out of wedlock was against the very moral foundation that Skye was raised to believe. She considered herself a family rebel of sorts, but not like that. Not in any way that could ruin her life or her family's faith in her.

Holy hell. The picnic table started to tilt again. She gripped it hard and tried to ride out the spinning and the accompanying lurch in her stomach.

"I'm not feeling so well," she croaked.

"I was just noticing how pale you looked. What can I do?"

Nothing, unless you have a pregnancy test in your pocket. She stood up, swaying. "I . . . I think I ate something that didn't agree with me. I have to go."

In an instant, Eddie was at her side, his hand on her elbow steadying her. "Where? I'll help."

"No!" she snapped. "I'm sorry. Look, it was so nice to meet you, Eddie, but I'm afraid I'm going to get sick to my stomach, and I like you, so I don't want you anywhere near me if I do."

He tugged her in the direction of the restrooms at the entrance to the resort's Winter Wonderland Garden. "I'm a doctor. That kind of thing doesn't faze me. Let me help."

Shit, he wasn't going to make this easy on her. "But it does me. Please, I'm going to handle this on my own." She shook herself free of his grip. "Call me, maybe?"

Okay, she was channeling Carly Rae Jepsen now, but whatever. She took off across the lawn as fast as her legs could take her. She felt Eddie's eyes on her and shook her head. She'd been on dozens of dates lately, but this was the first time she was the one who was the crappy date and not the guy. Unbelievable. After she took a pregnancy test and discovered that there was nothing to worry about, she'd get his number from Granny June and call him to apologize.

In her car, she sped along the twisty road to the highway and pushed the pedal to the floor. She wouldn't dare buy a pregnancy test in Dulcet. It'd get back to her family before Skye made it home to take the test. So instead, she headed to a drug store three towns over, where she was certain not to know a soul.

An hour later, she pulled into her garage. It didn't look like anyone else was home, not at her house or her parents' house across the street. Thank God for small favors. She did have three texts from Gloria, wondering where she was before deciding that Eddie must had been such a dud that Skye had skipped out on him, as she'd done with so many other men.

She took the tests out of the drug store bag and stuffed them into her purse, just in case someone was home that she hadn't anticipated, then crept through the house into the bathroom. When Gloria and the kids had moved in, Skye gave up the master bedroom and had relocated to the bedroom on the ground floor so Gloria and her kids could share rooms on the same level. She'd also given up a private bathroom. She'd never minded before, but now, she wished she could lock herself into a suite with a bed and attached bathroom for the rest of the night under the guise of food poisoning and check out of the world for a while.

In the downstairs bathroom, she ripped open the pregnancy test and sat on the toilet. It took more than a minute to rouse her body out of shock and fear to pee on command. Then, in the following the two minutes while the test developed, she flashed back to the last time she'd taken a pregnancy test, only three months into her marriage to Mike the Mistake.

She'd been so young. A child, really. But she hadn't been scared while she'd waited to read that test because she'd been married and in love, because she thought she knew exactly how her future would unfold.

Anger at the memory felt like fire sitting at the top of her throat. It stung her eyes. How dare this happen to her. How dare her desires betray her—again. All she'd wanted with Gentry was one last thrill, a fling with a hot guy whom she had great chemistry with. Was she not even allowed that? Every time she stuck a toe out of line, she was punished for it.

Bracing her hands on the rim of the sink, she looked in the mirror. She wasn't twenty anymore. As she'd reminded herself over and over the past two weeks, she was a grown-ass woman and it was time for her to start acting like one. She had enough money now and a home to call her own. If she was pregnant, this baby would be the most loved baby in the world. She would privately endure the shame of her sin without projecting it to her child. And she knew in her heart that Gentry, the man who'd told her outright that he never wanted to settle down or have a child, would still do the honorable thing and pay child support. She'd bet he'd want to be in the child's life, too, even if only a little bit.

She shook her head to clear it. She was getting ahead of herself.

She heard the garage door open, then slam shut. Children's chatter and laughter reverberated through the house along with the stomping of feet. Shit. This was the last thing she needed right now. As stealthily as she could, she locked the bathroom door.

Footsteps sounded in the hall. "Skye? Are you in there?"

It was Gloria.

"I'm in here."

"You okay? Mom said you got food poisoning, which explains why you didn't return my texts."

It was so tempting to lie to Gloria and run with the food poisoning story, as she'd planned to, but Gloria was the one person in the world who knew the truth about what Skye had gone through after leaving Mike. Skye hadn't told her sister right away, but she'd confided her story of grief to Gloria in the months after Ruben's death, on the night of Teresa's birthday, the first one since his passing. After the party and the kids had been tucked in, Gloria had crumbled in Skye's arms and the two had spent the night talking and trading secrets.

Gloria had taught Skye what it meant to lean and let others help her in her time of need—and it was time for Skye to give her the chance to return that gift. That's what sisters were for. She unlocked the bathroom door and opened it a foot.

Gloria peaked her head in. "Don't get puke on my new bathmat. That was the last blue one Costco had."

Though Skye didn't have the guts to look her sister in the eye quite yet, she held up the box that the test had come in. "Can you put a movie on for the kids and come back?"

Gloria's was silent for a beat. Then, "Yes. Absolutely. I'll be right back."

Skye slumped on the toilet seat lid, her head in her hands.

She could read the test before Gloria returned, but she wanted to wait so she could lean on her sister. Besides, reading them promptly when the two minutes were up wouldn't change the results. She either was or wasn't pregnant with Gentry Wells' baby.

Chapter Eleven

A minute later, Skye, who still sat on the toilet, her head in her hands, heard the bathroom door open, then close, then lock as Gloria rejoined her and flipped on the exhaust fan to mask their words in case the kids decided to listen in.

Gloria knelt on the bathmat and hugged Skye's knees. "Oh, shit, sis."

"Yeah."

"You're going to have a baby. I'm . . . I don't know what to say besides oh shit."

When her sister said it like that, fear started to edge out anger again. "I don't know if I am or not. I haven't looked at the result yet."

Gloria sat up straight and smacked her hard across the legs. "What? You got me going crazy and feeling awful for you, but you don't even know yet?" She smacked Skye again for good measure.

Skye held her hands out to defend herself. "I couldn't look by myself."

Gloria was on her feet. "Don't be a baby. Just get it

over with nice and quick. Like getting a bikini wax. Want me to look first and tell you?"

Only Gloria would compare a bikini wax with reading a pregnancy test. "No, I should be the one to do it. Hand it to me." If she were adult enough to get pregnant, she was adult enough to read her own damn test result.

On the other hand, it took a village to raise a kid, didn't it? There was no harm putting that philosophy into practice from conception. When Gloria held the test out to her, Skye jerked her face to the side and stared at her shoulder so she wouldn't see the result. "On second thought, you look."

With a tsk, Gloria turned away from Skye and looked at the test. "This guy, the country singer, you like him?"

At Gloria's tone, at the question, Skye's heart sank. She was pregnant. "He's a great guy." Would he still be, once he learned he'd gotten her pregnant? What if he had no interest in raising a child? Or worse, what if he refused to believe it was his?

But as soon as she thought the questions, she realized it didn't matter. She was tough enough to raise this baby alone. And, really, she wouldn't be doing it alone. She knew without a doubt that her family would always be there for her. As much grief as they'd given her about divorcing Mike, the whole family rallied around her, and not only Gloria, who'd been her rock during those tough first months. Her mom had rehired her for her old job at Polished Pros, she'd been invited to move back home with her parents until she'd gotten back on her feet, and Mama Lita had helped her find her fire again. She'd never wanted for love—and her baby wouldn't, either.

"Mm-hmm. If he's such a great guy, has he called you or texted you since that weekend?"

She supposed it was Gloria's sisterly right to interrogate her, and, honestly, it was keeping Skye from freaking out, so it was hard to mind. "No. But we'd agreed to go our separate ways, so I didn't expect to hear from him." Though it would have been nice. It would have been more than nice to know the night they'd spent together had meant something to him too. "But I guess I'll be calling him now to tell him the news."

How did one say something like that over the phone? Something that was going to change both of their lives forever. She wasn't ready to be a mom. For all her distant dreams of motherhood and starting a family, that dream was not to be a single mom knocked up by a famous musician during a one-night stand. All she'd wanted was to fall in love with the right guy and make good choices for a change. Choices she could be proud of, and that her mom could be proud of too. But in her mind she could already see the look of betrayal in her mom's eyes.

"Is he father material? Is he going to make a good dad?" Gloria asked, cutting into Skye's vision of her mother's face. *No. No, he really wasn't, by his own admission.*

Skye's head was swimming. How could this be? And yet . . . "I guess we'll find out."

Gloria bumped her shoulder against Skye's. "Nah, you won't. Not unless you two try to with another roll in the hay. Try poking some holes in the condom next time."

"What are you talking about? You're killing me here."

Gloria let out an utterly diabolical laugh and turned the test so Skye could see the result. "You're not pregnant."

Skye grabbed the test out of Gloria's hand. "What?"

Skye took one look at the single blue line and smacked Gloria on the shoulder as hard as Gloria had hit her knees earlier. Then again, harder. "You little bitch!"

Gloria never stopped laughing, even when Skye wrestled her into a headlock, just like she used to do when they were kids. Even from her prone position, Gloria could reach the faucet. She turned on the water and flicked Skye in the face. "Oh cowboy, take me home with you!" she said in a fake, breathy twang. "Give me your babies! And your child support!"

Skye was laughing now too, as she dug her thumb into Gloria's ribs for some tickle torture. Gloria howled.

"You squeal like a stuck pig!" Skye teased.

A knock sounded at the bathroom door.

"Occupied," Gloria said in a sing-song voice.

"What's going on in there? Are you two fighting?" Teresa asked with a note of worry in her voice.

Skye reached over and opened the door so the kids could see for themselves that nothing was wrong.

"It's a water tickle fight. I'm winning, mija!" Gloria said with glee as she filled a little paper cup and sloshed it on Skye's shirt. "Your soldier mama is getting Aunt Skye all wet!"

Skye cupped her hand under the faucet, then hurled a scoop of water through the air. It splatted against Gloria's chest. "But Auntie Skye's rallying!"

They battled back and forth while the kids cheered them on. Of course, both of them were rooting for their mama, but them were the breaks.

Skye went for the winning move by grabbing a cleaning bucket from under the sink, but she'd only managed to turn on the bathtub faucet when Gloria rushed her. "Oh no, you don't. You've got too far, lady! Now you must pay."

And before Skye knew what was happening, Gloria had performed some kind of army maneuver on her and had her facedown on the drenched bathmat with her arms and legs all but hog-tied behind her.

"I surrender!" Skye bellowed.

Gloria let her go, then pranced away with her fingers up in victory Vs. "And it's little sister for the win!"

With water streaming over her cheeks and down her neck, Skye mugged a cartoon villain face and shook her fist. "I'll get you next time, mark my words."

The kids giggled at that. "You look silly, Auntie," Chris said.

"Don't I know it, little man." Skye sank to the toilet seat lid again. She grabbed a towel to mop her face, which was when she realized that the water wasn't only from the fight, but from tears. Oh shit. She was crying and she couldn't stop. She tried holding her breath to keep it together for the sake of the kids, but a sob broke free despite her efforts.

"Okay, kids," Gloria said, standing in the doorway to block the kids' view of Skye. "Show's over. Go watch the movie. We'll be right out."

As soon as the bathroom door shut again, Skye let the tears flow free. They were tears of relief and release, purging her of the fear of getting pregnant again and the frustration that she'd gotten herself in such a jam. It was exhausting, this war between the normalcy she wanted for her life and the drumbeat of restless yearning she couldn't seem to shake. She couldn't stop craving more adventure like she'd had with Gentry, more nights that bucked the rules. She wanted wicked, rowdy sex with wicked, rowdy men. But look what happened to her when she gave in to that drumbeat?

Gloria pulled Skye into a hug. "You're okay."

She burrowed into Gloria's shoulder. "I know. Just coming down from it all. I was so sure I was pregnant. I felt it."

Gloria rubbed her back. "Did you buy more than one test? To double-check?"

"Yes." She sat up, sniffing. "Of course."

She'd no sooner sat up and reached for her purse where the other tests were when her phone sounded with a text.

Gloria said, "Is that going to be the almost-baby daddy?" She made a table under her chin with her fingers and fluttered her eyelashes. "The talented and dreamy Gentry Wells."

Skye plucked her phone from her purse. "As if you'd ever heard of him before I told you his name."

But Gloria's antics had their desired effect. Skye couldn't help but smile, even as her pulse sped at the idea that it might be Gentry texting her. Maybe he was in town again. Maybe she'd been on his mind as much as he'd been on hers.

I hope you don't mind me texting so soon. Granny June gave me your number and I wanted to make sure you're feeling all right.

So much for her high hopes. Skye let her arm drop. "It's the guy from the picnic, Eddie Rivera."

Gloria wrinkled her nose. "I saw you two together. He was the one with the neck-flap hat. He's not your type."

Skye gave Gloria a pointed look. "What if I wanted him to be? He's Catholic and a doctor."

That earned her an eye roll that was identical to their mother's. "Whatever. Granny June and Ma just want you to marry him so they can have a medical professional on hand. Ma wants free advice about Dad's health issues, and you know I'm right about that. Why do you think she tried to get me to be a medic when I got done with boot camp?"

She had a point. Then again, the fact Skye had been

flooded with crazy hope that it was Gentry on the phone was telling. It was also pathetic. Their fling had given her an awful pregnancy scare. And he'd told her himself that he wasn't interested in settling down or starting a family. Why would she want to keep pushing the envelope with him? How could she feel so little for guys like Eddie Rivera, who were textbook perfect for her in every way that mattered?

Gloria kissed the top of Skye's head. "I've got to get the kids started on their baths. They're all sticky from the cotton candy booth at the picnic. You got this?"

She smiled her gratitude to Gloria. "I got this. Thank you for being here."

"I'm always here for you. Whether you like it or not," she added with a shoulder shimmy full of faux attitude.

Skye took the second pregnancy test amid the deep rumbling sound of the upstairs bathtub filling and the chatter of Gloria trying to wrangle Chris out of his clothes and into a bath. A feat not so different from Remedy trying to herd cats at a wedding.

The test came back negative. Okay, then. Crisis averted. Skye's life was unchanged. It was time to take this experience as the lesson it was and move on. But lurking in the dark corners of her consciousness, a niggling disappointment threatened the sound logic of her relief.

What a ridiculous, immature feeling. Did a part of her want the shame that came with screwing up her life? Did a part of her want that inviolable connection to Gentry, a reason to bring him back into her life?

Stupid. Stupid. Stupid.

The only reason she felt a twinge of disappointment was because she wanted a family of her own. That had to be it. She refused to acknowledge it as anything more.

She should be so lucky to settle down with a nice man with a great career who cared more about sun safety than vanity. That was a good thing.

She exchanged the pregnancy test for her phone on the counter. *I'm feeling much better, thank you. Sorry I had to leave so fast. How was that perfect ear of corn?*

She tucked the phone back in her purse, thinking that she probably should have waited a couple days before texting him back, playing hard to get, the way the game was supposed to be played, but she was totally over the idea of playing games.

To her surprise, she heard the chime of another text.

That corn was good, but I know a barbecue restaurant that does even better. May I take you there sometime?

Smooth, yet right to the point. With no games. Eddie Rivera really did have a lot of checkmarks in the win column, even if his phrasing of *barbecue restaurant* was as dorky as his sense of style. The thought brought a smile to her lips.

Telling, that easy smile. It was high time for Skye to be with someone who brought out the best in her instead of someone who fed her most self-destructive impulses. Look at her tonight, hiding in her bathroom taking pregnancy tests after a one-night stand with a country rock star who'd never bothered to text her after the fact. She was nearing thirty, for pity's sake. It was past time for Skye Martinez, lifelong hell raiser with an insatiable taste for bad boys, to grow the hell up.

I'd love to go out with you, she texted Eddie. *How about Saturday night?* Saturday was the anniversary of her miscarriage, the worst day of her life. Going out with Eddie was bound to make the night bearable. She had to believe, anyway. She paused before sending the text, considering, then threw caution to the wind by adding, *You can pick me up at seven.*

The night of the ACMs, or, rather, early the next morning, Gentry returned to his ranch in the dead of the night. In years' past, he'd stayed and partied in Vegas for the whole ACM weekend, but no longer. He didn't much have an appetite for hanging out with drunk people—even Nick and the rest of the band—and, more important, he had an album to write, an album for which the due date was approaching as fast as a high-speed train.

The ACMs had gone well. At least, his performance had, anyway. He'd had to eat a lot of crow on the red carpet about not being up for any awards, and a few of the people he'd thought of as friends couldn't even look him in the eye. But there were also a lot of questions about the mystery woman he'd been caught on camera with.

He took Neil's advice and built up the mystery, offering little more than sly smiles and the promise that he was going to sing a song dedicated to her that night. Gentry might have had a rough spell recently, but that didn't mean he didn't know how to play the game. In that way, Larry was right that being a professional musician really was a lot like baseball. One lousy game, or even one lousy season, did not make the man.

The crowd had seemed to respond well to "Riding in the Dark." More important, Gentry had felt good singing it. He'd put his heart and soul into that song. Hell, he'd put his whole libido into it too. And it'd worked. The women in the backstage afterward were falling all over themselves to let him know how much they loved it, and Neil even gave him a thumbs-up.

He tried not to think too hard about whether Skye was watching. He'd considered texting her before the show so she'd tune in to his performance, but then he remembered the way Neil wanted him to capitalize on the gossip about them, and Gentry wasn't too keen on her seeing that part or getting the mistaken impression that he'd been using her in any way.

You did use her, man.

Gentry's conscience sure was a narrow-minded bastard. Because he hadn't used her, not really. Yes, she'd inspired him to write all kinds of fantastic new songs, but none of that would have been possible without the down-and-dirty chemistry that sizzled between them. Like the old adage said, you can't make smoke without a fire.

His trouble now was that it'd been more than two weeks since his and Skye's weekend in Nashville, and the fire inside him had definitely gone dim. Once he'd mined his imagination for all the songwriting gems from his weekend with Skye that he could, his creative well had turned dry and empty. He'd been spending nearly every day out on the range on Beaver, trying to force the magic, and he'd read every article about them in every gossip magazine that Neil had left behind. Still, nothing.

He hadn't written a single new song in ten days and he was still five songs short of enough material for an album. The thought made his stomach churn. It was two in morning, two weeks until his album was due, and his mind was blank except for the memory of Skye.

Restless with anxiety, he wandered through his empty house, flipping on lights as he went. He'd let Cheyanne redecorate the place, put her own touches on it so it felt more like home to her, but in the end, she'd taken it all with her. Just like his ex-wife had; just like they all had. Gentry supposed he could have hired a decorator after the breakup, but redecorating would only be buying into the lie that he could ever be the staying, settling-down kind. Rather, the blank walls and barren floors felt necessary. A reminder that he wasn't cut out for relationships. A reminder that he should sell this place and be done with it this settling-down lifestyle once and for all. If only he had any other place to go.

In the living room, on the coffee table right where Neil had left them, were the gossip magazines, along with a few more that Gentry had added to the pile since then, all flipped open to the photos of him and Skye whooping it up in Nashville. The speculation about whether he'd gotten married at the Islands in the Stream Chapel or if he'd gone off the deep end made him smile. Was he in Mexico on his honeymoon, one article pondered. Had he checked himself into rehab after his bender, wondered another. None of them came close to the truth. He'd spent the night with his muse, the hottest damn woman he'd ever been with, then he'd come home to memorialize the experience in song. And now it was over.

He gazed at the table, the proof of their weekend together. The emptiness of the house yawned around him. Loneliness oozed into the silent, empty spaces. All those feelings of being an imposter on the brink of being exposed came rushing up. "Hello, old friend," he said to the self-doubt. Or maybe he'd said it to the tequila bottle that was sitting next to all those magazines.

He grabbed the bottle and twisted off the cap. Nothing like tequila to mute those vicious insecurities and puff up a man's confidence. Could be that all Gentry needed to get his creative juices flowing was a little agave lubrication for his mind. He needed the help of something, that was for sure, because he was no good at writing songs on his own.

He had the bottle touching his lips when he got a whiff of alcohol and stopped. What the hell was he doing? This wasn't him. This wasn't who he wanted to be. Not anymore. He smeared his hand over the pile, sending the pages fluttering to the floor. And then he walked to his kitchen and poured the tequila down the drain.

Enough of this moping around. Enough daydreaming about the woman who haunted his every waking thought. She'd told him if he was ever in her neighborhood, he should look her up. That neighborhood was a solid eight-hour drive from his doorstep. Close enough. Just thinking that he could be standing in front of her in less than twenty-four hours was enough to propel him up the stairs and into his bedroom to pack.

He stuffed clothes in backpack, then stuffed himself into his leather riding jacket. A woman like Skye didn't need a boring drive in a pickup truck. She needed motorcycle rides under the stars. She needed the wind in her hair and the open road all around her. She could talk all she wanted about settling down with a quiet, respectable guy, but he knew she needed a man who could keep up with her insatiable wild side, whether she was able to admit it or not.

He strapped a spare helmet to the seatback of his Harley, then fired it up.

Probably, he was crazy for doing this. Certifiable. But maybe not. Maybe the crazier idea had been thinking he should let her go from his life so easily. Someday, he'd break her heart. He knew he would because he was a Wells man and that's what they did, but until that day, there was no one else on Earth that he wanted by his side.

Chapter Twelve

Saturday. The anniversary of Skye's miscarriage. She hadn't been scheduled to work, but she found herself there anyway. Mindlessly cleaning up after the hotel guests and listening to the gripes and gossip of her employees was far better than moping around the house, stewing with her own dark thoughts about the miscarriage and the pregnancy scare the previous weekend. And thinking of Gentry, who was never far from her mind.

Actually, that was an understatement. She couldn't stop thinking about him, with every song on the radio, every time she passed the villas at the resort, and every night alone in her bed. Yet she couldn't decide why his hold on her had lingered. Was it because she missed the thrill or the man? Or maybe she simply missed the distraction, that brief moment in time that she could forget about her worries.

She really could have used him as her distraction tonight. Her body felt physically wounded by the emotional turbulence that this anniversary brought. Her stomach churned and her muscles ached, and no amount of chocolate or tears seemed to help. What did help a little was reading back through the occasional texts that Eddie Rivera had sent her throughout the week in advance of their date that evening.

Every text made her laugh, they were so dorky and endearing. He even sent her a weather report and sent her a survey about her favorite candy since they were going to the drive-in movies. After that, she got a knock-knock joke—an actual, bona fide knock-knock joke that she'd then shared with her niece and nephew, much to their delight.

But despite that, she wasn't looking forward to their date like she should have been. Now that the anniversary was upon her, Eddie Rivera seemed a paltry distraction indeed. Her heart didn't race when she thought of him. Her mind didn't flood with electric, wicked thoughts, but rather, with . . . well, knock-knock jokes.

She took her lunch break later than usual, and arrived in the break room to find a handful of the housekeeping staff gathered around a cell phone watching a video, when they should have all been back to work already. Skye drew a deep breath and stemmed the urge to snap at them. Rather than break up their fun, it was time to make nice because she'd been short-tempered all week, which she hated because it made her feel like her mom.

Rather than look sheepish at the arrival of their boss, the ladies giggled when they saw her. Laura tried to hide the cell phone under the table.

I am not my mother . . . I am not my mother . . . "What's going on?" Skye asked as casually and carefree as possible.

"Is it true about you and Gentry Wells?" Laura asked.

Skye hadn't said word one to anyone at work about her weekend with Gentry, because she'd broken a lot of rules that night, and anyway, it wasn't professional for a boss to go blabbing about her hedonistic weekend, with a hotel guest or not. But, of course, the staff knew. One of her mom's favorite sayings was that nothing happened at the resort that the housekeeping staff didn't know about, and over the years, Skye had found that unequivocally to be true.

"We're friends, yes."

More tittering filled the room.

"What?" Skye pressed. "I'm feeling self-conscious here."

Laura held up her phone. "Did you see his performance last night on TV?"

Gentry had been on TV? If she'd had any idea, she would have been glued to her television set. Anything for another glimpse of him.

Laura handed her phone over. "Start it at the beginning."

Pulled up on the screen was a video recording. Heart racing, she pressed play. The first shot of an empty stage as the sound of an engine revving filled the air. Then a motorcycle drove right onto the stage from the wings, Gentry on it. Sure enough, her heart did all sorts of crazy acrobatics at the sight of him. Damn it all, he looked good on a motorcycle dressed in a black leather jacket, even better there than on a jet plane or in a club's VIP suite. He basked in the roar of the crowd as he took his place center stage at the front of a band of five. When he grabbed the microphone, Skye noticed the brass knuckles he wore on his right hand.

Then he started to sing. She expected another song like "Well Hung" or "Beer O'Clock," but this time the topic was a midnight horseback ride through the backwoods with a beautiful woman.

Skye's cheeks flushed hot. *My God, he really did write a song about us.* Not only that, but with the way his gaze seduced the camera, she would've sworn he was singing it right to her. Which was fine, as long as he sang about riding horseback, but the song turned real dirty, real fast.

Skye's employees giggled behind her as Skye's face turned from flush to on fire. And that was before he got to the part in the song where the woman in the song rode him in reverse cowgirl all the way to the finish line.

Five minutes later, Skye walked from the break room in a fog and down the stairs to her office in the basement. The guy she'd spent a night with nearly three weeks earlier, the one with whom she'd thought for a solid hour that she might be having a baby with, had written and performed a song about the intimate details of their night together—on live television for millions of viewers all around the world.

Without a greeting to her mom, who sat at her desk on the far side of the room, Skye sank into her desk chair, too stunned to do more than ruminate about what to do. Did she text him? Did she ignore it? Was she flattered? A little. But more than that, she was obnoxiously and indescribably aroused. Embarrassingly so.

She had to remind herself that of course she was into him. *Of course.* He had that "it" factor that all celebrities had. That was the whole point—you couldn't take your eyes off them. They made you want to let them into your heart and your life. After that ACM performance, there were probably thousands of women fantasizing they were the one he was singing about. And yet it was Skye, a no-name housekeeping manager who was pushing thirty in Dulcet, Texas, who was actually the lucky one who'd done all those things with him.

Before she knew it, a giggle was bubbling over in her throat, making her eyes water as she fought to hold her laughter back. She'd longed for a distraction that day, the anniversary of her loss, and, sweet Jesus, she'd gotten one. *Thank you, Gentry.*

Her mom looked up over her reading glasses. "What is going on with you? You've been snapping at everyone all week. Not just me, but our girls. And now you're laughing? What's so funny?"

Skye roused herself with a shudder. "I don't know. I'm sorry."

Her mom accepted her answer with a *hmph* and got back to work.

Skye was too distracted to work, so she did what any self-respecting woman would—she found the video of Gentry's ACM performance online and texted Remedy the link.

Ten minutes later, while Skye was still sitting there staring at the muted video she'd been watching ever since on a continuous loop, Remedy burst through the office door. "Oh. My. God."

Skye shot out of her chair, flashing Remedy a look of panic. "Let's talk outside. My mom's trying to work."

"Subtle," her mom murmured. "Very subtle."

They walked up the stairs from the basement level, through the lobby, Remedy squeezing Skye's arm the whole way, as though she was about to burst. They fast-walked out the front doors, where they found a private corner between two potted shrubs.

Remedy clapped her hands on her cheeks. "Did you two really do all of that?" she hissed in an exaggerated whisper. "Because oh my God!"

"Right? At first I was pissed because all that stuff he sang about, we actually did, but—"

Remedy gasped. "Shut up! Are you serious? All of it?"

There was no need to pull her punch with Remedy. "All of it."

"Okay, seriously, that performance. I mean, wow. I'd thought Gentry Wells was hot before, but this . . . this is a new level of scorching. Did you know he was going to sing that?"

If only. "No. We haven't talked since that weekend," Skye said.

"You haven't texted him today?"

"Texted, yes. Sent it? No." The text she'd written out had been simple—*great performance last night*—but it sounded hollow and impersonal. But what could she say that was real, that would capture the disparate jumble of emotions roiling around inside of her? Maybe, *Thanks for ruining me for other men. And, oh and by the way, I have a date tonight with a nice, dorky guy. Your complete opposite*. Or maybe she should write, *FYI, we dodged a bullet. The pregnancy test came up negative.*

Yeah, no.

Remedy said, "You have to text him. Let him know you got the message loud and clear."

"What message?" That he enjoyed their time together? That being with her had been lucrative for his career?

"That he wants you! Don't be dense." Remedy danced Skye around in a circle. "Gentry Wells wants you, Skye Martinez."

"He doesn't, at least not anymore. And I don't want him. And that's the end of it."

Remedy made like she was melting, with droopy shoulders, a long face, and eyes rolled up into the top of her head. "Sweetie, I love you. Which is why I feel comfortable telling you right now that you're full of shit."

The group of housekeeping staff that had been

watching the video in the break room picked that exact moment to walk through the front entrance, finally getting back to work, as it were. Even still, they stopped to flirt with Skye's cousin Marco, who was working the valet desk.

The next person out of the entrance was Skye's mom. She waved her cell phone at Skye. "Sorry to interrupt your little gossip session, but I just got a call from Gloria. She said that some man she didn't recognize just stopped by the house looking for you. She said he looked like he was bad news. Any idea who that could be?"

A motorcycle engine rumbled through the circular driveway, its engine so loud that it set off a car alarm. Remedy nodded to it, her eyes going wide as saucers. "Skye, look."

As though she conjured him right out of that video her employees had showed her, a man in aviator sunglasses and a black leather jacket set down the kickstand of the bike and swung his leg over it. Gentry. Hot as ever.

He leaned against the bike's seat, a thumb hitched behind his belt, and smiled at her. "Hey there."

Skye took a few steps closer, not sure her feet were touching the ground or if she was floating, the moment was so surreal. "What are you doing here?"

His gaze swept over her body. "You told me the next time I was in the neighborhood, I should stop by. So here I am."

"You just happened to be in my neighborhood?"

His lips pursed into a wicked, lopsided grin. "Not even close. I'm here for you."

Chapter Thirteen

Gentry came for her. He couldn't have known how badly she needed him today, of all days, but he'd somehow known to pick today to drive up on a motorcycle and sweep her off her feet. While Skye was still trying to figure out what to say in reply, her mom sidestepped closer to her.

Under her breath, she said, "From a lion tamer to a rock star. That's not a good trend. Why do you keep wasting your time with these bozos who aren't good for you now that you have so many fine men knocking down your door, thanks to the spell?"

Aside from the fact that Gentry was no bozo, her mom had a point—but Skye was in no mood to hear it. Exasperated, she walked closer to Gentry, out of her mom's earshot.

"How'd you know where to find me?" she asked.

"I stopped by your house and your roommate told me you were at work."

Her roommate. That just went to show how little they knew about each other and each other's lives. Oh, well. It wasn't like he was there today so the two of them could have deep, heart-to-heart conversations. She smothered the little voice in her head reminding her of what a bad idea this was, how it went against the promise she'd made herself to give him up.

Too many ears were cocked in their direction, taking in their every word and look, so she walked the rest of the way to him, until the rumble of the bike's engine was loud in her ears and the smell of motor oil took her back to the days when she used to visit her dad at the resort maintenance shed. She'd perch on the hood of whatever golf cart or riding mower he was tinkering with and watch him work while she pelted him with endless questions about his tools and saws and employees.

Gentry maintained his cool, bad boy vibe as she approached. His tongue darted out to wet his lower lip like she was dinner.

She assumed a femme fatale expression. "So you think I'll just drop everything and jump on the back of your motorcycle?" She didn't need to let him know just how tempting that idea was. Yet.

"I promise to make it worth your trouble."

"That's your pick-up line?" she teased. "Needs some work."

In one fluid move, he reached out and closed his fist around her thin white uniform belt. He tugged her right up against him, his knuckles pressing into her belly. Up this close, the odor of the bike's engine was eclipsed by the scent of oiled leather coming off his jacket and riding boots. Or maybe from the bike seat itself.

All of the above, she decided, moving her hand up to stroke his sleeve. Damn, she loved leather, the way it smelled, the way it felt against her skin. Growing up, leather meant long trail rides or quiet afternoons polishing saddles and organizing tack. And, now she was all grown up, she'd developed quite the appetite for leather on her men and in her bedroom.

With his free hand, Gentry lifted a strand of her hair off her shoulder and wound it around his finger. "Baby, you got it all wrong. I'm not tryin' to pick you up. I'm tryin' to lay you down."

That growling Oklahoma drawl lit her body up like wildfire as much as his words did.

She let her gaze crawl down his body in a brazen inspection, all the way to where his crotch rested against the shiny black leather seat. Such a fine body. If they hadn't been standing in front of an audience that included her mother and several members of her staff, Skye would've rewarded Gentry's smirking lips with a teasing kiss. Perhaps it was good that she couldn't follow her instinct, because there was something delicious about the idea of playing hard to get for this brazen alpha of a man who rolled up unannounced and expected to get exactly what he wanted, when he wanted.

Even though she knew she'd give him exactly what he wanted. Because she wanted it too. Nothing would help her forget her grief like a night with Gentry. Nothing.

She shoved playfully against him until he released her belt. With a toss of her hair, she strutted away from him back toward Remedy and the rest of the crowd that had gathered, swinging her hips. "I have to finish my shift, and then we'll see."

She didn't actually have a shift to finish because, technically, she had both today and Sunday off work, but he didn't need to know that.

"Fine. I'm still gonna be waiting here when it ends. That's a promise."

Carlotta, the graveyard shift manager, shuffled forward with flushed cheeks and one eye on Gentry. "I'll cover your shift. You go have some fun. Someone might as well."

That was sweet of her. Skye was ready to say as much when a throat cleared nearby. Skye didn't need to look to know who it was. She felt the icy needles of her mom's disapproving glare pricking on her skin. That alone would have been enough to propel Skye onto the back of Gentry's motorcycle, even if this weekend's devastating anniversary wasn't looming over her.

Call it childish, but over the years, Skye had developed quite the appetite for the sweet taste of rebellion against her mother.

"I'm with Carlotta. Why wait until your shift's over?" he mom said dryly. "We'll manage just fine without you. Don't let me hold you back."

Skye had to fight a wince. What her mom really meant was *don't let me hold you back from doing something stupid,* the trademarked line she'd created when Gloria was in high school. She'd lobbed the words at both sisters whenever she felt them in danger of making a choice that went against their family values. But what had started as a dig meant to convince them to do their homework or not attend a party being held by one of their classmates while their parents were out of town had morphed into a general criticism of how Skye conducted her life. Gloria, it seemed, had been exonerated from the cutting remarks by the death of her husband.

If they had not been surrounded by employees, her mom would have said as much today. But surrounded they were. Skye couldn't find it in her heart to care, not about the scene she was causing or her mom's concerns. On some days, survival by any means necessary won out over common sense, and today was one of those days. If she could ride out the tide of her grief with a kindred gypsy spirit, then so much the better.

"I guess I'm free, after all," she said. "But I still need to go home and change."

"No need for that. Like last time, I'll buy you whatever we need when we get where we're going."

"Where are we going?"

That wolfish grin reappeared. "No idea. Does it matter?"

"No."

He seared the air between them with a smoldering gaze that seemed to lock on the sway of her hips as she walked to the bike again. The appraisal rendered her breathless with anticipation. She could see clearly in his dark, hungry eyes all the plans he had for her body.

He was going to make her sing. The thought made her smile as she took in the guitar strapped to the back rest. *Of course he would.* After all, he was a professional, wasn't he? A country-bred rock star to his core.

"Tell me that smile's for me," he drawled.

She dipped her face close to his, letting her lips hover only inches from his. "What do you think?"

He angled up to kiss her, but she evaded his efforts. She didn't want to be the only one hot and bothered on their ride. She took the spare helmet from his hands and set it on her head as she swung behind him on the bike.

She felt twenty again. Twenty and invincible. Just as she had been back then before it all fell apart. *Every woman deserves this,* she thought. To be twenty and free again. Just a glimpse of what it might be like to be granted a do-over. It wasn't a time of innocence, but pure power. She had all the time in the world, and the freedom that came along with it.

There was no failed marriage or broken heart. No baby lost or parents' disappointment. No responsibilities, no shame. Just joy and freedom and the power of sexual discovery pulsing through her veins. Just for tonight, she was going to live in that space. She was going to let Gentry Wells take her there, wherever *there* happened to be. She honestly didn't care.

The wind in her hair, her arms around Gentry. She knew she would have second thoughts about letting him go. This man who was so far from what she needed, yet everything she wanted. Even before they'd reached the highway, she felt untamable. Her hair whipping in the wind, the open road stretched out in front of them.

Somewhere on a mountain pass near the Texas/Oklahoma border, where Gentry had pulled them off the road and onto a secluded lookout point, Skye spread a blanket over a concrete picnic table as a makeshift tablecloth. The lookout point they'd found was tucked away from the road, giving it the illusion of solitude along with sweeping views of lush, sprawling mountains and valleys of northern Texas.

While Gentry tinkered with his bike, Skye set out the chicken they'd picked up at a fast-food joint next to a gas station back in Vernon. She sat at the picnic table and plucked a leg from the top of the bucket. She sank her teeth into it, savoring the crunch of salty, oily goodness that made her hum with pleasure. Her focus drifted to the setting sun looming over the hills on the horizon, and she stretched her legs out in front of her, smiled at the contrast of the picture-perfect sunset to her terminally uncool, plain black work sneakers.

That's what she got for jumping on the back of a

motorcycle straight from work. Usually on work days in which she had a date immediately afterward, she brought a change of clothes, but—

She sat straight up on a gasp.

Eddie Rivera. Their date was tonight. With a muttered curse of shock at her forgetfulness, she pawed through her purse in search of her phone. She didn't let out a breath until she saw the time. It was only seven and he wasn't supposed to pick her up until eight. She still had time to text him, and, thankfully, she actually had cell-phone service, even though they were in the seemingly middle of nowhere.

"What are you up to? You look like you've got a bee in your bonnet," Gentry said from where he was tinkering with the motor.

She glanced up from texting. "Canceling a date I had tonight."

Gentry stood, looking utterly pleased with himself. "That's a cruel thing to do to a man. Especially in a text."

Skye made a show of looking at the time display on her phone. "There's still time to drop me off in time for the date, if you want to take me back."

"Like hell I do." He climbed onto the picnic table next to her and reached around her waist, tucking his hand under her hip to grab her ass and pull her close. "The only place I'm dropping you off tonight is onto a bed, right before I climb in with you."

She fed him a piece of chicken, popping it right past those gorgeous, full lips. He licked the grease and spices off her fingers.

"I've got to clear the air about something," she said with a smile, so he'd know it wasn't anything serious.

"Oh yeah? Make it fast because I'm ready to eat some

dinner." Judging by the look in his eyes and the way his hands were getting friendly with her backside, the dinner he was talking about was her.

"That wasn't my roommate you talked to today at my house. It was my sister Gloria."

He pretended to contemplate that. "That is a bombshell. So glad you cleared the air. Gloria . . . she's the one with those two kids I thought for a second were yours."

"That's her. I live with them. Or they live with me, actually."

"You and your sister are close?" he asked.

"Very. Gloria's husband died in combat four years ago, when Chris was just a baby. I asked her to move in with me, to be closer to the family, and I'm so grateful that she did. I wouldn't have it any other way."

"Does she work for your housekeeping company too?"

Mom had tried to convince her that nothing was as noble as joining the family business, but Gloria had known she wanted to be a solider since she'd been in middle school, and even though Mom was one of the most persuasive people Skye knew, Gloria had been even more stubborn. "No. She's in the army, stationed at Camp Bullis."

"You sound proud of her."

"Very. And her kids are great. I love being an auntie."

"But that love spell you had your mom conjure tells me you're ready for a family of your own," he said.

Her hand crept to her belly of its own accord. "I'd like to try. It's time."

"I still don't get it. You're not into these guys. You say you want to get married and settle down, but you sure don't act like it. Why push yourself like that when it clearly makes you miserable? Take it from me that some people aren't the marrying types."

"That's the thing, Gentry. I am the marrying type. A little too eager, my sister says. I've already tied the knot once. Briefly. When I was twenty. Don't you see? There will be no more divorces for me. I can't bear to bring any more shame to myself and my family. So the next time I get married, it has to be forever, and a forever kind of man has proven really hard to find. Impossible, actually."

Skye wasn't sure what had prompted her to overshare like that, but she had. For reasons she didn't want to analyze, she wanted him to know her. Maybe it was the anniversary of her miscarriage warping her emotions, but suddenly nothing was more important than coming clean to Gentry about who she was and all she'd been through.

She looked to him for support or questions or anything, but he stared blankly at her, and all he said was "Oh."

She'd been married. And divorced. Gentry wasn't sure why the news came as such a shock to him, but it did. With that nugget of information, all the pieces fell into place: Skye's serial dating, the desperation, and her dissatisfaction with every man she auditioned for the role of her forever mate.

She'd shed her suit coat and her bare shoulders glowed golden in the light of the setting sun. Flecks of red shone in her hair. She turned to look at him, taking in his posture and expression as though searching for signs of judgment. Just in case he was accidently projecting any, he sat up straighter and schooled his features.

"My first husband, Mike, he wasn't good for me in so many ways," she said. Her eyes radiated with pain.

Gentry could easily conjure an image of all the men who wouldn't be good for her using the exact traits she'd told him she was looking for in a man. Vanilla to a fault, a churchgoing, upstanding citizen, a true Texas gentleman. Like she'd said, what she wanted in a husband was wrong for her in every way.

"He was a performer with a traveling circus, living like a nomad. A flashy, macho"—she turned a pointed gaze at Gentry—"rock-star type of personality. Not religious, not into family. Barely into me. And I followed him anyway."

Boy, oh, boy, had he called that one wrong. No wonder she wasn't looking for a future with a man like Gentry. No wonder they could never be more than temporary.

"So what did he do? What was the final straw?" Gentry prompted. "Because you would never just throw up your hands and give up on a marriage for nothing. You may be a wild spirit, but you're not built to leave." *Not like me.*

But that was a thought for another time, not when the woman in his care had trusted him enough to open her heart and her past to him. The mask of stone she'd been wearing started to crumble. She chewed her lower lip hard enough that he wouldn't be surprised if she broke the skin soon.

"No, I'm not. Or, I didn't think I was. Not in my wildest dreams. But in the third month of our marriage, when I went to find him after a performance to tell him I was . . ." Her expression turned angry as her gaze shifted to the horizon beyond Gentry's shoulder. Her teeth gnawed her lower lip without mercy. In the stretching silence, she drew a sharp breath through her nose and sat straight up as her hand flew to her mouth. She really had drawn blood.

Gentry grabbed a napkin from the table and shooed

her hand away. He dabbed at the cut until the ooze of blood had subsided, then he cracked open a fresh water bottle and handed it over. She drank deeply, in rhythmic, noisy glugs, and he had to wonder if she was that thirsty or if she was stalling, debating if she really wanted to reveal to Gentry what she'd been about to.

"What were you about to tell him?" he prompted.

She crushed the empty water bottle in her hand, then hurled it in the direction of the trash can. It bounced off the side and landed in the dry red dirt with a puff.

"That I was pregnant," she bit out.

Well, shit. But she didn't have a kid. At least, she'd told Gentry she didn't. So . . . abortion? No, even as a lapsed Catholic, there was no way she'd do that. Then, she either had a miscarriage or gave the baby up for adoption? His imagination spun out the possibilities and he had to force himself back to the present, to her words.

"What happened to the—" *Shut the fuck up, man. She'll get there if she wants you to know.* It wasn't like she owed him total access to her life and her family, much less her past choices.

"I'd gone to a clinic that day after the half-dozen drugstore tests came back positive. When I walked into our trailer, he was on the couch, his hand wrapped around the long, blonde ponytail of the girl kneeling in front of him. One of the lighting techs. Someone I'd considered a friend."

"What a bastard." Then again, he'd known dozens of that kind of guy during all this years of touring. Dozens upon dozens of men who didn't consider a blowjob from a roadie to be cheating on their women. There was a time Gentry hadn't either. When he was young and stupid and thought the world was his for the taking. Before he figured out that partying and womanizing turned him into the kind of man he didn't want to be.

Skye cut a sideways glance at Gentry. A regal smile spread on her lips, causing a fresh smear of blood to appear in the cut. She darted her tongue out to taste the blood, and for a moment, Gentry thought again about wiping her lip clean. But he knew from experience that something about the taste of blood was grounding. Maybe she needed that tonight. To taste the blood and embrace the pain of memory. He knew all about that too.

"When I saw them like that, I went crazy. I threw everything in the room I could get my hands on at the two of them, and then I chased that bitch out of our trailer with one of the knives from the kitchen. I almost threw it at him, and I think he thought I would, too. But I told him, "You're not worth going to jail for, you piece of shit. But you don't get to have me anymore. And, guess what? You don't get this baby, either." I left him standing there blubbering like a fool. I stole his motorcycle and took off with nothing but the clothes on my back. I got about two hours away before the bike ran out of gas and I didn't have any money, so I had to swallow my pride and call Gloria. It was a ten-hour drive from Dulcet to that gas station in Arizona, but she picked me up and listened to me rage about Mike the whole way back to our parents' house. I never told her I was pregnant until years later. Not my parents either. I just couldn't deal with their reactions to that, on top of everything else.

"I'd been home two weeks when I miscarried. Two weeks of my mother urging me to return Mike's phone calls, to make things right. To try. A woman didn't just give up on her marriage, she said. No, actually she said that a *Catholic* woman didn't just give up on her marriage. Divorce is a sin, and God will punish you, she reminded me. Our priest reminded me of that too. But I hired a divorce attorney anyway. I had no interest in trying to work something out with a man I didn't trust, even if I'd thought I loved him for a while. The day I had the papers served to Mike, I started cramping and bleeding. And that was it. I went to the doctor and they told me the baby was gone. Maybe my mom was right, you know? Maybe God was punishing me for my sins."

She'd used the word *maybe*, but there was no mistaking the conviction behind her words.

Fucking hell. She really believed it. She believed that leaving her cheating husband had caused her miscarriage. No wonder she'd heaped so many rules onto herself about the man she'd end up with this time around.

He knelt before her and took her elbows in his hands. "Listen to me, Skye. It was not God's will that you lost the baby. That's not how it works, okay? You did not bring all that on yourself."

She stared daggers at the ground to his left, lost in her anger. He pushed on, feeling helpless and desperate to soothe her. "This Mike guy was the one who sinned. Not you."

He could practically see his argument float through her like an apparition.

She shifted her gaze to the horizon again, silent and trembling with rage. Then all of a sudden, she seemed to snap herself out of it. She slapped her knees and offered Gentry a forced smile. "This isn't a sexy topic for our weekend away together. Let's drop it. Please."

He tried to swallow, but the walls of his windpipe seemed to stick together, tacky and dry. No, it wasn't sexy. But who the fuck cared? Not him. Somehow, knowing her, this intimacy was better than sex. Deeper. It would last them both longer. This was the real Skye. Not the muse. Not the vixen. This was Skye Martinez, a real woman, with all the scars and feelings and needs of one. Somehow, that made her even sexier, that realness. The trust she gave him.

He kissed the palm of her hand, then left his lips there against her skin, breathing into her his gratitude that she'd trusted him with her secret. He rose and slid his fingers through her hair to cradle her head. He had to kiss her, to taste that blood and leech the pain from her.

He kissed her with all the tenderness he could pour into it, letting her know that she wasn't alone and that she was perfect in every way that counted, perfect in her flaws and failings and painful past. He knew what his role was in her life, his function as her lover. Escape. As much as he craved for her to connect with his true, creative self, she needed him to help her disconnect from her life, from her past and her pain. The two of them were the perfect yin and yang of need and release.

Not so different from the way his music was designed to pluck people out of their minds and their worries. Such was his lot in life, to offer himself up as a gift of forgetting, to be that illusion. Tonight, though, might have been the first time that he didn't feel used. He didn't feel like a tool or a puppet. What he felt was privileged to be the man Skye trusted with this job. "I'm gonna take you someplace soft tonight. Someplace nice. And I'm gonna fuck you so sweet, baby, that you're gonna forget everything but me."

Her eyes glittered with unshed tears and toughness. "Promise?"

His grand romantic plan had been to linger at the lookout point until the sunset, but that's not what she needed. And if he were being honest with himself, that wasn't what he needed either. Not romance or sunsets, but she needed kinky thrills that pushed her boundaries and lit up her kink for breaking the rules. He gripped the collar of her dress in his hands and tugged her toward him for another kiss, open-mouthed and urgent.

He slipped his hand beneath her skirt and took a firm grip of her ass.

She pushed into his hand. "I like that."

And he liked the sound of uplift in her voice. That determined joy, despite the quaver in her breath. This was why she'd jumped on the back of his Harley tonight. This, right here, was why he'd been compelled as though by angels back to Dulcet. To be here for her like this.

She didn't need another man in her life who tamped her wild spirit down. This was the woman who'd let him take her in that club, who'd got off on being watched while she was taken hard. He would give her this gift of escape. Hell, the way she whimpered against his mouth and inspired song after song after song, he'd give her whatever she wanted. Anything in the whole wide world.

He took his time strapping her helmet on, first combing back that thick mane of hair, then picking errant tendrils from where they tangled with the helmet strap. He held his leather jacket out in offering and she slipped her arms into the holes. He zipped her in, and when the zipper closure curved over her chest, he paused to plunge a finger between the swells of her breasts and trace the full shape up to her collar bone.

Her skin was soft and hot, as though she'd absorbed the heat of the sun.

He'd passed a place on his way down from Tulsa that had looked nice, a modest resort hotel on the other side of the mountains near the Oklahoma border that looked out over a wide expanse of the Red River, cutting through a valley. Right on the edge of wild. Perfect for the two of them to hide away from the world, if only for the night.

He straddled his bike and fired it up. The engine revved, ready to be unleashed on the highway again. She threaded her leg over the leather seat behind his back and tucked in behind him and held tight to his sides. He felt strong and good. Right with the world, exactly where he needed to be.

He got them back on the road, and he took the hairpin turns, smooth and in control, like he would with Skye's curves later that night. He'd ride each curve of hers just as hard and fast, just as daring. Until she clung to him as she was now. Was that laughter he heard?

"I love this," she said.

In his rearview mirror, he watched her chin tip up, eyes closed. Trusting him, loving the ride he was taking her on. Wind in their faces, the setting sun to their left.

His attention shifted to the road in front of him, and adrenaline and fear jolted through him with the strength of lightning. He opened his mouth to scream at the sight of a delivery truck barreling down on them.

Sounds were muffled, even the blare of the truck's horn.

Time stretched, giving him just enough space to process his choices. Hit the truck head on, go over the cliff or crash them into the mountain.

And then the choice was taken away from him.

So focused on the truck that he didn't see the slick patch on the road. The bike laid down, spinning. His left leg was consumed with pain. White hot, nauseating pain. Skye flipped up over him, her limbs as limp as a doll's. Her bare legs bright red. Blood? Everything was bright red. Red and black and hot white pain. He screamed her name. Or maybe that was all in his head. He couldn't get his jaw to work.

He heard the skid of truck brakes. The crumple of metal as the bike was eaten below the truck. The last thing he saw was Skye's body tumbling over the cliff.

Chapter Fourteen

Gentry woke up flailing, screaming. For real this time, not just in the movie playing in his mind about the crash every time he closed his eyes. He felt the vibrations of the scream in his throat, sandpaper against his raw, dry windpipe.

Tubes weighed down his arm. He was in a bed. A hospital.

The Life Flight and ambulance rides had been a blur of fuzzy shapes. He hadn't been able to speak or move. His whole body pulsed with the pain.

A familiar face came into focus next to his bed. "Nick. What are you doing here? I thought you'd be partying in Las Vegas for the rest of the weekend."

"The hospital called. I guess I'm your emergency contact, eh? That's cool. I know I've put you down as mine a few times over the years. I'm glad you're all right." But Nick's face was drawn tight, and his words rang hollow in Gentry's ears.

Something was really wrong with him because he could barely move his left arm, but none of that mattered until he learned Skye's fate. He'd never been much a praying man, but he was sure praying now. "Where's Skye? Please tell me she's okay."

"Skye? That's her name, the woman you were with in the crash?"

Gentry's heart contracted painfully. "Yes. And if you don't know her name, then I'm guessing you either don't know if she's all right or she's hurt really badly and you don't want to tell me."

"I'm not lying to you. I swear to God. The doctor wouldn't tell me anything except what was going on with you," Nick said. "But I'll find out about her for you. Just . . . stop moving, okay? You're going to hurt yourself worse if you keep this up."

"What's wrong with me? Everything hurts."

Nick sighed as though he carried the weight of the world on his shoulders. "Well, your injuries are mostly superficial. You hit your head pretty hard and scraped up your stomach. But other than that, it's just your hand, man. And that's messed up bad. Real bad."

A look down his body confirmed it. His left hand was wrapped in a thick bandage. "What's wrong with it?" But, really, it didn't matter, until he figured out if Skye was all right. "You know what? Never mind about that yet. Get a nurse in here, would you? I need to know about Skye."

Nick pressed a call button on the side rail, and not a minute later, a worried-looking nurse bustled into the room. "Looks like our patient's awake. Are you in pain?"

Hell, yes, he was in pain. "Skye, the woman who was in the crash with me, where is she? Is she all right?"

The nurse frowned down at him, which got his heart racing like crazy. Was she gravely injured? *Was she alive?* He tried to sit up, but only ended up flailing his arms, sending waves of pain through his left hand. "Tell me. I need to know. What's wrong with Skye? Don't you dare tell me she's . . . she's . . ."

"Sir, you need to calm down. I'll tell you, okay? But lie back and stop waving your arm before you hurt your hand any worse." The nurse glanced at the door as though to make sure they weren't being overheard. "I'm not really supposed to say anything to you about other patients unless you two are related."

"Yes, we are. She's my wife," he said, knowing that was the lie that would get him the information he needed about her. He shot Nick a warning glare.

To his surprise, the nurse bought it. "In that case, I can tell you that she's fine. You were both lucky. She has some minor injuries, but the baby's safe."

Gentry's relief quickly gave way to confusion. What baby? Skye wasn't pregnant. They'd used condoms. They'd done everything right and safe and consequence free. He'd spent a whole afternoon with Skye before the accident, and they'd even talked about her previous pregnancy, but she'd made no mention at all about a baby. Not only that, but he knew she'd never get on the back of a motorcycle and take that risk if she was pregnant. Unless she hadn't known either.

Nick stepped forward. "Baby? Gentry, what the hell?"

The nurse was staring wide-eyed and pale-faced down at Gentry with dawning awareness that she'd just stepped in it. "Oh, I shouldn't have said that in front of your friend. But you knew she was pregnant, right? I mean, of course you knew. I would never—"

"I need to see her," Gentry croaked, tugging at his IV tube.

Whatever the truth was and whatever their future held, he sure as hell wasn't going to figure it out alone while painkillers were being pumped into his blood. If she was pregnant, then she'd be freaking out. This was the anniversary of the baby she'd lost, the reason she'd needed an escape with Gentry that weekend. She already blamed herself for her miscarriage, so he could well imagine the torture she was putting herself through about the motorcycle accident.

The nurse stilled his arm, but it was Nick's hands braced on his shoulders that kept him pinned to the bed. "Stop that before you hurt yourself," Nick said. "Don't make me knock you out cold."

He would do it too. "She needs me," Gentry ground out. "You're not helping."

"You can't see her right now anyway," the nurse said. "She's in surgery."

Dear God. "What happened to her? I thought you said she and the baby were safe."

"It's minor surgery. The doctors needed to clean out the road rash wounds on her legs."

In his mind, he saw her bare legs flopping on the road as she skidded. Red flashed behind his eyelids. Red like raw beef. "Shit," he choked out.

"Other than the road rash and a sprained wrist, all her wounds are superficial."

In other words, she was pregnant and broken and he knew with absolute certainty that she would never forgive him—or herself.

He raised his hands to his face. Only then did he remember that his left hand had been hurt. Badly, according to Nick. Only his pinky finger and thumb were visible beneath the bandage, and now that he was looking at it and trying to move it, he was suddenly, acutely, aware that it hurt like a motherfucker—a stinging, awful pain that made his teeth throb in time with his whole left arm.

"My hand. What happened?"

He couldn't remember what his hands were doing during the accident, where they flailed, how they hit the road or knocked against the bike. He didn't remember his body at all. Only Skye. The contortion of her face in pain, the shredded, bloody flesh of her legs.

"Like I said, your left hand's pretty beat up," Nick said, his eyes brimming with pity that Gentry didn't want, didn't deserve. "You lost a finger, man. Your middle one."

He lost a finger on his left hand, his guitar-playing hand, which told him all he needed to know about the grief-stricken expression on Nick's face. In other words, he'd never play the guitar again.

"We won't know for sure until the surgeon's get in there how bad the damage is," the nurse added hastily. "But your friend is right. You lost your middle finger. It ripped clean off at the knuckle during the accident. The EMTs found it on the road and put it on ice, but the surgeon said it's too damaged."

His guitar playing hand. He may never play guitar again. His career might be over, but he couldn't muster up too much concern over that because the real crisis was that Skye was pregnant, and he knew how that would destroy her. She would think that this accident was punishment from God. He knew it as surely as he knew the sun rose in the east and set in the west. He needed to see her with his own two eyes, to talk her down from whatever ledge she was on after learning that she was pregnant.

He swallowed. "How soon will Skye be out of surgery?"

"Another hour or two, I'm guessing. Sometime during the night. I'm sorry, Mr. Wells," the nurse said. "There's nothing I can do to change that."

Nick braced a hand on Gentry's right shoulder. "I'll

find out which room she's in and keep checking with the nurses about her surgery, okay? For now, you just focus on healing."

Like hell he would. He would focus on Skye. On their baby. Whatever the fuck happened to him next didn't matter. Not one bit except in his ability to provide for them.

Goddamn it.

What the hell had he done?

At the sound of papers rustling and the distinct sensation that someone was watching her, Skye peeled her eyelids open a crack. The fuzzy silhouette of a dark-haired man wearing white gradually came into focus. A visitor. Fine, even though all she wanted was to sleep away the pounding pain in her head and the dull, throbbing ache of her body.

Every time she'd awoken that evening after a helicopter rescue had plucked her up off the side of the mountain, she'd had to piece together the facts. She was in the hospital. Which meant that the visitor in white was a doctor.

She was alive. Alive and in pain, but alive. *Gentry . . .*

All at once, her memory of the accident came rushing back. Gentry. His bike. That moving van. She remembered his guitar flipping up off the back of the bike, the blare of the moving van's horn, and Gentry calling her name as the bike swerved and tipped, launching her off of it. Time had slowed as she'd skidded over the blacktop, right to the edge of the road. The memory of those moments of skidding glowed like white-hot light in her mind and tasted like iron in her mouth, then black and pungent like dirt as she slipped over the edge of the road.

She'd drifted in and out of consciousness during the

Life Flight to the hospital, and then in the emergency room, but she vividly remembered the warring emotions of relief that she was alive and fear that Gentry wasn't. He was in the helicopter with her, but they'd kept her neck immobilized so her view had been reduced to the helicopter roof and whichever emergency worker was bent over her at the moment.

She hadn't been able to get a straight answer about his condition until right before she'd gone into surgery, and not until she'd wound herself up to hysterics over the hospital workers' inability to give her a straight answer about seemingly anything.

This doctor who was standing over her now so quietly might have an update for her about Gentry. She had to hope. The last she'd heard, he was going into surgery to try to save his badly damaged left hand.

With some effort, she forced her eyelids to open even more and her vision to clear, then blinked several times when she saw who it was.

Eddie Rivera. The man she was supposed to have been on a date with. What was this, a Ghost of Christmas Past moment? The man whose attention she'd spurned had come back to haunt her and help her see the error of her ways? Not necessary, because she was pretty damn clear about those errors.

"Eddie?" she croaked, pushing the word up through a tender throat and dry mouth.

His hand touched her arm. "You're in the hospital."

"I know. But why are you here?"

His lips quirked. "When you canceled our date, I decided to get some work done after hours."

That's right. Eddie worked at a hospital. This hospital, apparently. Just peachy.

She's detected a note of bitterness in his tone, which

made total sense. She'd lied to him about being too sick to go out. Worse, she'd lied because she'd wanted to be with a different man. She couldn't imagine the damage to Eddie's pride at that. He'd deserved better than her. Maybe he even felt like he'd dodged a bullet.

"I'm sorry," she rasped. "I lied to you. About tonight."

He tried to mask his flinch with a worried smile, but unlike her, he was a terrible liar. "Last night, actually. It's early Saturday morning. You're pregnant. Did you know that?"

The words hovered in the air above her bed. No, she was not pregnant. She'd taken a half-dozen tests that said she wasn't. Skye gaped at Eddie, waiting for him to crack a smile or take it back, but all he did was frown down at her with a tight jaw and sad eyes. "Who's lying now?"

His stiff shoulders dropped a few inches. "So, then, you didn't know. That explains a lot."

"I'm not pregnant." Which meant that either Eddie Rivera was pranking her—or he was a figment of her imagination, conjured by the meds she was on. He really was the Ghost of Christmas Past. "You're not real. This is a hallucination or a bad dream. Whatever freaky strong drugs they've got me on, they need to dial them back."

She reached for the nurse call button, but Eddie touched her wrist. "Skye. I'm real. I'm right here. And you're pregnant. I can show you the lab test to prove it. And I'm relieved to hear that you didn't know, because otherwise you wouldn't have gotten on that motorcycle, right?"

Exactly. If she'd been pregnant, she would have never, *ever* done anything so risky. If she'd been pregnant, she would have been at home, praying for repentance and trying to figure out what she was going to do to fix her disaster of a life. So if Eddie was there to tell her that she was pregnant, it had to be a hallucination. Or, better yet, a dream. Maybe she didn't even get in an accident. Maybe she'd fallen asleep at her desk. People had vivid dreams like this all the time, or so she was told.

But if her subconscious wanted to argue with her about whether or not she was pregnant, she could indulge it. "That's not possible. I took several pregnancy tests last weekend, and they were negative. Plus, it's been almost three weeks since I last had sex and we used protection."

"But your period is really late, I'm guessing? That's why you took the tests in the first place."

"Well, yeah, but I'm not a robot. Sometimes my cycle fluctuates."

Thank God this was a dream because she would not, never ever, want to talk about menstruation with the man she'd stood up for a date.

"That's probably because not enough time had passed," he said. "Those do-it-yourself tests need at least two weeks or more for a positive reading. The tests we do at the hospital can detect a pregnancy much sooner."

He held out a piece of paper for her to read, but she couldn't get her eyes to focus on the words. "It's too soon to hear a heartbeat, but the OB/GYN at the hospital says your vitals are fine and she'll monitor you in the hospital for the next couple days, because there's still a chance you could miscarry. But there's nothing else for you to do right now but rest and heal."

The word *miscarry* made nausea bubble in her throat, but she refused to succumb to the lure of hysteria. "Impossible, because I'm not pregnant," she said as much to herself as Eddie. "I can't be. I barely know him."

"Him . . . meaning the man you were on the motorcycle with? Gentry Wells, the musician?"

She closed her eyes at the sound of his name. "Is he all right? A nurse early said he was going into surgery."

"He's out of surgery, but he needs to rest and so do you. You can see him later today. One more thing, Skye. You should know that the accident made national news because of him. The hospital grounds and lobby are crawling with reporters and photographers."

I'll bet. Then a stab of dread made her gasp. Just like that, her mind cleared. She grabbed Eddie's sleeve. "You can't tell anyone. About the . . ." She couldn't say *baby.* "About this."

His smile was kind, in a professional, distant way. "Of course not. No one here is going to violate patient confidentiality, not for the media—and not even for worried families who are pacing in the hallway waiting for the green light to come visit you."

Oh God. Her family. What was she going to tell them? "Do I have to see them right now?"

"No, you don't, especially not everyone. But it might be nice to let your parents come see for themselves that you're all right. They've been here since before Life Flight landed and they're worried sick about you. And I think one of your aunts brought dinner, though it's probably stone cold by now."

Now that he'd mentioned it, the stomach-churning smell of grease, tomato sauce, and cumin hit her nose. She lifted a hand to cover her nose, and hit herself with her cast. With all that was going on, she'd forgotten she'd sprained her right wrist. Pain coursed through her. "I'm definitely not dreaming this. Any of it." Eddie, the accident, the baby . . .

He set a hand on her shoulder and gave it a sympathetic squeeze. "No, you're not. And for that, I'm sorry."

With her permission, Eddie opened the door and invited her family through. They rushed in, her mother leading the charge, followed by Gloria, several aunts and uncles,

Mama Lita, and her father shuffling in last. They swarmed the bed, chattering at Skye in English and Spanish, until Eddie's voice cut through the cacophony. "Quiet down! This is a hospital. And the best way to help a patient heal is to keep the atmosphere calm."

"You brought dinner. That's sweet but . . ." It was too late. Her aunt Sylvia was already setting up a buffet on the counter near the sink.

Eddie shot Skye a look of sympathy from the doorway. She attempted a shrug of resignation, but the movement hurt too much. The only way she was going to get through tonight was to shut it all down—her fear, her pain, the truth. She was pregnant and she'd almost killed her baby by getting on that motorcycle. Time to shove those facts in a tiny box, close the lid, and lock it up tight until she was alone again.

Skye's mom assumed the same place that Eddie had at her bedside, with her father next to her. Mom's eyes were red-rimmed and her whole body quivered with emotion.

"I'm okay, mama."

Except that you're pregnant.

No, she wasn't going to think about that right now.

Skye watched the expression on her mom's face morph from fear to anger. Her mouth contorted into a cringe, looking as though she was trying to swallow peanut butter, but her throat was too dry. Finally she spit out, "Are you happy now?"

"Yessica, don't do this," her father said.

Skye wasn't sure why she'd expected sympathy from her mom. She'd witnessed this reaction every time her dad hurt his back or suffered a medical setback and wound up in the hospital. Unable to handle the magnitude of her fear, her mom mutated it into anger. Skye would never forget the way her mom had raged for hours after her dad had a heart attack and had been admitted to the ICU.

Well, like mother, like daughter, because Skye could feel her anger rising, pulsing up through her like a delicious drug. “Yeah, I’m really happy, Mom. Thanks for asking. I love it when my master plan to torment you works out even better than expected.”

Her dad patted her leg. “It’s okay, mija. Don’t get yourself worked up.”

Her mom’s nostrils flared and her frown was on the cusp of being a sneer. “No, it’s not okay, Beto. Your daughter went against God, the commandments. She went against the old ways.” She turned her sharp eyes on Skye. “That charm we summoned for you was no simple magic. Did you think there wouldn’t be consequences for ignoring the path you’d committed to?”

Oh, brother. “Spare me your hocus pocus.”

Her dad put his arm around her mom’s shoulders and gave a pull. “All right. We have to let the patient rest. Gloria, Mama Lita, where are you? Come take Yessica for a walk.”

Her mom huffed and puffed, looking very much the part of a frazzled old wolf who’d just discovered that even all her hot air couldn’t blow a brick house down. For a minute, Skye didn’t think she’d leave. But her dad rarely ever issued commands, and when he did, Mom tended to follow them, especially with Mama Lita tugging her arm and issuing her own commands in whispered Spanish.

“Fine,” her mom said, spearing a finger toward Skye. “But we’re not through talking about this, young lady. You could have been killed. Do you know what that would have done to me?”

And there it was, the huge, loving heart that her mom fought to keep armored. It was almost enough to make

Skye apologize for scaring her like that by getting herself hurt. *Almost.*

Her mom let Gloria and Mama Lita pull her away, along with her two aunts. Leaving only her father and her mother's two brothers-in-law in the room, both of whom were busy eating and looking out the window.

Her dad perched at the edge of the bed near Skye's ribs, his posture stiff. He turned his head to look at her slowly, until a wince crossed his face as he reached the edge of his range of motion. He held her hand and shone kind eyes on her. "It's nice to be the one visiting the sick person instead of the one in the bed for a change. But I wish it wasn't my beautiful daughter."

In so many ways, her dad had gotten the short end of the stick in life. All those damn health problems, his back, his failing heart. Forced into dependence on his wife and girls, not only financially, but physically. So much had been robbed from him, but every time she looked at him—really looked—she saw hints of the larger-than-life giant he'd been to her when she was a little girl, before he got sick.

Once, when Skye was seven or eight, she'd wandered into a field of cattle on the farm across the street from their old house. The cows had trotted to her, perhaps thinking she was there to feed them. They'd scared her with their size and heft. They crowded her until she couldn't see the fence she'd jumped. She'd cried, stuck and small and helpless. Her dad's voice had found her there. At first she'd thought it was the voice of God. But it was only her dad.

"You're braver than this," he'd said. "You can save yourself, but not if you panic. You have to quiet your anger enough to listen."

He never said what she should be listening for and

over the years, her theory evolved from God to her inner wisdom. Or maybe the two were one-in-the-same.

She squeezed his hand. “I love you, Dad. Thank you for being here for me.”

“That must have been some ride,” he said. “I bet the sunset was beautiful up on that mountain.”

Without warning, she was hit by a sudden and overwhelming urge to weep. Something about her father’s quiet strength made her want to let herself dissolve in his arms. Ridiculous. She had too much to think about, too much to deal with, to get emotional. To panic. “Yeah. It was beautiful. I’d never been in that part of the state before. It’s incredible.”

“Are you okay? I mean, besides the sprained wrist and your beat-up legs?”

She mustered a grin. “I think so.”

“Your heart?”

Nope. They weren’t going to go there. “My heart is good.”

“Your mother is scared. She doesn’t mean to hurt you,” he said.

“I know. I didn’t mean to hurt her either.”

He snorted. “Of course not. I know I’ve told you this before, but you remind me of my mother. She never means to hurt anyone. She just can’t keep her feet tethered to the ground. It took me a lot of years to accept that about her. Her spirit is too wild. Just like yours.”

“I don’t want to have a wild spirit.”

His chuckle echoed in the quiet room. “I don’t know if you have a choice.”

Everybody had a choice. *You can save yourself, but not if you panic.*

She almost told him about the baby. But the words wouldn’t come.

She was saved by a knock at the open door. A tall, dark, handsome man dressed in navy-blue scrubs grinned at Skye. "Wow, it smells good in here. I'm Aiden. And this beautiful lady must be Skye. I stopped by to tell you that I'll be your nurse tonight."

Her father uttered a prayer under his breath, then smiled at Skye. "We have got to talk to your mother about that love spell."

She didn't have the heart to return his smile, not with her arm aching and her legs on fire, not with every cell of her being screaming out in horror at what she'd done to herself. She would have thought that getting pregnant would have canceled out the spell, because what man would want her now? More accurately, what would she want with a man? Hadn't the lot of them done enough damage to her life already?

Her father's words echoed in her ears. *You can save yourself . . .*

Damn right, she would. It was the only choice she had now that her world had come crashing down around her.

Chapter Fifteen

Even after her family left, sometime around dawn, Skye couldn't sleep—and not only because she jumped every time a nurse entered her room, fearing it was Gentry. No, she couldn't stop staring at her belly, watching it rise and fall beneath the blanket with every breath. She was having a baby. Even as she lay there, that baby was growing, cells dividing, the organs forming.

What a mess. And it was all because she was foolish enough to go against everything she believed in, against her morals, her family's advice, and against her faith—all so she could jump on the back of some random rock star's motorcycle for a temporary thrill.

She closed her eyes. *You can save yourself, but not if you panic.* The wisdom in those words hit her all over again. Instead of panicking, what she needed was a plan. There might be nothing she could do about the baby growing inside her, but there was definitely a way to help herself stop jumping out of her skin every time the door opened. It was time to clear the air with Gentry, right then and there in the relative privacy that the early morning hour provided, before her family returned later that day. Not that she planned to tell him about the baby right then and there. He had a right to know, of course he did. But she couldn't tell him, not yet. Not when she could barely think the words, much less say them out loud.

The nurses had kept her updated on Gentry's status, namely his recovery from the surgery on his hand. They'd even passed along his room number in case she wanted to call him. She had wanted to, about a million times since her surgery, but what she had to say needed to be said in person.

Slowed down by the fact that she could only use her right hand, she lowered the side rail on her bed and pulled back the covers. Her legs were covered in bandages and open sores that the doctors had told her would heal better if left unbandaged. She gingerly shifted her legs one at a time over the edge of the bed. All the blood rushed from her head straight into her legs. They throbbed with the pain of it, but that wasn't going to stop her from doing what she had to.

Gritting her teeth, she set one foot and then the other on the floor. Even through her socks, the cold chilled her all the way to her bones. Ignoring this added discomfort on top of everything else, she shuffled into the wheelchair that had been stationed bedside for her in case she needed to use the restroom. She grunted as she touched down in the seat. Her whole body felt like it was on fire. Probably, she was due for another round of pain meds, and the prudent thing would be to wait to go traversing the hallways until she'd had a fresh dose. But she couldn't wait. All she wanted to do was get this conversation over with.

She'd never used a wheelchair before, but she'd seen it done enough times to have the general idea of how it worked. She lowered both hands to the wheels' push rims, but she couldn't get her left hand to close around the rim without sending shooting pains through her arm. Without another option, she reached back to the bed and pressed the nurse's call button.

When a nurse appeared in the doorway, Skye said, "Would you help me push this? I need help getting to room 208. The man I was in the accident with, that's his room."

"Oh, honey, I think he's sleeping. You both should be sleeping. Healing takes rest."

Skye bit back her frustration. The last thing she needed at the moment was a lecture, even from a well-meaning nurse. "I know that, but you saw how my family hovered over me today. They'll be back later this morning, and I'd really like to go see Gentry before that so we can talk in peace. I haven't seen him since the accident. Please."

The nurse hesitated a moment longer, then nodded. "All right. Let's go."

The wheelchair rolled smoothly through the quiet hall. Skye was grateful that the nurse didn't try to talk her up, as busy as Skye was trying to figure out what she was going to say to Gentry.

Despite that it was only six in the morning, the hospital corridors and nursing stations were brightly lit and active with nurses, doctors, and the occasional patient shuffling down the hall.

At the closed door to room 208, the nurse stopped. "Wait here. Let me see if he's up for a visitor."

She slipped through the door and closed it behind her, but was out a moment later, smiling at Skye. "He was already awake, and he very much wants to see you too. I'll push you in and give you two some privacy. Just have him push the call button when you're ready for me to wheel you back to your room."

"Thank you."

Gentry's room was dimly lit with a light over the sink in the corner and the dawning sun beyond the window. Gentry was sitting up in bed, as though he'd been waiting for her.

"Skye," he croaked as her wheelchair crossed the threshold. "Are you all right? I've been so worried, but surgery wiped me out and I just couldn't get over to see you."

He did look weak. Weak and in pain. His face was scuffed up, and his left hand was wrapped in thick bandages. He pressed the button to turn a light on over the bed, wincing at the effort.

The nurse wheeled Skye to a stop close to the bed, close enough that she could reach out and touch Gentry's right hand, if she'd wanted. Then the nurse was gone, closing the door behind her.

"I think the better question is if you're all right?" Skye asked.

"Never better." He said it sincerely, rather than sarcastically, as though seeing her had made everything right in his world in a genuine way. He reached for her hand, but she evaded his efforts. If they connected like that, then she might lose all resolve, just as she did every time they touched.

He curled his hand into a weak fist, honoring her wishes. "Skye, listen. I'm so sorry about the accident. It was my fault and it's going to take me a long time to forgive myself for it. I should have gone slower. I should have seen that truck coming. And I can't tell you how relieved and grateful I am that you're not more hurt."

The apology was a balm for her battered heart, even though the truth was that she should have been the one issuing it. But she hadn't come to him that night in order to exchange apologies. "I was there. It wasn't your fault. Sometimes shit happens." Hopefully, he couldn't tell that she didn't believe her own words.

"It's not your fault either," he said pointedly.

So much for her attempt at dissembling. "Contrary to what you might believe, I was raised with the notion that there are consequences for our actions. And I screwed up, big time."

He swung his legs over the side of the bed. "Stop it, Skye. I know where you're going with this, but just stop it. God's not punishing you. You didn't bring this on yourself. I swear on my life, Skye. It was just a freak accident. You and I are going to be all right," he soothed. "All we have to do is stick together and—"

Time to nip that thought in the bud. "Listen, Gentry. That's why I'm here. Besides wanting to see for myself that you were all right, I came here to ask you to give me some space."

He stared at her, blank faced.

To fill the silence, she forged ahead. "We're not going to stick together because I can't be with you anymore. I need time to heal. Alone."

"I get it. You're scared and in pain, but you and I are in this together, okay?"

He wasn't getting it and it made her heart ache to have to say the words again. "No, Gentry, you're not listening to me. I'm supposed to be in the hospital for a couple more days, and I don't want to see you." There was no mistaking the tinge of desperation in her voice. The plea for him to stop pushing her and let her go. She cleared her throat and tried to infuse her voice anew with strength and pride. "Not for a while. I need space."

"The baby . . ."

The baby? She must have misheard him because there

was no way he could have known she was pregnant. She would tell him, but on her own time. She was going to cut herself that slack while she healed.

You can save yourself, but not if you panic.

Yes. And as soon as she could rid herself of this damn panic, she'd figure out a way to save herself, just like she always did.

"I'm not your baby, so don't call me that. And unlike you, I can't just take off whenever the urge strikes me. I risked my job and my life with you too much already. You're no good for me. And don't try to tell me otherwise."

"I agree. I'm no good for you. At least, I haven't been. But that's all going to change now. You're pissed off at me and scared, and that's understandable. But I'm here for you. Let me prove that to you."

"Are you kidding me? You almost got us in a head-on collision with a moving van. You almost killed us both." They'd already established that it wasn't his fault, but it felt so good to unleash her anger. "I didn't ask you to ride into my life yesterday and mess everything up. But that's exactly what happened. And now . . . now I can't work—" She held up her wrist brace. "And my legs feel like they're on fire. Have you seen them? This is going to leave permanent scars. My skin will never be the same."

She twisted to the side and showed off the oozing gashes, bruises and scrapes that weren't covered by bandages. He winced, and she could tell he was clenching his jaw. Good. He should feel bad for what he'd done to her. It had been his idea that she go with him that weekend to Nashville, and he hadn't taken no for an answer. Those had been his condoms. Her life had been fine before he'd barged his way into it.

"Don't you see? Our relationship has caused me nothing but pain and embarrassment. You might be living the high life in your celebrity fantasy world, but I have to go home and face my future. I have to do the dishes and get my niece and nephew ready for school, and I've got to help my mom with my dad's care. On top of all that, I can't work, so no paycheck, and even when I'm able to again, I'll have to bust my butt to make up for the time I took off to be with you plus the time off I'll need to take to recover from the accident. You and I aren't going to be together after this because I can't afford to be with you anymore. It nearly killed me already."

He drew a labored breath through his nose. His chest puffed with the effort. But his eyes weren't angry. They were sad. Was that . . . could that be *pity* she read in them?

"Don't you dare pity me," she spat. "I don't even know why you would. You're the one who's hurt worse than me."

He blinked his eyes wide and shook his head. "No pity. I swear. Take all the time you need. You have my phone number still, right?"

She had no idea. Did she even still have a cell phone or had it been destroyed in the crash too? Despite the excruciating pain in her left hand, she wheeled herself to the door. "I know how to find you. Just . . . don't come looking for me. You've done enough damage."

Chapter Sixteen

KTTX out of Texas is reporting this morning that the rumors of out-of-control drinking and partying surrounding award-winning country music artist Gentry Wells came to a head last weekend when the star and an unnamed woman were injured when their motorcycle collided with a moving van on a remote mountain pass in northern Texas. No word yet on whether alcohol was a factor, but Wells is best known for his—

Gentry clicked off the television and walked to the floor-to-ceiling window in his hospital room. His left hand still hurt like hell even though it had been four days since the accident, and even though the doctors had removed his bandages that morning and processed his discharge papers—but even that had nothing on the pain that plagued his heart. Earlier that day, he'd watched from that same window as Skye was wheeled out to the curb in a wheelchair. A newer model truck pulled around the circular drive and stopped in front of her and the hospital attendant, a man who had to be her father at the wheel. Her mother rushed around, barking orders, manic in her commitment to transfer Skye smoothly to the truck's passenger seat.

In the truck, Skye had rolled down the window and looked up at the hospital, angling her head as though searching Gentry's room out, as though she knew he was watching her. He'd set his good hand on the glass and concentrated his energy, willing her to sense him watching. But then the truck rolled away and she was gone.

Their last conversation would haunt him forever. It hadn't been the first time a woman had laid it out for him how much he'd hurt her and how he'd ruined her life, but this time, with this woman, the truth stung with a pain like no other. More painful than losing a finger. More painful than the collapse of his marriage.

When she'd told him that she couldn't afford to be with him anymore, all he'd been able to think was that she was right. She'd had a good life before he'd walked into it, and all he'd done was screw it up. He'd nearly ended it. He'd gone to her and used her because she'd helped him regain his creative spark, but it seemed that the better she made his life, the worse he made hers. It was as if their relationship was a teeter totter, and Skye kept coming out on the bottom. If only he could have seen that more clearly sooner, before . . .

He stopped himself mid-thought.

Before what, the accident? Because if the baby was his, and he knew in his heart that it was, then their lives had already been on a collision course, motorcycle accident or not. And now she was obviously so damn scared of that fact that she was in denial—or, at least, unwilling or unable to talk about it with Gentry.

Not that he blamed her. He was still in a fair bit of denial himself. They were having a baby, a sentence he'd repeated to himself over and over, but which never felt like anything other than a trite song lyric or the punch line of a joke that was not at all funny.

What the hell was a man supposed to do in a situation like that, where the mother of his child was so scared and angry that she wouldn't even come to him with the truth?

Marry her, a voice inside him said.

With as Catholic a family as she was from, marriage might be the choice that set her conscience at ease. The thought made his stomach churn. Just because getting married was the easiest and cleanest choice didn't mean it was the best choice for either of them. Yes, the air sizzled whenever they were near each other, and since the moment he'd met her, he'd thought about her every hour of every day, but he was still Gentry Wells, Mr. Born to Leave. Every women he'd ever tried to have a relationship with, he'd ended up breaking their hearts, often without even meaning to—and some that he had.

He hadn't been paying lip service when he'd told her he was lousy husband material. Especially now. He glared down at his bandage-covered left hand. His music career was over. He knew it as plain as he knew his own name. She didn't need to settle for a man who was a shell of his former self. She might have climbed onto the back of a rock star's motorcycle, but the minute he'd laid his bike down, life as he'd known it had ended.

At least you have a life.

True, that. But any way the future shook out, it was a raw deal for Skye. She'd either be a single mom or she'd be saddled with Gentry as a partner, the man who'd already hurt her in so many ways.

A few hours later, Gentry was the one being rolled out of the hospital lobby in a wheelchair, as was the hospital's protocol. Nick picked him up in a shiny black limo, this time with Larry by his side, along with a hulking driver who would probably double as Gentry's bodyguard in the airport, in case any paparazzi were lurking about. Larry's touch, no doubt.

Larry had flown in on the day after the accident. He'd been pale and stoic as Gentry had explained his injuries, no doubt arriving at the same conclusion that Nick and Gentry had about the future of Gentry's career. But whatever he thought, he sure hadn't mentioned it. In fact, Gentry, Larry, and Nick hadn't talked about Gentry's career at all. And nobody mentioned Skye—not her or the pregnancy. In no time, they'd fallen into their typical hang-out mode, watching ball games, talking shit about other celebrities, and keeping the conversation light. Gentry had no problem with that. The longer he could ignore the writing on the wall about his career, the better. As for the situation with Skye, he wasn't interested in Nick and Larry's advice. They didn't know her like he did.

In the limo, Larry didn't fuss over Gentry the way Skye's mom had over her, but he did press a highball glass full of bubbly clear liquid into his good hand as soon as his seatbelt was on. "Tonic with some lime still your drink of choice?" Larry said.

"You bet it is." He wrapped his left hand lightly around the glass, letting the cold soothe the itchy ache of his stitches and swelling.

Nick held his own glass up in a toast. Judging by the stench, Nick's and Larry's drinks were more gin than tonic. "To our boy, Gentry. One of the toughest fuckers I know."

Gentry didn't feel all that tough at the moment, but the cold, crisp drink went down fast and smooth. "I appreciate you doing this for me, you two. Dropping everything to help me like this."

Nick nodded. "Someone's got to get Gentry Fucking Wells back on his feet."

True enough, and Nick had had that job for a while, sobering him up and giving him the occasional career push when necessary. Friends like him were worth their weight in gold. He might have said as much, because the pain meds were making him punchy, but Larry rolled his eyes and waved off the gratitude.

"Don't go getting mushy on us. I'm just doing my job."

Right. Just doing his job by holding a bedside vigil for Gentry for the last four days while his hand healed.

Gentry raised his glass again. "In that case, I nominate you for Agent of the Year."

"There you go getting mushy again. Those must be some drugs they've got you on. Good thing you can sleep it off in the private jet I rented to take you back home."

"Private jet? That's fancy," Nick said.

"Yeah, well, there's no sense giving the media anything more to write about, Gentry. Laying low is going to be the name of the game for a while."

It was sound logic, but Gentry had gotten hung up on the word *home*. The problem was, his ranch had never really felt like home, and going back to that empty house held zero appeal. Not only that, but the longer Gentry considered it as he watched the rolling fields of bluebonnets pass outside the limo window, the more his instincts screamed that it was the wrong move to leave Texas or Skye, even temporarily. The trouble was, Skye had told him in no uncertain terms to keep his distance.

Maybe he'd just drive through her town, buying himself some time to figure out what to do. No harm in that. It wasn't like the private jet was going to leave without him. He tapped the driver on the shoulder. "Hey, make a right up there, would you? We're going to take a detour."

Larry looked at him like he was nuts. "Detour? What detour? Did you not hear what I said about lying low?"

"I heard you just fine." To the driver, he said, "Go on. Make the turn. We're headed to Dulcet."

To his relief, the driver bumped onto the off ramp and slowed around the curve, headed west toward Dulcet.

"Dulcet? Oh, hell no." Larry popped an antacid and washed it back with his gin and tonic. "Don't listen to him, Pauly. We're going to the airport. That girl has ruined your life enough as it is. If you're feeling guilty, then let's throw some money at her for her hospital bills and so she doesn't go blabbing to the press, and then we can get your life back on track."

Gentry's anger was instantaneous. He was in Larry's face in a flash. "*She* ruined my life? Are you sure that's the story you're going with, champ? You sure that's the tack you want to take with me right now?"

Larry just about climbed up the back of the seat, rattling the ice in his glass. "Hey now," he said as gentle as a hostage negotiator, his palms out as though in surrender, though his index finger and thumb remained wrapped around his drink.

Nick grabbed a hold of Gentry's shirt and shoved him back against the opposite seat, sloshing his gin and tonic on Gentry's pants in the process. "Hey, man. Stay cool."

Larry dropped back into the seat, his suit wrinkled and his tie askew. "May I remind you, Gentry, that you're only paying me for one job—and that's to look out for your best interests. That girl, she is not in your best interest. And if you need proof of that, I've had to hire a publicist because, between the accident and your drunken bender in Nashville, the shit's hitting the fan for you. The rumors are flying that Neil's label is gonna drop you and that you haven't even started the album that's due in less than a month."

Gentry's head of steam diffused. He batted Nick's restraining hand away from his shirt, then found his own spilled drink on the floor. He scooped the ice back into the glass and set it on the minibar. Everything Larry said was truer than Gentry was about to admit, save for one point. "I didn't go on a bender in Nashville. I didn't have one damn drink and I never lost control. And I was stone cold sober when I got in the accident too."

Nick resumed his carefree sprawl across the bench seat next to Larry. "Don't you see? It doesn't matter what actually happened. All that matters is what people think about you."

That was some bullshit logic right there.

Nick continued, "Look, man. We've got a tour coming up and a new album later this year. We can't—"

"I can't play the guitar anymore. Not like I used to. I'm missing a finger. It's not going to grow back." He held up his bandaged hand to drive the point home. "How am I going to tour, much less write and record an album?" And not only because of his hand. Gentry wasn't sure he wanted to get back to business as usual. Actually, he was pretty sure that he didn't.

A sign proclaiming that they were entering Dulcet's city limits. *The Jewel of the Hills!* the sign proclaimed.

"Don't you think I know that?" Nick said. "We can fix this too. We'll hire another guitarist."

"All you have to do is sing and shake those hips," Larry said. "You still got those hips, right?"

They rolled down Main Street. At a four-way stop, Gentry read the name of the familiar-looking church on the corner. Our Lady of Guadalupe. Skye's family's church.

Gentry knocked on the driver's shoulder. "Stop the car."

The driver swerved right, coming to a fast stop at the curb.

"What are we doing now? This isn't lying low." Larry said, spine snapping straight and looking ruffled again. "It's not good for you to be here. If there are reporters around, if they got a photo of you fresh out of the hospital, wandering around your Girl of the Week's small town . . ." He shook his head so hard his jowls jiggled. "Nope. I won't allow it."

"She's not my Girl of the Week. And how can you even say that when she's pregnant."

Larry nearly sloshed the ice right out of his highball glass. "She's *what*?"

Guess Nick hadn't spilled the beans about the baby to Larry on the sly, as Gentry had assumed he had. "She's pregnant. It's mine." And didn't that just bring it all home in a way Gentry hadn't internalized before. The baby was his as much as Skye's. His baby. His child. He couldn't stop repeating the words to himself, as though if he said them enough, the truth in them would somehow seem less surreal.

He looked at the church's tall, thick wooden entrance. Knowing Skye was nearby, that she was so scared by the pregnancy and the accident that she couldn't even admit it to Gentry filled him with despair. Never had he wanted so badly to be a different man, a new man, someone Skye could count on. But she wasn't looking for a guy like him, a rambling cowboy with a six string. She wanted a local man, a settling-down type. She'd probably want to raise their baby up Catholic too, just as she had been. He'd never wanted to be a father, but the thought of his child being a different religion than him, living in a different state than him, filled him with a whole new kind of disquiet.

"What do you think's involved with converting to Catholicism?" he mused.

"The hell kind of question is that?" Larry said. "Are you trying to get right with your Lord and Savior? Not that I blame you. I've done my fair share of praying for your salvation this week myself. But we can do that in Tulsa. We can sneak you in the back door of a church somewhere with no reporters hiding in the bushes. Not here, though."

Gentry took a look at shrubs that lined the sanctuary, pretty certain there were no paparazzi hiding behind them, waiting to snap an oh-so-scandalous photo of a grown man entering a church.

He popped the limo door open. "I'm going to go ask."

Larry was out of his seat, his hand on Gentry's arm. "Ask what? What are you doing? I told you, you can't get out here."

Gentry was sick and tired of people telling him what he could and could not do. Even though he loved Larry and they'd been together since the beginning, it was time for Gentry to cut all the puppet strings that were trying to control him, Larry's included. "Larry, you're fired. Nick, you too, along with the rest of the band. Trust me, it's all for your own good. I'm a mess. I'm not going to get that album done and Neil's going to drop me. He already told me as much. It'd be best for you both to get off this runaway train before it crashes and burns."

Larry deflated like a balloon in a cactus field. "But . . . your tour. Your new album. You can't just walk away . . . you owe me."

Like hell he did. So much for cutting those puppet strings; they just plum snapped off. "The only thing I owe you is the truth. And the truth is, you and I are done. I quit. You're free to go. Both of you." He ducked back down to look them both in the eye for good measure. "Oh, and thank you, Larry. You were a great agent." He extended his hand for Nick to shake. "We had a lot of fun over the years, made a lot of great records. I can't thank you enough for your loyalty and friendship over the years."

Nick shook Gentry's hand, even as he was shaking his head. "You're making a mistake. One you can't take back when you come to your senses."

Time would tell if he was making a mistake, but Gentry already knew in his heart that he wasn't.

Larry looked like someone just shot his dog. "You're serious?"

"As serious as a turkey on the first day of hunting season."

With that, Gentry walked away, his steps lighter and his heart freer than it'd ever been. He walked right up to the church door and saw a little sign with an arrow indicating that the office was around the corner. He turned in that direction, which is when he realized that the limo was still idling curbside.

"I'm not going to change my mind," he called. "Go on and get out of here. Stop wasting your time."

The back window rolled down. Larry stuck his head through the opening. "I'm not giving up on you." His voice cracked once. "We've come too far together to give up now. I'm not letting you go, you big, stupid lug."

What were they, star-crossed lovers at the end of a romantic comedy? "Goddamnit, Larry. Get a hold of yourself. Because I swear to God, I half expect you to pull out a ring and pop the question or some bullshit like that. You've got to let me handle this."

"What are you going to do about the bun?" Larry asked.

"The what?"

"The bun in the—" Larry pointed to his gut. "I'm trying to be discrete."

"You want to know what I'm going to do about my child?" Gentry called nice and loud, so the imaginary reporters in the bushes could hear. "I'll tell you. I'm going to teach it guitar and take it on the road with me. I mean, Jesus, Larry, what kind of question is that?"

Larry rubbed his chin. "That's not a bad plan."

"Come on, now. What do you think I'm going to do? I'm going to raise it. Like adults are supposed to do with the kids they sire."

Whatever he'd thought about fatherhood before, whatever he'd thought his future held, it all disappeared, along with the career that didn't suit him anymore. If he wanted to be in this child's life in a real way—and in Skye's life, for that matter—he'd have to relocate to Dulcet and convert to Catholicism. And why shouldn't he? It wasn't like he had much to keep him in Oklahoma, or anywhere else in the world, really. He hated his ranch and, contrary to Larry's desperate optimism, Gentry knew his career was over. Neil had granted him one last Hail Mary play, and Gentry had screwed that up beyond repair.

Then again, with Skye getting pregnant despite the condoms, maybe there was a higher power at work, pulling the strings. What if this was his big chance to completely change direction in his life? To start fresh. He wanted to rediscover his roots, who he was away from the guitar and microphone, and fatherhood definitely would show him that.

His life spooled out before him in straight, measured

lines of love and commitment—and healing for them both. If she'd let him into her life again.

She doesn't really have a choice. Neither of them did. Even if she couldn't love him, they were still bonded forever, for better or worse, through their child. Even if she wouldn't have him as a partner, he was going to take care of her and their child from there on out.

He eyed the real-estate office across the street. If he was going to prove to Skye that he was the settling down kind, then he was going to need to buy a house, preferably one with a stable. He'd seen the way riding had made Skye come alive. For the rest of his days, he'd be haunted by the dull pain he'd seen in her eyes when they'd argued at the hospital. He couldn't stand it, knowing that she was hurting so bad, knowing that he had a lot to do with it. He could truck all his horses down to Texas and gift them to her, if she wanted. He could give her whatever it took for her to put away her fears and come alive again.

A new house, a new truck, new clothes. Hell, he might even order some custom, left-handed guitars like the kind Jimmy Hendrix used to play. It was time for this Oklahoma boy to build himself a new homestead for his brand-new family.

"I appreciate your concern, but I've got this. You're free to go. I'll be in touch." *Or not.*

"I can't pick you up at the hospital and then just leave you on the side of the road out in the middle of nowhere. You're giving me heartburn."

"Well, gosh, Larry. I'm sorry that me making my own decisions is so tough on you," Gentry deadpanned.

Larry popped an antacid and gave a solemn nod. "Thank you. I appreciate that."

Gentry gave a tip of his cap. "See y'all later." And he turned toward Our Lady of Guadalupe's office. He didn't bother fighting the grin that spread on his lips. Crazy as it might be to be bursting with joy when he'd just hit rock bottom, but he couldn't help it. For the first time in a long time, he was a free man.

The office that Gentry was shown in to by the church secretary was crowded with books and as dusty-smelling as a library. The priest sat behind a large cherry-stained wood desk. A name placard read FATHER ELLWOOD.

He was a kindly looking older man. Pale, with wisps of white hair crossing his shiny bald head like rivers of ice. He had a welcoming smile and a firm handshake.

"So, Mr. Wells, my secretary told me that you want to be Catholic."

Frankly, Gentry had never give one single moment of thought to the idea before that day. But the Father might as well have been asking him if he wanted to be the best possible father for his child. And there was only one answer to that question. "Yes, sir. I do."

"I can tell, by the conviction in your voice. And it's a good thing, because there's only one true reason to take this journey. It has to come from the heart. It's my job to make sure you understand all that it entails. It's no small choice. And I'm not trying to scare you away. I wouldn't be very good at my job if I did." He paused to chuckle at his own joke. "But it's important for you to understand the magnitude of this decision. Let me assure you that this will be the most rewarding choice of your life, if you commit to it."

Again, Gentry heard the words, but thought about fatherhood, rather than faith. *The most rewarding choice of your life, if you commit to it.*

Yes, his mind boomed. *Yes,* his heart seconded. "I'm ready."

"What happened to your hand, son?"

Gentry held up his left hand, gnarled with dark stitches, scars, and fading bruises. "I was in a motorcycle accident last week. I lost a finger."

"Ah. Nothing gets a man thinking about eternity like seeing his life flash before his eyes. You're lucky to have escaped with only a finger lost."

"Yes, sir. I know it."

"But why our church?" the Father asked. "I don't recall seeing you at mass."

Gentry had attended Catholic mass a few times throughout his life, mostly for weddings, and not in many years. "I'm new to town, sir. Father. I haven't always lived an upstanding life that I could be proud of, and, honestly, I never thought of myself as a man capable of such a life. Of settling down and starting a family and living a quiet, normal life. But I'm having a baby with a woman here in town who's Catholic. Her faith is important to her family, which means it's important to me. I want us to be a family in every sense of the word, including how we practice our faith." He felt the power of his conviction in every cell of his being.

"That's wise of you."

"Yes, sir, Father. I'm trying my best. She and I, we're both divorced, but we're trying our best to change our lives." The priest's eyes went a little distant, as though he was calculating the total of their combined sins. Divorced, pregnant out of wedlock. What a pair they made.

The Father templed his hands and tapped his fingers together, considering. "I'm going to go out on a limb right now and guess that you've gotten Skye Martinez in a family way. I'm surprised you're alive to sit in my office today. Mrs. Martinez must be feeling merciful."

He'd sure put two and two together mighty quick. "How did you . . ."

Father Ellwood tapped his forehead.

Of course, he knew. Word about the motorcycle accident was probably all over town. "Her mom doesn't know yet about the baby. And, please, I'm begging you not to—"

"Relax, son. Keeping secrets is part of my job description. Besides, I like you. I don't want to see you get killed." He wagged a finger. "And Skye, neither. If the two of you are waiting for the perfect time to tell her family, then your child will be grown and married while you wait."

In other words, there would never be the right time. Gentry agreed, but he wasn't very well going to tell Father Ellwood that first he had to wait for Skye to admit as much to Gentry. "Point taken, sir. Now, about converting. I remember hearing something about a class I have to take."

"Yes. Back to business. The class, the Rite of Christian Initiation of Adults—or RCIA, as we call it—is only a part of the process that includes attending mass regularly and reading the Bible, among many other things. That way, you can experience each of our celebrations and holy days. By then, you'll have a much better understanding of what you're committing yourself to."

Sounded complicated. "How long does that take? Because we're in a bit of a time crunch with the baby on its way."

Father Ellwood's smile was benevolent. "A year. You'll be Catholic by next Easter. The perfect time to join our church."

Too long. That was way too long for what he needed to offer Skye so she would trust him with her heart. More than anything, as the man responsible for getting her pregnant, he wanted to be able to offer her marriage, if she wanted it—so she could give birth as a married woman, so she could reclaim the dignity in her community that he'd done his part to yank away from her.

"There isn't a fast track? I was hoping Skye and I could get married before the baby's born," Gentry asked.

The question evoked a chuckle from Father Ellwood. "Oh, there's a fast track to God, all right, and it seems that you avoided it by surviving that crash. My best advice to you is that you worry about your own salvation and the rest will fall into place."

Wise words. But the way Gentry saw it, he'd already spent far too much of his life only worrying about himself. That was partly to blame for how he'd gotten into this trouble. "Yes, sir. I hear what you're saying."

"That's good. One more question, and I'm not sure how to put this delicately," Father said. "But has Skye actually agreed to marry you? Or were you hoping that becoming a Catholic would persuade her? Because, let me tell you, as I've told many young men who've sat in that very chair, becoming Catholic to woo a woman is a faulty plan."

That old familiar insecurity came knocking at the door. That unshakeable awareness that he was nothing but an imposter, not worthy of Skye, not worthy of being a Catholic. Not worthy of being a father. He just couldn't stop screwing up, and there was no cure for it. He looked down at his left hand, where his middle finger used to be. He'd lost everything in that crash—his career, his identity, Skye's trust.

And then, out of nowhere, a wave of relief crashed through him.

His career was over, which meant he didn't have to pretend to be someone he wasn't anymore. He never had to be that hip-swiveling, beer-drinking showman again.

He didn't have to posture. He didn't have to bow to the almighty Neil Blevins' wishes. He didn't have to please the voracious fans who were never satisfied and didn't care about the real him. Gentry Wells, the Bad Boy of Country, was gone.

Hallelujah.

The best part was, he knew exactly who he wanted to be now that the pressure was off. He still had music running through his veins, but that didn't mean he had to take his songs on the road or wrap his music and himself up in a tidy package to sell to the masses. He had enough money and time to do whatever he wanted. And what he wanted was Skye. To be a family with her and their baby and to be the very best father he could.

The same ambition that had propelled him into church this morning consumed him once again. Dulcet, Texas, was going to be his new home. Our Lady of Guadalupe was his new church. And no matter what happened romantically between him and Skye, the vibrant, fierce-loving Martinez clan was going to be his new family because they would be his child's family.

Instead of pushing Skye to tell him about the baby before she was ready, he vowed to earn her trust until she felt brave and safe enough to tell him herself.

He would figure out how to play left-handed and he'd write whatever damn songs he wanted, without care if they'd get a lot of air time on the radio. He'd had a good run in the spotlight, and now it was done. But this wasn't rock bottom. Not even close. He still had his life and his health. He hadn't seriously injured Skye, and their baby was all right. He'd invested soundly and had a lot of money at his disposal, especially once he sold his ranch.

He would be at Skye's doctor appointments. He would see that little baby's heartbeat on the ultrasound monitor.

It was time for the rise of Gentry Wells, the settling-down kind, the marrying-his-sweetheart-and-raising-a-family kind. He was going to be a father, and he was going to be a damn good one, at that. And, with any luck, he'd turn himself into a damn fine husband too.

Gentry stood and set his hat on his head, then tipped the brim. "Thank you, Father, for helping see it all laid out so clearly and getting to the heart of the matter. I'll see you on Sunday at mass."

"Good man. I'll see you this Sunday. Until then, good luck and God bless you."

He was going to need all the blessings and luck he could get, because his entire plan hinged over convincing Skye of all of that.

He swallowed hard.

No problem.

Chapter Seventeen

For the first week after getting discharged from the hospital, Skye didn't have the stamina to work. Her legs were on fire, her wrist ached, and first trimester nausea was starting to set in, making her long to get back to Briscoe Ranch and all the many distractions it provided. But as it was, she had way too much time on her hands to stew about her reckless choices and the damn curse she'd allowed her mother to cast, the curse that somehow hadn't been nullified by her pregnancy.

It didn't help that her mom was watching her like a protective mother hawk who didn't trust her daughter one whit. All her life, Skye had watched her mom focus her nervous, caretaker energy on Skye's dad. She'd always felt sorry for him, being relentlessly fussed over and treated like he was helpless. But now that it was happening to Skye, she had a whole new appreciation for her dad's patience and kindness. There was an edge to her mother's caring, an unspoken "I told you so" vibe swirled in with her fierce love. But now her mother was the only manager at Polished Pros, doing double duty to cover for Skye, so it was pretty unfair for Skye to get annoyed with her.

The only way Skye had been able to contribute was getting Gloria's kids ready for school and onto the bus, since Gloria reported in at the army base before dawn each day.

The trouble was, Skye's injuries had put a real damper on her ability to do anything with speed, and by the time she'd fixed Teresa and Chris eggs and pancakes, then helped them get dressed, pack their lunches, and tie their shoes, they'd been late for the bus every single day that week. Today, they burst out of the house with only a couple minutes until the school bus was due down on the corner. She walked with stiff, pained steps behind them, wincing but managing. Her dad was already outside, waving to them from his driveway. Very little in life was worth the pain her dad experienced while walking any kind of distance, even to the end of the block, but he insisted on walking the kids to the bus stop each morning.

The kids skipped across the street and swarmed around him, giving excited hugs and squealing, "Grandpa!"

Skye shuffled across the street to join them. "Hey, Dad. How's the back today?"

"I have no complaints. Come on, kids. We don't want to make the bus wait. Again."

As quick as they'd bounded to her dad, the kids were off again along the sidewalk, skipping and trotting like a couple effervescent bundles of energy.

Skye's dad fell into step next to her and they trailed the kids at an increasing distance. They might have qualified as contenders in the sport of synchronized limping except that their stiff gaits weren't quite in unison. Unlike the grimaces on their faces, which Skye imagined were remarkably similar.

"What a pair we are," he joked on a wheezy chuckle.

That they were, but even still, they got those kids on the bus in time, with full bellies and finished homework, then shuffled back to their respective houses. Skye gave her dad a hug before crossing the street. "Thanks for your help."

"Wish I could do more. You know that. I hate to see you hurt."

Skye tried not to think about the baby growing inside her. She should tell her dad. Hell, she should tell her mom. Every time she tried, an overwhelming fear gripped her, though she wasn't sure why. The argument that she was going to hurt them with the revelation that their screw-up daughter had gotten pregnant out of wedlock and had nearly lost the baby by jumping recklessly onto the back of the motorcycle of some fly-by-night playboy was only a convenient excuse, seeing as how this wasn't a secret she could take to her grave. But she just couldn't shake the impending sense of doom that rendered her paralyzed. It was getting damned frustrating.

After getting the kids on the bus, she returned to her house and looked at the empty space, groaning at the idea of another day on the sofa watching daytime television shows while her body healed. Screw that. It was time to go back to work, even if all she did was show up, sit at her desk, and answer emails for a few hours.

By the time she pulled into the employee lot, she was feeling optimistic about the choice to work. Her body was warmed up now and feeling slightly better, and her mind was relieved to have something to do.

Emily Ford-Briscoe pulled in right after her and parked a few cars down. Emily was a long-time chef at the resort who'd recently married into the Briscoe family. She and Skye didn't travel in the same circles often, but Skye considered her a friend. She'd watched Emily's ambition and skill soar over the years and, along with the rest of the senior staff, had celebrated the opening of Subterranean, her signature restaurant at the resort, earlier that year.

Emily beat Skye out of her car and jogged around to Skye's open door. "Hey, heard about the accident. How are you?"

Skye gingerly unfolded one leg out of the car and then the other. She was bound to be asked that question a lot that day, and so she decided to channel her dad. "I have no complaints." Because if a man who was in as much chronic pain as he was didn't feel the need to complain, then neither did she.

"Glad to hear it. I'm headed to the main building. Can I give you a lift in a golf cart?"

Skye grabbed her purse and locked her car up. "That would be great."

The Briscoes staged golf carts at various points around the sprawling resort grounds for employee use, which was a true blessing today of all days. Skye squelched a wince as she hoisted her legs into the cart on the passenger side.

"You know, I'm sure you could have taken a few more days off," Emily said. "Rumor has it, your boss has a soft spot for you."

Obviously, Skye hadn't done a very convincing job of hiding her body's discomfort. "I'm not so sure I'd describe my mom as having a soft spot, but you're right. I could have taken more time if I'd wanted. I was going nuts sitting at home."

The wind in her hair felt great, even though it made

her long skirt whip around her legs. Her scraped-up skin smarted every time the fabric snapped against her, but the flowing skirt had been her only clothing option that week. The thought of wedging her beat-up legs into a pair of pants made her shudder.

"I know exactly what you mean," Emily said. "There were a few weeks while Subterranean was in the early planning stages that I didn't have anything to do, and I went totally stir crazy. My poor husband finally had to break it to me that the multi-course meals I was fixing him for breakfast, lunch, and dinner were starting to interfere with his productivity at work."

"Not to mention his waistline, I imagine."

They'd passed the stables and were winding their way around the golf course when the air sounded with a horn honking *La Cucaracha*. Granny June's riding scooter rolled to a stop in the path, blocking Emily and Skye's golf cart. Skye let out an exasperated breath, but Emily smiled and waved.

"Are you and Granny June having issues?" Emily asked as she slowed the golf cart.

"No, I love her, don't get me wrong. But she's a matchmaking fool."

"More like genius," Emily said. "She knew Knox and I were perfect for each other before we even did. I give her a lot of credit for the two of us getting together."

"Maybe she's lost her touch."

Emily's smile turned smug. "Or maybe you're in denial that she's right, like I was for a while?"

Skye shot her an *oh please* look, then turned her attention to Granny June, who was waving her cane at them. "Hey, Granny June. Good to see you." *Not.*

"I had to see for myself that you were all right after the accident," Granny June said, walking around to the passenger side of the cart. "And look at you, already back to work. It's a miracle."

Maybe Skye's judgment had been too hasty. "Thanks. I'm feeling all right. No complaints."

Granny June patted her arm. "That's good. That's good. Means we can get back to talking about you and Eddie Rivera."

Or not. It was all Skye could do not to groan. "It's over between us, Granny. He's a great guy, but my heart wasn't in it."

"He's a doctor, you know. He works at the very hospital you recuperated in. Tell me, did he come to visit you?"

"Yes, but—"

Granny June threw her arms up. "Then you've got to give the man a chance."

Enough was enough. "I blew off my date with Eddie to spend the weekend with another man, and Eddie found out precisely because he works at that hospital."

"Dang. Harsh," Emily muttered.

Skye nodded at her. "Exactly. It was harsh and embarrassing. And, anyway, it wouldn't have mattered if he'd found out or not because I've given up men for Lent."

"I don't believe that for a minute," Granny June said, crossing her arms over her chest with a scowl.

Skye tried on her most pious smile. "It's true." *Sort of. Maybe this year she'd actually keep a Lenten promise for once.* "Look, I've got to get to work, but thanks for checking in with me, Granny June."

Back on their drive to the main building, Skye spotted a large white special event tent near the chapel.

"Hey, Emily, I hate to do this to you, but could you let me off here? I'm going to pop in and see Remedy before I head to the office." Skye hadn't felt much like company in the hospital and then afterward, at home, she had not wanted to keep the truth about the baby from Remedy, but she did not know how to tell her—or anybody, really. Today, it felt right to check in with her friend and apologize for being such a hermit.

"No problem," Emily said, turning down the path that led to the tent.

They found Remedy in front of the tent, talking to a group of scantily clad Tahitian fire dancers. Their ripped, bare chests were oiled and ornamented with leis, the real deal with white and pink plumeria, not the bargain-store plastic flower variety.

When Remedy spotted her, she threw her arms open wide. "You're back at work!"

Skye thanked Emily for the ride, then walked with careful steps to Remedy's waiting arms, where she melted into a hug. "Sort of. Thanks for understanding about me not being up for visitors in the hospital."

"I get it, and I knew you had lots of people there taking care of you."

"Almost too many."

Remedy stepped back and gave Skye a studying once-over. "You're okay? Your leg, your wrist? I've been worried sick."

More than anything, Skye was determined to be okay—more than okay—even if her life seemed to be spiraling out of control. It was that determination that brought an easy smile to her lips. "Yes. I'm banged up, but I know how lucky I am that I wasn't hurt worse. I can't complain."

Remedy chewed her lower lip for a breath, then braced her hands on Skye's shoulders. The look in her eyes was intense and searching at the same time. "I know you, which is why I know I need to say this. You didn't do anything wrong. The crash was not your fault."

Shit. Skye *really* didn't want to go there. Because it

was her fault. She made her own choices—and they'd been terrible choices. But dwelling wasn't going to fix any of the problems she'd created, the pregnancy included. "Doesn't matter. What's done is done. All I can do is move on and try to change."

Remedy's thumbs started a slow massage of her shoulder. "No change necessary. Listen to me. We're all entitled to some fun sometimes. That's not why the accident happened."

If that was true, then why did it sometimes feel like a sense of impending doom was eating her alive?

They were interrupted by one of the dancers. He smiled suggestively at Skye and held out his dinner-plate sized hand for her to shake. "Excuse me, Remedy, but I couldn't take my eyes off your friend here, so I figured I'd come introduce myself. We haven't met yet. I'm Julio."

Unbelievable. Her face was visibly bruised and scraped, and she was wearing a cast on her arm. And certainly he'd noticed her limp, hadn't he? Then again, maybe not. Damn spell. As annoying as Skye's love life had become, she had to give her mom begrudging respect. Who would've guessed her mom was that powerful in the old ways?

"Aw, geez. Give it a rest, Julio," Remedy muttered.

Julio's gaze never wavered from his perusal of Skye's body. "When I see such a beautiful woman, rest is the last thing on my mind."

"Down boy!" Remedy gave his bare shoulder a push toward the rest of the dancers, who were all watching Julio's pathetic pick-up attempt and chuckling to themselves. "Don't you need to go light your torches or"—she grimaced at her palms—"oil yourself down again before show time?"

Only with great reluctance, and great prodding by

Remedy, did Julio leave them alone. As soon as Julio was out of earshot, Remedy wiped her hands on her dress. "You've got to get your mom to reverse that love potion."

"I wish, because I am so over men."

Remedy snorted. "I'll bet. But speaking of which, have you seen him yet? Are you okay with him being here or does that make it harder? I need details, woman! We haven't talked in way too long."

"Who? Eddie?" Because that had sucked. It'd sucked hard. And if he was at the resort today for whatever reason, she'd do her best to avoid him. "No, he and I never even made it to a first date."

And it wouldn't have mattered anyway, because she was pregnant. The truth would have outed itself soon enough and then they would have been over. And the stupid love spell wouldn't have mattered because nothing said *classy* like dating around while she was pregnant with another man's child—whom she couldn't bring herself to tell yet. That kind of soap opera drama only happened in Mama Lita's telanovelas.

Remedy cringed and wrung her hands together. "Not Eddie. Gentry Wells."

The sound of his name did weird things to her insides, even after all they'd been through. "He's not here. In the hospital, I told him I needed some space. I'm sure he's back home in Tulsa."

"You mean, your mom didn't tell you? Or any of your family? Oh, honey. Oh, my God." Remedy smacked her forehead.

"What are you talking about? Tell me what?"

"Apparently, Gentry didn't listen to you because he's been staying at the resort all week. He rented out the same villa he was in before, this time for two months."

"He *what*?" It didn't make sense. She'd told him to leave. How dare he disrespect her wishes like that?

Remedy shook her head. "I can't believe nobody told you. *I* would have told you, but I figured you already knew."

"I most certainly did not. And please don't feel bad. It's not your fault that I didn't know." But Skye knew exactly whose fault it was, which meant she couldn't decide who to yell at first. She could march—or limp, rather—to her mom to ream her out or go pounding on Gentry's door demanding answers.

Her mom.

Definitely.

The longer she could put off another confrontation with Gentry, the better. What was he even doing in Dulcet? Not just in Dulcet, but at her place of business? For two months? She'd been crystal clear that she needed space. She didn't need another person looking out for her. She didn't need another goddamn man inserting himself in her business. Above all, she had zero need for a swaggering, bad boy musician with a chip on his shoulder and a restless heart. She didn't need Gentry Wells.

Actually, you do. This baby needs its father.

"Shut up," she grumbled. At Remedy's wide eyes, she added, "Not you. My conscience. It has an agenda that doesn't line up with mine at the moment."

"Been there, done that. Hang in there."

With that, Skye took off to find an unused golf cart.

"Hey," Remedy called after her. "Don't go wearing yourself out by pitching a big fit. There'll be time for that later, after you heal. Right now, you need rest. Plus that limp doesn't make you very ferocious."

True, that. But she was too fired up to sit on the information.

She was passing between the villas and the swimming pool when she spotted Annika in her golf cart. She waved, but that seemed to send Annika into a panic spiral. Her golf cart surged forward, blocking the gate to the villas. "Oh. You're back," she said, trying to sound casual even though she was suddenly, mysteriously out of breath.

The villas hadn't been where Skye was headed—not until after she reamed out her mom, anyway—but Annika's attempt to keep Skye out of the villas and away from Gentry was like lemon juice in a cut. "I'm back," she said through her teeth. "And Gentry's staying here in the villas."

Annika had the stones to act surprised. "He is?"

Skye's fight wasn't with Annika, or any Polished Pro employee. They'd merely been doing what the company owner had required of them. Skye had never come so close to thinking of her mom as a bitch, but it had a certain ring to it today. "What kind of boss tells her employees to lie?"

Annika's eyes widened.

Skye hadn't meant to say that last part out loud. "Forget that. Out of my way please."

Looking pale and nervous, Annika raised her radio to her lips. "Yessica, you told me to call you if Skye came around the villas."

Gentry sat on the front patio of his villa and stared out at the lake nestled among bluebonnet-carpeted hills that stretched out before him like a storybook come to life. A fat brown duck and four yellow ducklings paddled along the shoreline, and a slight breeze rustled the reeds and cattails. Spring looked good on the landscape of Texas' Hill Country. A man could get used to this.

Only the day before, a full three weeks after the

accident, he'd gotten a voicemail from Neil. The message was a huge *fuck you* all wrapped up in a guise of sympathy and support. *I'm a fair man,* he'd said, *So I'll tell you what. I'll extend it another month because of your injuries. Good luck. I can't wait to see what Gentry Wells, singer-songwriter, comes up with.* Then he laughed. He fucking laughed.

At that sound, Gentry's self-pity crumbled. He'd already decided he was going to teach himself to play left-handed, but he'd written off his music career, at least with Neil's label. But when he heard that laugh, all he could think was *challenge accepted.*

He was not only going to relearn how to play the guitar with his opposite hand, and with the help of his physical therapist, but he was going to write and deliver a polished album to Neil well in advance of this new deadline. He had more than enough material, having single-handedly set fire to his life and with a baby on the way.

Hence, why Gentry had a pick in his left hand and a brand new customized, left-handed guitar resting on his thigh. On the small glass table beside him sat a notebook full of the song lyrics that Skye had inspired before the accident. The only trouble was, he wasn't a bullshitting, fake-ass party boy anymore. He felt like he'd aged a decade in the past two weeks. And all the songs he'd written before seemed irresponsible and immature now, the blueprint of a crash and burn. A blueprint for disaster.

He set down the guitar and pick and opened the new spiral notebook he'd picked up at the grocery store, pressing his pen to the top line of the first page. In slow, meticulous printing he wrote, *A Blueprint for Disaster.*

He frowned down at the words. So depressing—and so very wrong. Because this wasn't a disaster. More important, that wasn't the attitude he wanted to welcome his child into the world with. He was alive, and Skye was alive and unharmed, as was the child she carried. He still had all the resources of his successful career—the manager, the world-class producer, the money, and fans. What the fuck did he have to complain about? His new songs should be a celebration.

He flipped back a few pages in his notebook and reread the first draft scribbles of "Make Me Your Mardi Gras." He thought about the way Skye looked that first night on the horse and then on his bike, the freedom he saw in the wild whipping of her hair in the wind, her outstretched arms. He conjured a memory of the fire in her eyes that night together in the stable as she crowded against him for that first kiss.

What he and Skye had shared wasn't a disaster. It was perfection. *She* was perfection. Beauty in its best and purest form. She was the only woman who'd made him yearn for more in his life, who awakened a hunger in him for adventure and truth, and who pulled him up out of his inner darkness with her own blinding light. She'd stirred his creative energy up and turned his imagination electric.

The woman I never knew I needed, he wrote in the notepad. His throat tightened. *The baby I never knew I wanted.*

The woman. The baby. The life he never knew was waiting for him down a windy back country road in the Texas hills.

He wrote the word *Oasis*. Then he circled it. That was Skye, his paradise in the middle of the desert that his life—his heart, his very soul—had become. Sometime soon, tonight perhaps, he would seek her out. Although he was determined to let her tell him about the baby herself when she was ready, he would let her know his intentions and that she wasn't alone.

The peace of the lake was broken by the sound of women's voices shouting as though in argument. Gentry felt a duty to make sure all was well. Standing, he pocketed his pick, set the guitar just inside the front door, and went to see what the fuss was about.

The argument was happening on the far side of the villas' gate among three women—and one of them was Skye. His heart gave a painful pulse. She looked tired, and her arm was in a cast, but she was full of life. He had to hope that her presence at the resort meant that the road rash on her legs was healing. The fire in her eyes was back and directed at her mother. The two of them were shouting at each other in rapid Spanish while a young maid looked on, squirming anxiously.

When Mrs. Martinez noticed him, she stomped up, getting right in his face. "Don't you stand there and look at my daughter like she's fresh bait. You don't belong here. You've done enough harm."

"Yes, ma'am, I know."

"You're nothing but a user. A womanizer."

Skye put herself between Gentry and her mom. "Mom! Leave us."

"I'm not leaving without you. Do you think it's been easy, watching you get hurt by all these men? Do you think it's been easy to watch you dream and pray about love and starting a family of your own year after year? It breaks my heart, mija. I've worked too hard for this family for too long to allow my daughter to throw away her future for some flashy snake-oil salesman."

"Mom, you're not helping. I'm going to handle this, but you and Annika need to let me by giving us some privacy."

Mrs. Martinez looked like she wanted to argue that point, but after opening and closing her mouth a couple times, she nodded. "Fine. Don't let me hold you back."

With her back to Gentry, Skye watched her mom walk away, then she spun around and stormed past Gentry and through the villas' gate. "We can talk in your villa," she snapped, not waiting for his reply.

He probably should have been nervous about their impending conversation, but he couldn't get over how strong and healthy she looked, her tentatively taken steps notwithstanding. "Last time I saw you, you were in a wheelchair," he said when they'd reached his villa. "Your legs, they're healing okay?"

Skye whirled to face Gentry, her eyes even angrier than they had been when she'd been arguing with her mom. "You didn't listen to me. I told you I needed space, but here you are. Go back to Oklahoma where you belong."

"And if I told you I belonged right here in Dulcet?" It was all he could do not to look at her belly.

She flapped her arms with a huff, totally out of steam. "You can't just barge into the place I work and the town I live in and make yourself at home."

"See, that's the thing, Skye. I feel like I am home. I've felt that way since that first night in the stable with you." And he meant every word. He could feel the truth in that statement all the way to his bones. This was his new home. Nothing had ever felt so right. "I'm not trying to upset you or do you harm. I just . . ." How could he break down her defenses without letting on that he knew about the baby?

But something she said was rattling around in his mind, about him barging into her place of business. She'd told him before that her involvement with him while he was a guest at the resort had been in violation of her company's contract with Briscoe Ranch. He could have put her out of business. If he was trying to turn himself into a man who was good for her, then making her lose her job sure wouldn't help.

"I don't want to cause you trouble with your work. I really don't. I hired a realtor yesterday. I'm planning to buy a house nearby, but that takes time. Do you want me to relocate in the meantime?"

"You can't do that," she said breathlessly.

"Relocate?"

She shook her head. "Buy a house in Dulcet."

"There's nothing for me in Oklahoma. My ranch, it never felt like home after my ex-wife—"

"You're divorced?" She spit the words like the sin it was.

How little they knew about each other. He'd gotten to the point in his fame that he assumed the people around him knew his history. His divorce had made the front page of a lot of tabloids.

He motioned to the table and chairs on the patio in front of his villa. "Let's sit. I'll tell you anything you want to know."

To his relief, she accepted the invitation, eyeing his guitar as she sat.

He settled into the seat across from her. "I'm learning to play left-handed. And I'm going to finish that album."

She blinked, looking stunned. "I guess I've been so wrapped up in myself since the crash that I didn't really think about your hand and your music."

"Yeah, it sucks. But I'm grateful for this second chance, grateful to not be hurt any worse and that you're not hurt too badly. About my divorce . . . Look, Skye, I wasn't trying to hide from you the fact that I was divorced. Hell, all you would've needed to do was a Google search to get all the dirt on my past. I was married, for five years in my twenties, to an actress. We weren't right for each other and we knew it, but we stayed together for the sake of our careers. Which, looking back on it, was soul crushing."

When he thought about all the many ways he'd contorted himself and his life for the sake of his career, it made him sick to his stomach. All those wasted years trying to be someone he wasn't. The more he embraced his future with Skye and their baby, the less of a deadbeat, commitment-phobic wanderer he felt like. What if his failure in all his past relationships wasn't because he wasn't the staying kind, but because he wasn't being true to himself? It was as though the drive to be a successful musician had poisoned every aspect of his life.

Then he found it, the perfect way to inch him and Skye closer to the truth that was churning between them. "At least we didn't bring kids into that disaster of a relationship." He paused, choosing his next words carefully. "I never thought I wanted to be a father, but that accident brought me right up against my mortality. I saw my future flash before my eyes and now I know I got it wrong before, about living fast and loose and commitment-free. That isn't me anymore. I want be the kind of man my family and my children can count on, the staying kind."

Skye looked at him. Her lips parted. She wanted to tell him. He could feel it. But as quickly as that desire pulsed through her, it was replaced by fear. He reached across the table and took her hands.

"It's all right, baby. I'm gonna prove it to you. I'm gonna prove that you can trust me to stay. You can take that to the bank."

She pulled away from his touch and stood. "Stop it. Please. I can't . . ." She covered her eyes and forehead with her hand, and he had the sneaking suspicion it was to hide the tears that were gathering in her eyes. "The accident brought up a lot of shit for me and I'm trying. But I can't yet—with you, with this thing between us. I need space."

This thing between us. She might have meant the baby, but Gentry knew it was more. Today he finally understood that the ties that bound them went beyond having a baby together.

"Take all the time you need. I'll leave a light on. And my phone on too. Anything you need, anytime, you just give me a call."

She nodded, but he could tell that her mind was already far away. Without a word, she left back down the path. He watched the swish of her long skirt as she walked and sent up a thanks to God that only three weeks after watching her tumble over a cliff, she was upright and safe and so, so strong. And then he was alone, just him and his new guitar and a cluster of ducks in the lake.

He grabbed his guitar, then fished the pick out of his pocket. It slipped through the gap in the fingers of his left hand. He stared at the purple plastic triangle on the concrete between his boots. Yeah, he had a lot of work to do if he was going to learn to play again. Which he most certainly was. To hold himself accountable to that goal, he found his phone in his pocket and dialed Neil's number. It went to voicemail, as expected.

"You're trying to play a game a chicken with me, so all right. Game on. I'm gonna take that extension you're offering, and I'm going to deliver the best album of my life."

And in the meantime, if he had any prayer on following through with that declaration, he needed to get the rust off his work ethic and get back in musician mode.

Which meant he needed to write some more songs. And book some gigs to test out those new songs. Compared to the daunting task of winning over Skye and her family, rebuilding his career from the ground up would be easy as pie.

Chapter Eighteen

Skye didn't miss a day of work for the rest of the week. It was such a relief to be out of the house, her mind on her job instead of her aching wrist and the road rash on her legs that was itching like crazy. Her mom's perpetually grouchy disposition didn't even faze her.

On Friday, she was driving a golf cart to the chapel to give it a final clean before that night's wedding, her mind a million miles away, when Mama Lita stepped in front of her on the path, her legs out and a hand up in an international sign to stop, as if Skye had any choice, given that Mama Lita was blocking her passage. As it was, she had to slam on the brakes.

"Hey, Mama Lita! What are you doing here?"

As though the question offended her, Mama Lita gave a terse shrug. "What kind of question is that? This is practically our home. Walk with me. We need to talk."

Every now and then, Skye rebelled against Mama Lita's commands, but she usually lived to regret it. Since she wasn't looking forward to cleaning the chapel, she couldn't see any harm in finding out what was on Mama

Lita's mind. She negotiated the golf cart onto the close-cropped lawn and hopped out.

She fell into step with her grandmother's brisk pace toward the Winter Wonderland Garden. "What did you want to talk to me about?"

Mama Lita captured the cigarette between two fingers and brought it down to her side as though it was actually lit. "I want to commend you."

"For what?"

"For having this baby on your own, not using a man as a crutch. Good for you."

Skye stumbled over a crack in the concrete. *Having this baby?* Did that mean she knew? Impossible. "How did you know that I'm . . . I'm . . ." She couldn't get the words out. Not yet.

She winked. "You think that anally-retentive mother of yours is the only one with a few magic tricks up her sleeve?"

Skye grabbed Mama Lita's sleeve. "You won't tell her, or anyone, will you? I'm not ready."

She lifted the cigarette to her mouth again and placed it in the corner of her lips. "Of course, I won't. This is your life. It's past time for you to take charge of it."

Good. Okay. Crisis averted. Magic tricks. Now they were talking. "Then let me ask you a question, since you brought up magic. Do you know how to reverse the love spell my mom put on me?"

Mama Lita leaned in close. She smelled of burnt sage and Chanel No. 5. "I do."

An intense wave of relief rippled through Skye. "Then help me. Please. If I never get romanced by another man, it'll be too soon."

"That's the spirit! Gentry's a good man, better than most, but you're right not to let him woo you. Remember that it's a trap that no woman needs. Just imagine what Frida could have become if she hadn't had that dead weight of a man holding her back. He killed her, you know."

Frida was Frida Kahlo, the flamboyant Mexican painter and feminist icon, whom Mama Lita talked about as though she were an old friend from childhood. True, they'd grown up in the same neighborhood, but a solid thirty years apart in age. By the time Mama Lita had been born, Frida Kahlo was already living in the States, which was a fact that nobody dared mention. Nor the fact that Diego Rivera had nothing to do with her death. "You don't think the accident had anything to do with that?"

Mama Lita waved off the suggestion. "Bah. It was that man. It's always the man." She wrapped a hand around Skye's cast and gave it a shake that made Skye wince. "Look at how you were almost killed. Do you blame the moving van or the man?"

For some reason, Skye had never really internalized how vehemently Mama Lita felt about men. "The moving van."

But Mama Lita wasn't having it. "You show me a happily married man and I'll show you a woman in chains. Singledom is the key to living a long, happy life."

Remedy wasn't in chains. Gloria hadn't been in chains with Ruben. "My mom's married to your son, and she's not in chains." But as soon as she said it, she knew it wasn't true. Her mom was in all kinds of chains, but not because of Skye's dad. They were chains of her own making. Skye's heart sank. Was that really any different from the chains Skye had imposed on herself?

As soon as she thought it, she scrubbed the notion from her brain. Nope. She was not turning into her mother. No how, no way.

"Ha!" Mama Lita said. "You really are brainwashed."

"I'm not. I'm really not. So help me out, if you're so good with magic. Let's get rid of all these men."

Mama Lita skidded to a stop and squinted one eye. "You want to know the secret to ending the spell?"

Skye's breath caught in her lungs. "Please. My mom says I have to fall in love for the spell to end, but I can't. I won't."

Mama Lita snorted her disgust. "Your mother and June Briscoe are two of a kind. Here is the truth: stop listening to those windbags. While you're at it, stop valuing anyone else's opinions above your own. Go out. Have fun. Live your life."

"That's the worst advice ever. How do you think I got in this mess?"

Mama Lita looked her up and down, then shuffled behind her, getting a 360-degree view. "What mess? I don't see any mess."

"Mama Lita, please stop being obtuse. My life is nothing but one big hot mess right now. I'm all banged up, my wrist is hurt—" *And I'm pregnant.* Though she couldn't yet say the words, she set a hand on her belly. "If I'm supposed to ignore the opinions of others, then I guess I'll ignore yours too. Which is too bad because I thought you said you had some magic tricks up your sleeves that would help me."

"I do have magic, child. Same as you do. You don't need any spells. It's all in your heart. Stop pretending that the spell works and it will go away. Be happy with your life, just as it is, and believe in yourself."

Believe in herself? Was Mama Lita kidding with that shit? "You're the last person I expected to start spouting lessons like an afterschool special on TV."

"Maybe so, but there it is."

The sound of her radio made Skye jump. "Skye? Have you written next week's schedule yet? I can't find it on your desk," her mom said, tone sharp.

Mama Lita muttered a string of curse words under her breathe and shook her head. "That woman, your mother, needs to take that stick out of her ass. I've been asking my son to do that for her for years."

With a warning look at Mama Lita, Skye lifted the radio to her lips. "I haven't started it, but I'm on my way back to the office. I'll have it to you by the end of the day."

Her mom's silence said enough. She could practically feel her mom's eye roll through the air between them. Guilt settled like a rock in Skye's gut. Screw Mama Lita's advice, Skye would be better off doing the opposite—going to bed early after praying for forgiveness for her sins.

"Enough," Mama Lita said, as if reading her mind. "I have to go. June and I are scheduled for a cutthroat game of Bingo tonight, so I'll see you later. Remember, go have some fun."

Cutthroat Bingo? Skye wasn't sure she wanted to know. She gave Mama Lita a kiss on the cheek and bid her good-bye.

As if it'd been a coordinated attack on Skye's plans, the moment Mama Lita was gone, her phone chimed with an incoming text from Remedy. *Micah and I are going for burgers tonight at Hog Heaven. Wanna come?*

Hog Heaven. The site of so many fun nights. A bar and barbecue joint twenty minutes down the highway from Dulcet. It was the first place she'd tested out her fake ID when she was nineteen. It was where she learned how to two-step and the site of many wonderful memories with friends and boyfriends. Plus, they really did make a killer burger.

Her stomach growled.

Did Mama Lita put you up to this? she texted.

Your grandma? LOL. Your grandma would have invited herself along too.

True.

Skye blew a strand of hair from her cheeks with a puff of air. What if Mama Lita was right? What if the key to ending the spell was to stop believing in it? It was worth a try anyway. And Skye was going to need a little fun after an afternoon spent writing next week's schedule under the watchful eye of her mother.

She shook her head as she typed, *I'll meet you at your house. What time?*

Hog Heaven had the best burgers in Hill Country, hands down. Which was why it was jumping with people and music almost every night of the week. It was particularly packed on this Saturday night, moments before the Buck Riders, a band out of Dallas, took the stage.

Skye walked in behind Remedy and Micah, and one look at the Saturday-night party crowd had her feeling instantly optimistic about her life and future. For the first time since the accident, the dark cloud of dread that had been haunting her dissipated. She was going to be all right because she was going to make sure she was all right. She and the baby. Mama Lita was right. She had to let go of her irrational fears about the future and learn to love her hot mess of a life.

"Praise be, is that a table I see opening up?" Micah said, nodding toward the dance floor, where an older couple were rising from a tiny round table.

"On it," Remedy said, pushing through the crowd.

"I'll get us some drinks and order the food. No sense waiting for a server to come take our order. This place is slammed tonight. What do you want, Skye? Your usual, a burger with cheese and a Jack and Coke?" He wedged his shoulder into an opening at the bar, then looked back at Skye for her order.

Skye already knew pregnant women couldn't drink alcohol, but what about caffeine? She couldn't remember. Yet another question to ask her OB/GYN next week when she had her first official prenatal appointment. "A yes on the burger, and I'll take a Sprite."

He flickered his eyebrows at that, but she took off after Remedy before he could ask any questions.

Before Micah could join them at the table, though, a server came around to take their drink order. He was tall and good-looking, but young . . . and from the second he got to their table, he only had eyes for Skye. He lingered, hovering over them, even after Remedy explained that her husband was getting them drinks at the bar.

"So," he said to Remedy. "You're here alone?"

Here we go. Damn spell. "Not alone. My friend is right here."

With a roll of his head, he squatted down, getting a little too close for comfort. "Yeah, but I mean, you're not here with a guy. You're single."

"She is," Remedy said.

Gee, thanks. Skye kicked her lightly beneath the table.

"That's great to hear. Listen, I get off work in a half-hour. Would it be okay with you if I came back after my shift and asked you to dance?"

Skye tried to look disappointed when she said, "Sorry, but I gave up men for Lent."

He chuckled, as though he approved of the burn. "Yeah? My sister did that one year too. This year I gave up beer, so you can imagine how much fun it is working in a place like this." He tucked his pencil behind his ear, then extended his hand for her to shake. "I'm Adam."

She shook it, to be polite. "What's your favorite kind of beer, Adam?"

"I'm a Shiner Bock man. You're not going to tell me your name?"

Slick. He was paying attention. "Skye, and you can bring me a pint of Shiner Bock then." Obviously, she couldn't drink it, given that she was pregnant, but she couldn't pass up an opportunity to rub Adam's nose in his Lenten sacrifice, just for the hell of it.

He made a show of clutching his heart. "You're a cruel woman, Skye. But as you wish."

Micah arrived with their drinks just as Adam left. "Here we are, ladies. Remedy, your beer. And Skye, your Sprite."

Remedy tapped Skye's glass. "What's with the Sprite? You feeling okay?"

Skye took a long, slow drink, conjuring the response she'd prepared on her way to Remedy's house earlier that night. "Yep, but I'm still on antibiotics. That beer from Adam was all for show."

"Nice. Even though it sucks that you can't drink yet."

"I know." The truth sucked even more. She felt terrible leaving one of her dearest friends in the dark, but she wouldn't be the first pregnant woman to want to keep the news to herself until after the first trimester had passed. Moms-to-be did that all the time.

"Who was that guy you were talking to when I walked up?" Micah asked.

"Skye's new boyfriend," Remedy said.

"Yeah, right. That was Adam. He wants to dance with me when his shift is over."

Remedy sipped her beer. "It's all part of this spell that

her mom conjured for her." To Skye, she said, "Tell him about it."

Remedy told Micah the *Reader's Digest* version of the spell story. "And now I get asked out everywhere I go, leaving a trail of heartbroken puppies in my wake."

"I guess you don't mind too much because you hooked up with Gentry Wells," Micah said with a wink.

Remedy ribbed him. "Micah!"

"What? It's not like it's a secret. It's all over the news."

That it had been. But Gentry was different. He wasn't part of the spell. Which didn't explain what he was still doing in town. Or why she couldn't stop thinking about him. "If it's all the same for you two, I don't want to talk about Gentry tonight. I just want to have some fun and forget my troubles." Or at least try to.

Their burgers arrived just as the Buck Riders took the stage, along with Skye's Shiner Bock. The cheers in the bar reminded Skye of the Wild Beaver and the way the crowd had cheered Gentry onto the stage. What a night that had been. One of the best nights of her life in so many ways.

She loved being that wild, feeling so free. Frustration settled in her throat, tightening it painfully. Why did she crave that feeling so badly? Why couldn't she just settle down like a nice girl and be content with mundane routines and kind, if boring, men? But she couldn't seem to bring herself to give up her vices.

"Thank y'all for coming out to see us tonight," the lead singer said into the microphone. "We've got something special for you, a special guest singer who's gonna bring the house down. He contacted us this afternoon, looking for a last-minute gig, and I'm still pinching myself. I can't believe I have the privilege to stand on this stage with him and sing for y'all tonight. Now, I know there are a lot of haters who thought he'd be taking a break to recuperate after a motorcycle accident a couple weeks ago, but all of us fans knew better than to count out none other than the one, the only . . . Mr. Well Hung!"

Skye's head snapped up. No. Couldn't be.

The lead singer basked in the cheers, flapping his arms in a "raise the roof" gesture that made the crowd cheer even louder. "That's right, you know who I'm talkin' about. Put your hands together for the one, the only . . . Gentry Wells!"

Skye felt Remedy and Micah's eyes on her, but if she looked at them now, she'd lose all composure. *What the hell?*

"Did you know he'd be here?" Remedy called over the din.

"No clue. I told him I needed some space. This"—Skye gestured to the stage—"this is not space." What she wouldn't give for a shot of tequila. Good Lord, she was pissed. She glowered at the pint of beer on the table in front of her.

"Maybe he didn't know you'd be here. I mean, how could he?" Remedy said. "Coincidences do happen, you know."

She was right that there was no way Gentry could have known she'd be there, but that didn't stop her from feeling smothered in the worst possible way.

And then there he was, taking the stage. Mr. Goddamn Well Hung. Mr. Not Respecting Skye's Wishes. But also Mr. Sexy As Always, even with fresh scars on his hand and the missing finger. He played the crowd just like he had at the Wild Beaver, strutting around and slapping the hands of everyone in the front row. He'd told Skye he was a changed man, but up on stage he looked like the same old Gentry.

But then something happened. He brought the guitar that had been strapped to his back around to his front and from his pocket he took out a pick. Then he sat on a stool, paying the crowd no attention. The guitar looked awkward in his arms, like he was a beginner. His tongue poked out of the corner of his mouth.

Skye couldn't imagine how hard it would be to learn to play with the opposite hand. Heck, whenever Skye tried to write her name with her left hand, not only did it look like a kindergartner's scrawl, but she couldn't even get the "S" to point in the correct direction.

As the opening bars of a twangy song started up, Gentry's pick popped out of his now-four-fingered hand and bounced off his boot. There wasn't time to pick it up before the verse started. Ever the experienced showman, he let the guitar hang there and gripped the mic as he sang, looking unruffled, as though he'd planned that minor gaffe.

Skye didn't recognize the upbeat song, which was saying something because she'd given herself a crash course in Gentry's music since their first night together, and this song definitely wasn't his. But he sang it well and the crowd was into it.

When the song ended, the lead singer took to the mic again. "Thanks for starting us off with a little Garth Brooks, Gentry. But how about we get into your stuff? I know the crowd tonight would love to hear some of your classics. We've been covering your songs for years and it'd be an honor, man."

While he talked, Gentry bent down and discretely got the pic. "Sounds like a plan to me. Think y'all can handle that?" He smiled out at the audience, who whooped and cheered for him. "I taught these guys one of my new songs this afternoon, one that I previewed at the ACMs a couple weeks ago. Something that'll be on my next album. Want to hear it?"

They cheered again right on cue.

"All right then. I wrote this song after one of the best nights of my life. Any of you men in the bar tonight ever met a woman you knew you'd never forget? The kind of woman who haunts your dreams?"

She'd seen that performance on YouTube. She knew the song, about their horseback ride together. She braced herself to hear him sing such personal, sexy lyrics about her once more. Remedy snagged her attention. "Is this the one about you two?"

Skye was just about to answer, when Gentry said, "This song is about just such a—" He went silent.

Skye looked up to see him staring at her over the crowd. His shock at her presence seemed genuine. Had he really not known she was in the audience? Had he not staged this performance on purpose? She straightened. Her heart raced.

"Well, hello," he whispered into the mic through smiling lips. People in the crowd followed his line of sight to Skye, their stares curious. His eyes zeroed in on the Shiner Bock and his eyes narrowed—almost as if he knew she was pregnant. But there was no way . . .

He turned to talk to the band, seemingly giving them music instruction, and when he faced the mic again, he cleared his throat. "Change of plans. The Buck Riders are being gracious enough to let me try out some even newer material for you tonight. This song is called 'After the Crash.' Here we go."

Skye's whole body clenched. Had he really written a song about their accident? Had he honestly figured out a way to cash in on that nightmare of a day?

Concentrating hard on his guitar again, Gentry

strummed it with a simple chord and the band caught on. A ballad.

Skye sank to her seat again. Mesmerized. It *was* a song about the crash, sort of. But more of a song about a woman who'd crashed into his heart and changed everything. It was about two people whose lives crashed into each other, without warning, no seatbelts or safety nets. It was beautiful and vulnerable in a way that none of his other songs had been.

While he played and sang, he never once looked up from his guitar, concentrating on picking out the chords, until the very end. And at the end, when he did raise his eyes to the crowd on the final chorus, his gaze went straight to Skye. She felt like the only person in the room.

Remedy poked her arm. "Did he really write that about you? Because that was incredible. He's really talented."

Skye opened her mouth but no sound come out. She'd never been anyone's muse before and it filled her with a kind of warmth that crumbled her defenses—right up until the high wore off. Like the sun cleared out a morning fog with its blazing rays of light, anger rose inside. He'd written a song about her, about them. How dare he? Didn't he get it? This was her life he was messing with. She'd asked for space to figure out how she felt, but here he was in her face, broadcasting their personal life for everyone to hear.

That sense of impending doom crashed through her again. He was pushing her too far, too fast, and she wasn't ready to handle it yet. How could she plan for her future when she had no idea if her body was even capable of carrying a baby to term?

She swayed in her seat as the realization hit her hard. No wonder she'd been filled with dread. No wonder she couldn't bring herself to tell anyone she was pregnant.

She was carrying a baby inside her that may or may not survive. She'd already lost one baby when she was around this number of weeks pregnant—and that was on top of the fact that he and she had almost killed this baby themselves with their carelessness of getting on that motorcycle.

She'd been so wrapped up in her anger about getting pregnant by a virtual stranger, by the same kind of man she'd been trying to distance herself from, that she hadn't allowed herself the space to process how terrified she was of being robbed once again of the chance to become a mom. The problem wasn't that she wanted men and a life that wasn't good for her—it was that she hadn't been allowed to keep them. No matter how badly she'd wanted her marriage to work, how badly she'd wanted that baby, they'd been ripped away from her.

She wasn't afraid of having this baby or falling hard for Gentry. She was afraid that, in the end, loving either of them wouldn't matter, because she was powerless to control whether she got to keep either of them in her life or if they'd simply slip through her fingers.

"Beer's not working for you?"

It was Adam again. Skye roused herself from her thoughts and swallowed hard. A huge part of her was grateful for the distraction from her sudden shock of fear. She drew circles in the condensation on the pint glass and forced a smile to her lips. "Turns out I'm not a big fan of Shiner Bock," she said, pushing the still-full pint away. "I'd offer it to you, but . . ."

He chuckled. "Listen, I'm off work in a couple minutes. Mandy will be your new server after that. But, uh . . ." He whipped out a pen and scribbled on a cocktail napkin, then handed it to her. His phone number. "In case you change your mind about dancing with me."

She made a show of accepting the napkin and reading his number. "Thank you. It was a pleasure meeting you, Adam." She offered her hand for him to shake and he pressed a kiss to the back of it.

"For my next song, it's another new one," Gentry said on stage. "Y'all might be surprised to hear that this one's also about a girl."

"I'm sensing a theme," the lead singer joked.

Gentry tipped the brim of his ball cap. "Damn right. This one's called 'Take It.'" He squinted at the crowd. "We don't have any youngins in here tonight, do we? I hope not. Because this one's a little X-rated."

Skye didn't have it in her to sit and listen to Gentry sing an X-rated song, possibly about the two of them. She shot out of her seat. To Remedy and Micah, she said, "I have to go. I can call a cab if you're not ready, but I'm tired and I have to work tomorrow."

The two exchanged a knowing look. "No, we're ready too," Remedy said. She stood and wrapped her sweater around her shoulders.

Micah chugged his last sip of beer. "Yup, now's good. Let's roll."

"Whoa, whoa, whoa, stop the song," Gentry said. The band stopped playing and the crowd hushed.

"Skye Martinez, don't you leave yet." The words boomed over the speakers.

Skye turned and faced the stage, mortified.

Gentry's blue eyes bore into her. "Do you like the new songs? They're coming along, aren't they?"

She nodded. What else could she do with everyone watching?

"Good. Glad you liked them. I've just about got this whole album written. Looking forward to singing you the rest of it."

What was he thinking, talking to her like that as though they were the only two people in the room? She hooked her thumb toward the door and called, "I've got to go."

He remained unfazed. "Yeah, I know, but you forgot something."

Her pulse pounded and her cheek blazed. What did he want from her, a kiss? Was he going to ask her out? He wasn't going to try to make her drink that beer in front of everyone, was he?

He nodded to the table she'd been sitting at. "You forgot that cocktail napkin. The one with the waiter's number on it."

Um. He wanted her to take the napkin? He wanted her to see other guys? It didn't make sense. And the confusion must have shown on her face because he added, "Yeah, that don't bother me at all. I think it's kind of funny, actually. You can date every one of those lovesick clowns if it suits you. I'll still be here waiting for you when you're ready."

Fear coursed through her again. She couldn't fall for him. She refused. Not when he could slip through her fingers so easily. *Just like this baby.* He wasn't the staying kind. He wasn't husband material. He'd told her so himself. Hell, he'd written a whole damn song about it. How could she risk her heart to someone like that?

"I know you're scared, and you have every right to be," he said. "But that doesn't change the fact that we're . . ." He swallowed hard. "It doesn't change the connection we have. That's not going away, no matter how much you want to deny it. So I want you to know I'll be here waiting for you."

A few people in the bar got it in their heads to try to cajole Skye up on stage. They led a chant of "Kiss! Kiss! Kiss!" that spread like wildfire through the bar.

"Aw, come on, kids. Knock that off. Don't pressure the lady. Next time she kisses me, it'll be because she wants it as bad as I do."

She held his smoldering gaze, feeling his words all the way down to her toes. Every day since the first one they'd met, she'd been consumed with a gnawing hunger for his touch, for the chance to melt into the feel of his lips, his body, as she had in every juicy, toe-curling kiss they'd already shared. Every. Single. Day.

A whole-body shudder rocked her where she stood.

She forced herself to break eye contact. "Let's get out of here," she said to Micah and Remedy.

"See you soon, beautiful," he called after her as she walked through the door. "See you soon."

Chapter Nineteen

Gentry realized a lot of things while he'd been on stage at Hog Heaven the previous weekend.

Number one, he could connect with Skye through his songs in a way that he hadn't been able to do otherwise since the crash. Performing for Skye had been the best way to convey exactly what he was feeling, what she meant to him. That had always been his best way of expressing himself and now that his inspiration had returned in spades, he wanted to sing to her every chance he got, all the songs she'd inspired. Which brought him to his second realization.

He needed a backup band if he really wanted to make that deadline. They'd have to be local musicians and hired on the sly, so no one in Nashville would catch wind of his project. So he'd put up the call in town, leaving fliers all over Dulcet. Which is how he ended up with a line extending down Briscoe Ranch Resort's pathway leading to their special events barn where he was holding auditions. As he'd known they would, the fliers had brought in a lot of gawkers and fans that simply wanted his autograph, and a lot of townsfolk who treated the audition like he'd put out a call for *American Idol*—they may have no talent, but they wanted their five minutes of fame and to have a celebrity musician's attention for a few minutes.

That motley group included all the provocatively dressed young women who tried to convince him that he needed backup singers. One of the ladies left her phone number on the signup sheet. She circled it and added a heart.

"Just in case you might be holding some other auditions while you're in town," she'd said with a toss of her hair. There was a time that he would have been all over that. But never had he been so crystal clear in his focus about who he was and what he wanted with his life.

After two hours and talking to what seemed like more than a hundred Dulcet locals, he'd just about given up hope of finding any gems in the rough when a truck hauling a horse trailer pulled right up behind the barn on the maintenance road.

It only took a moment for Gentry to recognize the long-haired, tattooed driver. He strode out past the line of audition hopefuls to meet the truck. "Nick! What the hell you doin' here, man?"

They roped each other into a back-thumping one-armed hug. "Word on the street was that you decided to go ahead with writing a new album for Neil. And seeing as how I was just fired from my last band gig," he said with a wink, "I had plenty of time to burn."

Gentry had decided not to lasso any of his old band members to his current wagon, knowing it might go down in flames and not wanting to take anyone else down with him. But Nick's arrival and his touching offer got Gentry right in the heart.

"That means a lot, man. Thank you." He nodded to the horse trailer. "What's with that?"

Nick grinned. "Borrowed it from your ranch manager, Elias. He and I got to talking, and he said Wild Beaver hadn't been the same since you left. And I figured, since you wrote your best songs when you were out on the range with him, that you might be missing him too."

All Gentry could do was blink at him. "You brought me my horse?"

"Sure did. I stabled him here at the resort under your name."

"That's . . . damn, man, I don't know what to say."

Nick clapped a hand on Gentry's shoulder. "Say, let's get this fuckin' album lit up and let Neil Blevins know in no uncertain terms that he can kiss your ass."

With Nick and Wild Beaver there, Gentry had reason to hope again. "These auditions are rough. I've been at it for hours and haven't come up with anybody."

"Let's give it another hour or so. There's got to be someone in this line who can play, make this worth your while."

As they surveyed the line, a petite older woman strutted past the other auditioners, dragging a rolling black instrument case behind her.

She marched right up to Gentry and Nick, waving a flier in their faces. "What is all of this? What are you hoping to accomplish? Why won't you leave my granddaughter Skye alone?"

Well, that changed things. "You're Skye's grandmother?"

"Yes. Call me Mama Lita."

His head crowded with a hundred different questions about Skye. Was she all right? Were her legs all healed up yet? What about her wrist. *What about the baby?* "All right. Well, I'm holding auditions because I need a band."

She narrowed her eyes at him. "I've seen you on TV. You already have a band."

"And now he wants a new band. What's it to you?" Nick said.

Gentry added, "I wasn't sure how long my recovery would take and I couldn't leave them hanging like that. But this is Nick, my drummer. He's still around. I'm just looking for guitar and bass at this point."

She frowned at that answer. "What about a keyboardist?"

Gentry looked past her to her black rolling case. Was that a keyboard in there? "Er, yeah. I'd love to find an accomplished keyboardist to join the band."

The answer seemed to appease her. She rubbed her chin and nodded. "Okay. I've been looking for a new band to join up with for years. Not enough rock 'n' roll around here for my taste. I'd like to audition. Someone's got to keep tabs on you." She glared at Nick. "Both of you."

Er, okay. Gentry had had no idea that Skye had a rock 'n' roll granny, but he was intrigued. He hadn't put out the call for a keyboardist, nor did many of his songs feature a keyboard, but he wouldn't dare disrespect Skye's grandmother by turning her away. Besides, she talked like she knew what she was doing. He doubted that she was country rock-band material, but he was getting desperate. If he couldn't find a bass player, then a keyboardist would fit the bill just fine. Even if she was twice Gentry's age.

Nick helped her haul the keyboard up to the stage and set it up.

A commotion near the sign-up table had them all turning around to see an itty bitty old woman dressed in a yellow sequined track suit leap out of a hot pink riding scooter. Onto the table, she unloaded an armful of instruments that looked better suited for a grade school. "I'm here to audition, sonny, and I brought all my instruments. What'll it be? Tambourine? Kazoo? Cowbell? I play a wicked cowbell."

"God help us," Mama Lita spit out. "This is no place for you, you old bat! This is a serious audition."

The so-called old bat shook her cane at Mama Lita. "And I am seriously auditioning. You can't stop me!"

Nick leaned in close to his ear. "Dude, you can't have a full-on geriatric band. It's not right for the image."

Gentry didn't care much about his image any longer. The audition was already a bust, and so he didn't see any harm in humoring some old ladies, especially when one of them was Skye's grandma. He stuck his hand out for the newcomer to shake. "I'm Gentry, and you are?"

She gave him a hearty handshake that defied her age or petite stature. "Granny June Briscoe. This is my resort."

Then that settled it. "How about tambourine? You can accompany Mama Lita on her audition song."

Mama Lita snorted. "Over my dead body."

Granny June plucked up the tambourine and mounted the stage. "That can be arranged, Edalia."

Mama Lita cracked her knuckles and gave Gentry a pointed look. "If you're going to make this old bat perform with me, then I want Logan up on stage to drown out the sound." She nodded to a young man in line who held an electric guitar. "Logan, get up here. You know the song 'Light My Fire'?"

That was the last song he would have a grandmother to audition with.

The kid, Logan, scrambled up on stage. "Uh, yeah. The Doors. Got it." He cast Gentry a self-conscious look. "Is this okay with you if we play together?"

More than okay. Gentry was honestly intrigued.

"What's your full name, kid?"

"Logan Ryder."

"What class are you supposed to be in right now, Logan?"

A lopsided grin revealed a dimple. He bet the girls in town were crazy in love with this kid. He reminded Gentry a lot of himself when he was that age and dreaming of hitting it big as a musician. "Civics."

Gentry wasn't going to risk the liability of having an underage kid in his band, but since the guy had ditched school for this audition, Gentry owed him the chance to show his stuff. "You got a job?"

"I'm a lifeguard at the resort."

Another Briscoe Ranch employee. He should have guessed as much. Every local he'd met seemed to work there, save Granny June, who actually owned the place.

Nick grabbed a pair of drum sticks and took to the stage. "I've got drums on this one. And honestly? I can't wait to hear what you've all got."

That made two of them.

Mama Lita counted them down and Logan started in on those famous opening notes of the song, playing them with an ease and skill of a professional guitarist. Gentry hadn't expected Logan to sing, but he surprised him again by stepped right up to the mic and letting the words float out of his mouth in perfect pitch, his voice not too dissimilar from Jim Morrison himself. As Mama Lita had predicted, he completely drowned out Granny June's hopelessly off-rhythm tambourine.

But perhaps the biggest surprise of the day was Mama Lita, who tore into the first organ solo like she'd been performing in rock bands all her life. And maybe she had.

"Damn, she's good," said one of the other people in line. He was right—Mama Lita rocked it out.

When the organ solo ended, Logan stepped forward. He'd already proved he could play better than every other guitarist who'd auditioned combined—and that was before he ripped into an intricate solo that blew Gentry's mind. Gentry didn't realize he'd risen to his feet or that his mouth had fallen open until the solo ended. Gentry had performed with a lot of musicians over the years, which is why he knew with absolute certainty that it was only a matter of time before Logan Rider was a household name across the country. He was that good.

It wasn't until after the guitar solo ended that Gentry noticed that Granny June had either gotten bored with the tambourine or her arm had gotten tired, because the instrument was out of her hand and she'd taken to dancing and prancing around the stage, clearly having a hoot of a time, much to Mama Lita's obvious chagrin.

Gentry raised his hand for them to stop, which they all did except Granny June, who just kept on dancing to the music in her head until Mama Lita stuck her foot out and tried to trip her.

Nick had to do a bit of a dance himself to get around Granny June, but once he did, he jumped off the stage, leaned over the table, and whispered to Gentry, "Geriatric band, it is. Make the call, man. That chick on keyboards might be old, but she can rock."

So it seemed. "I don't need to hear any more. You're in. All three of you. Granny June, I'm taking you off tambourine and making you our—"

"Mascot," Mama Lita called. Granny June elbowed her in the ribs.

"Stage manager and go-go dancer," Gentry countered. Because what the hell? She owned the resort and she was mighty entertaining. "Band practice is Monday night at six, right here. See you there."

While Mama Lita and Logan packed up their instruments, and Granny June gathered her collection of grade-school instruments from the table, Gentry checked his phone and was startled at the time. He didn't know a lot about becoming a Catholic, but he was pretty sure being late to his first RCIA class wouldn't be a good start. He turned to the dozen or so people still in line. "I'm so sorry, but the audition is closed. I found all the players I need, and I have to go. I have an appointment that I can't be late to."

He was gathering up his notes when Mama Lita planted herself in front of him, her arms crossed. "You're putting together a band, you're buying a house, and you have important appointments to get to. You've lived in this town for, what, four weeks? What's your plan?"

What she probably meant was, what's your plan with my granddaughter? And the answer to that was, he had a lot of plans, but even though she was Skye's family, none of those plans were any of her business. Not yet, anyway. "I don't have time to talk right now, but we will. Soon. I'll see you at practice Monday night."

He shook a few of the hands of the people who'd only come to the audition for the chance to meet him, then hustled across the resort to the truck he'd bought a few days earlier and sped to town, arriving at the church just in the nick of time.

He was in such a hurry that he didn't recognize the greeter at the classroom door until he was right up on top of her. And when he saw who it was, he nearly put it in reverse and moonwalked out of the building and back to his truck. If only his future wasn't at stake. So he sucked it up and smiled in greeting. "Hello, Mrs. Martinez. What a surprise."

"I'll say," she groused. "What are you doing here? What are you trying to prove?"

Mr. Martinez appeared in the door. He put his arm around his wife. "Yessica, let's welcome this young man to class. Whatever brought him to Catholicism is a blessing."

"Your daughter, sir," Gentry said before he could think better of it. "I'm here because I want to be the kind of man your daughter wants in her life."

Mr. Martinez let out a genial laugh. "Who would have thought our baby girl would inspire a person to seek out God? That's an extra blessing. Come on in, Mr. Wells. We're happy you're here."

Mrs. Martinez drew a sharp breath through her nose, but she stood aside to let Gentry pass. He took off his hat and found a seat. Three other men and a woman smiled at him in greeting.

Father Ellwood looked up from the podium. A broad grin brightened his face. Gentry tried to return the smiles from everyone in the room, but he was having trouble shaking off Mrs. Martinez's accusations. Of all the obstacles that he faced in winning Skye over, he'd never considered how her family might feel about him, the resentment and blame for getting her in that accident and for stealing her away from her job at inconvenient times.

If converting to Catholicism wasn't enough to sway Skye's mother's view of him, then nothing would.

"You came, praise God!" Father Ellwood said as he

approached. He embraced Gentry in a strong hug full of warmth and acceptance.

Gentry tried to relax, wanting to be just as friendly in response, but all he could think to do was lean in to whisper from behind his clenched teeth, "You didn't mention that Mr. and Mrs. Martinez were teachers."

Father Ellwood stood up straighter. His eyes twinkled mischievously. "Oh, I must have forgotten. This mind sometimes. Can't be trusted. Why don't you take a seat because we're about to get started."

Skye's OB/GYN was located in a nondescript medical building two towns over. She'd been going to this doctor since she was twenty, after her miscarriage. She'd never seen an OB/GYN before that, never needed one. Dr. Ghosh had been there for her in the difficult months after she lost the baby and had held her hand throughout her painful divorce. Other than Father Ellwood, Dr. Ghosh probably knew the most about Skye's secrets and sins than anyone else in her life.

It was only fitting that she would face this new disaster with the doctor's help.

In the hospital, she'd seen the obstetrician who'd been on-call. She'd made sure the baby was unharmed by the accident and had approved the pain medication they'd prescribed to Skye, but this was her first real appointment.

She hadn't realized the depths of her fear that the doctor would check for a heartbeat and there wouldn't be any until she got lost twice on the way to the doctor's office, along familiar roads she'd driven her whole life. Dressed in a paper gown and sitting on the exam table, she couldn't even look at the baby on the cover of the parenting magazine in the plastic rack on the wall. What if she wasn't pregnant anymore? What if she'd already lost it?

It was possible. She didn't feel pregnant. She wasn't even sure how being pregnant felt, exactly, even though it'd happened to her twice. She was nauseous, but that could be psychosomatic from the stress of thinking she was pregnant.

"Hi, Skye."

Dr. Ghosh was only a few years older than Skye, with a youthful face and figure, with her black hair pulled in a youthful ponytail and jade post earrings that complemented her green eyes. She closed the door to the exam room and slid onto the rolling stool, Skye's file in her hands. "What can I do for you today?"

As though she didn't know why Skye was there. As though the hospital hadn't contacted her or she hadn't read Skye's chart, which she most certainly had.

"Why do doctors do that? Pretend they don't know why the patient's there? What if we're not up to spelling it out again? It's almost cruel." She heard the hitch in her voice, the plea to avoid this part. She had yet to speak the words aloud to anyone except Mama Lita, and even then, she hadn't been the one to speak them. Mama Lita had.

Dr. Ghosh's smile fell. She rolled forward and took Skye's hand. "Hey, you're okay. I've got you. We ask because we like to hear it from the patient instead of making assumptions. Didn't you ever play the game 'Telephone' when you were a kid? People screw up messages all the time."

And, furthermore, why did people keep telling Skye she was okay? She wasn't okay. She was anything but okay. "I got in an accident. A motorcycle accident. I was thrown from it."

Dr. Ghosh nodded. "You were in the hospital. Your legs, how are they? Still banged up?"

Skye held her right leg out for the doctor to see, the web of scars, scabs, and fading bruises. "A little. For the most part the scabs are going away. I'll always have some scars. And I've got another two weeks of this cast for my wrist, which is making work tough, but I'm managing."

"Good. What brings you here today?" she asked again, still holding fast to Skye's hand.

Skye drew a tremulous breath. "I screwed up. We used protection, but it didn't work. And you know what happened last time. You know I lost it and . . ." She shook her head and squeezed her eyes closed.

Dr. Ghosh jiggled their joined hands. "You know what? We're going to do things a little out of order today. Why don't you lie back? Let's get this ultrasound started and see what we can see."

Queasiness bubbled up her throat, making her gag. "We could wait."

"Come on, Skye. I know you're scared, and with good reason, but waiting isn't going to help."

She was right, so Skye steeled herself and laid back on the exam table. Dr. Ghosh helped her legs into stirrups.

"What we're going to do today is called a trans-vaginal ultrasound. I'm going to insert a wand into your vaginal canal and that should let us see what's going on in your uterus. With any luck, we can get a sound on that heartbeat even though you're only eight weeks along."

"Ultrasound?"

"Yes, ma'am. Thanks to the motorcycle accident, you get an early look at the little peanut with an ultrasound."

In an effort to completely ignore her fear or, worse, the blossoming excitement at the thought of actually getting to see the baby—*if it was there,* she reminded herself, refusing to get her hopes up—Skye closed her eyes and focused on the physical sensations between her legs. Cold jelly. The wand sliding inside her, invasive but not uncomfortable.

Within moments, the room filled with the sound of rhythmic bursts of electronic sound waves. A heartbeat.

Skye squeezed her eyes closed and tried not to weep. A heartbeat meant a baby. Her baby.

"Skye, open your eyes and look at the monitor." Dr. Ghosh's voice was quiet but optimistic. Surely she wouldn't tell Skye to look at the monitor if there was a problem.

She turned her head and looked at the screen. It was filled with gray and black grainy shapes. Skye remembered those types of images from Gloria's pregnancies, but she'd completely forgotten how to interpret the waves and splotches.

"Where is it?" she croaked.

Dr. Ghosh stretched her arm to the monitor from her position between Skye's legs. "See that peanut? That's your peanut. The head, the torso, the legs," she said, pointing out each body part in turn. Then she pointed at a black spot in the torso that seemed to be fluttering. "And its heart. Look at it go, so strong. The heart rate is perfect for this stage of development. Absolutely perfect."

The image blurred as tears crowded Skye's eyes as she was overcome with love. This was her baby. All these weeks, she'd been so ashamed of getting pregnant and so scared about the future. She'd thought this had ruined her life, this precious little baby inside her. But that wasn't true at all. Nothing so perfect was to be ashamed of and her future was going to be filled with more love and joy than she'd ever thought possible for herself. This baby was the biggest blessing of her life.

"Hi there," she said to the monitor in a quivering voice.

Dr. Ghosh patted her knee. "You're having a baby."

"Oh, my God. I am." Tears filled her eyes. This time, motherhood wasn't going to slip through her fingers like a dream she couldn't hold on to. This time, she and the baby were going to be all right.

"Say it, Skye. Say it loud and proud. What are you having?"

"A baby," she whispered, and then, louder, "I'm having a baby."

"Yes, you are. Congratulations, mama."

Skye closed her eyes and prayed. For strength, for patience—and for forgiveness that she'd ever been ashamed and afraid of such a miracle.

Her only shame now was that she'd deprived Gentry of this moment. This was his baby, too, and he was missing out because she'd been too scared to face the truth. But he had a right to know. Immediately. And then she would beg his forgiveness for letting fear control her for so long. Not just fear about the baby, but fear about her love life. What was she doing, holding herself back from the man she really wanted? How could she have been so afraid to take a chance on something with Gentry that felt too good to be true? What if it was true?

"I haven't told the father yet."

Dr. Ghosh nodded, nonplussed. "I hear that a lot, more than you might guess. Are you two an item?"

Skye held up her casted left arm and wiggled the empty ring finger, proving exactly how old-fashioned she was. No marriage, no baby. Except now, she had to decide what to do, if she even had a choice. What if Gentry offered to do the noble thing and marry her? Could she say *yes* to a man who didn't love her because it was the right thing to do for her and the baby? Could she take the chance that she could be happy with him for the rest of her life? Because the next time she got married, it was going to be forever. Or was she fated to be a single mom like Gloria?

"I'm not sure. I don't think so. I got pregnant the second day we'd known each other."

"Wow, fertile much?"

Skye let out a gasp of surprise. "Dr. Ghosh!"

"Hey, if you can't joke about this, then wait until you get a load of motherhood. You've got this, Skye. I know you. I know your family. This baby is going to be well loved. Get your phone out. Let's make a recording of the heartbeat for you to share with its daddy. And I've already printed out some ultrasound images for you to share with him too. If he gets mad at you, just show him these and have him listen to the heartbeat, and I'm sure he'll forget all about you not telling him promptly."

An hour later, Skye was back on the road, driving straight to the resort, before she had time to lose her nerve or second-guess her decision, armed with the printouts of the ultrasound images, grainy white silhouettes of a peanut with a heart. Instead of parking in the employee lot and risking seeing anyone she knew, she parked in the guest lot nearest the villas and let herself through the security gate.

Déjà vu spread like an ink stain inside her. The last time she'd sought out her man to tell him she was pregnant, she'd caught him with another woman. Skye's whole world had collapsed. As she raised her fist to Gentry's door, she couldn't stop the barrage of flashbacks. Pain and insecurities crowded her like ghosts. Her throat tightened with panic. She gasped for air and clutched the ultrasound images to her heart.

"I'm not twenty anymore," she soothed herself. "And Gentry is not Mike." It was an insult to Gentry that she'd been subconsciously comparing the two all this time.

And, furthermore, so what if she knocked on his door and discovered that he was entertaining another woman? Unlike with Mike, whom she was married to, she had no claim on Gentry and had even told him more than once to leave her alone and give her space. Skye was stronger, wiser, and more grounded than she'd been when she left Mike. Whatever happened next, she could handle it. As her father had told her, she could save herself. All she had to do was not panic.

Summoning every ounce of courage she could muster, she knocked on his door. And waited.

She strained an ear to the door, listening, but didn't hear anything. Technically, she could let herself in with her resort master key, but there was no way she'd take a chance at catching him in the act of something she didn't want to see. No need to invite heartache.

After a minute, she rang the doorbell.

Still, nothing.

A bubble of crazed laughter burst out of her, diffusing some of her tension. More than likely, he wasn't home and she'd worked herself up for nothing. She found her phone in her purse and texted him.

Where are you? I'm at your villa.

He didn't reply immediately, so she forced herself to draw a full breath, then another, getting her heart rate back down. She dropped into the nearest seat on the little patio out front and let her attention be drawn to Lake Bandit, which bordered the southeast corner of the resort.

She'd grown up skipping stones on that lake, and it had been where her dad had taught her to fish, but it had been years since she'd slowed down enough to really look at it. All this time, she'd had her head down, grinding out a daily existence.

Like her mom.

It was as though her mom believed that if she could just work even harder, give even more, and sacrifice enough, she could keep herself and the people she loved safe and healthy and happy, even if doing so meant that she, herself, wasn't. Even if her joy and sense of peace had to be sacrificed.

What a lie. What a terrible, destructive lie that her mother had perpetuated out of love. Out of fear of losing those she loved.

She dialed the Polished Pros office number. Her mom picked up on the second ring. "Polished Pros. This is Yessica."

"Hey, Mom."

"Are you okay? You don't sound okay."

Skye had to smile, her mom sounded so worried. "I'm more than okay. I just wanted to tell you thank you."

"For writing this week's schedule for you? You're welcome. But how'd you even know about that? You're off today."

"No. Thank you for just . . . for loving me so much."

"You're not okay. Where are you? I'll come get you."

"Mom, stop. I'm fine. I was just thinking about how hard you work and how I don't thank you enough. That's all," Skye said.

"Did you break something? Did you crash my car? That's it, isn't it? Oy, mjia. You're an accident waiting to happen."

Skye chuckled. It was a good life she was going to give

this child. A good, solid family—not without their problems, but what family wasn't?—and a good, solid faith foundation. No matter how Gentry reacted, no matter what the level of involvement he wanted with their child, she was going to be okay. Their baby was going to be okay. "I know."

Her phone chimed with an incoming text. "Mom, I've got to go. I'll talk to you soon. And for the last time, I'm fine. Love you."

The text was from Gentry. *In the special event barn. Come see me.*

She took another long look at the lake. Maybe her dad would teach their baby how to fish there too. Maybe Gentry would teach her or him how to play the guitar. And maybe Skye would teach her baby the best gift of all, how to stop worrying and let go and enjoy life. Maybe, by the time her baby was old enough to learn that lesson, Skye will have learned it too.

She tucked the ultrasound photos in her purse for safe keeping and set off along the path to the barn. With every step, she felt more sure of herself and more sure that telling Gentry was the right move. She heard the music before the barn even came into view, and it sounded terrific. Professional. As though Gentry had recruited the entire crew of the Buck Riders to be his backup band.

The door was ajar, so she pushed it all the way open. She wasn't sure who she expected to be in Gentry's band, but the shock of seeing her grandmother on stage rocking out on keyboard, and Granny June dancing around them without a care in the world, after the rollercoaster ride of a day she'd already had, knocked the wind right out of her. She sank to the nearest hay bale to listen in.

Mama Lita was in Gentry's band. Go figure.

At the sound of the keyboard's melody, Skye was instantly transported to her favorite childhood memories with Mama Lita, of listening to old records at her house. Skye and Gloria would sit on the orange shag carpet of Mama Lita's apartment while Rodrigo González, Los Nómadas, and other Mexican classic rock bands blared through the speakers, and Mama Lita regaled the girls with stories about her experiences in the La Onda movement. Sometimes, Mama Lita would play her keyboard along to the records. Sometimes, they would all dance and play air guitar along with Carlos Santana.

Back then, it had been a balm for the quiet of her own house. Her parents worked all the time. If Skye or Gloria wanted to be with them, they had to come to the resort. Mama Lita's eclectic apartment felt more like a home than any other home she'd known—right up until Gloria moved in with her after Ruben's death, giving her a new, loving image of home in her mind. Love and children's laughter. The clutter of living covering every horizontal surface. The smell of beans simmering on the stove blending with the smells of children—Elmer's glue, washable markers and soap and stinky shoes, the almost-real cheese scent of Goldfish crackers. The smells and sounds of home.

She'd never thought much about how music and the sound of grandmother's electric organ also conjured that feeling of home. And now, her baby's heartbeat joined those ranks. With every *thump*, she thought *home*.

Tears sprang to her eyes. *Shoot.* She didn't consider herself an emotional person, but she'd wept more in the past few weeks than in the past several years combined.

She dabbed at her eyes with her finger as discretely as possible. But still, she saw a shadow cross Gentry's face as he watched her while he sang. When she finally found the guts to meet his gaze, he flickered his eyebrows up in a silent question. *You okay?*

She gave him a thumbs-up.

At the end of the song, Gentry turned to the band. "Hey there. Everyone, this is Skye, Mama Lita's granddaughter."

The drummer, who looked strikingly similar to the drummer in Gentry's old band, and Logan Ryder both gave her a wave. "I know her," Logan said.

"It's a small town, bucko. We all know each other," Granny June added.

"Right. Okay, well, let's sing the lady a special song. How about the new one we've been working on? 'Built to Stay.' "

Had Skye heard that wrong? Or did Gentry actually just say he'd written a song about commitment—the antidote to his song "Built to Leave"? She searched out his gaze, and she found him already watching her. When their eyes met, he smiled, confident. Happy.

Logan set up the song with a twangy waltz of a melody. And then Gentry started to sing.

Skye barely heard the words to the song, her mind was spinning in so many different directions at once, but when she did tune in, when she could get past the affection and warmth in his eyes and the rich, soulful sound of his voice, she got the gist of it. The song was about building a life in a small town, one brick at a time. And about building himself into a better man, one prayer at a time. By the second run through the chorus, Skye couldn't stop the tears again. She clenched her teeth together to keep from dissolving into actual crying. He'd written that song—and he'd written it for her.

It's nothing you can buy ready-made
It's gonna take a lot of hard work

And I might stumble along the way
But when I come to you,
Wanting to put that diamond ring upon your hand
When you say yes to me
It'll because I built myself into a better man.

A man that you can love
And trust with all your heart.
There's no shortcuts I want to take
No prayer I wouldn't say
With my whole life ahead to spend loving you,
There's nothing that I wouldn't do
To be the kind of man who's built to stay.

When the song ended, she clapped, a sound that echoed through the barn.

"What do you think?" Gentry said, his expression intense and searching, maybe even a little insecure. "We sound pretty good, right? I still can't play worth a damn, but I don't need to with these guys having my back."

"Better than pretty good. You wrote that yourself?" Skye said.

His jaw rippled. "Yes, ma'am."

She might have asked, *Is it true? Is every word of it the truth?* But she could see in his eyes that it was.

"We rock, don't we?" Granny June asked.

We was a loose term, because Granny June herself hadn't done much rocking, but Skye was too taken by the song to do more than nod.

"I mean, it still needs work, but it's getting there," Gentry added, popping Logan's young man ego.

"No. It doesn't need work. It's incredible. I can't believe what you've all accomplished in such a short amount of time. All of you. Mama Lita, you put the rest of us mere mortals to shame."

She hung an unlit cigarette between her lips and winked. "That I know, dearie. That I know. But I think rehearsal's over. Time for me to hit the road." Turning to the rest of the band, she said, "Logan, can you give me a ride home?"

"Oh, sorry. I got a ride here from Nick."

She packed up her keyboard. "Ah, well, then you can both take me home. Granny June, too. Let's go, old bat. Maybe I could even stomach your company for an hour or two if you wanted to get a bite to eat in town."

Skye smiled at the two women's bickering. She got the sneaking suspicion that Mama Lita had orchestrated that maneuver to give her and Gentry some privacy. If so, she was grateful—and nervous. This was it. She was going to tell him and then everything was going to change between them forever.

On his way out of the barn, the drummer stopped in front of Skye. "You're the one, huh?" He offered his hand. "I'm Nick."

At the sound of his name, the pieces fell into place. "You're Nick, the drummer. I mean, from Gentry's old band. The one he's known since high school."

"That's me. And if you're Skye, then you're the chick from the songs, the reason he's in Dulcet."

Skye didn't know what to make of that, and Nick's expression didn't offer any clues. "I guess so."

Nick's face broke out in a smile. "Then thank you for that, for getting him to change for the better, and not just because he's written the best songs of his career about you." He nodded back to Gentry, who stood away from the group, breaking down the mic stands while the rest of the band stowed and buttoned up their instruments. "He's a good man. The best. You'll see."

Skye had already seen it and knew with her whole heart that Nick was right.

It wasn't until they were alone in the barn that Gentry spoke. "You okay? I mean, for real, now that everyone's gone. You don't look like yourself today."

"No. I'm not." She was so much more.

His gaze swept over her, assessing. "What happened? Did you not like the song? Because I know it needs work, but I wrote it for you. I mean, for me. About me."

She plunged her hand into her purse and closed her fingers around the ultrasound pictures. *Okay, little peanut, here we go . . .* "Gentry, I'm pregnant. It's yours."

Chapter Twenty

Skye held out the ultrasound images. He took the papers from her and sat on a hay bale. He had yet to speak, but that meant he hadn't yelled at her. He didn't look angry. He didn't even look confused. He looked humbled, like he was bowing his head in prayer instead of studying the images of the unborn baby he hadn't known he was having until moments earlier.

Babbling to fill in the silence, she took a seat next to him. "It's not much to see at six weeks, but you can just make out its head and its little peanut body. We won't be able to tell the sex for another twelve weeks, at the twenty-week ultrasound."

"The black spot there, is that the heart?"

"Yes. See? You're picking up how to interpret the images. And it's a real strong heartbeat too. The ultrasound tech said the baby's developing right on schedule, perfectly." She got her phone out and navigated to the sound recording. "We made a recording of the heartbeat for you."

And she pressed play.

On a huff that sounded a lot like relief, he closed his

eyes. When the recording ended, he peeled his eyes open again. They were glassy with tears. "That's . . . I don't know what to say."

He took the phone from her and replayed it as he looked at the pictures. His hand slid across her lap and onto her belly. When the recording ended this time, he cleared his throat, taking his hand back. "I didn't think that would hit me like that, but I've . . . I'm . . . I'm going to be a father. I mean, this is really happening."

"I'm so sorry I kept you from hearing it at the doctor today live and in person because of my lie. Please don't hate me."

He knelt before her and kissed her hand, then cradled it in both of his like a precious jewel. "Thank you for trusting me with this."

Maybe Skye was just stunned stupid by all that had happened, but there was something off about Gentry's response. "Shouldn't you be more surprised? I mean, this is a big deal."

He smiled up at her, his eyes glassy with wetness. "I know it is. Believe me. And, not to turn this back around on you, but please don't hate me for this. I already knew. I found out by accident in the hospital."

"What?"

He kissed her hands again. "Right after the accident, I was going crazy trying to get to you in the hospital, not knowing if you were okay, but hospitals usually only let immediate family in, so I told them we were married. Then one of the nurses let it slip that the baby was all right."

Skye gasped for air. "You knew this whole time?"

"Yeah."

With a groan, she dropped her head into her hands.

"You knew I was keeping it from you. I feel terrible about that."

"You gotta knock it off with that Catholic guilt, baby. Because I didn't think about it like you were keeping it from me. What I thought was, here's a woman who got pregnant by a man she barely knows, who told her he isn't interested in monogamy, and whose faith and family believe that getting pregnant out of wedlock is a sin. I can only imagine how scared you've been, and that's not even taking into account that you already lost one baby."

She dried her eyes. Enough tears. Enough apologies. They had a healthy growing baby, jobs they were each passionate about, and more than enough love to share with their child. "I did think that, but not anymore. This baby is a miracle. Our miracle."

He rose and wrapped his arms around her in a tight hug. "Got that right."

"Where do we go from here?"

He eased back to the hay bale again, contemplating that for a moment. "Well, it's getting late. I think I ought to cook you dinner."

Not what she was expecting. Not at all. "You cook?"

He feigned mock offense. "Do I look like I go hungry to you?"

She shook her head.

"Beyond deciding what to eat for dinner, I don't think we have to make any other grand decisions right exactly now. I need you to know that I'm here. For the long haul. It's why I'm buying a house in Dulcet. I don't want to miss another doctor's appointment, Skye. I don't want to miss out on anything with our child. I know I was a rambling man. I know I've spent my career branding myself as a rebel and a drifter, a bad seed and a womanizer.

"Part of that was true, part of it wasn't. I own up to hard living. There were a lot of years I was proud of the trouble I got into, proud of that reputation. But that's not me anymore. Actually, it hasn't been me for a long time, and I'm done pretending. Whatever happens next for my career will be on my terms, and it's gonna happen from right here in Dulcet, where my family is."

Skye's heart cracked wide open.

"And I'm serious about that, Skye. Whatever you need, whatever you want. All the doctor bills come to me too. You got that? Let's put all that useless money I make to some actual good for once. You promise me that?"

"I promise."

He adjusted the brim of his ball cap. "I only have one more question for you."

"Anything."

"Did getting pregnant put an end to that silly love spell?"

The question surprised her so much that she laughed. She could have kissed him for that, for the levity and the understanding and the lack of jealousy about her being constantly bombarded by eligible bachelors.

"No," she said. "I got hit on by my hot male nurse in the hospital. And you were there at Hog Heaven when the waiter gave me his number."

He let out a belly laugh. "That's right. Oh man, poor guy. He never stood a chance."

"That doesn't bother you?" she asked. "You're not the least bit jealous?"

"Like I said at Hog Heaven, I think it's kind of funny. And I also think your mama's in the wrong business. She should be bottling that stuff. She'd be a millionaire."

"I'll tell her you said that."

She almost thanked him again, but what she couldn't

stop thinking about was how badly she wanted to kiss him. So she did. She lassoed him into a hug and planted a kiss on his cheek. "Thank you."

He felt so good with his arms wrapped around her. He nuzzled his face into her hair and held on tight. She slipped her hands down over his back, reveling in every muscle.

She felt the moment that the energy humming between them shifted, charged with potency and purpose. "Gentry," she breathed.

His hold on her tightened, rocking them both where they sat. "Yeah, I feel that too. I've got you, baby," he said gruffly.

She turned her face in and pressed her lips to his jaw, breathing into him. Their eyes met, but only for an instant, before his lips found hers. The first touch of their mouths together rocked her whole body with shockwaves.

He stroked her back. "You're gonna stay with me tonight. Please. Don't make me let you go again."

Saturday morning, Gentry left a sleeping Skye in his bed and padded out of the room as quietly as he could to get ready for his RCIA class. The last few days with Skye had passed by in a haze. They'd laid in bed for hours, swapping stories and making love, breaking only to eat or for Gentry to serenade her with one of his new songs.

He walked to the safe in the hall closet. After another glance at the bedroom to make sure Skye was still asleep, he opened the safe and pulled out the ring inside, just to take a peak. He opened the lid of the little velvet box and stared at the ring he'd driven into Dallas to select for her earlier that week. Not that he planned to propose to Skye anytime soon, but it gave him peace, having a crystal-clear view of what he wanted for his future. Skye's love, their family thriving together in Dulcet, surrounded by her big, loving family.

Down boy. She ain't in love with you yet.

But he was ready for when, or if, that happened.

He'd never believed in anything as pie-in-the-sky as love at first sight, but damn it all if he hadn't fallen for Skye that first night in the stable. He'd thought he needed to get grounded in order to cut the puppet stings that held him back so he could find himself again. Never in a million years would he have guessed that what he really needed to do was push both feet off the ground and take to the sky—so to speak. Because the problem hadn't been not enough grounding, but that he'd been straddling two worlds, who he was supposed to be and who he wanted to be. Being with Skye, this freedom of the road, was the cure to all that ailed him.

Arms came around his waist. "Hey there. Where are you going? The bed's getting cold."

Gentry startled, then stuck the ring in his pocket. "Hey, yourself. I was trying not to wake you up. I have a class this morning, a surprise I've been holding off on telling you, but I'm not sure why anymore, because I think you'd be proud of me."

"A class? If it's in Dulcet, the only class outside of the resort is Mrs. Pratch's Zumba class at the senior center. Now that would be a sight to behold. Your hip gyrations would make all the old ladies swoon."

He put on a show, gyrating his hips for her. "Then I might have to try it one time, just for that. But that's not where I'm headed today." He held out the RCIA study book that Father Ellwood had presented them with during the first class. "With this baby, we're going to be a family, and I don't know how you were raised up, but for me, that includes how we worship."

Skye touched the cover, her lips parting, and when she looked up, her expression was pure love. "I don't know what to say other than thank you. Our baby is going to be the luckiest kid in Dulcet to have a dad as dedicated as you. But I want you to know that you don't have to change for me."

His arms came around her as he tipped her chin up and gazed into her eyes. "I'm not changing for you. I'm changing for me. This is what I have to do. New career direction, new home town, new family, new man. Don't you see? When you made that spell, you laid out some pretty clear parameters for what you're looking for in a man. And seeing as how there's never been anything or anyone I've wanted more than I want you—and for us to be a family—I'm setting out to do whatever it takes to be that man."

He kissed her again, then nuzzled her nose. "Be back soon, baby. With any luck, I'll find you in my bed again when I get home."

On his way out the door, he grabbed the padded envelope he'd packed the night before. A demo tape of all the songs he'd written for the album, packed up and ready to mail to Neil Blevins, five days ahead of schedule. Gentry could have sent them digitally, but there was something about an actual recording that appealed to his old-fashioned sense. He knew it would appeal to Neil's too. Along with the CD, Gentry had included a simple note: *Your move.*

He drove through town feeling like he was floating on air. Even the line at the post office couldn't drag him down.

What finally knocked the smile off his face and the spring out of his step was the sight of Mrs. Martinez standing as the greeter for RCIA class. She scowled at him. "We need to talk."

He swallowed hard. "Sure. What can I do for you?"

"Skye hasn't been home at night in almost a week. She's been with you, hasn't she?"

How did a man say *none of your business* to the woman who might someday be his mother-in-law? "Yes, she has. And we're happy." He'd like to see her argue with that point.

She sniffed, raising her chin, which only deepened her frown. "You want to be Catholic, but yet you're breaking God's rules every night by lying in sin together. Tell me how you reconcile that. Tell me how you can sit in this class every week, and then go home and sin with my daughter."

Well, he had to give it Mrs. Martinez. She'd certainly found a way to argue the point. He supposed, to her, some things were more important than her child's happiness.

Mr. Martinez appeared in the door. He rubbed his wife's back. "Yessica, please. It is not for us to judge."

Over the past few weeks, Gentry had gotten to know Beto Martinez fairly well and had developed a true affection for the man. He was the polar opposite of Gentry's father, which was a high compliment, indeed.

"Come in, Gentry. And welcome to class. We've got a great lesson planned for you all today."

Gentry had found his seat and stowed his book beneath it when the classroom door flew open. Skye stood in the threshold breathing hard and looking meaner than a bull at a rodeo. She pointed to her mom. "How *dare* you?"

Skye clutched the paper in her hand like a weapon. It'd fallen out of Gentry's RCIA book when he'd left, so she'd picked it up. But before she'd set it down, she'd taken a look. Under the Our Lady of Guadalupe letterhead, was the title:

RCIA Lesson Two: The Call of the Disciple.

Catechists: Yessica and Beto Martinez

She waved the paper in front of her mom's face. "All this time you've been harping on me about how Gentry was no good for me, you did so knowing that he was converting to Catholicism. For me. For us. But that's not enough for you to stop harping on me about the mistake I'm making in being with him? No one I choose to be with will ever be good enough for me unless you choose him, is that it? You don't get to ruin this for me, Mom."

When Gentry had left for RCIA class that morning, before she'd found the paper, she'd watched the pride in the set of his shoulders as he walked to the front door and slipped into his boots. He set his Stetson on his head. Love filled her heart more deeply than she'd ever experienced. She'd sank onto the sofa, drunk on her love for him.

"I'm in love with Gentry Wells," she'd said, just for the pleasure of saying it. The realization made her laugh out loud, it filled her with such joy. She'd laid back and stared up at the ceiling, her hands on her belly. "You hear that, baby? I'm in love with your daddy. I'm going to marry him." She'd closed her eyes. "I found my forever."

And yet this whole time, her mom had been working to sabotage Skye's happiness. Then she'd found the class notes on the floor. At the sight of her parents' names, she'd swayed back and leaned against the wall, stunned stupid. She'd been so focused on Gentry and the significance of his gesture that she'd forgotten her parents were the catechists. She'd been filled with an instant, potent rage and had been in her car on the road to town in minutes flat.

"I deserve answers," Skye said, her eyes on her mom. More than that, she deserved to have her family's support of her choice of partners. An old, forgotten fear slithered into the cracks of her anger, fear that she'd be forced to have to choose between them or Gentry, like she'd felt with Mike, torn between her wild heart and her devotion to her family. "I deserve your support, damn it."

Her mom had the gall to gape at Skye like she was the one out of line. "Skye, please. This is a place of worship. Control yourself."

"That's exactly it, Mom. I am in control of myself. I'm the one who's in control of my life, not some spell or mystic power. And definitely not you."

"I do what I have to do because you have no good sense at all. Never did. As soon as you figure out what's best for you, you do the exact opposite. There's no getting through to you."

"Maybe you're not getting through to me because you're lying. You keep telling me I'm too good for Gentry. That he's not a safe bet. That all he'll do is leave me. And all this time, you knew how committed he was to changing—for me. What's it going to be, Mom? Will any man ever be good enough for me, by your standards?"

"The right man's out there," her mom said. "We just haven't found him yet."

We? Since when did her life become a group project?

Since forever, she realized. Her whole damn life. No wonder Skye rebelled every chance she got. "He's right here, Mom." She gestured to Gentry. "I could go on and on about how he's everything I asked for in the spell. He moved to Dulcet for me. He's joining our family's church. For me. He has a good job and a good heart. But all of that is beside the point. The only thing that should matter to you is that I'm in love with him. Why isn't that enough for you?"

Gentry stepped forward. He draped a supportive arm across Skye's shoulders. "I'm trying, Mrs. Martinez. I will be the kind of man your daughter deserves. I'm going to take care of them."

"Them?"

"Yes, them, Mom," Skye said. "Because I'm pregnant, okay? I'm pregnant with Gentry's baby and I'm in love with him and there's nothing you can do about it."

Her mom froze, mouth lolling open. "You're pregnant?"

Skye's head of steam cooled down a little. Petty as it was, it felt good to be able to wound her mom like that—and finally unburden her secret while she was at it. "Yes. I wanted to wait to tell you because I knew all you'd do is judge me for it. And I thought, why put myself through all that scorn and shame when I can wait until after the first trimester, in case I lost the baby. I've miscarried before, when I was married to Mike. So I'm not even sure I can carry a baby to term."

Her mom shook her head in disbelief. Skye was half-surprised she didn't put her fingers in her ears to drown out Skye's voice. "You were? I had no idea."

Gentry stepped between them. "Mrs. Martinez, this baby wasn't anything we planned, but we're fully committed to being the best parents we can. And I'm in love with your daughter." He closed his eyes. "So very in love. Everything's going to be all right. You'll see."

Gentry's words seemed to snap her mother out of her trance. She screwed her mouth up and whirled to face Skye, her expression one of regret and anger and fear. "What else haven't you told me?"

"Nothing," Skye said. "That's everything."

"These men you fall in love with. You run off with them and they hurt you. And I hate that. I still have flashbacks from the last time you left to marry that idiot, Michael. You didn't call or write for weeks at a time. I thought I'd lost you forever."

"No, Mama. Never that."

"This man will take you away from me again. He's not like us. He's not from around here and he's no different from Mike. Same user, different skin."

"I'm not taking her away from you," Gentry said. "Why would I want to leave Dulcet? I love it here. My life is here. In case you hadn't noticed, my career crashed and burned along with me in that crash. I'm still a musician, but not a jet-setter anymore. This is where I want to be. This is the woman that I am going to spend the rest of my life loving."

That stopped her mom up short. Honestly, it stopped Skye up short too. It wasn't until the room went quiet and Skye went still that she realized she had a stitch in her side. She rubbed her kidney, trying to work the cramp out.

"You okay, Skye?" Gentry said.

"Yeah, just . . . I don't know." By the time she got to that last word, her head had started to spin. The cramp pulsated, doubling her over. "Ow."

Gentry was at her side in an instant. "What's going on? I don't like this."

Skye let out a slow stream, refusing to let fear take hold of her. It was just a cramp, nothing more. Happened to pregnant women all the time. She heard her dad's voice in her head. *You can save yourself, but only if you don't panic.* "I'm trying, but I can't help it."

"What? Who are you talking to?," her mom said. "You're scaring me, Skye."

Gentry wrapped his arms around her and walked to a chair, but before she could sit, she felt wetness on her leg.

She lurched at the sight of blood trickling down the inside of her thigh. "Gentry. Oh no. Oh God."

Fear made her knees buckle. She collapsed, and she would have hit the floor, but Gentry caught her before she could. She surrendered to his arms and to the pain in her belly. She knew this would happen. She just knew it. This baby was going to slip through her fingers like the last one, and then she wouldn't be able to hold onto Gentry, either.

"Jesus, Skye, hang on," she heard Gentry say. His voice sounded a million miles away. She closed her eyes, feeling his strong arms holding her up. She didn't even startle at the sound of his voice bellowing for all to hear, "Somebody call 9-1-1!"

Chapter Twenty-One

The only other time that Gentry could recall being this scared was right after the motorcycle accident, before he knew if Skye was alive or dead. He sat bedside in the emergency room while nurses came and went, taking readings off of the monitors, asking questions, and assuring them that Skye's OB/GYN was on her way.

Skye's pain had subsided, which was a relief, except that the absence of it had seemed to give her way too much opportunity to worry. "We're back in the hospital," she croaked. "I can't decide if I still feel pregnant or not. I have no idea."

He kissed her hand. "I've got to believe the best. If I start thinking the worst, then I'll go crazy waiting for that doctor to get here."

They bent their heads together, praying and offering each other reassurances until a slim, dark-haired doctor in a lab coat who looked about Skye's age threw the curtain open and wheeled in a machine.

"Dr. Ghosh, finally!" Skye said.

"It took me a little bit longer because I wanted to have one of these puppies here with me." She patted the machine, then turned and offered her hand to Gentry. "You must be the father."

"I am. Gentry Wells."

"Oh, I know," the doctor said with a wink. "I'm a huge fan. Huge. But enough about that." She snapped on a pair of gloves. "I hear you two devised an elaborate plan to get another ultrasound look at your baby. Clever, you two. Very clever."

Gentry liked this doctor a lot. She had a way about her that put everyone in the room at ease. Except maybe Skye today. "Doctor, please don't joke like that. We don't even know if I'm still pregnant and I can't . . ."

Dr. Ghosh got right down to Skye's level and looked her in the eye. "I know, honey. We're going to find out right now. But I've got to tell you, given the small amount of blood loss and your stable vitals, I have a lot of hope. Twenty-five percent of pregnant women experience moderate blood loss and cramping during their first trimester and still deliver healthy, full-term babies. But let's see for ourselves, shall we?"

Gentry watched with curiosity as the doctor prepped Skye, then ran a wand over her belly. Immediately, grainy gray images appeared on the screen and the *woo-woo-woo* sound of a heartbeat filled the air.

Skye burst out crying. Gentry held her hand and tried to soothe her the best he could, but he couldn't tear his gaze away from the monitor and the sight of his little baby growing there inside of the woman he loved. He'd never truly understood the word *miracle* before.

"Hi, baby," the doctor cooed. "You made your mama worry. That wasn't very nice. But look at your strong heart. And look at those legs kick. Dad, are you seeing this?"

"I am," he croaked. He cleared his throat. "But what about the blood?"

"Not as uncommon as you might think during the first trimester. Sometimes it can be something as benign as having a lot of sex or an undiagnosed fibroid, for example. I'll run some more tests to make sure the prognosis is as optimistic as I'm thinking it is. But the baby's heartbeat is strong, your uterus looks healthy, and all your vitals are normal."

Gentry collapsed over Skye, his forehead against hers. "Thank God. I was so scared. So damn scared."

Foreheads together, they shifted to look at their wiggling baby and its strong, perfect heartbeat. "Mama Lita once told me that the only kind of real magic was the kind a person made for themselves, but this . . . this is real magic, right here."

Gentry knew exactly what she meant. Looking at his baby, Gentry's heart felt too huge for his chest, it was filled with so much love. Skye must have been feeling the same way, because she asked, "Do you believe in love at first sight?"

He smiled at her. "I didn't used to, but I changed my tune when I saw you. Just today, I fell in love at first sight of you in my bed. And I fell in love at first sight of you on that horse under the moonlight, and then love at first sight of you taking my hand and letting me pull you onto my jet. I feel like I've fallen in love with you a thousand different times since that first night in the stable."

She stroked his cheek. "I love you, Gentry Wells."

"I love you, Skye Martinez. You and this little peanut." He leaned in and kissed her reverently. The mother of his child. His lover. His life.

"After the accident, you told me that you'd give me whatever I wanted. Does that offer still stand?" she said.

"Yes. Always."

She bit her bottom lip as though working up the courage to ask. "Marry me."

He blinked hard. Okay, that hadn't been what he'd expected. "Are you proposing to me?"

"I am. Marry me. I don't want to wait until the baby's born. I want to marry you as soon as humanly possible."

He wanted with all his heart to say yes, because there wasn't anything in the world he wanted more, but there was just one thing that made the moment less than perfect. "But if we get married before my conversion is complete, the wedding won't be in a Catholic church. It won't be blessed by God in the way you need it to be. I want to give that to you, Skye."

"I don't care about that. I want us to be together. I want you. I love you."

He would never tire of hearing that. Never. "In that case, did you bring me a ring? It's not a real proposal if you don't have a ring."

She tousled his hair. "Then I guess you'll just have to wait a little longer while I acquire you one."

From his pocket, he pulled the little black box he'd accidentally walked out of his house with that morning. He popped open the lid. "Or you could borrow mine. I mean, if you want to make it official today."

Her hand went to her mouth. "You didn't . . ."

"I did. I told you I believed in love at first sight. I was saving it for the right time. Waiting for you to fall in love with me as deeply as I'm in love with you."

She only had eyes for the ring. Not that he blamed her. He'd picked out the biggest, most beautiful diamond he could find in the whole Dallas area.

She reached out and worshipfully touched one of the

points of the diamond. "That's a generous offer, but I don't think I should borrow that ring to give to you to wear. I think it belongs on the ring finger of the person it was meant for."

"Is that so." He liked the way she thought.

"I think it's only right."

Gentry carefully lifted the ring out the box and held it up. "Skye, would you do me the honor of—"

The hospital room door flew open. Skye's family stood in the hall behind her mom and dad. "We can't wait any longer," her mom said. "We need to know what's going on. Skye, you okay? What about the baby?"

Skye gave Gentry a look of panic, but he knew what had to be done. "Talk to your mom. Introduce her to her new grandbaby. I'll still be here, with this, when you're done." Yet another reason she loved him so much. He would never make her choose between him and her family.

"Mama, the baby's fine. It was a false alarm. Come look at it yourself. Dr. Ghosh brought an ultrasound machine."

Skye's mom walked with cautious steps to Skye, as though the rug might be pulled out from under her at any moment. Her dad shuffled behind them. When her mom got to Skye's bedside, Skye took her hand and held it tight. Even Gentry could see that her mom's hand was shaking. Mr. Martinez stood behind his wife and rubbed her back, his eyes on the monitor.

"Look, Mom. There it is. It's too soon to tell if it's a boy or a girl, but Dr. Ghosh says he's perfect."

"Or she," Dr. Ghosh added. "And yes, she's perfect in every way. Strong heart, correct length, and moving just as she should."

Her mom stared at the monitor until her lower lip

started to tremble. Her eyes filled with tears. "I'm so sorry, mija. I haven't been what you needed. I haven't been there for you. I was so scared of losing you that I screwed everything up. As much love as you're feeling right now for your own little baby, that's what I feel for you. Can you imagine that?"

"If you feel for me a fraction of the love I feel for this baby, then that's a lot of love, indeed. And I love you too."

Her mom bent down and hugged her tight. The two of them cried and trembled and embraced.

Gentry looked around him to see that there wasn't a dry eye in the room. The perfect mood for what he wanted to do next. He cleared his throat. "Now that everybody's here, I'd like to finish asking Skye a question that I started to before y'all busted into the room."

Skye's mom backed up to give them space. As for Skye, she couldn't stop smiling.

When her mom saw the ring in Gentry's hand, she gasped and did the sign of the cross. "I told you I was going to do this right, Mrs. Martinez. I love your daughter more than anything and it's my vow to you and to Skye's father that I will take care of her and love her for the rest of my life."

"I believe you," Mrs. Martinez said. "And I'm sorry to you too. For what I've put you through."

He shook his head. "I can't accept that because there's no apology needed. Thank you for raising such a magnificent person. I am humbled by your family."

She nodded, then pulled him into a hug. When it was done, Mrs. Martinez stepped aside. Gentry turned to Skye. "Skye, darlin', where was I?"

"I believe you were about to get on bended knee."

"Oh, was that it? I don't remember that part, but here I go." He knelt beside the bed and took her hand. "Skye, will you make me the luckiest man in the world? Will you be my bride?"

"Yes. Of course. Nothing would make me happier. Now get that huge rock on my finger."

The family clapped and whistled as Gentry slid the ring on, then stood to kiss his fiancée.

Mama Lita dabbed at her eye with a bright yellow handkerchief. "We did it, June."

Granny June put her arm around Mama Lita. "We did it, Edalia. Nice work." And then they high-fived.

"Wait a gosh-darn second," Skye called from the bed. "You two have been working together this whole time? I thought only Granny June was into matchmaking. Mama Lita, you told me you didn't believe in marriage."

Mama Lita only gave her a wink. "Old ladies never share their secrets."

Granny June planed her hands on her hips. "Does this mean we get to put on a wedding now?"

"No, it means I get to put on a wedding now," Gloria said. "She's my sister."

Skye's mom waved her hands. "You're all wrong. This is my wedding to plan."

And then all the women in the Martinez family started talking at once. Gentry and the other men in the room all took a giant step back, then another. "Yeah, it's best if we just leave them to it."

This big, loud, hard-loving family was now his. They and their children would never want for love. He wouldn't have wanted it any other way.

Skye's dad cupped a hand on Gentry's shoulder. "Welcome to the family, son. Glad to have you aboard."

Chapter Twenty-Two

Two months later . . .

Skye pushed the stable door open and disappeared in its dusty depths. The horses poked their heads over their stall doors, curious about the intruder. Who would've guessed that she, of all people, would have had a wedding-day meltdown? She wanted to marry Gentry. More than anything, actually.

They were having a baby girl together. Heck, they'd already started brainstorming names, even though their daughter's arrival wouldn't be for another four months or so. But her wedding had turned into a bona-fide circus. And who was its ringleader—or rather, ringleaders? Her mom and Gloria, with a little help from Remedy.

Skye didn't remember her mom going quite this nuts for Gloria's wedding. Probably because it had been held in the church. In fact, this wedding was the first in her family as far back as anyone could remember, that was not going to be in the church. They would have another wedding at the church once Gentry had been baptized Catholic next spring. Meanwhile, Skye's father had been ordained so that he could be the one to marry them.

On paper, everything was going as planned—except that, in reality, Skye was miserable.

Her mom and Gloria wouldn't stop bickering about wedding details. The bridesmaids' dresses were gaudy shades of orange and blue, but her aunt had insisted on sewing them herself, so there was nothing she could do. The mariachi band hired to perform before the ceremony sounded atrocious, but her cousin Marco played in the band, so she had no choice.

That seemed to be the common refrain throughout the wedding process. Skye had no choice. About anything of consequence, except for who she was marrying.

The final straw had been at the pre-wedding photographs, when her trio of uncles who always got hammered before weddings, sang "*Besame Mucho*" at the top of their lungs, sloshing flasks of tequila around as they danced. Actually, everyone in her family was partying so hard in the reception area, she wasn't sure they'd notice whether a wedding had taken place or not. All her family, that was, except for her mom and Gloria. As for those two, they were so consumed by planning that Skye doubted they'd hold up the ceremony for her if she or Gentry were late.

When she'd confessed to her bickering mom and sister in the bridal suite that she needed some space, they'd told her, "You don't have time for space. You're getting married in an hour!"

Well, too bad. Guess they'd see if they held the ceremony up for her or not, because Skye had to get out of there.

Gentry, for his part, had been a champ throughout the past two months, accompanying Skye to her doctor's appointments, writing blank checks to her mom for the expenses, and calming Skye's nerves when the pressure got too much. Add to that the news that their offer had been accepted on the ranch house around the corner from Skye's current house, the one with the property large enough to build a stable on and house horses of their own. Gloria and the kids would continue to rent out Skye's old house for a bargain-basement price, and Skye couldn't be happier.

So, no, she hadn't escaped to the stable on her wedding day because she didn't want to marry Gentry, which she did with all her heart, but just to catch her breath and regroup in a place that held a lot of wonderful memories of her and Gentry together.

She walked to Vixen's stall and stuck her hand out for the horse to sniff. "Hey, girl. What do you think of my dress?"

Vixen snorted and licked Skye's hand.

The dress was a simple ivory sheath, form-fitting enough to show her burgeoning baby bump. It was such a relief not to feel like she had to hide the pregnancy out of shame anymore. With every outfit she chose these days, she judged it by whether it proudly showed off her belly.

She stroked Vixen's nose as tears streamed down her cheeks, ruining the make-up that Gloria had worked so hard on.

After a few minutes, the stable door opened again. A shaft of sunlight kissed her slippers.

Skye mashed her eyelids closed. "Whoever it is, I need some space. Can you come back later?"

"If that's what you want, but I'd like to say something first."

Gentry.

She turned to find him standing just inside the doorway, looking devastatingly handsome in a black tuxedo, a black Stetson, and shiny black cowboy boots. A fresh wave of despair crashed over her at the wedding circus they were supposed to go through with. It simply wasn't right for them. Maybe they shouldn't have rushed it. Maybe they should have waited until Gentry was baptized in their church so they could have had a proper wedding and start their life off on the right foot.

"Oh, Gentry, I'm so sorry. This wedding is all wrong," she choked. "This isn't what I wanted. But my mother and Gloria took over, and now they won't stop fighting. Maybe we should postpone the wedding so we can do this our way, not anybody else's. Because I don't think my family got that memo."

Worry lines appeared on his forehead and, even though he was trying to hide it, she could tell she'd upset him, which only made her tears fall harder. "That's a load of bull. We're not getting married for the wrong reasons, because we're not getting married because of the baby or to make you a respectable woman or any of that BS. We're going to love that little peanut with all our hearts either way, marriage or not. If we do this wedding, we're doing this for us. You and me."

So, then, he did understand where she was coming from. "Exactly. I want this to be about us and our love, not what my family expects."

His shoulders relaxed and the worry lines on his face vanished. He stepped to her and gathered her in his arms. "Come here, baby."

She sank into his arms, cringing against a sob.

He rocked her slowly. "You had me worried there for a minute. I thought maybe you'd decided you didn't love me and didn't want to marry me."

Sniffing, she offered him a watery smile. "Now who's spouting the bullshit?"

He dried her eyes, then cupped her cheeks and angled his lips over hers. She would never stop loving his kisses, from the dirty, midnight ones to the lazy Sunday morning ones. If only they could skip to that part in the wedding ceremony and forget the rest.

When the kiss ended, Gentry held her out away from him so he could look at her. "You know, we don't have to get married here. We have options."

"Options? There are three hundred guests arriving as we speak. My father is set to officiate. Are we supposed to tell them all that we're moving it across town?"

He shrugged. "I've heard Nashville is one of the best places to whisk away a runaway bride to. I even know a place that does a real nice ceremony, dancing waters, Dolly Parton, and all."

Awareness dawned over her. Was he really talking about eloping? Anticipation blossomed, intoxicating her with the prospect of breaking that many rules. "You're not serious . . . are you? Don't tease me about this."

"Does this sound like I'm teasing?" And he broke out with the chorus to "Islands in the Stream," much to the horses' delight, who stamped their hooves and snorted in appreciation.

Skye's mind was racing, trying to get all the details worked out. "We do have a private plane on standby for the honeymoon." That was one luxury Gentry had suggested that Skye had fully approved of.

"And I know firsthand the best ways to commandeer a limousine."

She paused, setting a hand on his chest. "We can't ditch our own wedding, can we?"

"Can you think of a reason why we shouldn't?"

The faces of her drunk uncles sprang to mind. "No, no I can't. Oh, my mother is going to be so mad." And that was reason enough, right there.

Gentry smoothed his hands up and down her arms. "I know. Isn't it wonderful?"

She threw her head back and laughed. "We're going to make our own magic."

He took her hand. "Let's go. There's no time to waste."

But another thought had occurred to her and she stopped in her tracks. Her eyes pricked with tears again. "Gentry, I just thought of something."

"What? What's wrong?"

"Nothing's wrong. It's just . . . the spell worked. The love spell that my mom and I cast that night. I can't believe it, but it worked. You're everything I ever wanted in a husband. And here you are, with me. And we're having a baby. I mean, look at us." She spread her arms wide and looked down at her wedding dress and her beautiful belly.

"Yeah, baby, look at us." His voice was gruff with emotion. Then he offered her his hand once more. "Skye Martinez, are you ready to run away with me?"

"I'm ready. More ready than I'd ever thought I'd be, thanks to you and your love." With the horses looking on, she set her hand in his and let him pull her out the door and right into her destiny.

Epilogue

One year later . . .

"I've never walked a red carpet before, but I could get used to this," Skye said as she stepped from the limo out into the red carpet staging area at the Academy of Country Music Awards in Las Vegas. Gentry let his gaze linger on her long legs and strappy heels right up until she twirled for him, a vision in gold. "How do I look?"

"Like you were born for this. I love that dress. Feels like I've already won an award tonight, with you on my arm."

She strutted his way and straightened his bow tie. "You're going to win, you know. You're up for just about every ACM award you're eligible for. It's an incredible album."

He pulled her close and kissed her temple. "Thanks to my incredible muse."

"Okay, team. This is the big leagues, so let's be on our A-game," they heard behind them and turned to see Larry and Nick striding their way along with Gentry's backup band, which included one very uncomfortable looking young man.

Skye was all smiles. "Hi, Larry and Nick. Logan, you look so handsome!"

Logan tugged at his tie. "Thanks, I guess. I can't wait to get this suit off."

It hadn't taken much for Nick and Gentry to convince Neil to give Logan a shot. Not only had Logan gone to Nashville with Gentry to record the final cut of the album, but Neil had invited him to go on tour with Gentry's band that summer—just as soon as he'd graduated high school. As Gentry had known he would, Logan jumped at the chance. Gentry had been there. He knew what it meant to want something so badly that he was willing to sacrifice anything and everything for it. He looked at the woman by his side as proof.

"We're behind schedule," Larry said. "Time to walk the red carpet. Logan, you remember the answers we practiced?"

Gentry hadn't thought it possible, but Logan looked even more uncomfortable at that prospect. "I guess. I don't have to say much, though. Right?"

Larry slapped Logan's back. "As much as you can. You're an All-Star in the making, kid, so go out there and promote yourself."

Gentry squeezed Skye's hand. "You ready for this?"

The smile she gave him hit him right in the gut. "Like I was born for it."

"Then here we go." Arm-in-arm, they rounded the corner and into a noisy sea of people and camera flashes. Larry directed them to their first media station, this one for a cable-news channel.

The reporter was a tiny young woman who gesticulated as though she'd downed two Red Bulls before show time. "I'm standing with Entertainer of the Year nominee

Gentry Wells and his wife Skye. Gentry, where's your cute little baby girl tonight? Little Miss Ruby Wells."

She stuck the microphone under his nose.

As Larry might have said, that was a nice softball question to get him warmed up with. "Home with the best babysitters in the world, Skye's parents." It was amazing how much Yessica and Beto had warmed up to Gentry over the past year.

It'd taken a little time for them to get over the fact that Gentry and Skye had ditched the wedding that Yessica had so meticulously planned, but all had been forgiven the first time they held Ruby in their arms. It was safe to say that the entire Martinez family, Gentry, Nick, and all the other Briscoe Ranch friends and employees who'd come out to the hospital that day had fallen in love with the baby girl the first moment they laid eyes on her. Truly, she had them all wrapped around her little finger with eyes the color of the earth after a rain and the most beautiful black hair in the world next to her mama's.

"Want to announce right here on the red carpet any plans for more kids?"

Nice try. Both Gentry and Skye afforded the reporter an indulgent smile. Of course, they had plans to add at least one more kid, maybe two, to their family, but they refused to make their family part of an entertainment-news show's exclusive scoop.

"Aw, now, don't go putting ideas in my bride's head. Let me get through our world tour first."

"Speaking of that tour, there's been talk that you're taking the whole family?"

"You bet. It is called the 'Coming Home' tour, and for me, home is wherever my little Ruby and my beautiful bride are." Bride twice over, actually, since he'd been baptized Catholic the month before, and they'd had a second ceremony, this one during mass and blessed by Father Ellwood himself. Gentry wasn't sure he'd ever seen Skye so happy as she'd been that day.

For once, the reporter extended the microphone to Skye. "Are you looking forward to hitting the road?"

Skye didn't hesitate. "You know, I am. I was born with a wild heart, ready to hit the road, and there's no one I'd rather do that with than this guy. And then, at the end of the tour, it'll be nice to settle in back home in Texas for a while. It's the best of both worlds."

Gentry was so profoundly grateful that she'd come to see it that way. He would've been content to never leave Dulcet again as long as she was by his side, but this tour had been her idea and he couldn't be prouder to have her and Ruby on the road with him. He loved it even more that she'd accepted that side of herself, the wild side of her that longed-for adventure. He'd like to think he really was the best of both worlds as her partner, providing her with just the right amount of settling down and the right amount of rule breaking to keep that spark in her eye and that spring in her step.

Then the mic was back in Gentry's face. "What do you think your chances are for Album of the Year?"

But Skye wasn't done and pulled the microphone back her way. "He's going to win. I know it."

He loved her confidence in him, but still . . . "It doesn't matter to me if I win or lose. I know it sounds corny, but I feel like I've already won, with my family healthy and happy, and I'm making the best music of my career. Honest music."

"One last question. I think it's safe to say that your sound has evolved a lot in the last year. If I may be so blunt, you went from 'Built to Leave' to 'Built to Stay.'

Was there a moment you can pinpoint where everything changed? Maybe when you lost your finger or your alleged tiff with Neil Blevins?"

Nice try, but he was going to let that particular rumor about him and Neil fizzle out and die. The two men would never be best friends—or friends at all—but without Neil pushing him and challenging him at every turn, Gentry wouldn't be the man he was today. "Come on. Don't play me. You've got to know the story by now. It's in all my hit songs on the new album, starting with the one that's up for Song of the Year."

"You're talking about 'Riding in the Dark'?"

"That's the one. Everything I have in my life, all the riches a man could want, started with one wild night, a midnight horseback ride, and the prettiest girl I'd ever laid eyes on."

"Just like that?"

Gentry hugged Skye close. "Just like that. And life has never been sweeter."

Catch up on the
One and Only Texas series!

BOOK 1

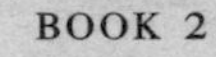

BOOK 2

E-NOVELLA

E-NOVELLA

Available now!